D.H.

pinkpigpublishing

pinkpigpublishing

First published in Great Britain by pinkpigpublishing in 2017

A catalogue record for this book is available in the British Library

ISBN 978-0-9957741-0-0

Book Design by Tamsin Slatter

Printed and bound in Great Britain by Clays Ltd, St Ives plc

Find out more at www.pinkpigpublishing.com

Life is for living, for sharing, for giving.

In memory of David,
and all those who have, do, and will struggle with the journey,
may they never be forgotten…

The inspiration for this novel was my dad, more precisely the journey we walked as he battled against cancer. Ours was not a journey dominated by sadness but one filled with hope, inspiration and most importantly love. We connected with each other in a way as never before. We learned things about each other and ourselves. We became friends.

Every person battling against a terminal illness requires support. They need help in many guises; physical, mental, emotional and spiritual. Sometimes they need one person with whom they can bare their inner most thoughts; someone who they do not need to protect from the reality of who they are and what they are thinking. This person is their saviour, for they can help to release the fear of the end before they depart.

In memory of the support my father received from various organisations during his battle, I am supporting charities which are responsible for providing support to those with cancer. Details of charities and contributions can be found at pinkpigpublishing.com.

Your Father

He cradled you in his arms,
He cared for you through the years,
He was there when you needed help,
He was your father.
He believed in you when no one else did,
He could tell stories about you no one else knew,
He loved you more than he could ever say,
He was your father.
He is still here,
He is in a different form,
He will always be in your heart,
He is your father.

CHAPTER 1 — BEE

Bee had never been like other people and probably never would. She walked through life just on the edge of isolation. Had the ability to know things others did not. This made her very different. Sometimes the knowledge hindered her life and other times it helped. She had never shared her knowledge, had not told anyone of her ability. Long ago, in childhood, she had learned to keep her thoughts to herself. But recently, there had been a change in her state; the choice to remain silent had been revoked. As with all directives the message was intense, delivered to her head, constantly repeated until accepted. She had to deliver support. There was no escaping the fact. A phone call had to be made to her dad. He needed her help. She did not know all of the details, did not need to know. All she knew was his journey had become difficult to manage alone, the cancer he fought on a daily basis was wearing away at his belief in life and his chances for survival.

The relationship she had with her father was similar to many other daughters, they only spoke a few times a year, mainly at family functions but rarely on the phone. To call her dad and begin a deep and meaningful conversation would be somewhat out of the ordinary. To broach the subject of his illness and drag it out in the open would be challenging. But had to be done. All protocol must be discarded. A man's life was at stake. The assistance he required was not in the general domain. Only she could provide the help required. Her father was a proud man and would never ask her for help. Which meant she had to be strong, believe in the support she could provide and approach him. There had never been anyone quite like herself. No one had ever mentioned they were privy to information which had never been spoken out loud; the gift of silent communication from which there was no escape, where messages could not be ignored. The current unspoken message, which dominated all thought, was to contact Dad and open up the channel of communication. But how? They had not spoken in a long time. Perhaps she could open a conversation by talking about herself? Distraction from his situation could be a good thing. However, he must not for one moment think she was trying to fix him. If he suspected assistance he may shut her out.

The news of his illness had arrived a few years earlier like a bolt from the blue. Her response had been paralysis; caused by the fear of losing her father, information not easily digested. There had been little opportunity to help him in his time of need, for she'd been supporting her two year old son and expecting another, with no extra capacity for additional emotional support. Luckily he had not encouraged assistance. In fact he had refused all support, isolated himself, thus preventing anyone from accessing his painful existence. Along with the rest of the family, she had watched from the side-line. During his period of self-enforced solitude he had received treatment to eliminate the tumours, and she had eventually come to terms with the fact she could lose her father. A reality not easily accepted. However, she had no other choice because there was nothing she could do. That was until the present day, the moment she received knowledge. There was a way. But this would involve telling him the truth about herself. She would have to bring him into her world, a place of infinite possibilities. No easy choice to make. She had successfully hidden all communication with the living, dead and everything in between. If she allowed another to view this side of her life could they be trusted to handle the information? Would she be believed? Could she really help him? There was only one way to find out. But where to start? Should she tell him of her ability to communicate with a silent channel? Would this help him? How was she to communicate to another person the feelings and knowledge received from something she could not see? There were no words to describe awareness of the unseen presence. One which she could never quite see but could feel in close proximity behind her when she washed the dishes or in the shadows of her bedroom as she lay in bed contemplating sleep. Whenever she chose to interact with the unusual force, the full extent of its power surged through her body—transported electrical energy which ignited every nerve ending. Thankfully this didn't occur in every waking moment—there were times when it took a back seat, providing respite, enabling her to maintain a level of normality in her life.

Bee had never really made sense of who she was and why she was different. She existed in a lonely space. One just outside of everyone else's experience of life. Although uncomfortable with the idea of letting her dad in on the secret, Bee knew she had to step into the unknown, boldly move forward and share her knowledge. There was one small problem. She was torn between the need to help, and paralysed by fear of humiliation which could follow an explanation of the unusual occurrences in her life. There had been many times when she had thought about sharing her truth but she had never been brave enough to follow through. Adam should be the one to share her secrets. They had been married for six years, together for ten, had two sons, and were bound together by their love for each other and for their children. As much as she wanted to, she could not share the reality of her existence with him. She didn't want to displace his love. She did not want to complicate their relationship. She didn't want to threaten their existence. Bee could not test their relationship to this level.

But the step had to be taken. The secret shared. One person needed to hear her truth and needed to hear it soon. With a dominant thought, there was no time like the present, she prepared to make the call. Her eldest son, five year old James, had been delivered to school. Two year old

Edward had fallen back to sleep, clearly in need of a morning nap. Instead of focusing on the endless list of tasks which required completion she made the choice to call him. The midsummer sun had begun to warm the chill early morning air, rays of golden light streamed through French doors at the rear of the house, Bee paused for a moment and soaked up the warmth. She did not really have the time to waste. He had to be called. Why had she never told anyone? There had never been a need. Even though she had shared everything else with Adam she had not felt comfortable telling him and testing their love for each other. But what about the others? Her mum? She had never seen the need to share. In the present Bee knew there was enough on her plate and besides, she did not think her mum would have the capacity to deal with the unusual events, would not be able to analyse the experiences from an objective viewpoint. What about her sister Lizzie? They had been close as children but Bee had never shared. She wasn't sure why. In the present day her sister had the unenviable job of raising three small children. Bee feared Lizzie did not have the capacity for the truth of her existence and in order to make sense of it might discuss the details with others. Bee worried about this most of all. Having very little understanding of why she was different, she did not want strangers to know. There had never been anyone to tell. But now she had to do it, in order to support a life, maybe even save a life.

Although driven by a notion, Bee was still unconvinced. She had spent her whole life keeping secrets and for good reason, this kept her safe. But what if she were the answer to his prayers? What if she made a difference to his journey? What if she could save him? With this final thought at the fore of her mind she picked up the phone. Excitement waltzed through her mind at the thought of helping him—then fear threatened the moment with paralysis. She took a deep breath and dialled his telephone number. As the ringing tone warbled in her ear, an image of the home of her parents presented inside her head. Last time she had visited the 1960's-styled vicarage, surrounded by lawn, it had been bathed in sunshine. The dwelling occupied an enviable plot midway between the village pub and the church. Suddenly the image was erased by the power of doubt and her confidence slumped. How was she going to introduce the conversation? What possible reason could she have for calling? Then an idea flashed into her thought-stream. The strange encounter a few weeks earlier. With any luck the unusual nature of her experience would open the door to more conversations and she would learn how to help him.

Chapter 2 — ARTHUR

Arthur sat in a large mahogany carver in the study of his rented home, his slight, medium-height frame supported by a large burgundy cushion at his back. There he considered his lot. He and his wife Sheila were forced to sell their dream home because he, the major breadwinner, had been unable to continue working in the cutthroat world of executive life. He had exited the world of work. A place in which he had once thrived. Unable to deal with the politics and pressure of constant delivery, continuously focused on making more money for faceless people for whom he did not care. In the upper echelons of management he had lost sight of the agronomist role in which he had begun his career, a job he had loved. Driven by a desperate need to leave before the stress of his job dragged him into the darkness of depression, he had been left with only one choice—retirement. But without a job he had been unable to pay the household bills. The house he and Sheila had lovingly restored had to be sold so they could release the capital. They were left with little option but to rent whilst they found a cheaper home to purchase, one which would allow them to use the profit from their house sale to support his meagre pension. However, this had not been the only trauma in his life. Arthur had also learned he was shackled with the sentence of death. At the grand old age of sixty-one he had been dealt a devastating blow. Prostate cancer had taken up residence inside his body. In response to this news Arthur had followed a similar path to all others. He recalled the period of time, almost three years earlier when he had been delivered the news.

Firstly, he had walked the path of denial. This stage had made him an unbearable person to live with and yet Sheila had somehow managed to support him with the patience of a saint. He had not been able to accept the information delivered. Had not easily come to terms with his terminal illness. On a daily basis he had asked the same questions. How can this be true? How can someone of my young years be under threat of death? The denial had transformed into anger. During this time Arthur had felt angrier than at any other point in his life. He had been ready to slow down and enjoy retirement but instead had been dealt a painfully heavy blow. His life could be over within five years, or worse, he had been told that only one in six people survived for five years. Upon receiving this news, a deep sadness had crept into every crevice of his body, numbing all his senses and darkening each day. This inescapable reality had caused him to remain in the state of denial for months. During this time Arthur had spent many hours considering his luck-less life. Why him? What had he done to deserve this bitter end? He had wallowed unreservedly in the berating of life and all he had been delivered. Towards the end of this first stage, denial,

Arthur vowed no matter what, he would fight the cancer and not allow it the pleasure of erasing his life.

Next had come grief, which delivered further countless days of darkness and despair. He had not wanted to converse with another living soul. Arthur had attempted to battle the overwhelming sadness by attending church and connecting with God. Each day he had summoned the energy to make the pilgrimage to the church only a few minutes from his home. Each visit entailed a walk through the churchyard where the reality of death lay beneath his feet. He prayed with all his might that he would not end up a corpse, a neighbour to the silent residents who lay in the ground. Entry to the church delivered a powerful connection with his God. Silently inside his head he pleaded to be saved. This heart wrenching plea resulted in tears, which rolled silently down his face, but they did not stifle the relentless repetition of prayer, the desperate cries to be pardoned from his sentence.

Then came acceptance. Once Arthur had passed through the horror of denial and felt the excruciating pain of grief, eventually, with the help of medical professionals he had come to terms with his illness. Even though he was determined never to give up hope of fighting off the cancer, he had found a state of acceptance, that it was part of his existence. During this phase Arthur had spoken with each of his children about the reality of the cancerous cells which marched steadily through his body. But he had not been able to share his feelings on the life which would be stolen from him. In fact, Arthur had found the act of sharing very difficult. Mainly because all conversations ended the same way, with Arthur making his illness okay for the other person.

Three years on he had come to terms with the reality of his life and found a relatively peaceful existence in the rented home he shared with Sheila. Each day he pottered through his list of chores: checking the accounts, making ends meet, searching out properties to buy and taking the odd furniture restoration job. Each evening he prepared a meal for Sheila who worked as a manager in a medical practice a half hour drive from their home. Arthur loved to cook, thoroughly enjoyed the process of mixing ingredients together and delivering a taste sensation. His was not a creative experience but more a scientific experiment. Each new recipe created was recorded in a database on his computer; with a view to creating a cookbook for his family, the product of his relationship with Sheila, his reason for being. His four offspring lived in the south of England; Bee and Lizzie in a market town in west Surrey, Richard in south London and Andrew in Bristol. Thankfully they were all close enough to allow him the chance to see them regularly. Although in reality he didn't see them often, for they had busy lives of their own. Richard, his eldest child, he saw the least. He lived and worked in London and spent the majority of his waking hours working. Arthur was happy his son had created success but was sad he didn't get to hear his news. Bee, his second child, he saw fairly regularly when she bought the grandchildren to visit. Before children she had also been too busy working to visit with any regularity. His third child Lizzie, he also saw when she visited with the grandchildren. But before creating her family she had lived and worked in south London, with little time for visiting parents. He was glad of their success. They were hardworking and had been successful in the careers they had chosen. When the first three children had been in their teenage years, he and Sheila had been delivered a very welcome surprise—the birth of Andrew, his fourth child. Andrew had recently finished university and his hectic work life meant Arthur did not see him often. He was a lucky man in that he still had a relationship with his children. However, he did not see them as regularly as he would have liked.

From his position at the old mahogany desk Arthur gazed out of the window onto the freshly mown lawn and pondered the meaning of life. Was there any point in fighting the illness that sapped strength from him daily? Inside his head an answer shouted loud and clear. Yes. He could not yet give up hope in a future. He had been told five years and at the very least, five years it would be. Suddenly, the telephone on his desk burst into life, the ringing tone bought his thoughts back to the moment and he lifted the handset.

CHAPTER 3 — BEE

He answered the phone and to begin with they talked about him. Every conversation since his diagnosis began with an enquiry about his health. Although superficial, the discussion had to take place, followed the etiquette required of a family member.

'Hi Dad, how are you doing?' she asked.

Bee had no idea how she would react if he laid bare his true feelings on the cancer which nibbled away at his lifeline. Thankfully his answer was brief.

'I'm okay, the doc has given me some new tablets which have the side effect of making me feel a bit sick but it is better than the alternative.'

She didn't know the right thing to say in response and yet she must not hide from the truth of his illness, as there were very few people with whom he could share details of his battle. As a very private man he struggled to communicate his innermost thoughts with anyone, even with his own daughter. Although this lack of ability to express his emotion had never been a problem because she knew how much he cared. He had demonstrated his love by supporting her when she needed him most. She did not need him to utter words of love. However, there was no time to dwell on this distraction. He needed her. Although he did not know it. She had spent too long in thought, before she had a chance to speak he had moved the conversation away from himself.

'Anyway, let's not talk about me. How are you and the kids?'

But they were supposed to talk about him. That is why she had called. She was being driven to assist. Electrical energy surged through her body communicating that she must find a way to connect with him.

'We are all well. But poor Adam's working all hours. We drop him at the station early each morning and pick him up late in the evening. The boys love seeing the trains, so this is the highlight of their day. Life is pretty tiring. But then I am sure you remember the days of young children. However, that said, the boys are fun and we play lots of games together. Our current favourite is building the wooden train set and pushing Thomas the Tank Engine round and round. I know I shouldn't complain, the time will go quickly and before I know it they will both be grown up, so I am trying to enjoy my time with them. However, the 5:30am wakeup call every morning is becoming a little wearing. Although I don't know why I'm surprised they wake early—both you and I are early risers. I also remember Grandad being an early bird too.'

This was the moment she could connect with him. The secret to share related to his parents. She grabbed the chance.

'The mention of your dad reminds me. Something unusual happened the other day which relates to you. Do you have time to listen?'

He responded immediately, 'Of course. There are only chores to fill my day. A distraction would be most welcome.'

Bee had no idea where the conversation would lead but she had been dealt an opportunity, one which could not be wasted. She had not done anything with the information delivered a few weeks before. She had never done anything with information delivered. Had never been brave enough to share. But this time it seemed the right thing to do. This was an important communication.

How could she explain herself and the depth of feelings present? How would her dad respond? Would he believe her? Bee leant against the windowsill and looked out across the valley. She took a deep breath and broached the new topic of conversation.

'Dad, did your mum whistle many tunes?'

She could hear a lightness to his voice as if he was smiling, 'Yes, she loved to whistle.'

His response caused a change in her state, she felt more confident, as if she now believed there was a message to pass on.

Assertively she asked, 'Have you had any experiences with your parents since their passing?'

He answered, 'No, never.'

He sounded confused by the question. But this didn't stop her. With new found confidence she began the recount of her experience.

'A few weeks ago I experienced an unusual encounter which I need to share with you. We've never spoken of these events but they happen in my life with regularity. I have never spoken to anyone on this subject but feel it would be wrong of me to keep this to myself because it relates to you.' She took a deep breath and continued, 'I feel really uncomfortable about telling you because I'm not sure how you are going to take the information. Do you think you will be able to listen with an open mind?'

He responded with an interested edge to his voice, 'Yes of course, how mysterious.'

She readied herself to begin but realised she couldn't tell him the whole story. The day of the encounter had begun with a need to connect with her grandparents. She had tuned into the silent space inside her head, the place where she heard all communication, then requested their support. She had no idea why. She had never needed to connect with her departed grandparents, and yet a driving need had pushed her toward communication. Within the quiet space of her head she had pleaded, 'Please help Dad. He needs you to show him the way forward, to know there is something at the end of his path.' Bee could not tell him this element of the story. She did not want him to know about her request to the departed for help. Instead she began the recount with details from later in the day when she had been cleaning.

'A couple of weeks ago when I was vacuuming the entrance hall, without any warning my head filled with a tune and I began to whistle 'Pack up your Troubles'. Obviously, I never sing this old war song so I was slightly taken aback when I randomly began to whistle it. Once I had begun to whistle I couldn't stop. The tune played over and over inside my head, it wouldn't be banished. Then followed a thought of Grandma—your mum. This was not the end of it though. Then, an electrical tingling sensation travelled from the top of my head all the way down the left hand side of my body to my feet.'

Bee remembered the moment and couldn't help but smile at the thought, she loved the magic of contact with the departed. Although, this time Grandma had presented almost within the bounds of her own body. Bee had been surprised by the development but had felt no fear, only excitement. She could not fear Edith, her Grandma. A jolly, short, rotund woman with a blue rinse and roller-curled hair. A lovable old lady with smiling blue eyes. Although when required Edith had presented a stern exterior. She had been a strong woman who had not tolerated misbehaviour in her grandchildren. There were many memories of times together during Christmas, Easter and school holidays. Even though Edith had not been an emotionally demonstrative woman the moments shared had always been fun, thanks to her sense of humour, which had manifested in a willingness to play games with her grandchildren. Bee had loved this playtime and recollected the time her Grandma had chased her with a rolled up newspaper and once caught, held her by the top of her tights lifting her high up into the air. Suddenly the flow of thought halted as she reconnected with her purpose, to communicate, time was not to be wasted on memories.

'When I accepted the communication had come from Grandma, then I received an inescapable thought. I needed to share the experience with you. I tried to quash the need but couldn't. I had to call you. A force unseen controlled my thoughts. To be honest it was a bit unnerving, I didn't like it one bit. I've never felt this level of interaction before and so, in response to the controlling force I shut down the communication channel, denying it a voice. All I could think was. How can I call Dad? For what reason? There is nothing tangible to share? In my mind all I had experienced was a vague connection to Grandma, nothing more. But all attempts to stem the flow of thoughts was futile; the presence remained alongside me throughout all of my cleaning duties. However much I tried to ignore it and fill my head with other thoughts and songs, I could not banish the song, could not stop the words from breaking through. 'Pack up your troubles in your old kit bag and smile, smile, smile.' Still there were no other words delivered, just the one line presented over and over again. As I fought against the message the stronger and more insistent the message became. There is only one other time when I have felt the fearsome power of the unseen at this level. It was a day when I had to acknowledge a message for myself. One day I will tell you about it but not now. From experience, I knew the force and the electrical energy which flowed through my body would persist until I accepted the message. Yet still I could not take ownership of the communication. In response to my lack of acceptance an additional control came into play. Each time I walked past a telephone the electrical energy increased in supply, coupled with an insistent message, 'Call your dad. Now!'

She paused for a moment to see if he wanted to respond to the rush of words just shared.

'Sorry, I have gushed a bit, I can't help myself. I have to release all the information in my head.'

He responded with love,

'Don't worry, I'm happy listening. I'll butt in if I want to ask a question.'

'OK. Where was I? Well, it didn't matter that I was battered by unrelenting electrical energy, words of the song and the tune, I still refused to give in to the unseen. I felt no fear at all. Instead I clung to a strong sense that I did not have to do what was ordered. I continued to challenge the connection. 'This song doesn't seem enough as a message and it doesn't make sense.' In response to the internal conversation my mind was cleared, as if a vacuum cleaner sucked out all that had once been there, everything which challenged the persistent force. Then in a moment of clarity I realised I had no choice, I had to surrender and must not waste time fighting the connection. I must act upon the message received. But I had no idea how to tell you.'

The truth, which she could not communicate, was that she had agreed to find a way to share the experience in order to stop the controlling communication. However, during the week which followed she had not fulfilled her promise. So another directive had been received. The next communication demanded she face up to reality. He needed her help. This stronger message, which had forced her to face up to the fact she might be able to help him in his battle against cancer, had driven the need to communicate. All of a sudden she recognised the magic of the flow. The first message had been delivered to give her a topic with which to connect. The second had been the instruction to communicate. She was going to have to learn fast if she were deliver the appropriate messages in a timely manner. She had never communicated all that had been received before, never had to. In order to exist, to fit in with all others in the world she had allowed everything which had come before to be released from the confines of her mind, lost to the intended recipients. But not anymore. She had an obligation to help her dad and had made the brave step to fulfil her responsibilities.

'This morning I decided I must waste no more time. I had to call you. So here I am.'

With her job complete Bee waited for a response. Silence. The quiet phone line fuelled her fear of not having a meaningful message for him. What if she had not delivered the message correctly? After what seemed like minutes but must have only been seconds, his voice halted her thought processing.

'This could be a massive coincidence but I actually sung the song 'Pack Up Your Troubles' at a local function one Saturday night, a couple of weeks ago.'

Catching her unaware a communication thrust forth with a greater supply of electrical impulses. She had to manage the situation. She tried to halt the overwhelming electrical surges but could not. There was no denying the force. In the moment she became aware of the importance of the electrical energy, it needed to flow, to enable her acceptance of all parts of the message. Bee took a deep breath and calmed her thoughts, released the need to control the flow and then spoke,

'Do you realise Grandma was with you the Saturday night a few weeks ago? She witnessed your singing. She wants you to know she is here.'

Had she gone too far? Was contact with the departed too much for him to deal with?

Once more there was silence. Bee felt compelled to fill the empty space, to convey the state of her mind and body during the connection. She needed to explain what it felt like to have control of your thoughts removed, to be a conduit for something else. But it was hopeless. She could never explain what it felt like when an unknown factor was in charge of her mind. However, she felt compelled to try. He had to understand what the message meant. Had to take responsibility, to make sense of it for himself. A question sprang from out of the blue.

'Grandma came to me for a reason, what are your feelings right now, about her communicating in this way?'

After a moment of hesitation he replied,

'I don't know what to think. There is a part of me wants to believe my mother is there somewhere. But to be perfectly honest I am stunned by what you have told me. Not only am I having trouble making sense of it but also coming to terms with the tune you were singing because I sang the song myself.'

He paused as if in thought then continued,

'I do actually think I need to hear the message and see the magic in it. But I have no idea why. Right now I am overwhelmed by the thought of the existence of the departed and why I would need to interact with them. This whole episode has raised a whole load of questions inside my head.'

Bee smiled and then spoke,

'Maybe this was the intention. We've both been tested. I have been asked to vocalise and trust in the communication with the departed, in my ability to hear and deliver a message.

You have been tested in your belief in the departed, of life after death. There are some big questions for you to answer. How are you going to move forward? Will you accept and believe in all you have been told or will you turn your back on all that has been delivered?'

His voice conveyed unease,

'I'm not sure what this means. I've had some pretty powerful experiences in my life, messages which I believe have been sent by God. There were times when I was pretty low after the death of my best friend Bob. I am sure God spoke to me then and I also believe the power of God has helped with my battle against the cancer. However, your experience has created more questions than it answers. In the church they do not believe in the departed. They believe and I have always believed, those who die go to be reunited with the maker. How then is it possible that a departed person can speak through a living person? The unseen power of which you speak is not God. Therefore what is it?'

She had no answer to the question but knew her connection was not with the God in which he believed. Then her thought flow stopped and changed direction. She heard something in his voice. He wanted to believe in his God. But she sensed a fragment of doubt. Many would have missed the vibration but she did not. She had sensed frailty in his words, which meant only one thing; he desperately wanted to, but did not truly believe in his God. Bee received this understanding through vibrations in his voice. This was not a new phenomenon, there had been many similar messages over the years, but this day was the first in a long time when she had accepted the gift. Knowledge of his lack of belief caused the chill of fear to creep into her mind and then a thought. If he did not truly believe what was waiting for him then how could he deliver himself to the place which could be coming to him soon? Was she the answer to the fracture in his belief? Was this the beginning of a journey together, where she could shed light on his path? Confirmation to this final question flowed through her body in the form of electrical tingling which travelled to every nerve ending and in accompaniment a 'knowing.' The mist which had once clouded her view cleared and an image became visible. A vision of father and daughter inextricably linked together. They needed each other, would travel together. Bee could sense the journey would not be easy but journeying together was their only hope. She had only taken a few seconds to process the message in his voice but it had been too long. He was waiting for a response,

'Bee, are you okay?'

She had to think of a way of ending the conversation so she did not have to answer the question. She needed time.

'Dad, I really need to go. I have just realised Edward has been sleeping the whole time we have been talking and I really should wake him. Can we talk again very soon?'

Bee was pleased to hear his eager response,

‘I would love to continue the discussion. Give me a call whenever you have time. Take care Sweetie. Cheerio.’

They had conversed for well over an hour. With the conversation at an end Bee noticed a change in state. Her heart felt unburdened and shoulders lighter, as if a heavy weight had been removed. The process of sharing the details of the incident with Grandma had been easier than she imagined. She had trusted it was the right thing to do. She had stepped over the threshold of fear which had been in existence for as long as she could remember, and walked right into the darkened room of the unknown. Without realising, the moment she shared this small part of herself she opened up a powerful channel of communication, one that could not be shut down, one that would grow in strength. She had unlocked a channel to her dad and his connection to the afterlife.

Chapter 4 — ARTHUR

Arthur felt uneasy. He had not spoken with Bee for a few months and then out of the blue she called with an incredible story to tell. How was it possible? The Church with which he was associated did not believe in such things. There was no possibility of a person who had died conversing with the living. No, he had always been led to believe a soul left the body and was reinstated with the power of God. Never had he thought he could converse once again with his mother. Yet Bee had delivered a message. Arthur recalled the conversation once more, tried to make sense of the connection with his mum. He could not escape the thought his mum had been with him when he sang 'Pack Up Your Troubles' on the Saturday night, a couple of weeks earlier. When Bee had spoken of the event he had felt a tingling chill develop down the left hand side of his body. A sensation that had not left his body for a full ten minutes; Arthur knew the exact time because he had watched the clock on the wall in disbelief as Bee continued speaking. He felt paralysed, unsure what to do with his new awareness of life after death. Not in all his years had he felt the presence of a member of the departed, not until this day when his mother had touched his life once again. As he recalled the presence, he challenged his belief in the existence of the departed, of a situation that could not be proved, one which defied all logic. He was torn, wanted to disbelieve as much as he wanted to believe. To believe meant there was something for him after his life ended. Yet disbelief threw him back into the uncomfortable void of the unknown. Had he really felt the cold chill of his mother or had there been a draft in his study? Had he forced himself to accept the tingling chill because he wanted to believe there was life after death?

He had a choice. To learn from their conversation of experiences he did not understand, or wander aimlessly through his life never quite knowing what awaited him at the end of his days. Since learning of his cancer he had entertained many ideas of what might be waiting for him if the cancer did actually strike him down. If he were being totally honest with himself, Arthur had to admit to confusion. He had thought his strong sense of belief in a lifetime's learning of God would be enough. But an element of doubt had crept into his daily existence and lodged there. He was no longer sure what was going to meet him if he died. This scared him more than death itself. He had come to terms with the fact he would die at some point. He had no choice but to accept his body may come to a point where it could no longer sustain its function, after all he had cancer. But he had not come to terms with the reality of what would actually happen to his soul when he died. Who would be there for him at the end of his days? His mum? He had no idea. The conversation with Bee had stirred up a hornet's nest of unknowns. He did not where to turn. His only hope was to continue conversing with Bee on the matter. But she had spoken of unseen forces. Something he knew very little about. What on earth was he to do? Had his daughter made up the story? Arthur didn't think so. He knew her well; she had nothing to gain from making up stories. But the events she described were unbelievable.

He recollected her childhood and remembered how she had never followed the crowd, had always taken her own path. She had spent many hours caring for ponies, in the village where they lived, seemingly preferring their company to family and friends. As Arthur further reflected on the past he recalled how Bee had stood out from her siblings. Even at her birth there had been an unusual occurrence. The day of her birth was fairly straightforward but snow fell the day after, not just a flutter, a total white out, which had confused the weathermen as it rarely snowed at the end of April. At the time Arthur had believed the snow had come with his daughter, the purity of her life had been followed by the purity of snow. However, thanks to a constant scowl in the early years, Bee had not endeared people to her. But as time passed she transformed into the sunniest child, with a smile that could engage anyone and an overwhelmingly caring demeanour. Arthur recalled how Bee had balanced the household in her position as middle child to the three which existed as the family for many years before her youngest brother arrived. Suddenly a thought was plucked from deep in his memory. He remembered her ability to know details of her siblings. Arthur reflected on the times he and Sheila had discussed their daughter, questioning how she was able to find her brother when no one knew where he was. How she was able to know what present she and her siblings were getting for Christmas. How she knew what they had been talking about in private. How she knew details of subjects of which she should have no knowledge. Arthur stopped his thought flow. There had been numerous events which for one reason or another had never been collated and analysed. Arthur supposed this had something to do with the effort required to raise three children and the small amount of time available to each.

Arthur considered the past and the present. He realised the connection just made, may well provide him with an opportunity to learn more about the complex individual he called his daughter. Bee was different but it was these differences which were intoxicating. Also, he could not escape the thought, she might have a connection to an unseen power, a link to his final destination, the place he would go when his body eventually gave up the fight. Arthur made a decision to keep an open mind.

Chapter 5 — BEE

Bee was acutely aware of the moment she shared the truth of her existence with her dad. She had felt the channel of communication develop and increase in strength. In the days before, she had received messages via a thread of a connection, but since their conversation this thread had developed to the size of an electrical appliance cable. The stream of communication had intensified as if she were downloading his present thoughts, his past and future. There was no escape. No option to shut down that which had been set in place. She had accepted her part and now had to deliver. There existed only a positive mental state at thought of such a connection, as if it would deliver benefit to both. He would open his eyes to the possibility of extending his life. She would learn to trust and develop her connection with the unseen force to deliver support to him.

To prepare herself for the journey Bee scoured bookshops, both on the Internet and in her local town. She searched for other people's experiences with that which could not be explained. The most recent encounter with the departed had inspired her to find out more. There had to be a reason for the heightened interaction with the departed and the force she could not see. After spending weeks gleaning information from books on Angels, Guides, God and other phenomena, Bee realised she was not alone in the interaction with an unseen existence. But even though there were other people who had similar experiences to herself, a sad fact remained—the text within the books did not satisfy her thirst for understanding, did not map to the unknown quantity with whom she conversed. She felt immense gratitude for the books, as they assisted her learning, but they did not hold the key to her search for answers. Instead, an absolute certainty pursued her through each day, knowledge that only she, through her own experience would be able to fathom why she had been immersed in this realm of change and acceptance of all things that could be heard but rarely seen. Trust was the key to unlocking a greater understanding. The next step became obvious. She had to release all doubt and allow messages to flow as they once had in childhood. This reinstatement of conversation with the unknown seemed bound to her dad. A thought led to a distinct possibility, she could actually assist his journey and make a difference. But could she save him from death?

Although she understood her role, Bee did not feel entirely comfortable with the idea of trusting everything which came via the unseen channel. However, she knew it was imperative to believe in the presence in order to help her dad. In response to this new responsibility she employed the process of affirmation. She spoke words both out loud and silently inside her head. No one had given her the instruction. She just 'knew' this was the way forward. Over and over during the course of a day she spoke the words, 'I trust the presence.' Although the words were easy to speak they were much harder to believe. Whenever she uttered the affirmation and then challenged it, a message presented in her conscious thought, 'It is the only way forward; in trusting you will learn, you will change beyond your current comprehension and you will be able to alter the world which surrounds you.' Accompanying the strange message came further isolation. Bee was acutely aware of how different she was to others. Her thoughts were different. This set her aside from other people. She had often asked the same question of herself. Why? There had never been an answer. Not in all her thirty-seven years. She could not escape the thought, maybe the newfound association with her dad would help her find an answer. But this was not supposed to be her focus. Instead she was to focus on him, to develop their relationship and understand him better. To achieve this she knew they needed an opportunity to meet face to face. To be given the chance to spend hours together talking, exploring why there was sudden contact with the departed and how she could help him. Also, more importantly, to find out if there was a way to release him from the bonds of death.

As if it had been orchestrated an opportunity presented. Her parents purchased a new home within half a mile of her own holiday home in Dorset. In order to reduce the cost of the move, her dad planned to transfer as many of his possessions in his own van prior to the main removal day. With her mum unable to assist, as she still had a few weeks work to see out at the doctor's surgery, Bee offered to support with the ferrying of possessions from the van to the new home in Dorset. Her reward for the gesture was alone time together. Affording them a chance to discuss life, death and all that was not visible. Providing Bee with an opportunity to get to know better the man she called her father. A man who had always been focused on work, with little time for playing with his children. He had worked away from home during the week when she had been a very young child, but when she was secondary school age there had been a change and he had mostly worked from home. However, this did not mean she saw any more of him. He had locked himself away in the home office at the back of the house from dawn till the late hours of the night. He had toiled endlessly to deliver a comfortable existence for his family. This golden opportunity for time together was not to be missed, would enable a deeper connection where she might better understand how she could help him. With this in mind she planned regular trips to her holiday home to coincide with his delivery of furniture. The days were planned in advance; mornings spent unloading his van and carting furniture to new positions. Then lunchtimes either involved a picnic of sandwiches, crisps and Jaffa cakes or an indulgent trip to the local pub for a either steak pie or scampi and chips. Afternoons were spent separately; she would take the boys down to the beach to play and he was afforded the chance to rest. The cancer cells which challenged his body depleted his energy levels, the effort required to carry furniture took its toll and he required an afternoon sleep to maintain a level of stamina for their evening discussions. The cherished evenings were spent in the comfort of her cottage where their routine followed the same pattern; he arrived at the house in the early evening and read a story to the boys, then together they put them to bed. With the children asleep, seated at the dining table they consumed a home cooked dinner. One which had been prepared by their team effort in the kitchen to the rear of the house. During this time they explored conversation, learned more about each other, shared thoughts on life, death and all that seemed inexplicable.

Bee understood her father more than she had at any other point in her life. She developed a greater awareness of his beliefs, vulnerabilities, hopes and dreams. During their time together they identified one common goal, to gain a greater understanding of the spiritual nature of their relationship. He was desperate to know if he could save himself from his fate but at the same time gain knowledge of what might happen if he died. She was keen to understand how she could use her connection with the departed to help him. Having read a great many texts on the existence of spirit Bee decided to approach her dad with an idea, one which might deliver him a greater understanding of the spiritual world. She had never delved into her past but had recently read a book on past lives and been attracted to the idea of investigating the possibility of a past existence. If it were true that you had lived before then maybe you would live again. Bee felt sure this was an important learning point for her dad and could strengthen his belief. As much as she wanted to save him from his illness, she did not know how. But she did know how to connect with spirit. Her guiding thought drove her to believe this connection would be enough to project them forward. With this in mind they planned a regression, a step back in time.

From a shelf in the sitting room she retrieved a book on how to return to a past life. They each took a role. Bee was the subject of the regression because she had a connection with the departed and he was in control of the text which led her into and out of the journey to the past. With roles agreed, Bee turned the dimmer switch down to reduce the lighting and sat in an armchair near the door. Arthur took a seat on the sofa opposite. Bee adjusted the cushions in the small of her back in the hope it would assist relaxation but the act did little to reduce the nervous fluttering which had developed in the pit of her stomach. Why did she have a sudden case of nerves? What harm could there be in the exercise they were about to undertake? Surely this was a game, a bit of fun, a chance to develop their knowledge? Out of the blue a question formed in the fore of her mind. Was she ready for a step into the past? Bee had absolutely no idea what would transpire during the minutes to come, but she was sure this was a step she needed to take. With this in mind Bee looked across the room, smiled and nodded to communicate it was time to begin. Her dad began reading text from the pages of the book. His voice deep, soft and relaxing as he explained the objective of the exercise. As his calming tones floated through the airwaves Bee closed her eyes, placed her hands by her side and attempted relaxation. The instructions filtered into her consciousness and Bee followed each of them to the letter. Her body became part of the chair and awareness of the room diminished. She was encompassed by the meditation, with all else forgotten. With each further step Bee moved deeper and deeper within. As she moved away from conscious interaction with the outside world her heart beat more rapidly and when it reached break neck speed she asked a question inside her head, 'Do I really want to do this?' Before she had time to back out, the meditation pulled her even deeper and she crossed a bridge.

His voice floated into the imagery which now presented inside her head, 'Where are you?' he asked.

She was in the dark. Walking down the cobbled street of a town, with houses on each side. She felt only fear, as if someone was searching for her, that the only safe time to leave her home was at night. From the look of her surroundings, the timber built houses with overhanging 1st floor windows, Bee knew she was not walking along a street in the twenty-first century. But she had no understanding of the exact date, almost as if it didn't really matter. Instead she was consumed by the fear of being found.

As if Bee were not allowed to look any further, her thoughts were directed by another question, 'What are you wearing on your feet?' he asked.

She looked down at her feet and observed a pair of smart, black shiny shoes adorned with a large silver buckle. An understanding formed. She was a man. Wearing black half-length trousers to the knee with the rest of the leg covered in black stockings.

Then another question penetrated through into her thoughts, 'What is the most significant event of your life?' he asked.

This question caused a giant a wave of emotion to engulf her senses. She found herself gazing upon the image of a woman giving birth to a child. A golden light surrounded the newborn child. The sight caused her heart to be filled with joy, but accompanying the happiness was another feeling, one of discomfort. This one dominated her thoughts. Something was wrong but she did not know what. Then a feeling of sadness descended and rested on her heart.

'How do you die?' he asked.

An image of an old man was presented. He wore a long white night gown and lay upon a bed in a large, sparsely furnished room. She felt an overwhelming sense of sorrow. She was truly alone. No one shared her life. She had lost everything. There was no one to care for her when she died. Her heart felt empty and cold.

Thankfully the final question took her away from the image of a lonely death, 'What did you learn?'

Even though she had witnessed a view of extreme loneliness at the point of death. She knew with absolute certainty death was not as dreadful as people thought, was not the most horrific event that could happen to a person in their lifetime. There was more but she could not see it, no more information was communicated to explain her 'knowing'. She knew there was more. She sensed another question needed to be asked in order to access another memory. But there were no more questions. All that remained was fear—that she was missing a vital piece of information associated with the message.

Somewhere outside of her conscious thought, Bee could hear a faint and distant voice bringing her back to an awareness of the room. On opening her eyes, the imagery present in her mind only minutes before, suddenly vanished. All that had seemed real was gone and in its place, a view of the sitting room. Any discomfort experienced during the regression had been replaced by a sense of gladness. She had been returned to her home in the present day and was very thankful to be free of the wretched feelings of fear and loneliness. A wealth of emotion had arisen as part of the regression, she could feel tears pushing for release. But she suppressed the need to cry and instead turned attention toward her dad. She smiled,

'I'm back now. Shall we go through the questions again so I can tell you what I saw?'

Earlier they had agreed she would not speak out loud until the exercise had been completed. To speak whilst in meditation would have affected the imagery.

Arthur spoke,

'Are you sure you are okay to continue? You look a little shell-shocked.'

Bee did feel drained by the emotion which had been present during the session but answered,

'I'm fine. I really want to share the experience before I forget any of the details.'

Having been given the go-ahead, he read the questions once more. This time Bee spoke of what she had seen, attempted to communicate the imagery which had played inside her head. She described every last detail of the regression, what she had seen, felt and known. In so doing she became conscious of the astonishing experience. How could the memory of a past life feel so real? There was little doubt in her mind everything presented was genuine. As she laid bare and discussed each point, an undeniable connection with the past grew stronger. A nauseous feeling developed in her stomach and Bee felt a sudden urge to run away from this past which had been dredged up. Prior to this evening she had never believed there was such a thing as a past life. What about now? A question dominated her thoughts. If there had been no past event then how could the memories have been presented inside her mind? What exactly had she connected to? Were these details from her memory or had she attached to another member of the departed? Was this member of the departed now present in her house? There were no answers to the multitude of questions that bombarded her thoughts. She halted the stream of questions inside her head and turned attention to her dad. He had been waiting patiently for the opportunity to discuss the meditation.

'Well, that was unusual, I'm not sure I understand what all those visions mean. Are they departed spirits? Was that really your life?'

There was one element in which he was particularly interested.

'Why do you think there was a golden light associated with the birth of the child?'

Bee knew why he had asked but did not know how to answer. He thought it related to the birth of Jesus, he wanted the experience to relate to God. The pressure to find an answer, coupled with overwhelming electrical energy pulses to every nerve ending, culminated in tears which forced their way to the point of eruption. She tried in vain to control the flow. Then to make sense of her reaction she silently interrogated herself. Why am I crying? Is it the reference to the birth and the golden light, or the sensation of death? With tears still rolling down her face Bee looked up towards her dad and in a voice strained with emotion asked,

'Why am I so upset?'

No sooner had the question been voiced than fresh tears fell. There was no rational explanation for the emotional outburst. No answers present in her head. So she accepted the need to cry and released all emotion until there was nothing left but emptiness.

Arthur waited quietly for her to regain composure. When the flow of tears had ceased they engaged in discussion, in search of answers.

'Bee, do you believe everything presented inside your head was from a past life or was it a communication of some kind?'

Bee had no idea,

'I don't know. It all seemed so real and yet I felt disconnected, as if it were me and not me all at the same time.'

He carried on pressing for answers.

'Let's assume it was a message. What do you think it means? Consider the first image where you felt really fearful, what could that mean?'

Bee felt the need to divulge everything and she answered with brutal honesty,

'My overriding feeling was fear, as if someone was looking for me and I had to stay hidden, except at night when I could move about. I guess I could relate this to my current situation. I have been hiding my ability to connect to the departed and know things others do not. I do fear people knowing about me. I'm not sure how to handle my gifts and certainly don't feel comfortable sharing with anyone but you.'

He moved the conversation along with more questions,

'What about you being a man, does that mean anything?'

Bee had an inkling to the reason for this,

'All I can think is the man relates to power. This message relates to my power.'

Without waiting for any more details he charged forwards with another question,

'Okay, but what about the significant event, the birth of a child, the golden light, the discomfort?'

Carried along by the flow of questions Bee continued finding answers.

'The whole experience is more than a little strange because I feel as if this is my birth. That in sharing I am reborn and the power of light has a part to play in my life. But as soon as I contemplate the wonder of finding all of which I am capable, I am paralysed by fear that chokes my throat and prevents me from speaking. I am consumed by dread that everything coming will be too overwhelming for me to deal with. In all honesty, I'm very scared. I think this is why I can't stop crying. I'm really glad you're here. Thank you for listening to my rambling. I think I have waited my whole life for this moment of release.'

Arthur responded, 'I don't know what to say. I'm not sure I really understand what has transpired tonight. But I too am glad I was here.'

He paused for a moment then asked,

'Do you have any thoughts on the last image, the one with the dying man?'

Bee stopped short of blurting, 'It's you, a message for you.' Instead, she shared the next best thing,

'Dad, I am not entirely sure of the message. I think the image is the communication of death being a lonely experience, a path you must walk alone but this does not make it bad. Death is final but is not the worst experience you will face.'

Bee could not tell him the truth. She knew the suffering and pain he would endure to the end would be much worse than the moment of death. But she could not share this secret. When all questions had been exhausted they agreed to call it a night. With concern for his fatigued appearance, Bee asked,

'Are you OK Dad?'

He responded, 'I'm tired. I think I need my bed.'

At the front door, after exchanging a goodnight kiss on the cheek, he pulled back and asked,

'Are you okay now? Will you be alright tonight?'

Bee smiled in response and sent him on his way, 'I'll be fine, just need sleep, as do you. Night-night, see you tomorrow.'

She locked the front door behind him, switched off the lights and climbed the stairs.

After tiptoeing along the landing she entered the boys' room, tucked covers around their bodies and gave each a kiss on the forehead. Love for the precious beings filled her heart with a warm and fuzzy feeling; at this time of night they looked perfect, almost as if when they slept an angelic appearance changed their form. A sense of gratitude filled her insides as it did every night, for the chance she had been given to share their beautiful lives and to experience the joy of motherhood. After turning focus of thought inwards Bee realised how desperately she needed rest. Within minutes she changed into pyjamas, completed bathroom duties and was snuggled under the warmth of the 10tog duvet. As she lay on her back, with her 5ft 3-inch frame swamped by the king-size duvet, she sought warmth and tucked the bedding around her body until only the top of her head and eyes were visible. Her thoughts wandered. The exercise of regression had dragged up thoughts maybe she should have left hidden. She was unsure if any benefit had been gained. Unexpectedly, unease crept into her thoughts. She did not feel relaxed or anywhere near sleep. Instead her head filled with dark shadowy images. As the unease grew her focus turned to the house in which she lay. Her holiday cottage had once served as an old 'Passage Pub' and was situated on an ancient Roman road, frequented by many a traveller. The front door of the house was located more or less on the street and a passage ran from the front to the back door through the middle of the building; on each side of the passage a room that had once served as a pub room. Her imagination ran riot as she contemplated the numerous visitors to the space below. Thoughts strayed to the possibility that over the years there had been more than a few deaths in the old building and maybe those departed spirits were in existence in the shadows of the house. Insecurity froze her thoughts, the icy chill of fear deposited in her mind and fog descended so she could no longer see. The resident dread led to one belief—she had become more connected to the dark side of that which could not be seen than ever before. The regression had opened a door she should have left shut.

Why had she thought regressing to the past was such a good idea? The notion had been placed in her head and she had followed like an over-excited puppy. But it had not been a fun game. Instead she had dredged up stored emotions, thoughts and the shadowy existence of an unknown quantity. Her lack of confidence in how to deal with the unseen generated further anxiety. In accompaniment, darkened shadows hovered in close proximity, dominated the space both inside and outside her mind. Bee felt out of control. As if she were being manipulated by something devious. Fear gathered strength, grasped at her thoughts and attempted to take control. But she would not allow it. Would not allow herself to be fearful of all she did not truly understand. Instead she turned to her tried and tested method of banishing darkness by imagining a large white light engulfing her wholly in its beam. Inside her head there existed an imaginary street lamp, under which she stood, bathed in white light. She focused on the light until it dispersed all fear. Once all darkness had been eliminated and just before sleep took her to places unknown, when the last thoughts of the night floated through her head, Bee contemplated the regression and realised she would never ever do it again. She would find another way to help her dad, in the hope of making a difference to his life.

Chapter 6 — ARTHUR

Arthur travelled the short journey back to his home in record time, parked his van on the sloped concrete drive and stepped out into the darkness of the night. As he took a slow, steady walk along the unlit pathway leading to his front door he became more aware of the isolated location. He allowed dark and shadowy plumes of fear to cling to his conscious thought. Were there shadows in the darkness? Was there something there, almost within reach? He had never been scared of the dark. What had changed? The regression? Arthur pushed the dark thoughts away and as he reached the front door, felt immense gratitude for the small lamp which illuminated his entry. Once inside he felt safe again. There were few home comforts but that didn't bother him. The sitting room had enough to supply him with all he needed, a 1970's metal framed deck chair and fold-away camping table. The sparsely furnished room which filled his eye-line caused Arthur to question his choice for a two phase move; to transfer a number of belongings into the house prior to the main removal date. But he didn't question himself for long. He felt certain the decision had been an excellent one. Firstly giving him a purpose in life and secondly allowing him to connect with Bee. The house, although lacking in furniture and carpets, provided a resting place that suited him perfectly; gifted him the precious space and peace he craved during his physical and mental battle against the cancer. He was glad to be there. Having spent the best part of the day on his feet, and with his energy reserves depleted, he headed straight to the bedroom to prepare his body for sleep.

Arthur lay on his back and looked up at the ceiling. As he relaxed towards sleep he couldn't stop the flow of thoughts related to the regression. At the fore of his mind was one dominant thought. He had not shared the whole truth of his experience. He could not. During the regression Bee had almost disappeared when a mist like substance shrouded her body. What had happened? Why? How could she manifest a cloud to hide behind? None of it made sense. Arthur struggled to rationalise all he had seen. He had no previous experience with which to compare the events of the evening. Logic could not be applied. But he felt desperately inquisitive, wanted to understand where she had been and who she had been. However, Arthur was a realist, was well aware he would never fully understand. Although this reality did not stop him from wanting to know more. In the moment before sleep claimed his thoughts he considered their relationship and the unusual path travelled together. Bee had somehow delivered him to a greater comprehension of himself and all he had chosen not to accept.

CHAPTER 7 — BEE

Bee hesitantly opened her eyes, not really believing morning had arrived. But there was no escaping the harsh reality of the sunlight which streamed into the room through the gap between the curtain and the wall, heralding the start of another day. In the bedroom next door she heard James and Edward giggling, then silence, followed by delicate footsteps on the landing. Bee was absolutely certain James was on his way to her bedroom as he had the lightest of steps. His sleepy face peered around the door checking to see if she was awake. On seeing her eyes open he raced across the room, clambered onto the high iron framed bed and wrapped his short slender arms around her neck. Snuggled together and encased in the warmth of the duvet neither wanted to respond to the call from next door, however they could no longer ignore the insistent sound,

'Me, me.'

Bee reluctantly slipped from the warmth and crept quietly down the landing towards the insistent voice. She had never lost the sense of excitement of connecting with her children, which had first been delivered on the day of their birth and then every day that followed. She peered around the door and connected with Edward, his eyes communicated silent gratitude at being remembered. As she lifted him from the cot she felt the warmth of mother love and snuggled him close. Back in her bedroom she lay Edward down next to James, climbed back into bed and drew both boys into the warmth of her body, a luxury she knew would not last long. All too soon the pleasure of cuddles was replaced by the need for sustenance. In response, all three slipped from the bed into the chill morning air and then carefully negotiated the ancient, uneven wooden stairs where splinters threatened to catch their toes. Once at the bottom of the perilous staircase her bare feet connected with the stone cold slate slabs which covered the ground floor, a shock to the system which encouraged a faster step towards the sitting room where she settled the boys on a chair in front of the television. Then she tiptoed back across the cold floor to the base of the stairs and collected her slippers. Once her feet were encased in the warmth of her towelled mule slippers, not pretty but very practical, she felt better able to cross the chill slabs of the dining room and make it to the kitchen at the back of the house. Here the contents of the sink cried out for attention but she had a more pressing task to fulfil first. Only when the boys had been delivered a snack and drink could she apply herself to the chore of washing up, a tiresome job which reared its ugly head every morning.

With hands deep in the Belfast sink and soapsuds up to her elbows Bee washed up the dishes. Then, unexpectedly, a change occurred in her thought process. Knowledge was planted inside her head. She knew her dad needed to feel his parents were waiting for him. Amused by this random thought with an absolute knowing attached, Bee followed the train of thought presented and found herself in receipt of a message which required interpretation. She left her mind open to the receipt of information and the detail was delivered to her conscious thought. He would gain comfort if he believed that as he passed over to the other side he would not be met by strangers, but instead be delivered to those he recognised. The connection had been made. Bee understood how he was feeling. He wanted assurance of his departure. He needed to know he would be welcomed with open arms by someone he knew. He had never expressed such a wish but Bee knew these thoughts were on his mind. In response to the knowledge, she tuned into a connection with the unseen channel, shifted her mind from a controlling position and transferred communication to another receiver. Silently, inside the space in her head she asked a question, 'Grandma, is that you?' Electrical impulses flowed through the left hand side of her body as confirmation was received. Next, still speaking within the confines of her head, 'Can you channel a message to me?' Instantaneously she doubted her ability to converse with the departed. Surely it was not as easy as speaking silently in her head and then waiting for an answer. Could it be that easy? It seemed so. With new found confidence she delivered the next communication, 'Grandma, the message you pass through me has to be something dad will believe without doubt. Which in turn will lead him to believe in the departed. The content has to be something of which I have no knowledge.'

Bee felt her confidence grow as the communication with Grandma developed. Her head filled with words spoken in her mother tongue. Emotions not her own were delivered to her awareness and electricity flowed as if she were a conduit. Each message transported to her consciousness required interpretation. This was the easy part. But how would she communicate the meaning of the message to her dad? A dominant thought was present. She must try. With little time to waste she faced up to her responsibility. Her dad needed to know his mum was in existence. As Bee allowed the communication to develop further, she was overwhelmed by a sense of warmth and love, along with a warm tingling as electrical impulses flowed from the top of her head and down the left side of her body. Once accustomed to the sensation of Grandma she pushed all thought aside. Instinctively, as if guided, she mentally walked through the 1930's, suburban Surrey house in which her Grandparents had lived. An external image of the house became present in her mind then Bee was thrust back in time. A child, she stood in the reception hallway and looked downwards at the highly polished parquet wooden floor. When she looked up, to her left Bee viewed the dark wood hat stand with four curled prongs pointing up to the ceiling, then to her right the dark wood hall table with mirror stand. She knew none of these visions were the message; their purpose was only to define the space in which she now existed. The connection with Grandma grew stronger as she walked forwards across the parquet floor. Then all of a sudden Grandma appeared in the doorway to the kitchen, dressed in a nylon blue and white checked housecoat, with hands on hips. As if the forward view was blocked, Bee turned to the right and looked in the toy cupboard under the stairs. Unexpectedly a communication presented in fore of her mind. In response Bee conversed silently but firmly with Grandma, 'No this cannot be the message. I have experience of the toy cupboard and its contents.' A few moments before, when the communication was in its infancy, she had felt a novice. But with each step she grew in confidence, became happier to challenge the information passed through her mind. The stream of thought continued as Grandma directed her to the sitting room at the front of the house. She was presented with an image of an old fashioned 1970's mock wooden television set, positioned next to a cut glass bowl full of sweets purchased from the Pick and Mix at Woolworth's. Next, thought control passed back to Bee, 'This cannot be the message as I remember the old TV and sweets.' As if in response Grandma led her toward the back of the house, to the dining room door. Bee stood facing the door. She was a child, at child height the door loomed large above her. She felt troubled. Something was very wrong. There was something going on behind the closed door. Then the message was delivered. 'Marbles.' Once the word had been placed inside her head it could not be ignored, electrical energy raced through her body, a 'knowing' presented, this word must be communicated to her dad.

The communication with Grandma ended abruptly and left Bee feeling deflated. All of the electrical impulses once present had vanished and she no longer felt the reality of a presence in the kitchen. What had happened? What had she gained from the communication? Was there a message to pass on to her dad? Thoughts careered through her head and the seemingly never ending electrical force ignited all nerve endings. Then her mind emptied and only one thought remained. 'You must call your dad now.' The pattern of behaviour which followed was exactly the same as the first time she had conversed with Grandma. She could not concentrate on anything else. Whenever she attempted banishment of the directive she was forcefully encouraged to pick up the phone and deliver the message. Although she had become used to the new sensation, where an unknown factor took control of her thought flow and drove her towards an activity, Bee still felt slightly overwhelmed and vulnerable. This was not an insignificant step. She was required to deliver a message to another person and admit every thought inside her head, to ultimately show her true self. The act of crossing the Grand Canyon in one stride seemed an easier task than the one presented, one which involved the interpretation of feelings, images and words presented in her head and transformation into an understandable message. She smiled at the ridiculousness of her fear, and within this lightened state developed 'a knowing.' If she must learn how to interpret and communicate messages then her dad was the best person on whom to practise. The 'knowing' delivered safety and confidence. She would know what to do.

Even though she had been greatly distracted by the communication Bee still managed to complete the washing up. But the hour was still early for most. The clock on the wall displayed 6:45 am. A little too early to call her dad. She made breakfast for herself and the boys in an effort to fill the time and push the hour past seven before calling him. Although still early Bee knew her dad would be up and about, as for the best part of his life he had risen each morning at 6 am. Nevertheless, when the hour hit seven she felt the confidence in the timing of her call and her ability to deliver a message drain away. But there was little choice. She had to call. There was no avoiding her responsibility. Reluctantly, Bee picked up the telephone handset positioned on the windowsill in the dining room and dialled his number. She stared out onto the road which ran along the front of the house, listened to the ringing tone and waited. Her heart raced and nerves danced in her belly. Eventually his voice answered the call,

'Hello Sweetie.'

He knew who it was, must have seen her number appear on the phone display. All physical symptoms of fear dissolved as she recognised amusement in his voice in response to the early morning call. Although devoid of fear, her confidence was still diminished and she was unsure how to begin. Then as if controlled by the unknown she asked,

'How are you this morning?'

He responded, 'I'm fine thank you, much better for a good night's sleep.'

They both knew there was more to the call but each played along with the niceties of exchange until they were ready to approach the real topic of conversation. As Bee readied for release of the message, her heart raced and confidence diminished. There was no way she could deliver the message. She heard the silent voice cry out in her head. 'You must try. This is for your dad. This is not about you.' Conflict took up residence in her mind and tension transformed her physical stature, she began to shake, arms and legs lost to her control as they became receptacles for the fear of failure. Bee felt glad for the distance between them, she did not feel able to deliver this information to his face.

Bee took control of her thoughts and after a deep intake of breath she spoke,

'Dad, I tried to contact your mum this morning.'

She had begun. It would be easier now. He responded eagerly,

'Oh yes?'

His positive response delivered a state of greater confidence, the way was clear to transfer the details of the communication, the message from his mum. However, she could not tell him of the actual flow of messages which involved knowledge of his private thoughts, his need to feel his parents were waiting for him. This gift of knowledge maybe too much for him to digest. As a child she had often used her knowledge of another person, but had utilised it more carefully as an adult. There had been times when her knowledge upset adults. They did not know how to manage the truth that seemingly another could connect to their thoughts. Adults always worried about how much she knew, as if they had a wealth of secrets to keep hidden, as if her knowledge of their real selves would somehow make them unappealing. The truth of the gift was, she only saw what they were willing to share. But adults never believed. They found this hard to comprehend. Bee understood perfectly well. When she connected to another person they were crying out for all to hear, they were communicating with everyone. Incredibly, only a few people were able to hear the transmission. She was one of them.

She released the thoughts which dominated the space in her head and turned focus to the conversation in hand.

'I had the weirdest experience this morning which I wold love to tell you about. I connected to Grandma. It was a strange encounter, where I could feel her inside my mind and body, a really clear communication, like a conversation. Then a message was delivered for you.'

Bee spent a few minutes explaining how she communicated with his mother through visualisation, the way she walked through the home of his childhood. The act of sharing the entire experience seemed important, as if it would assist his belief in the message. He had to believe the communication had come from his mother and not her own imagination. When she had finished the recount, when the word 'marbles' had been shared, Bee still had no clear idea what the message meant. But she knew how to find out. She would ask him a series of questions and wait for a response in her body. She was absolutely certain an electrical tingling would confirm the correct understanding. With this belief in the process Bee asked,

'In the context of your mum and your childhood home does the word marbles mean anything to you?'

Almost immediately he responded,

'As a child I played marbles in the house.'

No. This was not the message. There were no electrical impulses sent as confirmation, no emotion thrust to the fore. Bee responded,

'No, that's not the message.' Then he offered, 'My mum lost her marbles.'

That was it. Electrical impulses sped through the length of her body, down the left side, up the right side and then into her head as if a box of fireworks had been ignited. This was the message communicated. His mum had 'lost her marbles.'

Bee listened as he recounted the memory of a night when he was a young boy.

'On a night long ago, the family doctor visited our house. He entered the dining room, closed the door and spent what seemed like hours with my mum and dad. During this time, unbeknown to me, the doctor diagnosed my mum with having a serious mental illness and explained she had to be admitted to hospital. All the time, whilst they were in the room, I sat at the bottom of the stairs paralysed by fear of what would happen to my mum. When the doctor left, my dad explained how my mum had 'lost her marbles' and needed to be looked after by nurses.'

Bee could not deny the smile on her face. They had understood the message, made the connection between the dining room and the marbles.

'Dad, it really was your mum. There is no mistaking the reference to marbles.'

A fresh set of electrical impulses travelled along the left hand side of her body and in accompaniment happiness, an emotion transferred from Grandma. Communication between the two worlds had been successful.

'I have to admit, I'm amazed by the way you received the details from my mum. The word 'marbles.' It had to be her. But how?'

His voice contained both excitement and disbelief.

'What is she trying to communicate and why? I'm not sure what this means to me. She is dead but also in existence somewhere. How can this be possible? What am I supposed to do now?'

Bee could hear the frustration in his voice and so attempted to relieve his lack of understanding,

'Dad, I don't think you are supposed to do anything. I think this is part of our learning. We are on a journey of discovery. This is just a step along the path. We accept it happened and move forwards together. Last time the communication was through a song, this time through imagery and words. We are developing our connection. Are you okay to continue?'

He took a breath,

'I think so. I enjoy our conversations, they bring a whole new dimension to my life, encourage me to think about unknown quantities which I have never considered before. I do want us to continue exploring this realm, I'm just not sure how helpful I am going to be. It seems you have all the connections.'

Even though the connection had ended, there still remained a sense of energy and excitement which kept a smile on her face. Bee wished she could transfer this feeling, help him feel the incredible sensation of the departed. Although, she felt sure he would not want to experience the fatigue which remained following a high level of contact with the departed, or the emotion which was transferred during a connection. As this thought was processed her throat tightened and tears fell, accompanied by an unusual tingling sensation throughout her body. A 'knowing' was delivered. This is not my emotion. An imposter exists within, is still in control of my senses. She accepted the fact. With acceptance came comprehension that emotion was just another method of communication. Bee released the sentiment and spoke,

'I am glad we have conversed with Grandma. I'm glad she is here for you and me. But unfortunately I have to return to the world of the living and get the boys washed and dressed. Would it be okay if we catch up later?'

He sounded reluctant to release her from the conversation but they both knew there were practical considerations to be met.

'You go, I can hear those rascals in the background and they are clearly in need of a run about. I'll give you a call tomorrow when you're back at home in Surrey.'

With the conversation at an end Bee returned to her duties as a mother, all thoughts of the spirit world parked until a time when they could be reinstated.

Chapter 8 — ARTHUR

The old deck chair creaked as Arthur sat down in his partially furnished sitting room. He leaned back and considered the telephone conversation. One thought dominated all others. Could this be true? Had his mother communicated? It had to be true. Bee had described something she could not have known. This admittance delivered a heady mix of emotion. He wanted to be pleased for Bee, excited for her ability to communicate with the other side, but he was not. Instead he was overwhelmed by an alternative emotion. Terror. He was suffering with cancer and had no idea if there would be a miraculous cure. Currently, the possibility was slim, which meant he had to face the grim reality that he could soon depart the earth. How soon he could not be sure. But time was short. He had already spent three years fighting the battle against the murderous cells in his body. He had been told five years. Which meant he may only have two left. When his time came he could be reunited with his mother, who he now believed was waiting. Did he really want this? There were too many memories, both painful and joyful. Would they all be rekindled when he met her again? Arthur did not want to dwell on the relationship with his mother. Whenever he pondered on his childhood he was flooded with painful memories, confusion, and then hit a brick wall where he felt nothing at all. Arthur understood he needed to address this issue but he did not know how. He had enjoyed a good relationship with his mother in latter years but these were not the years that tore a hole in his heart. Arthur braved the sense of dread which often prevented him from going back in time. He took a step into the past and inside his head travelled to childhood. From toddler until the age of six he had spent many happy years following his mother around the house, helping her in the kitchen and cuddling up at night under the warm, soft eiderdown. But the heavenly existence had been stolen from him the day his father returned from the war. A stranger had entered the home and stolen his loving, caring mother. She had been replaced by a tired and argumentative woman, a person he had never seen before. After a period of time, following bouts of weeping and outbursts of anger, she had slipped to the murky depths of insanity. His mother had been taken away to a quiet place where she could be treated. During this time of depression his mother had shut him out. Arthur had never felt so alone. Not until this day when the reality of death seemed too close. He was not ready to go. It didn't matter if life had become a drag, ingesting drugs with horrendous side effects. He didn't want to leave his life behind, he could not release his grip. Once gone he would be forgotten. Of all the things which frightened Arthur the most, he did not want to be forgotten. He wanted to live forever. However, he did not believe he had any control of his body and the fight against the enemy that raged within. But Arthur refused to yield. He had made the decision to live the five years predicted and this is what he would do. For Arthur it was irrelevant whether this choice served him or not, he was determined to find a way to stay alive for as long as possible. When he could hold on to life no longer, and it was 'his time,' only then would he meet with his mother.

Chapter 9 — BEE

On the last trip to Dorset to assist the removal process, Bee arranged a lunch outing to nearby Lyme Regis. Although short, the time they had spent together in house moving activities and evening discussions provided them with an opportunity to connect as never before. Had delivered more knowledge of each other than the expansive period, the lifetime, which had come before. They had been gifted the space to share; Bee had spoken freely of communications with the departed and he had spoken unreservedly on the subject of his demise without the need to protect the listener from the truth of his feelings. Father and daughter had formed a close bond, learned to love one another again; were reconnected.

With lunch on their mind the party of four followed the road into Lyme, a quaint fishing town full of history and hordes of tourists during the summer months. The school summer holidays were almost at an end which meant there were fewer tourists and therefore more parking spaces. Bee found parking not too far from the sea front, in the small car park opposite the sweet shop. She was very aware her dad may tire easily, so to be able to make a quick return to the car was of utmost importance. The summer weather was still with them, warm and balmy with clear blue skies, which meant they could take full advantage of the promenade and sandy beach. Bee linked arms with her dad as they strolled along the sea front and the boys ran ahead towards the amusement arcade, which always had to be visited. Still coupled by arm, they stood and watched James and Edward enjoy the Bob the Builder ride, a pleasure which seemingly could never be exhausted. When the money to feed the machine ran out, the boys scampered off along the tarmac towards the harbour and they followed, stopping only to purchase fish cake and chips for the boys and fish and chips for the adults. With warm food wrapped in paper, held carefully in hands, they found a seat against the harbour wall on which to sit and using the wooden fork provided, proceeded to tuck into the lunchtime feast. From their position there was plenty to see. Men cleaning down their boats, tidying up the nets or passing the time of the day with fellow fishermen. Both adult and child alike thoroughly enjoyed the act of people watching whilst tucking into a lunch cradled in their laps. When they were finished and the seagulls had eaten their share of any chips which had dropped to the ground, Bee agreed to the boy's demands and followed them onto the beach. Having found a couple of deck chairs for hire, Bee and her dad sat once more, this time watching the children at play. Bee stole a sideways glance towards him. He looked tired, but seemed happy enough to be out with them in the sunshine. As if he knew she were watching, he turned and smiled.

'I love this place. There is something about this town and the region as a whole, that makes me feel good, injects me with energy. With each day this becomes more and more important. Time feels short. As if I should take advantage of every minute. Only be where I want to be, with whom I want to be, to ensure I don't sacrifice my needs for other people's happiness. I really believe I can follow my dream here. Live a simple life, in a home I can afford, with albeit a small amount of money to support my lifestyle. I know the dream is likely to be short-lived but I can still be happy here.'

He paused, his face tanned from outdoor chores reflected his sadness,

'Sorry, I didn't mean to be gloomy.'

Bee didn't want him to stop, she could tell he needed to offload,

'Dad, it is okay to say whatever you want. I'm here for you as a friend. I won't be saddened by your words. We have agreed, there will only be truth between us. I tell you mine and you tell me yours.'

He smiled,

'I know we agreed to share everything and I am very grateful for that because I don't want to deposit my gloom on your mum. She's had enough to deal with. The closer we get to the end of my days the more I don't want to tell her of my thoughts.'

Bee stemmed tears at the thought of his reality but she had to be strong for him, had to provide the safe harbour he needed.

'Keep talking. It's important you share how you feel. Maybe we will be able to find a way to save you. This area is full of spiritually-minded people, why don't we take advantage of this positive energy, find an alternative way of dealing with illness.'

He brightened, 'It's a good idea and would certainly bring more hope into my life. At the moment the only hope I have is in the possibility of a drug trial which is starting up in London and a vitamin treatment to boost the immune system. One could be really difficult to get on and the other too expensive for my small savings pot.'

He paused and smiled, 'Don't worry, I won't give up, not yet. Sitting here with you and the boys on this perfect summer day allows me to forget the reality of my life, of the cancer. However, when I see you and the kids beginning your family life together I can't help but want that time back. To be at the beginning with my family. Second time round I would make different choices. I would not waste so much time at work, toiling for money to support a lifestyle I never really enjoyed. All I really need to be happy is to have my wife and family, the ability to enjoy a pint, fine wine, good food and an endless landscape to walk. If only I'd known that years ago.'

Bee could not let him wallow. She needed to help him. She could help him. There was a way. But in order to succeed she must move him along the path of belief in the power of his spirit. Maybe she should divulge more of her life secrets. Would it help him to hear more of her stories of the unknown factor which was present in her life? Would this drive a greater belief in all that seemed so impossible? She knew there was a fracture in his belief in God. Perhaps she should tell him of another experience. Surely it wouldn't do any harm.

'Dad, I sense you feel very lonely with your thoughts of death. You feel alone in your battle. Obviously I don't know what it feels like to battle cancer. But I do know what it feels like to be alone. To walk alone without support, not really knowing the why or where you are going, or even how you are going to achieve what you know you must. If you want to hear it, I would like to tell you about something that happened to me about six months after Edward was born. I'm not really sure why but I think it would help to tell you.'

Bee was still unsure how to tell the story. It was more than unusual and quite hard to describe. But knew she must and so began,

'Do you remember I went on a spa trip with my best friend Katy, nearly two years ago? We stayed in that stunning place, nestled deep within rolling Hampshire countryside, somewhere near Liphook. As I'm sure you are aware, it is quite unlike me to agree to this level of indulgence and to stay away from home. But Katy talked me into it. She told me it would do me good. Well, at the end of our first day, when I had finished my treatments, I looked for an activity to fill in time while I waited for Katy to complete her treatments. I spotted a poster advertising a free admission talk from a local Medium, and I thought, enough money had been spent on indulgence so I would sit and listen to the ramblings of this stranger. I have to admit, the moment I entered the room I questioned my choice. But I stayed. There was nothing else to do, so I made myself comfortable alongside the other eight occupants of the room. Then it began. Something that had never happened before. I have to say, I'm not sure I ever want it to happen again. Suddenly, without warning a feeling of desperation smothered me. All thoughts in my head were drowned out by images of red and white warning signs. With them came a need. I desperately wanted to leave the room. I tried in vain to leave. It was as if I were possessed. The more I fought to control the power, the more control it took. Eventually, every one of my conscious thoughts was encompassed by the unknown factor. I could not leave. I was not allowed to leave. I have to say I was petrified of what might happen next and asked question after question inside my head. "What is happening? How can something stop me from moving? How are my thoughts being controlled? Why do I feel so scared?" Then panic set in. Silently, inside my head I screamed out for help. I tried again to leave the room but I was too late, the Medium Barbara Bright entered. With the entrance of the subject of the talk, there was a brief respite from my sense of unease, my thoughts turned to the grey haired middle-aged lady who entered the room. But as soon as Barbara was seated and speaking of her life story, the silent voice inside my head struck up conversation again, this time pleading. "What am I doing here?"' Bee checked her dad for a response to the story told so far, his eyes were engaged which she took as interest. She smiled awkwardly, 'Dad, I don't think I will ever be able to describe the feeling, the battle that raged within, the fight for control. The experience was so physical and yet there was nothing there. Nothing that could be seen. There are so few people who would believe such a story, yet alone understand it. I'm not really sure why I'm telling you but I'm going to keep on because I think it will help us in some way.'

He agreed,

'Keep talking. Tell me what happened next, I'm intrigued to know.'

Bee continued,

'I'm still unsure why I chose to go to the talk in the first place. I'm not keen on spending time with strangers, it was almost as if I had been placed there. Once there, something ensured I stayed until the very end. Anyway, all of a sudden, as I sat on the sofa all alone, I 'knew' why I was there. I was

unhappy. I needed to hear the life story. The story unravelling was filled with heartache, sadness and struggle. I understood that I, too, had not felt happiness within myself for a long time. Suddenly I recognised my problem. In not sharing my thoughts with anyone I had been spiralling ever deeper into a pool of negativity. I had created a large and unmanageable mess inside myself. I understood. I needed to find out why I was so sad. How I could lift the dark cloud which existed inside. However, I knew my current situation was not the place to address such issues. Instead I had to continue listening to Barbara. I could not help but be engaged by her words, she was very much alive with strong-held beliefs.
As I listened to the tale, I softened, relaxed and truly heard the words shared. I must admit I did find it hard to believe everything. But whenever I questioned any part of the story I heard words inside my head. These were not spoken out loud. But were made 'known' to me. Over and over I kept being told, 'keep your mind open.' Now you of all people know I don't appreciate being told what to do. I like to figure life out for myself. But for some reason I stayed there and I listened. No sooner had I entered a state of calm and acceptance then I was thrust back into panic. I heard Barbara speak directly to me. She had no idea it was me but I knew the moment she uttered the words, the message was for me only. "My guide is telling me there is someone here who is filled with negativity and they feel very sad about this." On hearing these words I

was held in a stranglehold of terror, which wrapped around my throat preventing me from breathing. I felt every kind of emotion, followed by pressure which bore down on my shoulders. There was only one response available to me. Yet another discussion inside my head. I could have invented excuses to project the focus on one of the other women in the room but I knew without doubt the message was for me. Almost as if a large sign had been erected in my mind displaying the words, "It is you." There was no argument allowed. When I accepted my part there came a change, as if I had been awoken from a deep sleep. On acceptance I was overwhelmed by a sensation never felt before, one which consumed my entire body. I tried to flee from the dominating force by getting up off the sofa. But I could not move. I craved to leave, but to no avail. I can still feel the strength of the desire now as I relate the story to you. I wanted to run away, as far away as possible, yet my limbs would not respond. As if they were controlled by a powerful immobilising force, I had to remain. There was no lessening of my desperation to leave the room, and although I had no power against the force, every single part of me fought on. Again and again I tried to raise myself from the sofa. As my efforts increased so did the pressure from the unseen. In the end I gave up. I submitted to that which held me in place. There was nothing I could do. Fear dominated every single thought, crushed my heart and occupied my head until there was no more space to think. All control of my body seemed to have been revoked. With this knowledge I panicked. The anxiety and desperation I had once felt were replaced by sheer terror, at a level I had never experienced before. I truly believed my life was about to be taken. I remember tears fell and no matter how hard I tried they did not stop.' Bee paused as she remembered the depth of emotion felt that day. 'I don't cry often, even now I can feel tears pricking at my eyes when I recall the level of fear I endured. What happened? What could possibly create such a physical experience? How could I have been held in place? I was really terrified. My heart sill races at the thought of the whole experience.' Without waiting for a response or answers to her questions Bee moved onto the next stage of the story. 'In my state of fear and confusion I glanced upward to see if any of the other people had noticed my tears. I felt sure someone must have seen all that was happening to me and yet, as I sneaked a look around the room I could see no reaction. I existed alone. As if in an isolation bubble. As a distraction from the reality of my situation I re-tuned into Barbara's voice, the recount of a life story. The words spoken were audible and yet I could not really hear them. My thoughts still dominated by an overwhelming need to leave, to escape my reality. But the pressure was maintained. I was held in place. Fear threatened to drown me. I was helpless. As if this was not enough, then a peculiar electrical tingling travelled throughout my body. This began at the top of my head and spread all the way down to my toes. I was terrified, which in turn caused my mind to race. Firstly, I had been held in place by a force I could not see. Secondly, my body appeared to be conducting electricity from who knew where. I couldn't control my body or my thoughts. My heart raced, faster and faster until I felt sure it would explode. I asked the most obvious of questions, "Am I about to die?" The sound of laughter echoed inside my head with the words, "Not today." But that wasn't enough, I needed answers, so I fired another question into my consciousness. "If I'm not going to die then what the hell is happening to me?" This time there was no response. I was left alone, pinned to the sofa with my heart beating at an unnatural speed. There seemed to be no other choice. I sat, listened and learned.'

Bee took another break from the story, this time to check on the boys. They were still merrily building sandcastles and driving cars through the sand. Her dad was sitting quietly by her side and took his turn to speak,

'Wow, I have to admit this is an unusual tale. I've never heard of an experience quite like it. Keep going, I want to know what happened.'

Bee wasn't really sure if the encounter had any meaning for him but she continued, something drove her to tell the whole story.

'As you well know, I've faced many challenges in my life and each time I've walked away seemingly unaffected. But this is different. I can still feel the fear, which was dominant, which caused me to lose all control.' But she did not dwell on this, instead she moved onto the end of the recount. 'When Barbara finished sharing her life story, a sense of relief blanketed my thoughts. Finally I could escape the room. My heart slowed, the pressure was released and I raised myself from the sofa. Although my legs were extremely weak from the tension of the hour past, I managed to stand. As I regained control of my body I became consumed by a need for answers. I felt sure Barbara would understand my experience as she was used to communication with the non-visible. With this in mind, hoping for clarification, I approached Barbara to ask the questions which clamoured for release. But Barbara didn't have the time to speak with me on the matter. My reaction to this lack of support was unusual. I felt enraged. As if she were the only person who would understand. As if she was letting me down. However, I had no choice but to accept her response. In turn my anger was replaced by panic. Without guidance how could I understand what had occurred and why? Then an answer was delivered, the panic slipped away and a 'knowing' presented in my mind, I would have to find help elsewhere.' Bee hadn't quite completed the story, there was a point to the tale. 'Afterwards I felt so lonely. There was no one to tell. How could I explain the power of the encounter? I knew I had to talk to someone because I could feel the burden of the experience pressing down, suffocating me. I knew then and still believe, I must share the unusual part of me, that which I have kept hidden. I have to speak of this event to unlock everything else I have concealed. And in recent days I have come to a conclusion, my interactions with an invisible force might somehow link to your situation. I have no idea how. But I think a journey of discovery might help us both. Release the sense of loneliness we endure on our journey through life. Would you be happy to explore the unknown together?'

His eyes lit up and face communicated a positive response was forthcoming,

'The more we talk about all that occurs in your life, the more mystified I become. But at the same time I'm more excited. As if life still has some magic to deliver, is not over yet. I never dreamed I would feel like this again. Full of hope for a new day.' He smiled at her, the wrinkles round his eyes creased and he looked happier than in a long time. 'I'm glad we've had this time together, to get to know one another again. Let's keep talking and discover what life still has left for me.'

Bee felt immensely grateful for the time they had been gifted and for the product of their interaction. They were alone no more. They still had no clear idea of what occurred the day she visited the health spa but it didn't seem to matter. The process of talking was all that was needed. A bond of trust had been formed. However, responsibility for the two young boys dragged them back to reality. They could not spend all day sitting and talking about strange occurrences. Instead they must return to the car and then home. On the stroll back along the sea front they stopped at the ice cream seller to add yet another treat to their day.

Chapter 10 — ARTHUR

Bee had long since returned home to Surrey. He was still in Dorset and would return to Wiltshire the following day after a night of rest. There was no way he could have driven home that afternoon, the strain in his body evident, his prostate region ached from the activity of the day. Having consumed a light meal comprised of a cheese and tomato sandwich followed by an apple, he sat under an old apple tree tucked away in the corner of his back garden. The worn deck chair which usually provided a seat in the unfurnished sitting room was just as useful in the garden. He smiled at the simplicity of his life and how much it pleased him to be alone with his thoughts. The late summer warmth still hung in the air and although he could hear faint road noise nothing, could spoil the moment of tranquility. These opportunities of quiet reflection usually took him to a shadowy zone, one where he wallowed in the unfairness of his situation. He was so young, in his mid-sixties. If he had known twenty years ago, ten years even, that he would be facing the possibility of death, what would he have done differently? He couldn't answer. Would he have done anything different? He could have given up work earlier. But then he didn't really have the funds to support his retirement as it was, so that might have been impractical. In all honesty he was unsure whether he would have changed a thing. His life was his life. He had made decisions in the moment and they counted for something. They were his decisions and in fairness they had been good. Maybe he would have chosen to return to the job he loved, relinquish the role of responsibility as the managing director. But he wanted the salary which came with the job and didn't want to be managed by any other, so it was a vicious circle which he could never resolve. His focus turned to the line of thought which always followed the questioning of life decisions. He didn't want to die. He didn't want to be forgotten. This scared him. He would be wiped off the planet, never to be seen again, never to be heard. He struggled with this reality. Sometimes he wished he had been struck dead. He envied those who had not had to walk through to the end of their life knowing they would die. But if he had died suddenly then he would never have been given the chance to say goodbye to his family, which would have been sad for all concerned. But on the flip side, he would have had the benefit of avoiding countless days of not knowing, the uncertainty of how much more of life was left. At this point in a reflection he would often cry but not this day. His self-pity was cut short by a strong sense of hope. One that had not been present in any of the preceding days. She had an effect on him which he could not quantify. The conversations they shared seemed to have remapped his thought processes, the way he dealt with his situation. He actually had hope. For what he could not say. But he had hope.

He had thoroughly enjoyed their day together. Arthur loved the opportunity to converse at an intellectual level. The conversations he shared with Bee always caused him to consider events and life in an entirely different way, today was no exception. Her story had inspired him and he could not tell why. There was clearly another avenue to life he had never explored, one that intrigued him. The product of their discussions was an unmistakable warm sense of hope, which dwelled in his chest. He felt excited. Life had more to deliver. Then his thoughts were redirected by the scent of a rotting apple which had fallen into the grass at his feet. A wasp hovered over the fruit searching for food. Normally he would have swiped at the worst of all insects, encouraged it elsewhere or struck it dead. But not this time. Instead he watched as it fed from the fruit. For the first time, in a long time, he realised every life was precious, not just his own. What had caused such a change in his behaviour? He could not say. But something had shifted his perception of life. He saw beauty where he had never seen it before. Even in the wasp, the most hated of species. It was her, she did it. But he did not know how. He smiled. He didn't care how. He was just glad. Glad to have her in his life. He could not escape the thought she would help him. There was no rhyme or reason to the thought. Just belief. He was no longer alone.

Chapter 11— BEE

Bee had shared more of herself, thoughts and secrets about the reality of her existence. Information which had never before escaped her conscious stream had been released. This act had initiated a new flow from a channel unseen. She was bombarded with communications. The only way to handle the volume of interactions was to record them within the bounds of a journal. This allowed the offloading of all thoughts inside her head and thus relieved the small space of clutter. The recording took many forms. She never controlled the flow. Sometimes a picture would be drawn, other times a series of words written, seemingly making no sense at all. On occasion entire paragraphs of text were scribed, meaningless to anyone else. These were her purest thoughts. She felt sure these communications, in some way, were part of the solution to help her dad escape the chains that bound him to cancer. Alone, without a true understanding of where she was heading, Bee drove herself forward with a hazy awareness there was a reason for the communications and eventually, within the bounds of time, the reason would be uncovered. But in order to be successful she knew her path required the mastery of life balance; to balance the demands of her family along with the many interactions from the unseen. Even though demands were great, Bee managed to juggle every day chores alongside the messages received. She learned to deal with the challenge of being overwhelmed or absorbed by the messages which flowed through her conscious thought. They always came without warning and would not leave until they had been accepted and understood. Although bombarded, Bee enjoyed the high delivered when she conversed with the unseen. Even so, she understood there must be no impact on family life. She must never forget her role as wife and mother, for it was these roles which created balance, held her together and made her journey whole.

No moment was empty; as she washed the dishes, drove the car, shopped in the supermarket, walked through the local town, watched a film or shared a coffee with a friend, and even the moments before sleep. The communication channel existed at all times. Messages could not be ignored. They impacted every daily activity. The most recent occurred as she waited at the Sainsbury's checkout desk, when a message had been communicated for an elderly lady in the queue. Bee had become used to interactions at any moment in her life but did not enjoy those which occurred in public places; when she would be thrown into emotional overload in front of strangers. As Bee unloaded her shopping onto the belt she felt the power of the energy surge as it passed through her body. Desperately she fought to contain any outward reaction and instead smiled at Edward who was seated in the trolley. Unfortunately the focus on Edward did nothing to release the force present. The energy transformed to the presence of an elderly man, the departed husband of the elderly lady in front of her at the checkout. Bee immediately instigated a conversation inside her head and asked the elderly gentleman to reduce the impact of his message. But he seemed either unwilling or unable. He was driven only by the need to deliver a message of love to his wife, to communicate with her. Bee felt the undeniable depth of love this man felt for the woman standing only a few feet away and she desperately wanted to share the emotion. But she could not. The act of shared emotion would release the electricity which set every nerve ending on fire, and yet she could not embrace the woman and pass on the message of love. As there was no other option available Bee chose to communicate silently. She looked straight at the elderly lady, then inside her head told the lady her husband was present and he wanted to share his love. For a magical moment she connected the pair. With the message of love delivered, the electrical energy in her nervous system diminished and the presence of the elderly man receded. Once more Bee was alone. She watched as the elderly lady walked away and felt sadness for all she could not share out loud. If she had made the choice to embrace the old lady, to explain all that had been communicated, then she would have been looked upon with disbelief or worse, been arrested for hassling and upsetting the old woman. Bee was acutely aware this type of contact from the departed would continue and she had to learn to deal with each instance, to understand there was not always a need to physically speak the words of the message.

The experience with the departed in Sainsbury's caused Bee to think on how she could transfer the feeling of an interaction to her dad, so that he too could feel the reality of the afterlife. He needed to believe in its existence in order to have faith in the journey he would make. The problem was, no matter how much she spoke of the existence of the departed it was hard for him to accept because he had not felt the connection. There was only one way forward, she had to find someone else who could deliver a message from that which so many chose to ignore. This fact had always amused Bee. She could never fathom why people chose to ignore interactions with that which they could clearly sense in existence. Seemingly they switched off the receptors because they could never quite process the contact. She smiled at the thought of all they missed. If only they followed the thought then they would learn so much more about themselves and the possibilities in life. She hoped her dad would achieve this state. She had to help him. There was no way she would sit by and watch him travel the path alone, without belief. With this in mind she searched through the listings in his local area and found a Medium named Marjorie, who it seemed, in addition to conversing with the departed also drew a picture of those who communicated. Bee hoped this pictorial proof and further contact with those in spirit would help him see there was something at the end of his life on earth.

On the day of their visit to see Marjorie, the weather turned and autumn presented a cold and wet front. But Bee did not feel the chill in the air—instead she felt only excitement for their outing. He eased himself gently into the front passenger seat of the car and she looked on helplessly, for there was nothing she could do to assist with the discomfort he felt when travelling. She knew sitting in one position for any length of time irritated the tumour in his prostate, caused intolerable levels of discomfort, along with the need for frequent urination. Eventually he found a comfortable position and they began the journey. After a very pleasant hour driving through Dorset and Somerset countryside whilst chatting about the state of the world, they arrived at their destination, a cul-de-sac of well-kept 1960's era bungalows. Having parked the car they searched for the bungalow displaying an oval slate with the number ten painted in white. Bee knocked on the side door. The sound summoned a response from a tall and wiry lady with grey shoulder length hair. Marjorie greeted them with a warm welcome and a smile,

'Hello, I'm Marjorie. Please follow me.'

As instructed they followed, to a prefabricated outbuilding in the garden—an aged structure which seemed older than the bungalow. On entry to the building Bee was overcome by the warmth emanating from an old-fashioned oil tower heater in the centre of the room. The smell of burning fuel sent her back in time to the 1970's, a time when her family had used the same type of heater to heat the house during power cuts. Bee caught her thought stream and returned to the present. There was much to process. The pink walls were clean and bright, vibrant pink and green flowered coordinated accessories were dotted throughout the room, but it was not these items which called for attention. No, it was the subjects which adorned the walls. A collection of black and white sketches, predominantly Native American Indians. Although these were not the only inhabitants, there were many faces from a multitude of origins scattered across a pink backdrop. Bee was captivated. But she was not there to look at pictures. She was there for him, in the hope he would gain another connection with the departed. Bee stepped away from the gallery of pictures and selected a wicker chair to sit upon, the type most often found in a conservatory. As she sat upon the comfy floral cushion pad, simultaneously she placed a mug of black coffee on the small glazed table to one side. She had been quick to accept the generous offer of caffeine to invigorate her senses after an early morning wake up, followed by a two hour drive to the house of her parents, then a further hour to their current location. She sipped at the warm drink as she waited for Marjorie and her dad to find their seats. When all three were seated Marjorie began.

‘Okay, I am going to start with you Arthur. I will connect to spirit and relay any messages which come through the channel. Often there are a number of spirits attempting communication, so be prepared for a few. As I receive a message I may also be presented with an image of that person, in which case I will sketch a likeness of the individual. Although I have to warn you, sometimes you may not recognise the person immediately. Are you ready?’

Arthur nodded and Marjorie started the process of connecting to the afterlife. Although Bee herself could converse with the unseen, she was unsettled by the session with Marjorie. But she did not allow her thoughts to spoil the encounter. With interest in what would follow she put pen to paper ready to take notes of the reading. Looking directly at Arthur, Marjorie launched into sharing details on the first visitor of the day,

‘I’ve had a strange morning. Ever since I woke a dog has been following me, a dog in spirit, he is black and white and looks a like a working sheep dog.’

Arthur and Bee stared at each other in disbelief.

Chapter 12 — ARTHUR

Arthur knew the dog. He could not contain his reaction to the information just delivered. His eyes welled up with tears and terror gripped at his throat as if he were being strangled. He recalled Rex. Arthur had loved his dog. Rex had never hurt him. Other than the day he passed to spirit. On that day Arthur had hurt badly, the day his trustworthy friend had been ripped from his life. He found the moment difficult to rationalise. Could Rex really be there in spirit? He answered his own question. If he believed a spirit passed on to another existence then this must be true for dogs as well as humans. Activity to his left drew his eye and Arthur caught sight of Bee as she scribbled notes. He turned his attention back to Marjorie. The reference to Rex caused his interest to be stirred, he had greater belief in the Medium. Marjorie had waited for him to regain composure and then moved on,

'The dog is here to show you he is still around, you can connect with him if you need to.' Then Marjorie paused, looked into a space in the corner of the room and then spoke, 'But now I must move onto relaying a message from the next visitor. There is an elderly man present who has poor eyesight and diabetes, he is very important to you and therefore I must sketch his likeness.'

She picked up a pencil and sketched furiously on a pad. The sketching of the face took five minutes, during which time

Marjorie encouraged discussion on the identity of the man. Arthur did not know anyone with the ailments identified, other than possibly his father-in-law. But when the sketch was complete and turned toward him Arthur realised this was not Sheila's father. Instead a stranger stared at him. He felt frustrated, an all too common feeling these days. He could not mask his response as he struggled to contain the bitter disappointment of not knowing the individual on paper. As if she sensed his frustration Marjorie spoke,

'This man could be someone from your recent or distant past, maybe a much older family member, you should dig out old photos and see if they help with the identification.' Then Marjorie stopped talking, looked as if she were listening to an invisible person and then spoke once more, 'Seemingly there are a number of spirits who want to converse with you Arthur. There is another man, again he is elderly. A man with a drink problem. He died in hospital. You and he did not end on good terms. I think this is your father.'

Arthur was horrified. How could he possibly be expected to deal with a connection to his departed father? Yet more emotion welled up in his eyes, once more an unseen hand gripped him by the throat and prevented any form of speech. This time the emotion which struck him dumb was different. With Rex there had been sadness for the loss. However, for his father there was only anger. The pain associated with the death reared its ugly head as Arthur recollected the last visit to the hospital to see his ninety-two year old father.

He had witnessed a person without hope, a man ready to be collected. Arthur recalled his deep seated frustration at the sight of a man who had given up. He had willed his father to fight for life. But his father had not fought. Instead, he had chosen to starve himself in order to finish the job the bowel cancer had begun. Arthur had been unable to accept this choice. He had tried in vain to persuade his father to fight, to live. But the act of persuasion had a detrimental effect, and that was to turn his father away. Arthur recalled the last words spoken in anger and frustration,

'Don't give up Dad, you can't just give up.'

His father had made his thoughts very clear,

'I don't want to see you again. Leave me to die. This is all I've ever wanted since your mother died. I want to be removed from this life, to be gone.'

At the time Arthur had felt greatly aggrieved, shocked by the truth his father did not love him enough to want to live, or even to allow him to visit. This issue had never been resolved. There had been no further conversation between them. His father had died.

His thought flow was interrupted by Marjorie,

'If your Dad comes to you, will you accept him?'

Arthur could not answer the question. There was too much history. An answer to that difficult question would have to wait. Then, rather abruptly, Marjorie finished his session, which she communicated by ceremonially handing over the sketch. Arthur felt his heart sink as he looked down at the piece of paper in his hands, still he did not recognise the face. He had hoped his departed best friend Bob would appear, but no, the man who had once been his drinking buddy seemed lost forever. Again his thoughts were interrupted as Marjorie asked,

'Would you like to use the toilet before we begin the next session?'

Arthur accepted the kind offer. The cancer tumour and expanding bladder did not share the space well, each wanting to inflate into the restricted area, resulting in more pain and discomfort. Once he had been relieved of pain and pressure, Arthur resettled himself with a notebook and pen, ready to record the details of the next session.

Chapter 13 — BEE & ARTHUR

Bee sat opposite Marjorie ready for her turn. She felt nothing. Absolutely no connection with the stranger. The sensation felt odd. She always connected to people and could see inside their souls with ease. Bee couldn't quite understand why Marjorie did not want to connect. Marjorie seemed unaware of any issue and launched into the next reading,

'An older lady wants to be made known. I am not getting any details of the woman, only that she wants you to know she is there.'

Bee had absolutely no idea of who it could be and questioned which of her departed female relatives would want to come back and converse. Having processed the list she still had no idea. She felt cheated. When she communicated with the departed she always knew who they were, there were many levels of information transmitted to her conscious thought stream. Why could Marjorie not do the same? Equally, why could she herself, not see or feel who it was? There were no answers. The voice of Marjorie interrupted her thoughts,

'Another old lady is here in spirit and wants to give you a message. You must forge ahead with your ideas and not be persuaded otherwise. You must stand up for yourself. This is a really important message for you. She is desperate that you listen to the advice.'

On hearing this Bee accepted the message was appropriate for her. Did it matter if she was not sure of the source? Next, Marjorie picked up pad and pencil to sketch a picture of the elderly lady. As her hands raced across the page in an effort to represent the face which needed to be presented, Marjorie described the old lady in spirit. But Bee still had no idea as to the identity of the person. Could it be the same lady who had delivered the message earlier? When the sketch was complete and had been turned to face them, her heart dropped, a face she did not recognise stared back at her. She felt huge disappointment. Marjorie must have sensed the negative response,

'It is not always immediately obvious who comes through the communication channel. Sometimes the passing of time is required to identify the person.'

This sounded like a cop-out. Bee wanted to see a physical likeness of Grandma. With proof on paper she could prove to herself and others, the person with whom she had communicated was actually in existence. This need, her craving for evidence took Bee by surprise. Had she not stepped past the need for proof? Was she not in a space of understanding and trust? With the delivery of the sketch, the session reached its conclusion. They politely thanked Marjorie for her time, made the agreed payment for services delivered and left the bungalow.

Once out of ear shot Arthur communicated his astonishment.

'I couldn't believe it when Marjorie described Rex. I'm still stunned. I didn't expect to connect with my dog. I had no idea it would mean so much to reconnect with the love I once felt for him. I'm not really sure why but I feel a deep sense of joy in the thought he still exists in some form. I feel really happy. Although, I had been hoping to hear from Bob. I wanted proof he was in existence. But I guess I will never hear from him again will I?' Without waiting for an answer he continued, 'I have to confess I'm still none the wiser on the identity of the old man in the sketch. The diabetes and eyesight problems don't match anyone from my family. I can't help feeling a bit frustrated, almost cheated.'

Bee had to agree with him, she felt cheated too. But the trip had not really been about her, it had been for him. Although he was unsure of the identity of his sketch, he had received clear messages from the session and contact from his dog. On the drive back to his house they kept revisiting the identification of the sketch he had been given. After reviewing the whole of his family and also the family of Sheila there was still no result. Then Bee understood. It mattered not who the spirit was. Someone had come through the unseen channel for him and this action alone had elevated his belief in the departed. Bee felt pleased for him. Any contact with those in spirit had to be a good thing. He was dying and there was no cure on the horizon. Knowledge in an unseen entity, waiting for him, would surely bring comfort.

Arthur sat in silence as he assimilated every element of the session. He still found the concept of his dog in spirit hard to believe but at the same time felt comforted by the presence. His love for Rex had no bounds. The unconditional love Arthur had afforded his dog had been reciprocated and was the one of the strongest experiences of love he had experienced in his life. Crazy as this sounded, Arthur could not deny his feelings. During his early life he had suffered at the hands of clumsy, heart breaking and double-crossing love. His experiences had hurt deeply. Long ago he had chosen to let no one in, this way no one could hurt him. Arthur was unaware how detrimental this decision had been on his life, love and health. Bitterness and hatred for all those who had hurt him had moved slowly through his body and poisoned everything in its path. Had Bee spoken? What had she said?

'Sorry Sweetie, what did you say?'

Bee repeated the question,

'Do you remember Marjorie asked if you would accept your dad if he came to you?'

No. Arthur did not remember this question. The words had not registered. Why not? He responded,

'No, I don't.'

Bee felt all external input paused, a metaphorical cloud blocked out all sound, she was detached, as if deposited in an empty vacuum with no connection to her earthly life. In the quiet of her mind there was a communication. Repeat the question, make sure he understands. This is crucial to his development. He has to hear loud and clear. Bee continued to drive. She was on autopilot, could still see and automatically respond to the function of driving but did not process any of the inputs, the road or cars. The communication had to be delivered. She spoke in a firm tone so he would not be mistaken as to the importance of what she had to say,

'It is important for you to consider whether you will accept your Dad if he comes to greet you when you pass into spirit.'

Arthur remembered a night in the past, when they had discussed the likelihood of family members at the collection point when you passed into spirit. As a result, it came as no surprise he might meet his family again. Even so, he felt awkward thinking about the proposition and was in no position to answer the question. The issues which surrounded the departure of his father had not been resolved but Arthur knew he had to say something, Bee would not drop the conversation until she had a response. Arthur answered unsurely,

'I suppose so.'

He actually had no idea what he would do. But hoped his response would stop the question being repeated. But no, although he had responded to the question, his answer was not sufficient to stop the line of enquiry. Bee spoke more firmly this time,

'It is very important for you to address this question. To understand how you feel about your Dad is a critical issue for you. When you pass over you need to travel with peace and as little angst as possible.'

Once the words were out Bee wondered why she felt so strongly. Where had the message originated? How could she speak with such knowing? There was no denying all that had to be communicated was important. He must address the issue. There would be no other way to make it across the divide safely.

Arthur looked across at Bee. She surprised him with her ability to connect with the unseen. To know the right question to ask. The right thing to say. How did she know? Surely she should be as much in the dark about the subject of death and passage into spirit as he was? But it seemed not. Bee had a connection he found hard to comprehend and could communicate messages in such a way he could not ignore. He would have to agree to consider everything delivered in the session, although he was unsure of what good it would do. After all, he could never speak with his dad again and put right all that had gone before. Could he really be expected to meet his dad again with love and peace? Bee seemed to think so. Arthur admired her belief in him. But only he knew the level of work required before the fateful day. The possibility of resolving past issues seemed hopeless.

Chapter 14 — ARTHUR

The session with Marjorie had both a positive and negative effect on his life. He definitely felt more enthusiasm for life. The connection with Rex had fuelled his belief in an afterlife, which in turn fed his thought processes with hope. But he had also been thrown into a vat of negativity when encouraged to think about his dad. He did not like the idea of combing over the past. Was he really supposed to forgive and accept his dad if he turned up to collect him at the end? This was not a subject on which he wanted to dwell. There were far more interesting spiritual experiences to seek out. His dad would have to wait.

Seeing as they had both enjoyed delving into the world of spirit it had been agreed they would follow up with further investigations, but his time stay closer to home. Arthur had spotted an advertisement for a spiritual centre in the 'Other Interests' section of his local newspaper. The headline had enticed him, 'Awareness Centre,' he liked the sound of the name, liked the easy read and welcoming copy. He had made it his mission to progress an enquiry into the organisation. Having parked his car in the shopper's car park in the centre of his local town, he walked away from the high street in a northerly direction, towards the hospital. After five minutes of brisk walking he found the entrance door to the double fronted Victorian building, the Awareness Centre. He followed the instructions displayed on a painted sign on the door. 'All Are Welcome. Please Come In.' Even though he had been invited to enter, the warm welcome did little to settle the nerves in his stomach. All of a sudden Arthur felt unsure of his venture into the unknown. But he dug deep. He found the courage to open the door and stepped into the unfamiliar house. Once inside Arthur turned left towards the reception area. A petite, dark haired, middle-aged woman walked towards him, smiled and continued on past. As the stranger brushed past him an electrical current originated at the base of his torso and fired all the way up to his scalp. The sensation was quite unlike anything Arthur had felt before. Nothing like a normal male reaction to a woman. Something he never felt anymore thanks to the prostate cancer, which had prohibited all reaction in his loins and the ability to have physical relations with a woman. This loss of manhood had been one of the most difficult elements of his illness to accept; he still became infuriated whenever he contemplated all that had been stolen. He would never again be able to enjoy one of the greatest reasons for being alive, the ability to have a sexual relationship with his wife. Arthur had loved this part of his life with a passion but he would never again experience the thrill. His natural reaction, sadness, dominated his thoughts. There was so little pleasure left in his life. Then a new thought interrupted the flow. He had a job to do. Arthur banished the sorrow and turned his focus to the task in hand. A small glimmer of light illuminated his path and he realised there were more simple pleasures to be found. The building in which he stood was the key to finding them.

With his attention back in the room Arthur considered the strange physical sensation he had experienced when the brunette had passed. He felt sure electricity had travelled through his body. However, he did not have time to dwell on the encounter and pushed all thoughts aside as he arrived in the reception area. An elderly woman wearing a pair of dark framed glasses sat at a desk reading a book held in her lap. Upon hearing his footsteps she looked up and smiled. This action caused a reaction and his earlier anxiety slip away.

'Hello there, how can I help you?' enquired the woman.

How indeed? How could he describe what he was after? He and Bee had decided to find like-minded people who could make sense of her communications, whilst at the same time provide greater knowledge into that which might be waiting for him. Arthur considered how strange his words might sound. He hoped the elderly woman had an open mind. Arthur found his voice,

'Hi, I was hoping to find a contact number for a person who could help my daughter with the spiritual messages she is receiving.'

Within the confines of his head he calmed himself with a few words, 'It's okay. Sounds alright, not too rambling, and fairly normal.' The woman at the desk paused in thought for a moment and then asked,

'Is your daughter looking for help in a private consultation or would she like to join a group to develop her gifts?'

Arthur was amazed by the response. This woman had not looked at him as if he were from another planet, instead she understood. With newfound confidence Arthur responded,

'She would probably like to do both.'

The receptionist replied,

'Well then, you could do with meeting Carrie, who holds private consultations and runs a development group every other week on a Thursday afternoon.'

Somewhere behind, Arthur was aware another person had entered the room. He turned and saw the attractive brunette he had passed earlier.

'Ah, here she is,' exclaimed the receptionist, 'This is the lady I was speaking of. Meet Carrie.'

He held out his right hand to greet Carrie.

'Hello, I'm Arthur.'

He found an immediate bond with the woman. She could be trusted. Her gentle brown eyes encouraged him to speak without fear. He quickly summarised the experiences to date and then asked Carrie if she were able to assist. She responded enthusiastically,

'I run a development group meeting on a Thursday for people like your daughter, people able to converse with unseen energies. There is one next week if you would both like to come.'

Arthur felt overwhelmed by an urge to spend more time with the woman called Carrie and boldly included himself in the arrangements.

'I think we would both be really interested in attending.' He gathered details of cost, time and location, then expressed his gratitude, 'Thank you for your time. I look forward to seeing you next week.'

He turned on his heels and retraced his steps to the front door. Once out on the street he mused over the interactions. Had the meeting with Carrie been a coincidence? There were many other practitioners who worked in the centre. But on the day and time he entered the building Carrie had been in place. A strong sense of knowing collected in his stomach, warm and filling. He had been placed there at the right moment. Arthur was not entirely clear of the actual effect Carrie would have on their lives, but he was conscious she held the key to moving beyond the current understanding that bound Bee and himself together in the present.

As he drove through Devonshire countryside which bordered his home in Dorset, Arthur couldn't help but smile as he considered the events of the morning. Who would have thought there were people like Bee? Over the past months he had tried his best to comprehend everything she spoke of, but he didn't really understand many of her experiences. Having visited the Awareness Centre he had developed a newfound optimism, belief that Carrie could provide support not only for Bee, but also himself. A need which had been building for a few weeks. He had told no one, not Bee or Sheila. He couldn't tell them the thoughts which dominated his waking hours, but he might be able to tell a stranger like Carrie. This troublesome thought stream had begun one morning a few weeks earlier. He had awoken with a sense of death knocking at the door. Every day since he had woken with this same thought, followed by another, he knew his passage would not be easy.

Chapter 15 — BEE

Bee was excited at the prospect of meeting a person who could shed light on the communications which dominated her life and help her dad to develop a greater connection with the departed. Since the moment she told him of her secrets, the second she connected to provide the support he needed, there had been an increase in the information passing through her conscious stream. Bee hoped Carrie would provide an outlet for this build up, a place of release, someone with whom to converse on matters of the unseen. She reached the front door of the Awareness Centre and took a deep breath, grabbed hold of the worn brass doorknob and pushed the door inwards. With her dad one step behind, she entered a long and dimly lit corridor which stretched away to the back of the building. A sign to the left directed her to the reception area where she met a short, middle-aged brunette woman, whom she presumed was Carrie. Suddenly all confidence in her ability slipped away. What if this doesn't get us anywhere? But she had to try. She had to help him. Bee mentally calmed her mind, smiled and introduced herself,

'Hi, I'm Bee. I'm here with my dad for your Development Group.'

Carrie welcomed her with open arms,

'Welcome. It is very nice to meet you Bee. Please follow me.'

Then they were led to a room at the top of the stairs. Her eyes consumed the peach coloured woodchip wallpaper, clearly once a bedroom, one that would easily have accommodated a king-size bed and numerous pieces of large furniture. But in its current state, a meeting room, housed eight chrome-framed, brown hessian fabric-covered chairs which looked as if they had been rescued from the 1970's. Bee took a seat next to her dad. Soon they were joined by five like-minded individuals, all of whom were female. Bee checked her dad's face for a reaction to the influx of women but he didn't show any outward signs of concern. In fact he looked as if he rather enjoyed the idea of an hour spent with a group of women. Lastly, Carrie entered the room, took a seat and began the session.

'For our newcomers I'll explain what we do here. This is a Development Group, also known as a Circle. We meet regularly to share experiences and practise skills like healing or clairvoyance. Today, first of all, we'll practice the art of filling our body with light and then try a guided meditation.'

Bee felt a warm sense of excitement—hope for a session which could deliver her further forward to a greater understanding of herself. She relaxed into the session, slipped off her shoes and placed her feet on the bobbled, man-made fibre carpet. Once comfortable she tuned in to Carrie's voice, which encouraged her to imagine white light filling every cell of her body. This was easy for Bee, very much like the process she followed to banish shadows from her thoughts. She wondered how her dad was getting on. But as her eyes were closed she could not check on him. Then Carrie asked them to breathe deeply, in and out, slowly taking air into every cell. Bee slipped into a deeper sate of relaxation. Then came instructions.

'You are walking in a beautiful green forest…'

Bee had no problem visualising a forest. As soon as the words were spoken she was catapulted into Savernake Forest, a place from childhood, where she had spent many hours riding horses. But Bee was not riding; she was racing on foot along a wide luscious green grass track. Compelled to run. Her legs carried her further and further. Never stopping. Each stride taking her deeper and deeper into the forest of beech, oak, birch and pine trees. Eventually the grassy track transformed into a tunnel of trees, at the end of which was a clearing and in the centre stood a building. A small chapel built from large sandstone blocks, with one large arched oak door in the centre and a small arched leaded window to the right. Bee stopped running and viewed the clearing, drinking in the heavenly green grass where groups of daisies broke the surface. There was no time to waste. She walked softly across the carpet of lush grass toward the oak door. On opening the door she was embraced by a calming energy, one that encouraged her to enter. She was safe in the small building. Once inside Bee found a large, dark brown leather bound book with pages edged in gold. As she stepped forward to take a closer look she was overwhelmed by its size. Before her was the largest, thickest and most magnificent book she had ever seen. Not one to be lifted. The book had been designed to stay where it had been placed. Then a voice filtered through into her consciousness. Carrie spoke,

'Write in the book and set boundaries for all of the people with whom you interact: family, friends, husbands, wives and children.'

Almost immediately her head filled with images of people she had allowed to trample over her path through life. There followed the chilling grip of fear which grasped hold of her heart and turned it to ice. She was not ready to address this issue. Bee looked down at the large book and her eyes filled with tears. But she would not give in to the fear. Instead she took hold of a pen and attempted the definition of boundaries. But she could not. The task seemed too daunting. Tears rolled ever so slowly down her face. She felt isolated, lost with an impossible mountain to climb. The voice of Carrie once more drifted into her consciousness,

'Now it's time to come back to the room and join the rest of the group.'

Bee opened her eyes as instructed and became aware of the room. The illumination and vivid colours of the meditation space inside her head had been replaced by a heavy blanket of darkness, which steadily developed into a sense of despondency. This unwelcome change reminded Bee of a time before, a period in her life when she had been lost. Bee deduced the feelings now present meant only one thing. Pain. A type of darkness which consumed all light. The reality of this presence in her life instigated a response, utter dread. An upsurge of panic rose from a place inside and Bee was transported back in time, to a point when all of life's tests had been too much, a time when she had considered the best solution was to end her time on the earth. Was this horrifying episode in her life about to be repeated? What had she done? What can of worms had been opened? Then as suddenly as the panic had arrived it receded. Replaced by something much worse. Another level of fear altogether. Terror. This crawled into every last space within her mind, body and soul. The last remnant of light was snuffed out; she was lost.

Bee could not return to the group as instructed, no matter how hard she tried. In the background, somewhere outside of her thoughts, she could hear the voice of Carrie.

'Okay, we are all done. I hope to see you all at the next session.'

But she could not move. Could not bring her awareness back to the room. She was trapped somewhere dark, in a place she did not wish to be but from where she could not escape. With eyes open, rooted to the chair, Bee remained seated. Carrie appeared by her side,

'Bee, are you okay?'

She wanted to scream out loud for all to hear, 'No I am not. I'm lost somewhere. I can't get back to where you are. It's too dark here.' But the only words which actually came forth were,

'Not good.' Her eyes connected with Carrie. Surely she could see the darkness, would know what to do. Bee offloaded the thoughts in her head, 'I'm sorry Carrie but I feel really unwell. I'm not sure what has happened to me. I feel as if an immobilising fog has descended and trapped me. I don't know where to go. I can't move. I'm absolutely petrified. The meditation has unleashed an avalanche of fear which has swept me away and consumed me wholly.'

Carrie remained calm, as if she had dealt with this problem before,

'Talk to me, tell me what happened in the meditation.'

Bee didn't want to explain, she wanted to escape the room and return to her life. But she knew the sensible way forward was to offload,

'Everything was fine until you asked me to define boundaries. I can't. I'm paralysed by the notion. I feel as if I have slipped into an abyss with absolutely no control or ability to get out of the situation.'

Once the words had been spoken then calm descended, the fear and panic dissipated, she was able to relax once more. Bee sat quietly for five minutes with her dad alongside, only then did she feel ready to leave the room.

'Thank you Carrie. I'm really sorry I caused a scene. I've never been in a meditation like that. It felt so powerful, so real. I'll try not to do that next time!'

Carrie didn't seem to mind the strange reaction to the mediation, as if she had seen it many times before.

'Don't worry, at least you're okay now. See you at the next session.'

Bee left the Awareness Centre with her dad alongside and they walked in silence up the street towards the car park.

She settled herself in the car and then waited for him to take his seat. Once the doors were closed, he spoke,

'Are you okay?'

Bee wanted to allay any fears he may have,

'Yes. I feel much better than I did immediately after the meditation. I still feel a bit shell shocked but I guess that will wear off.'

She did not want to dwell on her state and so turned focus on to him.

'How was the meditation for you?'

His voice was full of excitement as he recounted the experience,

'Well it was an experience that's for sure. I'm not sure my first meditation was very successful. I followed the instructions. I really tried to imagine a light which filled me entirely but I confess it was difficult. Then I imagined the beautiful forest. As I took my first steps through lush green grass I felt a strong desire to lie down. No sooner had I made myself comfortable on my back then I fell asleep. I don't remember anything else except Carrie asking us to come back out of the meditation.' He smiled at the recollection then continued, 'As you can imagine, I was slightly confused at the end when Carrie asked everyone if they had set boundaries. I had absolutely no idea what she was talking about.'

Bee smiled at him,

'Dad, you are funny. Maybe it's what you needed from the session. When do you ever allow your head to empty of all the concerns which clutter the space? Do you feel more refreshed thanks to a total shutdown?'

Arthur thought for a moment and then spoke,

'Well yes, I guess I do. The session was quite something. I feel as if I released control of my life for a short time. On reflection it was quite liberating and I definitely feel better for it. What about you? I assume from your reaction at the end that it was not good for you?'

Bee did not want to discuss her experience. She did not believe her dad was ready for the reality, but had to respond,

'No it was not good. I felt really wretched. In fact I'm still overwhelmed by sadness. I'm in possession of a dominant belief which tells me I've opened a door on my true feelings. What I see does not fill me with joy. This vision is dominated by shadows of the past, by a multitude of unresolved issues. The mere thought of putting myself first, of identifying boundaries to prevent other people from negating my needs, fills me with dread; reminds me of a time when I tried and failed. I'm absolutely terrified of attempting such a daunting task again.'

Bee felt her voice crack and throat constrict. She had to stop talking and drive. She could not break down in front of him. For the rest of the journey to his house she focused the conversation on small talk relating to the Development Group, Carrie and the attendees. When they arrived at their destination, his home, Bee deposited him outside the house and then turned the car eastwards for the long drive home.

In the silence of the car Bee reflected on the day. She could not escape the distress the emotional overload had delivered. Questions ricocheted off the walls inside her head. All required an answer. How could she possibly return home and be the same person? She could not. But what could she do? She did not understand how to change, how to adopt a new method of dealing with people and their effect on her life. How on earth could she be expected to tread through the minefield that was present in the confines of her head? The reason for attendance at the Awareness Centre was to obtain assistance in how to deal with messages so she could help her dad. A realisation embraced her thoughts. Clearly, first she must contend with the reality of choices made over the past thirty-seven years. As Bee drove along dark country roads, alone, on a journey meant only for her, she knew the only route to success was to face her fears head on and then come to terms with the past. A 'knowing' seeped into her consciousness; the resolution of the past would set her free, deliver her to a brighter future. Although she was aware of the glimmer of a positive outcome, fear still dominated every thought. She had been to the darkness before, had been consumed by it and almost lost in it. Could this happen again? She had never considered boundaries. Never believed she could put her needs above others. Instead she had allowed people, especially males, to take control. Quite how she was going to change this entrenched behaviour she did not know. The boundary setting seemed a huge and unachievable task. But this was not the worst of it. Bee feared the past much more. She dreaded the resurfacing of memories, those she had hoped would never be present in her conscious thought stream again. The meditation that afternoon had unlocked a door to a desperately miserable period in her life, one which had been hidden away, a place she did not care to revisit.

Ten years earlier she had chosen a path through life which delivered her to a series of consultations with a psychologist. The break-up of a long-term relationship and the fall out of the event had caused many changes in her life. She had been overwhelmed with conflicting emotions and had toppled off the edge of her world. Inside her head Bee unwillingly journeyed back and recalled the trauma which had surfaced within the psychologist sessions. Every element of her life had been dug over. She had uncovered details from childhood and young adult years which had been locked away for good reason. As she raked over the past she had tumbled into an undesirable space, a dark miserable place where the only valid escape was to end her life. This phase of darkness, where she harboured the desire to snuff out her existence, seemed to last for an eternity. During this period, whenever she became overwhelmed by the noise in her head or the reality of all she had become, she presented herself with the option of shut down, to quiet her mind. Thankfully, in recent years she had found a way out of the darkness. She had embraced the love of her husband and boys. Allowed them to love her and allowed herself to love them. She had found peace. Surely with this strength of love to support, this time there was a flicker of hope for a brighter future. Bee embraced this thought and vowed to release all of the darkness which had been stored. Although she sensed hope for the future, the challenge of returning to the past still sat like a heavy stone in her stomach. From past experience Bee knew there would be a turbulent time ahead, not only for herself but also Adam. She would not be an easy person to live with; last time Adam had managed the fallout and stayed by her side, but would he do it again? She hoped so with all her heart.

Her mind wandered as she pondered over the first step towards dealing with the past. First came the word 'protection.' Bee laughed out loud. The sound of her voice broke the silence of the car. Why the word protection? She did not understand. But she didn't have to wait long for the reason to flow through her conscious thought. It was simple really, the vast majority of her relationships were unhealthy, she always, without fail, put other people first. But how could she possibly change a behaviour that had been with her from the earliest of memories, was ingrained in her make up? Surely this was integral to her being? A cacophony of thoughts bounced off one another. Change felt unachievable. She had attempted this feat once already and failed miserably. But there was only one option. To jump into a metaphorical dark chasm with no knowledge of the depths to which she would plummet. Could she do it and survive? How could she possibly let go of all that defined her person? Then from the silence of the night came another word, 'boundaries.' With this word came clarity of thought. All of a sudden she understood exactly what to do. Bee turned her focus on the task communicated and mentally drew an imaginary line in the shape of sphere around her entire body. This process whereby she defined her own space had an outcome; tears spilled, emotions emerged and settled as a lump in her throat. Then finally, the chill of isolation embraced her mind, body and soul. She was lost and alone. Panic was her next response. How could she define something, a boundary, which could not be seen? But there was no let up. Onwards she progressed to the next focus point where she had to identify each person in her life, what they meant to her and what harm they caused each and every day. Bee continued to drive forward and followed the next train of thought, one which delivered yet more tears. She delved deep and gained greater insight into her relationships. Slowly she realised how she had allowed the very definition of herself to be trampled upon and abused. The person in the now bore very little resemblance to the person she had been in late childhood. But how could she take on the mammoth task and change her behaviour? Surely she was too far along the path of life to achieve such a colossal goal. One which meant standing true to herself—a precious element she had lost sight of years ago. As if on autopilot she drove onwards, then received another strong message in the form of a realisation. She would have to modify behaviour with everyone, including her husband, mother, father, sister and brothers, in fact all those who were central to her life. This choice she had made, to place other people and their wishes before her own, had allowed her life to flow more harmoniously, with less conflict and seemingly greater peace. But the reality of all she had endured reared up in full view. She knew these past behaviours had not served her well. Alone on the A31, having just crossed the county border into Hampshire, Bee reconnected with a part of herself not seen in years. The process was irreversible. She could not turn her back on the process of change, no matter how daunting. With acceptance of her new path she felt one dominant emotion. Anger. Bee felt as if she had opened the lid to a rage box, a place where she had stored a life's-worth of anger. As the fury escaped the confines of the vessel it overwhelmed her senses and threatened to drown out all hope. The result of release caused more tears but no more thought. Seemingly, she had followed the thought flow to the end of the line, left with only the fallout of everything which had passed through her mind.

Eventually she turned the car into the steep driveway which led to the top of the hill, where her house stood for all to see. As Bee parked alongside Adam's BMW, she let go of all the thoughts which had filled the journey home. There would be plenty of time to dredge through everything raised that day. For now she wanted nothing more than to be wrapped in the blanket of home and to forget the challenges ahead. Once inside, she slipped off her shoes, dropped her bag on the floor and padded barefoot through to the kitchen. There she found Adam standing at the sink, with jumper sleeves rolled up to his elbows and soapsuds covering his hands. He turned away from his task to welcome her home, dried his hands and then wrapped his strong arms around her body. The painful events of the day slipped away as she became encased in his strength, love and warmth. In the heat of his embrace she disconnected from all thoughts of her dad, the development at the Awareness Centre and thoughts which had dominated her mind on the journey home. She slipped back into her life and focused only on the enjoyment of being in the company of her husband. Once reconnected, they worked together to prepare a homemade curry. With cooking complete, they each carried food on a tray to the sitting room, where they consumed their dinner in front of the television. Bee chatted about the progress her dad had made but did not mention her own situation. She was unsure if Adam would understand and did not have the energy to explain. After an hour and a half of relaxed conversation Bee felt the call to the comfort of her bed. Once prepared for sleep, she climbed into bed and snuggled under the duvet. As soon as her head hit the pillow she felt sleep claim the remains of the day, all thought slipped away except for one. This time she would be okay.

Chapter 16 — ARTHUR

He stood in the warmth of the porch as he watched Bee pull out of the drive and turn left towards home. Once the car had disappeared from sight he turned to the sanctuary of his study. A sacred space which protected him from the outside world, allowed him to indulge in his love of music, either playing the piano or listening to the great classics. Arthur settled onto the plump cushion on the seat of his desk chair, leant against the back, clasped his fingers together at his lips and mused over the events of the day. He had enjoyed the Development Group tremendously, had been given the opportunity to venture past his closed mind, which had allowed him to connect with the unseen. His first ever meditation had delivered him to another plane of existence, a peaceful place where a blanket had covered him, delivered sleep and protection from the outside world. There had been no words of instruction placed in his consciousness, only peace and quiet. Something he searched for daily but rarely found. The session had most definitely delivered him much further than he expected. He felt regenerated. His mind and body more able to push ahead, with renewed energy to fight the cancer head on. Arthur had really enjoyed the whole experience. That was until the end when he witnessed Bee slip into darkness. The memory replayed inside his head and fear stepped forward, reminded him of years before, a time when she had existed in a lonely and dark space, untouchable by anyone on the outside.

Arthur recalled the day Bee had visited the medical centre where she had been diagnosed with a breakdown. Within two hours she had arrived at his house. She stayed for six weeks. During this time he and Sheila had looked after Bee. They had shared responsibility for a constant vigil, based on their knowledge of her threat to remove herself from the earth. His current state of fear reminded him of the time his daughter had sunk to unimaginable depths. Her innocence gone. The girl he remembered from childhood hurt and lost. Arthur could see she was hurting again. He hoped and prayed this time she would be able to cope with everything thrown in her direction. Then his thoughts strayed to her parting comment.

'Dad, maybe you should think about booking a session with Carrie. She holds one to one sessions. She may be able to help you access your past or connect with your parents.'

He would have to give careful consideration to this suggestion. Did he really want to delve into his past? In his long and full life he had stored double the hurt of his daughter. Could he really expect to clear it and move on? Without warning his past appeared as a series of images within his head. Memories, encounters and emotional traumas, all too painful to recount. In response to these visions, which threatened to overwhelm, Arthur switched off the rolling film in his head and extinguished any reminder of what had been. He did not want to dredge up all he had hidden out of sight. He made a decision never to venture back. Instead he would move onwards to his unknown future. Even though he did not want to talk to Carrie about the past, he might converse with her on the subject of death. He could discuss the march of death which was ever present in his life and his bitterness at the thought of having his future ripped away. He did not want to die. He would never give up his fight for existence. Within the quiet of his mind, nature dominated, a single-minded drive to preserve his life at all costs.

CHAPTER 17 — BEE

The eventful visit to the Awareness Centre raised many questions. Was she stable enough to support her dad? Were the messages clear enough? These were communications which must not be misunderstood. A man's life was at stake. She had hoped the visit would give her a better understanding of how to channel all the information available. But instead she had been thrown into a confused state. Her dad was not the only one who needed help dealing with the past. The session had highlighted she too had to visit the past and sift through her relationships to have any hope of a balanced life in the future and more importantly, to support him on his journey. There was no option available but to get on with it. Time was short. She had to be strong enough for him. Boundaries needed to be set. Bee was determined to deliver to her promise and so settled in an armchair in the sitting room. No sooner was she seated, with focus on herself, then fear reared up into full view and dominated every thought. What have I become? How have I allowed this to happen? How have I allowed other people to cause me so much pain?' There were no answers. As Bee took a stroll through the landscape of her past, a realisation occurred, she had not passed through life easily. She had allowed other peoples choices to affect her existence and then felt let down when they had stuck in a metaphorical knife. As dramatic as the scenario sounded, Bee knew this to be true. She was much more sensitive to others' actions than she had realised. Throughout her life she had endeavoured to resolve other people's issues, to make situations right for them even if this did not serve her needs. As Bee acknowledged this behaviour a change occurred, electrical energy coursed through her body followed by a 'knowing' inside her head. She possessed a very real gift. The ability to know what other people were thinking. She had spent most of her life using this gift to learn other people's thoughts. Then she had tried to deliver all they asked. She had tried to make their lives better. Bee felt deeply saddened by the thought she had been drowning in a sea of need. A serious threat which had almost snuffed out her light.

On the surface all appeared to be well. She never complained about her life. After all she had a wonderful husband and two lovely children, a fabulous family home and no worries financially. The depths of despair she had stored shocked her to the core. How could she have hidden her feelings so deeply? Why did they matter as much as they did? They really mattered. How much she had given to others, and not to herself, mattered. Tears escaped as proof. She reflected on the serene beauty of her external existence and the mess hidden inside her head. Bee thought of herself as a wardrobe. A pristine and elegant ivory wardrobe, perfect on the outside, but only when the door was opened did it become obvious there were no ordered clean clothes hanging on the rail. Instead there was a pile of crumpled clothes at the bottom which spilled out into a heap on the floor, waiting to be sorted. Her heart pained at the sight but this did not deter her progress. She followed the stream of memories which flooded her thoughts. There were too many to process. Tears fell in response to the volume. Surely she couldn't do it. But she had to. Bee battled the fear and the desire to give up. Inside her head she took control. 'Please stop.' Then miraculously, as if in response to the request, the pent up emotion released, the pain subsided and the grip on her heart loosened. Her head cleared of questions and she was catapulted to memories of childhood. As far as Bee could recall she had never really suffered. Or had she? With a focus on this period Bee vividly recalled a time when she craved love, an elevating love, one beyond description. The love she desired had never been delivered. An ache developed in her heart and then a 'knowing' settled within her conscious mind. Bee had been loved by members of her family but had not felt the intensity of love she knew waited for her. As clarity settled, her relationships made sense. When old enough she had looked for love outside of her family; she had searched desperately for the love she knew was waiting and had made the mistake of looking for it in another. This trip to her past delivered greater insight. She realised love was not to be found in another but could only be found within herself.

She smiled, and in so doing, the tears dried up and her thoughts cleared. She had processed some of the past and understood why she had put other people's needs before her own. She had not been required to visit each and every memory. But instead had witnessed a steady flow of images and felt each associated emotion. Subsequently, the emotions were erased and she no longer felt any form of sadness for this part of her life. The sense of joy and progression inspired her to want to share the process of emotion clearing. She wanted to help her dad. Surely he would benefit from exactly the same process. If he could address and clear the emotion feeding his cancer then maybe he could release himself from his death sentence. She wasted no time, the call had to be made.

Chapter 18 — ARTHUR

Arthur sat on a weathered wooden chair under the boughs of the apple tree in his garden. There he sipped from his cup of afternoon tea and pondered over his conversation with Bee. She had spoken of the ability to release memories from the past, to see them flash by, to acknowledge the emotion and then to release the memory; never again to reconnect with the pain stored. Could this be true? Had she really managed to rid herself of the pain, anger and hurt once associated with her memories? She had asked him to travel the same path and go to his past, to dredge up all stored emotions. He was not convinced. What good would it do? Bee had told him she believed he had stored emotion which did not serve, which could be feeding his illness. Really? What did she know? He understood why she made the suggestion. She was trying to save him from his death sentence. But he did not believe such a simple process would do any good whatsoever. He knew she only wanted the best for him. She wanted to use all of her knowledge to support and possibly save him. Except he did not believe she, or he, had the power to achieve such a feat.

He turned his focus away from stored emotion, towards his daughter and the other elements of the conversation. With care and consideration for his feelings she had spoken of her own emotional issues and the love she sought as a child. She passionately described a love she had searched for throughout her life; one she knew was beyond the understanding of many, but one she had to find. Arthur felt a twinge of recognition; the love his daughter spoke of, he had found as a religious man through the love of God. But Arthur knew from their conversation Bee was not looking for this type of love. She had explained many times before, her path was not to find a God to love. He considered her need for love and his thoughts turned to her early years. Had he let her down? Had he loved her enough? Arthur knew he had done his very best as a father and there was no going back to put wrongs right. Even if he had not shown her enough love there was little he could do.

Would he follow her suggestion? He still felt uncomfortable about addressing the burden of his past? Surely he was too old? Would the process really have any effect on his cancer? Bee was absolutely adamant it would help but Arthur was not convinced. Although, he was slightly attracted to the thought of an offloading session with a stranger, someone like Carrie. Bee had done it; made a brave step toward the clearance of her past. As much as he did not want to, he had to try for her sake. What if he was missing a trick? What if she was right? His latest focus on curing the cancer was directed at the opportunity to purchase vitamin injections from a private hospital in Hampshire, a costly process. Maybe he should try a cheaper option and arrange a consultation with Carrie.

Even if she could not help him resolve the past, she would undoubtedly be able to provide greater insight into life after death. He would not admit this out loud to anyone but Arthur knew all of the physical remedies he searched for would not save him. When the doctors completed the radiotherapy treatment, he had been told this was his only chance for an extended life but would not to save his life. Nothing could save his life. Instead he ingested numerous pills to extend his existence. Even so, he could not accept there was nothing that could be done. Every day he scoured the internet searching for an alternative solution. An opportunity had been placed right in front of him, but he could not see or accept it because it did not follow the medical process he knew and understood. This was a step away from the norm and was not something he could embrace easily. But as uncomfortable as it made him feel, he had nothing to lose. He would follow the medical option to fix his physical state with the help of the vitamin injections, and he would follow the suggestion made by Bee. Having sipped the last of his tea Arthur sealed the decision in his own mind. He would arrange a session with Carrie and if it did not serve his needs then he would not arrange another.

Chapter 19 — BEE

Having understood the only way to help her dad was to clear painful memories from the past, Bee set about revisiting events from years earlier to clear away stored emotion. The action caused a dramatic change. Her life altered, as if the pieces of her whole had been reshuffled to form another pattern. Not the final pattern but one which would serve better over the days and months to follow. With this change came a greater connection to the invisible presence. Now it was always close by, manifesting as someone standing alongside, a fleeting shadow past an open door, or even existing within her body. The appearances could not be ignored, nor disclosed. Bee felt sure another person would find it hard to digest the reality. How could anyone understand that she felt a presence as if it were in the room? She found it difficult enough to understand and even more difficult to explain a manifestation, one not in physical form and yet could be easily seen. In order to manage the activity she adopted a compromise position, to discuss the majority of the experiences with her dad. He needed to hear about the existence of another dimension. This would aid his journey. But she could not tell him everything. Many of the instances of manifestation could not be divulged to any other living soul. How could she speak of the weird goings-on in her life? She couldn't. There were times when she was overwhelmed by the activity of the unseen but mostly she was able to process the communication, accept the presence and associated message.

The most successful location for interaction with the unknown entity was at the kitchen sink. A place frequently visited during the day. In moments of meditation at this spot in the kitchen, Bee shifted her thoughts from the daily toil of life and focused her mind, then connected with energy in the space around her body. Next, she followed her thoughts in whichever direction they travelled. With each connection and reflection Bee uncovered stored memories, times when she had felt the pain of another or suffered at the hands of clumsy love. Frequently, tears accompanied the visited memory. There were many. One dominant reminiscence was of failure, particularly the one time in her life when she had truly failed, at school. Why had she not realised her work level had dropped before it was too late? Where had she gone for a whole year when she had lost sight of her school goals? Why the need to revisit this aspect of her life? Had she closed the window on this phase of her life to erase the memory of lack of achievement? Following on from this recollection came further instances of failure, both in work and relationships. Although they pained her thoughts, she would not allow them to demoralise. Instead, she maintained a balanced view. They were the past. They would no longer be able to affect her present. She boldly processed each painful memory.

Considered the event and then released all associated emotion from her clutches. Bee felt power return. This enabled her to place her needs before others and her self-belief returned to a state not seen in years. Surprised by the power and success of the simple but effective way of cleansing her past Bee vowed to continue investing time in her reflections for as long as necessary. No thought would ever be shut out, no matter how frightening or seemingly insignificant, for she concluded there was always a reason for the presentation in her head. She had to accept every single part of herself whether she liked it or not. No matter whether the part shone like a bright light reflecting her good side or a dark and ugly part of herself she would rather ignore. Each step delivered Bee closer to her goals. To understand why she was able to hear and see things others could not. To find out who or what was communicating. But most important of all, to understand how she could use her knowledge to save her dad from his demise.

Since allowing the flow of communication to develop, the concealed entity, which she did not yet fully understand, communicated regularly. Often during interactions with her family, friends or people in the shops. As a child she had been confused by her ability to pick up transmissions from an unknown sender. She had felt desperately alone. There had been no one with whom she could talk, no one like her. In the present day there was still no one like her. Only people who wanted to understand, to help. But no one fully understood what it was like to 'know', and it was the 'knowing', which if she were honest, was the hardest burden to carry. She knew details about anyone and everyone, it did not matter who they were or where. They could be one of her boys transmitting a feeling of nervousness or sadness. A shop assistant silently telling her they had a rough night or a friend who unknowingly communicated details of an argument with their spouse, financial problems, pregnancy or a deep dark secret. The activity was endless. For some people she knew details of their death, one of the hardest levels of information to deal with. But there was nothing she could do to help because telling them would only cause distress. She coped with being privy to this knowledge, by holding on to the hope they would make a change to their life and save themselves. But there were many more levels. There were also messages on a global scale. These were delivered in dreams, both terrorist attacks and natural disasters. There had been many. There was nothing she could do about any of them, other than to know they were to happen.

This heavy burden of 'knowing' manifested daily and made it almost impossible to fully connect with another person. She could not let them see who she really was and all she knew. She had tried. But the response was always the same and resulted in an outbreak of fear and loathing for all she knew. Then she would turn the hatred of her knowledge upon herself and bury the feeling deep inside so no one could see the fallout. Those who did not understand her ability feared their lack of knowledge, or more importantly feared her knowledge of them. Many times Bee had told a person what they were feeling. Their faces endeavoured to show amusement but Bee could see beyond the facial expression, their eyes communicated alarm. She couldn't help it, people had no idea they were transmitting information about themselves. They feared her telling others of their secrets. But she would never do that. Their information was not hers to share and the details communicated were not kept. She had absolutely no desire to carry information about other people around in the confines of her head for evermore. Therefore, as soon as the information was processed, she released the details from her conscious thought. However, there was one exception to this rule; for reasons still unknown, details of those in her close network of family and friends remained accessible whether she liked it or not.

Chapter 20 — ARTHUR

His life had taken a down-turn. There was very little to amuse. His physical stature had changed. Once slim and agile he now resembled a person quite unlike himself, a rotund man with too much padding in his chest and midriff. Along with the disappointment in his physique, on most days his thoughts were heavily laden with the prospect of death, the pain of his journey to the end and a large helping of disappointment. Except for the days when he attended the Awareness Centre, where a stimulating spiritual experience filled his life with a modicum of light. Within the bounds of the Victorian red brick town house anything was possible. Life had new meaning. There were new avenues to follow and there was hope that one day greater knowledge would be found which might save him from death. Although Bee could not accompany him to every Development Group, Arthur still attended every other week. The attendance was a luxury in his life, taking two hours out of a day to sit within a group and consider all that comprised life. Earlier that day, whilst seated on a brown plastic chair in a ground floor room of the Awareness Centre, Carrie had asked him to pick a Flower Card from a silver tray. There had been nothing unusual about the request, for he was used to picking a variety of divination cards at the group session. This time however, an unusual event occurred. When Arthur cast his eyes over the picture on the card he had been consumed by thoughts of a naked woman. No matter how many times he looked at the very tasteful painting of a near naked earth woman, surrounded by flowers, his only thoughts were of a naked woman and sexual activity. Arthur had been shocked by his focus on the sexual nature of the card and hoped no one else had any idea of his keen interest. Unfortunately for Arthur there had been no escape. Carrie had asked all members to look at their card to understand the message conveyed. Arthur had laughed silently to himself. Could he share the very personal message he received? There was no place to hide in the Development Group, the whole point of the session was to share and learn from each other. But Arthur had not been brave enough to divulge his message. He had pretended there was no message received and looked to Carrie for assistance. As always Carrie had a response,

'Arthur, you need to embrace your understanding of the female element of your life, you have some relationship issues that need addressing.'

Arthur had silently laughed once more. Surely this was not his message. He had received an entirely different communication regarding the female. Not wanting to develop further interest in his card Arthur had accepted the advice and allowed the group to progress. But he had not forgotten his sexual focus on the female. He had sat quietly and listened to the rest of the group and made a decision to call Bee for advice when he got home.

As Arthur waited for Bee to answer the telephone he questioned his rationale in asking for help. Bee was his daughter, she was not necessarily the ideal candidate with whom he should discuss a sexual matter. Yet there seemed no other choice. He had no one else to speak with on the subject of divination cards, which is why he remained with the telephone to his ear. She answered. As soon as polite exchange had taken place Arthur bravely pressed on with his need for answers.

'I went to the Development Group at the Awareness Centre today. Carrie asked us to pick a flower card from the deck and interpret the meaning. I picked a card but didn't understand the message delivered. Do you think you could help?'

Bee responded quickly,

'Did Carrie not have an answer for you?'

Arthur had hoped she would not ask this question. He could not lie.

'She did give me an idea, saying I needed to embrace the female element of my life, but I'm not sure what that means.'

Conversations with Bee always had the same outcome, she had an answer.

'I think Carrie has a point. When you look at your life and the cause of your bitterness, most of the events relate to a female. Maybe you need to address some of your relationships and issues with women.'

Arthur heard her words but did not believe they were his message. He felt very differently about the card. Driven by a desperate need for greater understanding and knowing Bee had her own pack of flower cards, he asked for more,

'Could you take a look at the card and check the message for me?'

He knew she would help him and was not surprised when she responded positively,

'Okay, I'll have a look later when I have finished giving the boys their tea.'

With the promise of more information being delivered, Arthur released Bee to her motherly duties then turned his attention to the sitting room where he tidied cushions in readiness for his guests.

Bee called back whilst Arthur was entertaining his visitors, an elderly couple from the village who he had first met at the local church. Although he did not have time to chat, Arthur could not allow the call to go unanswered.

'Hi Dad, I've done as you asked and connected to the flower card. Do you have time to discuss it now?' asked Bee.

Arthur replied hesitantly,

'I have guests here but I can spare five minutes if that's okay?'

He desperately wanted to hear all Bee had to convey but felt torn between the needs of the people waiting in the other room and enlightenment from his daughter. Arthur sat on a chair in his study and listened. 'I connected with the card and a message came through with an immense amount of strength and power. You need to connect to the female, to embrace female. The strength of the message increased when I progressed my understanding to the fact, you need to address your relationship with women. This same message keeps being presented in my conscious thought and a constant supply of electrical impulses are transmitted too. This is a really powerful message and one you need to hear.' Arthur did not know how to respond. But this did not matter because Bee did not wait for a response,

'How does that sound? Does the message make more sense to you?'

He did not know what to say, she seemed to be expressing the same sentiment he felt at first sight of the card. Awkwardly he responded,

'Sort of, but I feel like there is more, maybe we can talk about it tomorrow?'

Without time to clarify the true meaning of the message, due to the need to return to his guests, the call ended quickly and Arthur hurried back to the sitting room to reconnect with his friends.

Arthur was surprised to hear the telephone ring again late that evening and even more surprised to hear her voice.

'Hi Dad. I'm really sorry to call again but I feel as if I have not delivered the entire message. Consequently, the information is replaying over and over in my head. Unless I release the contents I will not be able to sleep tonight.' Her voice sounded awkward, 'I'm not really sure how to deliver this message because the detail is so clear and strong, yet the content conflicts with our relationship as father and daughter.'

Arthur heard the strain in her voice and offered support,

'Bee, you can say absolutely anything to me. Please could you try?'

Arthur sensed her prepare for delivery and inhale deeply,

'When I received the message I was also in receipt of an image, a woman. All I could focus on were her breasts and the sexual element of her persona.' Bee paused for a moment then continued, 'This image communicates your desire for a sexual relationship with a woman.'

Arthur could not speak, his only response was uncomfortable laughter and then he fell silent not knowing what to say. But he had to respond. After a short silence he spoke,

'You've come closer to what I think the message means than you could have imagined possible.'

Arthur stood silently, staring at the telephone in his hand. He could hardly believe the conversation which had just taken place. How could Bee have seen so clearly and known the depth of his thoughts? If his daughter were aware of this level of detail then what more did she know? Arthur felt prickles of unease creep through his body, which caused him to shudder. He wasn't sure he liked the idea of his own daughter knowing his intimate thoughts. But it was he who had asked for her input, he who had invited her to look into his personal life by requesting she connect with the card. He had no right to feel upset at her ability to see into his soul. A sense of horror descended. If she knew the absolute truth about him, all of his dark inner thoughts, then she might choose to have nothing more to do with him. Arthur was terrified of losing his precious connection with Bee. She created another dimension to his life, one not found with any another, he did not want to lose this gift. The conversation inside his head continued to flow. Would knowledge of his thoughts actually cause a problem between them? Had they not discussed many times the value of truth, it was better not to have secrets from one another. Bee had hit the nail on the head with regard to the message. In the days prior he had been solely focused on his need for a sexual relationship. He desperately wanted his body back, fully functioning, where everything worked as it should and allowed him the opportunity for sex. A dream never to be delivered, thanks to the wretched cancer which had stolen away his opportunity for a sex life.

Arthur was left in no doubt. Bee had the gift of 'knowing.' She had been able to connect to his dominant thoughts. Any doubt he had harboured was replaced by acceptance. In equal measure he was both pleased for the gift and horrified by it. He had not been a saint throughout his life. There were a great many secrets hidden in the depths of his soul which he did not want to uncover. Would Bee see them? Would she see the real him? Following the latest interaction he believed she would. He did not relish the thought of her knowing the truth. This latest encounter concerning her knowledge boosted his awareness of the power she possessed. Not only had she picked up his thoughts from the card but she had also delivered the same message as Carrie. He needed to address his relationships with women. What if she was right? Would the addressing of this area of his life make any difference to the battle against cancer, or was this imperative for his journey across to the other side? He had no idea. She would know of course. But she would not tell him. He was fast coming to the conclusion Bee knew more than she was letting on. Was she trying to protect him from the truth?

Chapter 21 — BEE

However hard she tried Bee had been unable to erase the details. The information present inside her head had been too sensitive to process and yet had to be communicated. The discomfort had to be overcome and content of the communication passed on. She could not choose how much to impart. Her responsibility was to deliver a message in its entirety and leave the recipient to decide what to do with the information. Bee did not always fully understand the gift of knowledge but knew it must be trusted. Unusually, on this occasion there had been a change in delivery method. As if the content had been delivered directly from his thoughts and not the unseen entity. Why the change? Why had there been greater strength and power associated with the connection? Then her thoughts were illuminated and she saw more clearly. The thrust of the communication had been to make sure he resolved his relationships with women. This message had greatest significance and therefore the delivery was stronger than usual. Unfortunately, all he could focus upon was the sexual element because this excited him, but Bee knew this was not the main point. Over the course of his life he had experienced a number of unhealthy relationships with women, had controlled them, made sure he held the position of power. This very private and personal information had manifested inside her conscious mind. She knew addressing his unhealthy relationships with women was the key to unlocking his problems. Could he rectify his state before it was too late? She felt sure he could change the course of his life. But was he was too stubborn?

She would not give up hope. There had to be a way. If he would not take the giant leap of faith and release his emotional baggage then she had only one choice, to look for another solution. She bought a book Carrie had recommended, 'You Can Heal Your Life', written by Louise Hay. A woman who had cured herself of cancer. Bee scoured every page, absorbed all of the words in search of guidance. Louise spoke a language Bee understood, the idea that people store emotion in their body. If you were able to understand the symptoms exhibited by the body and release all associated emotion then an area could be healed. This model of healing made perfect sense. The positive input in her life instilled fresh hope for her dad. If she were able to focus on and address emotional issues stored in the recesses of her body, to heal her own past, then she would have mastered the art of healing and could apply the knowledge to assist his situation. She had nothing to lose. With newfound hope and enthusiasm, she embraced the first step in the process of healing. The difficult task of affirming she did in fact love her whole self. Bee knew if she could not achieve this first phase then no others would follow and she would not be able to help him. This thought drove her forward, placed her in a situation she would not normally have chosen, the use of affirmations. This uncommon practice was not something she had ever attempted and as far as she was aware, no one she knew had ever tried this method of healing. But this did not dissuade her from attempting the unusual. With great resolve she addressed the seemingly impossible task of speaking the words, 'I love and approve of myself.' On paper the task sounded easy but the words were difficult to speak. She did not love herself. Even after months of clearing sad memories there still existed an ugly part which Bee dared not love. She wholeheartedly believed the inability to love herself stemmed from the result of male interactions across her early years; her dad, brother and a series of boyfriends had each reinforced her belief that she was imperfect or unworthy. Even though history told Bee she was not someone who could be loved, she persisted. She spoke the affirmation over and over inside her head in the hope, that in time, she would feel some form of love for herself.

When she began, the act of speaking the simple words silently in her head seemed ludicrous and she was glad no one else could hear. Although ridiculous, she continued to persevere and push back on any resistance to the bizarre but simple process. Once the words of the affirmation flowed easily, the next step was to come face to face with the mirror, to look at all she had become physically and speak the words, 'I love and approve of myself.' The first time Bee attempted this task, she failed. She couldn't say those words to her reflection. She was appalled by the undeniable reality of the face staring back from the bathroom mirror. The fine lines around her eyes, extra flesh on her cheeks, grey hairs protruding through the dark brown hair on top of her head and bags beneath her eyes. Could she really look upon herself and utter the words? There was no choice. There was no escape. To have any chance of healing herself of the past and then to assist him with the same process, she had to keep following the steps. She took a deep breath and spoke the words inside her head whilst looking at her reflection in the mirror. It didn't take long for old familiar emotions to erupt. They came from out of nowhere and popped into her thoughts in an uncontrollable stream. A torrent of painful memories from a time when she had suffered with physical and self-worth issues, manifested in the form of an eating and exercise disorder. The deep rooted sense of unworthiness had been driven by a belief that she could only be loved if she were of perfect physical form. Because of this past, which still hovered within reach, Bee found the words of the affirmation almost impossible to speak. Did she love the reflection in the mirror? No, not really. But there existed a sliver of hope, which encouraged Bee to persevere and maintain trust in the force which had driven her to this point. She held onto faith in the steps followed, in the hope they would one day reap benefit for both herself and her dad. For this reason and this reason only, Bee kept persevering with the affirmations. Sometimes she would look in the mirror and speak out loud, other times speak quietly to herself during daily activities. After weeks of effort she felt ready to impart her knowledge and tell him of a new way to help his situation. She longed for him to see the possibilities which still existed in his life, to attempt the impossible and heal himself of cancer. Did she really, truly believe in this possibility? Could a person actually heal their own body? Was the process as simple as addressing stored emotion? Louise Hay had succeeded. The time had come to find out if he could do the same.

Their conversation began in much the same way as all previous exchanges. He relieved himself of his angst and offloaded details of his battle. Bee listened as he explained his latest research into alternative ways to eliminate the cancer.

'You won't believe what I've found on the Internet. A supplier in the U.S. who can provide me with apricot kernels. I've carried out extensive research on their usage and found they have proven to be effective. Although, the more I uncover regarding their benefits, the angrier I become. It seems that in the sixties and seventies there were a number of trials using natural medicines such as apricot kernels. But the big drug companies who sat on the board of reviewers quashed the findings.' His voice grew angrier, 'What if this is another option to cure my cancer? A much less intrusive way. This could be an answer to my problems. But I can't get any support on the NHS for the use of natural therapies. The only thing on offer is one invasive treatment after another. Well, I don't want to harm my body any more than it's harmed already. But equally, I can't afford to pour more of my dwindling funds into the battle. What can I do? I'm stuck, stuck with medication produced for the masses, making vast sums of money for the few. Drugs that are not going to save me. All they offer is an extension to my life but at what cost? They only make me feel worse thanks to the numerous side effects. You should see my bloated physique. I have bloody man-boobs. Why is there not more information on how to heal yourself using more natural means?' He paused momentarily, his voice quieter, more contemplative, 'I have fast come to the conclusion that I need to be kinder to my body, not bombard it with alien substances. Seeing as I can't easily get hold of the apricot kernels I have decided to follow a vegan diet. After much research it seems this approach may provide benefit to my situation. I have to try. I have no other choice. I don't want to die. I am desperate to do everything possible to save myself.'

His voice was weighed down by sadness and desperation, to a depth she had not heard before. But there was little she could offer in response. After all, she was not the one with a sentence of death casting a shadow over her life. She desperately wanted to help him, to make the illness disappear, to give him back the life he had once enjoyed. But she could not magic his cancer away. However, she might be able to shed a light on a way forward. She dearly hoped, on hearing her news, he would take charge of his own recovery. She slipped into autopilot and allowed the stream of thought to flow,

'Dad, I can't wave a magic wand to eliminate your cancer but I do have an idea based on a new book I've just read.'

Firstly, she introduced him to the idea of healing on an emotional level, explained everything gleaned from the book. Then described her experiments and how the process had worked on her own body. Finally, she broached the idea of him embracing the method of healing,

'I don't see why you couldn't use this technique to heal yourself. I've had a remarkable response from my body in a very short space of time. It really is as simple as identification of a painful part of your body then apply the affirmation for that area. Surely you have nothing to lose?' She didn't wait for a response, instead she forged ahead with enthusiasm for the idea, 'I have to be honest, it is a simple process but it is not easy. Speaking the affirmations is difficult because they push against your natural thought process. You really have to believe in the repeated words. I mean really believe. But I think you can do it. You are mentally strong like me. All it needs is focus and belief in yourself.'

Arthur considered the suggestion for a moment, the idea sounded reasonable, after all the author had cured herself of cancer. He guessed he had nothing to lose. Although agreeable to the process, he still doubted it would work in his situation,

'I'm not convinced I'll be successful. You seem to have the ability to do anything. I on the other hand haven't been successful with any of our dalliances. But I promise, at least, to try. After all, I've no other option right now.'

The semi-positive response received was all she needed,

'I know funds are short, so why I don't I buy the book and have it sent to your house. That way you won't have to worry about a thing.'

Their conversation came to a natural conclusion and she left him to process the suggestion.

Chapter 22 — ARTHUR

Another conversation with Bee and another level of knowledge delivered. How did she suddenly know so much about healing? How was she able to progress at a phenomenal speed and heal herself? Could he really be expected to do the same? Whenever they conversed she brimmed full of inspiring thoughts, hope and knowledge. But Arthur lacked the hope of which she spoke. Although he couldn't deny the fact he was extremely attracted to the idea of affirmations, he didn't really believe they would lift him out of his current predicament. All that had been discussed seemed impossible, unachievable. He admired her belief in him but he did not share it. There were sound reasons for his lack of confidence. Experience told him so. He had already attempted addressing past issues and emotions a week or so earlier during a session with Carrie, where he had discussed many issues from early on in his life. As each detail had been disclosed, pain had reared its ugly head. He had been shocked by the realisation that he still harboured pain from the relationship with his mother, particularly the moment she let him down by turning her attention to his father. The woman who nurtured him had disappeared and he had never been able to forgive her. With the past dredged up and accessible, Arthur had uncovered a truth about his behaviour. He had turned the hostility towards his mother into anger against all women. But he had not been brave enough to admit this to Carrie. He did not want her to know the truth. Therefore he had not actually worked through the emotion and released it. He had also attended the Development Group and picked the card, which both Carrie and Bee determined was related to his relationships with women. The message could not be clearer. He needed to consider this area of his life. What if they were right? Carrie had made a recommendation, told him to break his cycle of behaviour toward women that it was never too late to change. But he was not sure. He could not see how to change. He was in his sixties. Too much had gone before. There was no way he could put right all that had gone wrong. A much easier choice would be to remain as he was, as he always had been. What was the point of change? Why not accept his fate? Let the cancer take him and leave as he was. This would be a much easier option. Why was Bee not able to understand? He did not possess her strength. Surely addressing pain in his body with affirmations would not make a difference to his health? Also, was he really able to change and break the cycle of behaviour? Halt his need to have power over women? The need had become integral to his life. Whereby he reduced them to weak and needy creatures, as he too had been made to feel all those years ago. He felt sure change would not cure him of cancer. The identification of stored emotions couldn't eradicate the tumour that continued to grow and slowly suck away his life. Fear gripped his heart, clutched at the organ and turned it to stone. He could not embrace the idea of healing and yet did not want to go to the place where the shadows lived. He did not possess the courage of his daughter who had jumped into the darkest abyss with the faith all would be well.

Arthur struggled to embrace all of the positive methods Bee was so willing to encircle. Inside his head he pleaded to whoever was listening, 'If anyone can hear me. I am trying. I just don't know how to change, nothing seems worth the effort. I just want the nightmare that is my life to be over.' He didn't like the man he had become. Maybe he should have noticed earlier, the dangerous path he had taken. Why had it taken him so long to see? Arthur considered the use of the word 'should' and chuckled to himself. If Bee had heard she would have scolded him and explained, 'There is no *should*, you can use the word *could* but not *should*.' He smiled at the thought of her dominant character but couldn't smile at the thought of what he had become. Arthur didn't like himself very much. Could this be the reason for his cancer? Who knew? Bee firmly believed his stored emotions impacted his recovery from his condition. Arthur was still unconvinced. Even on the days when he was partially convinced, Arthur still didn't desire a trip to the depths of his soul to drag up events from the past. He felt lost and alone, with no belief in any treatment for the cancerous cells dominant in his body. There seemed to be only one option, a reoccurring thought, he would be better off dead. Recently he had found life overwhelmingly tiring, coming to the conclusion that maybe the fight wasn't worth it. He most definitely did not share her enthusiasm that anything was possible. He was not sure he could heal himself. However, when the book came through the post he would read it, but he could not promise he would follow the process.

Chapter 23 — BEE

On hearing his voice Bee realised he was not in a good space. Although not able to see him she heard misery weighing heavy on his vocal chords. This was not a good day. Bee readied herself for the worst,

'You don't sound good today, what's wrong?'

His cheerless response did little to allay her fears,

'The pain is getting worse.' He coughed to clear his throat and continued, 'I've got excruciating pain in my kidneys; feels as if someone is wringing the liquid out of them. It's constant, unbearable, a living torment.' Bee heard him take a sip of water. 'The doc told me these buggers are going to give up on me way before the cancer gets me.'

What could she say to help? Her heart was consumed by an aching sadness. Bee knew dwelling on the reality of his situation would not help, so she took charge of her thoughts and responded,

'I'm really sorry. I'm not sure what I can do to help.'

What could she do for him? An answer was delivered. 'Listen to his words. When he has released all the sadness inside help him to find a new way forward.' Bee knew this next stage of their journey would be tough for them both. Which meant she had to maintain belief in her ability to deliver all that was required. He was dependent on her strength of belief. At times like these, initially she felt powerless to help him rise from the pit of despair, then miraculously she would know. The latest communication cast a beam of light upon the focus required. The time had come to boost his belief, so he believed in his own power to change his physical and mental state.

Switching off the thought stream in her head Bee focused on the conversation in hand. The solution lay before her as clear as day, as if she had always known what to do. She spoke with a firmness to her voice,

'Firstly, I believe you would benefit from meditating daily. Don't worry about how to do it because I will explain, it's really easy, something you can do anywhere.'

Bee knew a regular meditative state would be instrumental in assisting him through the dark days to follow. Arthur responded to the suggestion with little enthusiasm,

'I'm not sure I can summon the energy and interest for meditation. What good will it do?'

The activity would require him to make time and apply effort. Something she did not think he would readily agree to. But she would not allow him to give in to the lethargy which had taken hold. A 'knowing' drove her forward. He needed to find peace. The best way to achieve this was to connect to his inner peace, to a place he had yet to find. Bee maintained her strength of hope, ignored his lack of enthusiasm and ploughed ahead with instructions. She could not and would not allow him to give up.

'First you have to find a quiet place to sit. This can be anywhere; in your study, bedroom or garden,' he seemed to be listening, so she continued, 'Close your eyes and take yourself to a beautiful place, a meadow, a beach, absolutely anywhere. When you have found your place then listen to every thought presented. You should feel emotions along with associated thoughts. You must follow these thoughts wherever they take you. When you have finished, reflect on all that occurred during the meditation.'

Arthur sighed and with resignation in his voice responded,

'Okay, I'll give meditation a try but I'm not sure I'm going to be very good at it.'

Bee could not argue with him. This was his life. She was only a supporter. But she had one more nugget to share before they finished the call,

'Whatever you do, don't hold back. This is really important. A way for you to find inner peace. But you have to be willing to give the process everything in order to reap the reward.'

Bee did not labour the point, instead she left him to his thoughts.

Chapter 24 — ARTHUR

Inner peace? He didn't need to find inner peace. He needed a cure to the cancer. Resigned to the fact he should process her suggestions Arthur rested his head on the pillow, stared up at the ceiling and reflected on their latest interaction. Even though he did not agree wholeheartedly with her ideas, he still felt lighter, his spirit buoyed by their discussion. This wasn't the first time she had this effect on him. No matter how low he sunk, she could lift him up. Although he did not want to, he had to admit her ideas and thoughts delivered a breath of freshness to his life of stale and putrid air. He had been glad to speak with her, pleased to have a forum whereby he could vent his anger and frustration. As always they had found a way forward. This time through meditation. Her positive attitude that all could be healed was extremely irritating at times. He knew she meant well. But she did not understand what it was like to be living under a sentence of death, in a place without hope. However annoying, it was this positive attitude which enabled him to find a way to face another day of his turgid existence. He did not necessarily believe in all that had been suggested. He wasn't even sure if he would be successful at meditation. But she believed he could achieve anything. She expressed faith in him, it was this belief which helped him more than he cared to admit. He would be lost without her alongside. He valued the spiritual support and had developed this area of his life, learned how to trust the feelings inside, to find his path. In recent days he had been delivered a vague picture of his end, the moment of transition to another existence. But there were no details. This thought concerned him. The concept of disappearing from one existence and reappearing in another was confusing and terrifying in equal measure. He held on tight to one certainty in the whole process. She would be there to support him until the end. He would not be alone. How he loved his daughter! But how difficult the task of revealing this affection. Expression of love did not come easily. Arthur hoped Bee knew how he felt, hoped she could sense the depth of love he carried in his heart.

He closed his eyes and made an attempt at meditation. What had she said he needed to do? He couldn't remember. He encouraged his mind to empty but this was difficult as there were so many thoughts spinning around his head. Pain was dominant. His mind focused on the pain in his kidney. Then a thought popped into his head. Death. No surprise this was in the fore of his mind. Bee said he should follow every thought and so he did. Death was always on his mind no matter what he was doing, he could never eradicate its presence. Was this the same for every person who had a terminal illness? How had Louise Hay, the author of the book on healing, managed this thought? Then it came to him. She had filled her head with something else, with positive thoughts toward her body rather than a negative focus on the cancer. Very clever. Why had he not figured this out before? Bee had introduced him to the idea of healing but he had not embraced the process. Was he able to now? Having understood how the healing process could work, he made a decision to give it a go. One positive thought followed another. This would give him control. He would be in charge of his existence and not governed by the constant nagging pain. There would be hope for a brighter day. A decision was made. When he awoke from the sleep, which had been induced by the peaceful state of meditation, then he would begin the art of affirmations. He would change his thought process away from the negative spiral. Even if this did not cure him of cancer, it would at least make every day a little more bearable. As he slipped ever closer to sleep he smiled, this is what peace felt like, he would try meditation again.

Chapter 25 — BEE

She had vowed to help. She would never give up on him. But in order to provide support she had to learn to protect herself. Although strong, Bee questioned her own ability to manage what was coming down the line. But there was no choice. She was the only one who could help him. She had a connection to him and to a channel of knowledge. She was the one who could guide him towards safety. The gift of 'knowing' led her to an understanding; she must address all outstanding emotion associated with her dad. Everything which had been stored away. The message was clear. The time had come to release another portion of her past. Because if she did not, this would be a problem for him at the end. But if she were able to resolve all issues between them then he would be able to leave without needing to make amends for his actions. Seemingly without a choice, Bee made the difficult and painful decision to return to the past.

She sat down on the bedroom floor and faced west, crossed her legs, arms relaxed by her sides and then closed her eyes. When all was quiet inside her mind she began the first clearing. Bee connected to the quiet space inside her head and crossed into the realm of understanding. She sensed energy increasing around her body, as if creating a protective barrier. Within the confines of the void, a soft white light enveloped her entirely and a sense of calm descended. In this new state she was ready to move back in time, to a place where the relationship with her dad had not been healthy. Although her family life had generally been happy and supportive there had been times when it had not delivered all she required. As with many men of his generation her dad had been placed on a pedestal within the family unit and Bee had been raised to please him and all other males, as if they were the powerful race. Inside the space of recollection, Bee remembered how her dad had constantly played women off against one another, almost as a sport, fuelling a need within. Then as her brother grew older and verbally more able, her dad found an ally. Most often this masculine dominance manifested around the dinner table. Between them they abused Bee, Lizzie and their mother by making each of them feel inadequate. Bee wanted to see the good in each of them, her dad and brother, that maybe they had no idea what they were doing. But she knew the clearing session was not about making their behaviour acceptable. Instead she had to find the pain stored long ago, the hurt hidden from sight so as not to fuel their fire. Bee felt sure her dad and brother must have seen the hurt on her face. Then all of a sudden she understood. The pain and hurt reflected in the faces of the females had fuelled their male power. Once the weakness had been found, the men poked and jabbed verbally, until the recipient became emotionally distraught. Many times Bee had held back tears to show their taunts didn't matter and they couldn't touch her.

But they did. Inside she had cried out for the stream of abuse to stop. The childhood taunting had damaged Bee. But not physically. Instead she had been damaged mentally—left with a belief she was not physically perfect enough for any male, that all her female attributes were weak and unattractive.

On receipt of this greater comprehension Bee returned conscious thought to the present day. During the many years since childhood she had attempted to rebuild a view of herself as a beautiful woman. She wasn't quite there but was getting closer with help from Adam. She hoped the clearing would deliver her closer still. In the present, the relationship with her dad was very different. There were still times when he flexed his masculine force, tried to weaken her with comments about her body. During these moments she was transported back in time, connected to a sense of feeling unimportant and ugly. But this didn't happen with any regularity. Bee caught the thought stream and returned to the focus of the clearing. She must revisit the pain incurred years before. Whilst in this sorrowful space she must attach to all emotions experienced. Bee didn't need anyone to tell her this would be a difficult exercise. She already knew. The problem was, everything stored had provided the basis for relationships with men. The action of cleansing would remove all that had been, leaving behind a void, a need to redefine all male interaction. Despite this awareness she could not turn back. She would revisit all of the times he had hurt her with his words and then release all emotion stored. Because this baggage, carried around for years, no longer served. Bee maintained her strength of purpose and stepped into the past. Immediately an image of a mealtime displayed inside her head. Next, she recalled the pain felt as a child and then as a young woman. Tears followed, a few to begin with, then a steady flow rolled down her cheeks. A 'knowing' presented. Her father was not the only male relationship in which she had struggled. She realised almost all of her male relationships had been troubled in one way or another. A light illuminated her past. Whilst growing up she had been encouraged to see males as all-knowing, powerful beings and that she ought to be good—be her very best for each and every one. During childhood and transition to adulthood Bee had missed acquiring a vital skill, the ability to stand up for herself within male relationships. She had not been allowed to stand up for herself within the family unit and so there had been little chance of success outside of the unit. Determined to release herself from the manacles which bound her to unhealthy male relationships, Bee attached to past experiences with males and allowed a torrent of emotion to pass through her consciousness. The result was more tears which she allowed to fall, in fact she welcomed them, for in each tear was release from the shackles which held her captive. Once all emotion had been cleared Bee redefined each male boundary. Then released the need to please men in order to be loved or accepted. Having completed the cleansing of the past she was in a much better position to support her dad through the months to come.

Chapter 26 — ARTHUR

Arthur had so much time to contemplate his life or what was left of it. He was no longer able to over-exert himself and therefore spent many hours sitting or lying. He had come to the conclusion continuing his vegan diet was pointless. This lifestyle choice had made no obvious difference to his life whatsoever, other than removing meat from his plate, which in his mind was one of life's greatest pleasures. With each week came further disappointment. He had tried to battle the cancer head on and signed up for a drug trial. But he held out very little hope in this avenue. Also, he had attempted the art of speaking healing affirmations. Although they did place him in a more positive state of mind they had not delivered a cure. He had also embraced the idea of meditation but had not progressed far in identifying past issues to resolve. However, he had achieved many states of peace and fallen asleep numerous times. In his lack-lustre life, a silver lining loomed: soon he would be visiting Bee. Arthur looked forward to the places their conversations would take them. He wondered if he should tell her of his latest thought. The idea of finishing his life before the cancer took him. He hated being out of control and had tried every last method to save himself. But none had delivered success. Arthur did not look forward to the end. He sensed, with every fibre in his body, it would not be a pleasant one. But he did have a choice. He was still physically able to make the journey to Switzerland to have his life ended for him. Although, he sensed this window of opportunity would not exist for much longer. Would she help him? Would Bee be willing to assist in his transportation to the airport? She would have to keep the secret. She could not tell a soul. Was that fair on her? Then again was the cost of the procedure fair on Sheila? She was already going to have diminished funds on which to live. Could he really spend so much on ending his life? This was a dilemma indeed. If he had all the money in the world, would he be able to do it? End his life. The choice did not sit well with his religion. He had been told a person who killed themselves would not be reunited with God. Could he test this theory? He was undecided. Although the thought of avoiding a painful end currently outweighed the concern over whether God would accept him. Maybe he would discuss the option with Bee. They had agreed to speak on any subject regarding his illness or demise. Yes, he would ask Bee. He was desperate to talk the idea through with someone. But he could not tell Sheila. There was no one else but Bee. She would help. She would not be bound by her own emotion. She would only focus on what was best for him. He had to talk to someone.

Chapter 27 — BEE

Standing at the kitchen sink, looking out over the front lawn towards the apple tree with gnarled and twisted limbs heavily laden with fruit, Bee connected to the reality of his demise. She knew the day would come. Every day the message grew stronger but this did not make the reality any easier to accept. The despair which consumed his mind, also crept inside her own mind, as if she were connected to him. A week earlier she had given in to the hopelessness and stockpiled tears. She had wept for all that had been and all yet to come. The departure would not be immediate. There were still more battles to fight. But it would happen, and when it did, Bee had absolutely no idea how she would cope with losing her dear friend. In the present there was still only one focus, she had to save him. Not for herself but for him. Bee still believed there was a way. But how could he be saved when she had knowledge he would soon be gone? The conflict didn't make sense. What did it mean? Then she knew. She would not be saving his life. Instead she would be saving him from a torturous and lonely death. Was that enough? Is that what she had been engaged to do? Surely this was not the gift of support she was supposed to deliver. Was she not supposed to save him from death itself? How cruel the hand that dealt her this card. She had followed the guidance, firstly believing she had the power to connect him to the departed to regenerate his belief in another life, secondly she had connected him to the possibility of healing his past to make a difference to his future, to heal himself. She had thought she could save him. But now she knew. There had never been a possibility of saving him. But she had believed. She had given everything of herself to connect him to a power that could save him. But the reality present told a different story. As she reflected on recent interactions with him she understood. She had not been saving, instead she had been propping, supporting, guiding. She was not his saviour. She was his guide. She had been delivered to the truth. The moment had come to accept the reality. Her throat became swollen with emotion and silently she wept. As she grabbed a tissue from the box on the counter top she screamed silently to release the pain. She had believed she could do it. Believed he had a chance. She had been wrong.

From her position at the kitchen window she witnessed his car arrive, sweep up the steep drive and park outside the window. There was no time for self-pity or to dwell on the misery which would surely follow his death. She needed to be strong. She wiped away the remaining tears, blew her nose and checked the mirror in the hallway to make sure there were no signs she had been crying. Once over the front door threshold she ambled slowly towards the old man easing himself out of the front passenger seat. His physical appearance almost stopped her in her tracks. His face displayed undeniable fatigue and body exhibited a painful frailness. The man she approached was not the man she had last seen. Bee employed every ounce of self-control to conceal the shock and heart-breaking sadness which threatened to overwhelm. She stepped forward and hugged him with great care so as not to crush the diminished man in her arms. Bee shared her love but did not share the 'knowing' which had made a home inside her head; she did not tell him there was very little time left for physical contact. This knowledge could not be communicated, for he was still attempting what now seemed impossible, to save his body from the clutches of death.

To lift his spirits and to provide them with time alone, Bee invited him to join her on one of her favourite walks. He did not need to be asked twice. Throughout his life he had maintained a passion for walking and readily agreed to the idea. With the decision made, Bee drove them to a village five miles from her home. With every mile consumed, her delight increased at the thought of alone time, time to connect face to face. As they reached their destination she was overcome by a mixture of feelings, excitement at sharing her special place and dread as she knew this would be their last ever walk together. But she could not let him see. He must not know what she knew. She looked on as he eased his body out of the car and realised her immense sadness was due not only to her knowing he would depart within the year, but looking at his frame she could see that soon he wouldn't even have the strength to take a walk through the countryside. In order to prevent him from seeing the truth she pushed all thought and emotion aside and directed him toward the lane ahead. Almost hidden from the road the narrow, uneven sandy lane led from the hustle and bustle of daily life to the great outdoors, a secret treasure hidden from view. Bee loved this walk and was pleased to be sharing the space with him. As they exited the lane the view opened up to heath land, with groups of trees dotted across the landscape as far as the eye could see. She slipped her arm through his, as much for the comfort gained from physical contact, as the need to support him whilst he walked. They strolled across the uneven ground, where the colour of sand varied dramatically depending on the geographical lay of the land. In some places, shades of the lightest grey to almost charcoal, and in others, a multitude of shades of orange. Bee steered her dad towards a rusty orange coloured track which ran along the edge of the common. An easy route that would provide them with a gradual incline to reach the summit of the mount.

Soon the orange sand underfoot was transformed to a charcoal shade and the track edged with heather in all shades of pink and purple. They were surrounded by a sea of colour which covered the ground in a splendid carpet. Eventually, after half an hour of effort they reached the summit of their climb. The journey had been slow but the view from the peak was worth the exertion. Silently, they took a moment to admire the beauty of the flat rusty coloured sandstone rock which jutted up out of the soil at a jaunty angle. The product of mother nature pushing forth from under the surface of the earth many years before. Next, they turned to view the evergreen trees in the distance and allowed their eyes to feast on a 360 degrees view of forest. Finally, they absorbed the splendour of the great expanse of blue sky dotted with small white clouds. There were not many places in the locale where you didn't need to say a word, where you could silently appreciate the beauty. High up, on top of the world, this was one of her very special and magical places, a place she felt in touch with all of life's beauty. When in this heavenly spot her life achieved perfection. Her dad would live forever. A state of peace and beauty filled her entirely. But she could not hide from the reality of what needed to be said. Bee dragged her thoughts away from the escape delivered by the tranquillity of the summit and turned her attention toward her dad. Even though the walk had been relatively flat he looked exhausted from the exertion. He was no longer the fit and strong man he had once been. He was a shadow of the man. How had it happened so quickly? Last time she had seen him he had much more energy. The man alongside was depleted, almost lost.

Bee suggested they sit down on the deep orange and brown, horizontal striped sandstone rock. After shuffling their bottoms to find a comfortable spot on ridges hewn out by wind and rain, they sat and admired the inspirational view of pine treetops which surrounded them for miles. Bee felt driven to speak of the very special spiritual spot in which they were seated.

'There is so much beauty to be found on earth. Look. We are surrounded by so much right now. I truly believe this beauty exists everywhere, even in the darkest of places, the most inhospitable situation and most shadowy part of your existence.' Once in the flow Bee found she could not stop, as if everything inside needed to come out, had to be aired, 'I feel as if you need to see this beauty. Over the past months I've learned to see it in everything, even in the darkest moments of my life. Now I need to help you see. In seeing everything within your reach you will understand the way in which you can embrace and enjoy all you have left. This will enable you to see your path when you make the final transition to your next existence.' Bee felt compelled to continue and raise the subject of his parents. 'Dad, you really need to address your feelings for your parents. This is an issue which has arisen many times and I think you would be foolish not to confront it.'

Bee knew he held onto painful memories and emotions from his past. This knowledge drove her onwards. She had absolutely no doubt, this was his only chance of moving forward. But even with the strong and absolute 'knowing' that he must reflect on this area of his life, Bee still found the subject hard to tackle. What did she really know about his life and the anger and bitterness which consumed him? None of this mattered. She had undertaken responsibility for his wellbeing. After thoughts had been organised in her head Bee prepared to speak as coherently and with as much respect for his condition as she could muster. Seated on top of the world, in a place she loved and from which she drew strength, Bee attached to her internal power. As a child she had lived with knowledge and then as an adult, hidden it. The time had arrived to share the full strength of her 'knowing.' Her heart raced as if she had run a mile and her stomach felt as if weighed down by a piece of lead. How could she help him? She so desperately wanted to keep him alive. Bee could see as clear as day the shadows lurking within his structure; shadows which seemed to be outside of his line of sight. She was his only hope. She had to be brave, to push headlong through the barriers he had erected. Firstly, she connected to the invisible channel and in response felt electrical tingling throughout her body. Then in a quiet but firm voice she asked,

'How do you feel about your relationship with your parents?' Without waiting for an answer to the question she asked another, 'Is there any issue with them which you might have stored?'

He turned his head and their eyes connected. She witnessed pain and confusion. His voice was tired when he responded,

‘I can’t think of anything other than what we have covered before. The time when I was a young boy and they let me down badly,’ he continued, ‘From that moment I felt rejected. I chose to become independent even though I was very young. I can’t think of anything else.’

He offered no more insight into his life. Her heart sank. She could see so much more hidden in the depths of his eyes. Could he not feel what she could? Could he not see all she could? She wanted to shout out loud, ‘I can see the problem. I can see your pain. I feel your misery. But I’m powerless to show you. You will not engage. You will not listen. Why?’ Bee was consumed by despair. Not an uncommon sensation, but never to this level and never for someone who meant so much. How could she let him take the path he had chosen? But she had to. There was only one person who could go to the depths of his soul. Himself.

A sad realisation developed. He had most definitely made the choice to leave. He did not believe as she did in the clearing of the past. Bee saw clearly in her head his acceptance of death. She pushed the dark thought aside. There was a more pressing need. Had she heard him correctly? Had he not just said he was considering taking control of his own death?

‘I’m sorry dad, what did you just say?’

He looked uncomfortable at having to repeat himself,

‘I have thought about taking control of my ending, of going to Switzerland for an assisted death. I have researched the practicalities. I’m still fit enough to get there and of sound mind to make the decision. It is an option for me.’ He smiled, ‘Let’s be honest. We both know I’ll be gone within a year. I am the 1 in 6. I will survive the five year estimate but it will not be pleasant. I’m already falling apart. I’m not sure how much more pain I can bear.’ He paused for a moment. ‘The idea of ending my life is very attractive. A way out before the pain becomes untreatable. What do you think?’

Bee struggled to take everything in. She had known he had given up on life but she had not considered him ending his life. What did she think? She didn’t want him to die. Whether it was through his own choice or not. Could she help him? What would the rest of the family think? She wouldn’t be able to tell a soul. She caught her thoughts. This was his decision. Her views were irrelevant. She needed to be a sounding board, to be supportive,

‘I completely understand why you might consider this option. I can only imagine the pain you endure on a daily basis. If you are serious about it, then of course I will be there for you. I will support you in any way I can. You would have to tread carefully though. There’ve been a few stories in the news lately, where family members have been charged for helping loved ones to end their lives. I could not be seen to be assisting.’

He smiled, as if he had known she would answer this way,

'I have thought about that. I would only need you to take me to the airport. We could rustle up a story to say I had always wanted to visit Geneva. Once on the plane it would be easy for me to look after myself and get where I need to be at the other end.'

Bee contained the tears she felt building,

'What I would really like to do is to travel with you, to be there at the end, so you are not alone. But I can't risk it. I have to think of Adam and the boys. As much as I would like to support you, I can't be arrested for helping you end your life.'

He put his hand on top of hers,

'Thanks Bee. Thank you for being there for me. Who knows, I may do it without any help at all. If you get a call from me and I say I'm at the airport then you'll know where I'm going and what I'm doing.'

Bee was left speechless, she had no further response. She had to accept his very real choice. But she could not be part of it. With nothing more to say, her thoughts turned to the time. They had been perched on top of the world for an hour or more. The discomfort of sitting on the hard, ridged sandstone rock was too much to continue. Reluctantly they left. With slow and steady steps so as not to tire him out, arm in arm they walked back towards the car. Carefully they negotiated the sandy track and as they neared the edge of the common she released all negative thoughts on the reality of his situation. There was a positive outcome. Although not able to help him resolve the troubles he had stored, she had shown him heaven on earth. This was going to have to be enough.

The morning which followed the walk began as every other, with a trip to the kitchen to boil the kettle. As Bee contemplated the first cup of tea of the day she heard a sound from behind and looked away from the window toward a man in pain.

'How are you feeling this morning?' she asked.

He did not look well and she was not surprised by his response.

'I'm not feeling so good today,' his voice dry and shrivelled, 'I have an abominable pain searing through my prostate. It's crippling me. I'm in bloody agony.'

Bee felt twinges of guilt as she thought of her selfishness the previous day. She had taken him to her special place. Had the walk been too strenuous for him? Bee caught her train of thought. Instead of focusing on the previous day she turned her thought to the present. What could she do for him now? A 'knowing' slowly filtered into her consciousness and in accompaniment electrical impulses gently rippled through her body. There was only one solution which she voiced immediately,

'I could try channelling energy to see if that would help.'

He responded with a fatigue-laden voice,

'Whatever that is. If it will get rid of the pain. The answer is, yes please. Otherwise I've no idea how I will survive the journey home.'

She had never channelled energy to him before. This was something she had only practised on the boys. They seemed to enjoy the sense of relaxation delivered by the warmth of her hands. The art of channelling had been learned from a book but she had never had cause to use it on him before. Could she remember how to do it? Would it have any effect on him whatsoever? Bee knew this was the right thing to do. She had to believe she could deliver. He needed her to believe. He needed her to deliver.

They found a quiet place in the study at the very end of the house where the rest of the family wouldn't disturb them. Once he was seated on the swivel desk chair, Bee encouraged him to relax and then stood behind him, closed her eyes and prepared for all that would pass through her body. She cleared her mind of clutter, of everything which had been resident only moments before. The place to start was his head. She positioned her hands over the top of his head and imagined light and love flowing from her hands to his body. There she stayed until the area needed no more focus. Next, as if guided, she moved around the chair to face his front and placed her hands just above the heart region. Once connected to the heart she felt a blockage. A heavy weight that pressed down upon her own heart. A word passed into her consciousness, 'blockage', and was repeated over and over again. The dominant word meant only one thing, the blockage was sizeable. She needed to clear his soul. The instruction was as clear as if it had been spoken out loud. His soul was lost, had been hidden. The nature of his illness made it virtually impossible for him to see past the physical pain. She had to help him feel his soul. Bee channelled electrical energy from her body into his soul. What was she doing? How could this unseen transaction make a difference? Was it her right to make this choice for another? There were no answers. But there was a warm sense of right resident in her head and heart, telling her everything was okay. She was doing the right thing. She did not possess the power to do the wrong thing. Once the act of holding her hands over various parts of his body was complete, with warmth still pouring from her palms, Bee returned to the top of his head. There she remained with hands over his crown until the moment she knew enough had been shared. At which point she lightly rested her hands on top of his head to indicate the session had ended. Next, she knelt down on the carpeted floor in front of him and gently asked,

'How are you feeling now?'

A voice filled with disbelief spoke,

'This is really quite strange. The pain is subsiding. As if it has been ghosted. What I mean is, I can still feel a sensation of where the pain once was, but I can't actually feel the pain.'

She could never have predicted such an outcome on her first channelling session. What had she done? What was she capable of? There was no time to lose herself in thought. He needed her attention,

'I'm really pleased I could help. I would do this every day if I could, if it were possible.'

They both knew this was not practical as they lived too far apart. A knowing smile was shared. Then a gentle knock on the door reminded them there were other people in the house and they needed to re-join the rest of the household for breakfast.

CHAPTER 28 — ARTHUR

Arthur slipped into the passenger seat of the car and settled himself for the long journey ahead. The one night stopover had been very enjoyable, not the most comfortable night, but then nowhere was comfortable for him these days. However, the discomfort had been worth it. The time spent together would remain in his memory for all the time he had left. Their walk had taken him to heights he had not been for a long time, to a place which looked a lot like heaven on earth. Once again she had delivered elevation to his life. No more so than the session delivered that very morning. His thoughts strayed to the intense pain felt earlier in the day, pain which had not reappeared. Strangely, Arthur knew the pain sensors were sending messages to his brain and yet he could not process the transmissions. Somehow Bee had managed to place him in a pain-free state, one which made him fit enough to travel the two hours back home. How would he have managed the journey otherwise? He dared not contemplate an answer. Arthur came to the conclusion Bee was his angel. Always there for him when he needed extra support, relief from pain or mental angst. This support was different to that which Sheila provided. He and Sheila had always been there for one another emotionally and physically throughout their lives. Their relationship was not lacking in any way. Even during the period of his illness there had not been a change to this behaviour. However, Bee provided something that no one else could. Insight. Energy. Connection. She had an incredible gift. Their latest encounter in channelling energy caused Arthur to entertain the idea of magic, although he would never admit this to any other living soul.

Arthur had heard the insistent message Bee delivered. His need to connect with his soul and unblock emotions associated with his parents. But he did not feel able to achieve this enormous task. Bee did not understand. Life was very different for him. He could not return to the past and dismantle the dark barricade he had built to block out his childhood. Of course Arthur understood where Bee was trying to lead him. Fundamentally he agreed the process of breaking down the wall might be good for him, but he did not seem able to attach to the emotion stored. Was this because of his male characteristics? After all men did not store emotion in the same way as women. A man's life experiences were not about their emotional context. What seemed so easy for Bee to achieve, by attaching to stored emotion then feeling into the depths of the soul and releasing the past, was not so easy for him because he had stored an unmanageable pile of bitterness and resentment. Arthur did not understand why. But every event he revisited in his life created the same bitter reaction. Based on research into alternative therapies, namely through the Louise Hay method of healing, Bee had suggested his feelings had probably manifested into the cancer which now terrorised his body. In response to this thought Arthur felt even greater bitterness and resentment. Was there any hope for him? How was he to escape the reality of his existence? Arthur doubted he could. If the harsh reality of life proved there was no cure. At least there was one element at the end of his sad life he could depend on. Bee would deliver him to his end. She had promised to help him to the place of peace which beckoned and he was certain she would use everything in her power to deliver him there safely.

Chapter 29 — ARTHUR

Bee had called to check on his status but he was not in good form. However, he welcomed the opportunity to describe his rapid decline into a state of ill health. Although he possessed a weak and hoarse voice, he found enough strength to convey the details of his sorrowful day.

'I managed to coax myself out of bed at 11am. Then attempted to get the day started by having a bath. Which did little to freshen me as I expended ridiculous levels of effort just getting myself in and out. In need of refreshment I made the short journey to the kitchen to make a cup of tea.' Arthur paused for a moment to refresh his dried throat and then continued, 'The effect of all this activity was utter exhaustion. So, I took myself back to bed. Which is where you find me.'

Once the process of unloading had begun he could not stop. There was a willing ear on the end of the line and so he persisted with his tale of woe,

'I can't explain how frustrating my life is without any energy. I already feel as if I'm on my last legs. I might as well be dead. There is nothing left for me if I can't get out of bed before 11am and enjoy a simple cup of tea.'

He had once been an energetic man who had risen early and enjoyed every moment of the day. Currently, there was nothing to look forward to. Absolutely nothing. The only glimmer of light, ounce of hope, was that in unburdening his sorrow Bee might be able to assist with relieving the pain and misery which consumed his existence. He didn't have to wait long for her to deliver.

'Why don't I try to deliver a session of energy channelling from here? We have nothing to lose by trying a remote session, it may just work. I tell you what, when we've finished our conversation I'll find some quiet time to deliver the energy to you. I can't promise exactly when this will be, but I'll do it before the end of the day.'

Arthur could barely contain his excitement; this was the best news he'd heard all day. She was his only hope of relief from the position in which he found himself. With a weary but appreciative voice he spoke,

'Thank you Bee. I know you're busy and the kids demand much of your time but I would be really grateful if you could. I'm not sure I can bear this existence much longer. The pain turns my day into a living nightmare. I'm positive the drugs I take make me feel worse, not better. This is no life. I am not living. I am clinging onto a pointless existence.'

Then he stopped. He had unloaded enough. Bee had offered to help. He must release her to the task. Just before the call ended she touched his heart.

'I love you dad. I promise I'll do everything I can to help.'

Could she relieve his pain? He had to believe. There was no other way out of his current dilemma. During their conversation he had kept one thought to himself. His depth of fear. Fear of all that was to come weighed heavily within the darkened shadows of his body. A sense of dread which had risen to new levels, fuelled the belief he was fighting a losing battle. But Arthur dared not tell Bee. He could not tell anyone. If he admitted this out loud then maybe the reality would be delivered. On some days he was most agreeable to being taken from his dreadful existence, yet on others, he wanted to hold firm to the precious threads of his life. On this particular day he could feel the hopelessness of his situation but could not share the information. Instead he carried the burden of secrecy. Accompanying the fear was a thought, one which grew stronger every day. Time was short. He would be lucky to see another six months. From somewhere in the shadows of his mind a diminutive voice cried out, 'Don't give up yet. You never know.' But he did know. With each day that passed the reality became clearer. Maybe he should leave immediately. End his life. Take control of his own departure. He had the option of Switzerland. Was he brave enough? Could he actually deliver himself to his death? He had no idea. Arthur felt helpless once more and so turned to his source of strength, his prayers. He selected a favourite from the book next to his bed and as he spoke the words out loud, tears flowed the length of his face and his voice broke under the strain of his existence.

O Christ tirelessly you seek out those who are looking for you and who think you are far away.
Teach us at every moment to place ourselves in your hands because while we are still looking, already you have found us.
No matter how poor we are at our devotion, you listen far beyond what we can imagine or believe.
Speak to us in our thinking, our reading and our discussion, and grant us minds and hearts ever ready to hear what you have to say.
We ask this in your blessed name. Amen.

The words repeated over and over inside his head long after he had spoken them. He faced his reality. Soon he would be exiting his life. Even with his strong faith in God, Arthur was still terrified by the finality of death. All he had to assist his journey was a warm feeling, like a comforting blanket wrapped around his shoulders, communicating that he would be cared for. He had no real comprehension of what this meant. Was this enough? Could he go to his death believing in a warm feeling? With grave acceptance Arthur realised he might have to. The sensation was better than no feeling at all.

Chapter 30 — BEE

A promise had been made and she must deliver. Bee lay down on the bed, closed her eyes and relaxed, within moments she was connected to the unseen energy. An electrical current travelled to each of her nerve sensors causing them to tingle, at which point her whole body felt alive with electricity. Then she was ready to step into the unknown. She had read a book on how to channel remotely but had never really believed in the possibility of it working. There was only one way to find out. But where to start? Then as if guided, she knew. She had to travel. Had to identify a way of reaching him. Bee allowed her mind to clear and then imagined being able to lift up out of the roof of her house and up into the sky. With this thought she left her body and journeyed along an imaginary super highway. A blur of light indicated the speed of travel as she sped towards his location. Then she was there. She could see his house. She was in his bedroom. There was no space for conscious thought to allow consideration of her position. Instead, Bee permitted the experience to continue as if this was something she had encountered many times before. She trusted the flow of light, embraced faith in her ability and connected to the man on his bed. Next, she encouraged her mind to empty of all thought to make space for a message. She did not have to wait long. He required air to assist with his breathlessness. Immediately she moved focus to his solar plexus and once there, attempted to channel energy to this region. When finished, she turned attention to the top of his head. After focusing on this area she moved along his body and was drawn to concentrate on the sacral energy point and kidney. Strangely, the focus on this part felt very different to the sensations experienced previously. She was coupled to the region, as if a large magnet had been placed there with such force she was bound by an unbreakable attraction. Only after an extended period of attention, when enough energy had been transferred and the area had been fully balanced, was she released. The channelling session was like no other. Never before had she been able to visualise passing through another body. But she was doing just that. She actually seemed to be travelling within the physical cells of his body. Bee continued with the connection regardless of the unusual sensations, for she knew the process would harm neither of them, so long as she maintained protection from his shadows.

Following on from the focus on his kidney, Bee was encouraged to connect with all four elements of earth. She had no control. There was no choice but to follow the process. She must flow with everything presented. This was the only way to help him. She must not alter the flow to follow her will, no matter what. Firstly, she connected to fire and imagined lightning passing through his neurons, regenerating all connections. Next, she imagined water flowing through every cell, purifying and cleansing him of toxins. Then she thought of air passing through his major organs to oxygenate all of the cells. Finally, she connected him to earth in order to provide love and support. He was grounded and reunited with his spirit. Then there was nothing. All of the visions and knowledge which had filled her head slipped away, as if nothing had occurred. Bee opened her eyes and reconnected with the reality of her surroundings. She had no idea if there had been any improvement in his state but she had delivered what had been promised. There was no time to dwell further on the matter and with no additional effort required, Bee left the comfort of her bedroom and returned to responsibilities which awaited in the kitchen. She had two meals to prepare. Firstly, something for her boys. Knowing how much they loved pasta and mince, a decision was made to make their favourite meal, Spaghetti Bolognese. She could hardly wait to see the delight on their faces when she announced their tea. Bee would never tire of their youthful enthusiasm for life. How she loved them, loved being a mother. Once the homemade offering had been consumed the bedtime routine would follow, and when they were fast asleep, then she would turn her attention to preparing a meal for herself and Adam. The same ritual played out most evenings. As Adam stepped through the front door she kissed him and they reconnected. Once he had changed out of office clothes and into something more comfortable the evening truly began. They connected at another level through discussion of the trivialities of the day, mulled over decisions which needed to be made jointly and shared laughter. She loved nothing more than to prepare a meal for him. As if this were an offering of love, to show she cared, had not forgotten. What should she make him this evening? She would make his favourite, Chilli.

Chapter 31 — ARTHUR

Arthur could hardly believe the change in his physical state, unbelievably he was able to move from his bed. Not only did he have physical energy to get out of bed but he also possessed renewed mental energy. Totally mystified by the miraculous shift in circumstance, Arthur pondered the channelling which Bee had promised to deliver. Had she done it? Was his improved energy level the product of her effort? He could not prove this either way. But he felt pretty sure it was her. Did it matter if there was no proof? Not to him. Whatever had occurred made a considerable difference to his quality of life. He had a life. Arthur smiled. His heart warmed at the thought of his daughter. Not only was she the single person he had ever met, who knew how to live with love, how to share love. But she also possessed the ability to fully listen, to hear every single element of a conversation. She did not miss a thing. Her levels of observation were beyond anyone he had ever met. She saw and heard things in every situation which no one else could. She visualised options invisible to anyone else. Without fail she had an answer and could shine a light on a darkened path.

Prior to their last call he had been adrift, floating in a sea of misery. His thoughts consumed by the idea that all people were worthless, did not deserve a life and the chance to fulfil their existence. Effortlessly Bee had extinguished the burning flames of hatred for his life and the lives of others. How did she do it? Shed light so effortlessly? Seemingly she had an answer for all of his troubles. This latest situation a proof point. She had clearly managed to channel energy to him from her home in Surrey. He had absolutely no comprehension of how this was possible. But it must be, because he had not implemented a single change to his circumstances since their call the day before. The smile still remained on his face. He was a lucky man. Not everyone had their very own angel on earth to support them through the darkest of days. Or did they? Maybe he had been missing something, perhaps everyone did but they weren't aware of it. There was still much to learn about his daughter. Arthur was acutely aware that the little he did know was only a fraction of all there was to know. This triggered a chain of thought which caused profound sadness to develop, sorrow threatened to consume his every thought, until he settled on one. He would not be sharing many more moments of her life. His path would soon deliver him to the exit point. When the time came she would no longer be bound to support his life and therefore free of responsibility. But who would replace him as her opportunity for discussion on matters of the unseen? Could her friends possibly provide the support and unconditional love he supplied? He hoped so. With this thought at the fore of his mind he prayed. Having closed his eyes, Arthur requested for someone to replace him, someone who would support her in his absence. The harsh reality of the plea caused tears, and in accompaniment pain dominated the very centre of his heart.

Arthur had always wanted to be a father. There had been nothing else in his life to match the extremes of emotion encountered in fatherhood. The euphoria of the baby delivered into his arms, the delight of witnessing his child learning a new step in the lessons of life and the heartache of seeing them fall when they chose unwisely. In a moment of reflection Arthur savoured the joy of his daughter, their friendship and the journey they had travelled together. He was a lucky man. He caught the thought. In the past few minutes, twice he had recognised his lucky position. How strange the thought. Surely he was not a lucky man. He was a very unlucky man. His life was to be stolen from him. But no, he could not accept the unlucky status. He was a lucky man. There were very few people in the world who had achieved all he had in his life. For he had achieved. He had found a special person to share his life, Sheila. He had been responsible for creating four incredible children. He had watched them grow. He still had contact with them all, albeit on an infrequent basis. He had a roof over his head and enough money to feed himself. The only thing to spoil his lucky status was that his time was up. He had seen the best of life. The time had come to accept with grace, he was a lucky man.

CHAPTER 32 — BEE

No one warned Bee of the growing need. She just knew. Each day the need grew stronger as her dad edged closer to the free fall which would be his end. This reality, the one which lived within a domain in her mind, was almost too much to bear, too much detail to know. She struggled to maintain balance in life. The only way to cope with the knowledge was to shut out the despair, to hide from the misery she knew would be present the day he left, and focus on all that was required in the moment. This mechanism of survival focused on the promise made long before. She would always be there when he needed support. This pledge meant she had no choice but to maintain emotional strength. There was no room for self-pity. No time to dwell on her loss. She had a role to play.

A message came as she stood at the kitchen sink. You need to understand the meaning of the word 'matter.' Next came a question. What is happening to the physical makeup of his body to make him terminally ill? Then another question popped into her head. Why has his matter changed? There followed an immediate need to record the communication. She grabbed a towel to dry her hands, then picked up a pen and wrote the message on the first scrap of paper that came to hand. An answer to the latest question stood boldly upon the page.

Because his matter doesn't matter.
His matter is angry.
He could shed his leaves as a tree.
Release all to earth and then prepare for dormancy.

With the task of washing up forgotten, Bee turned her focus to the words recorded. A sense of bemusement caused her to smile. Where had the words come from? She knew the answer. They came from the place they always came. A place unseen. She re-read the words and attempted an interpretation by asking a series of questions silently inside her head, as if she knew someone was listening and would help her understand. Can he release all of the anger stored inside? Release all that does not serve him? An answer sprung into her consciousness as if it had always been there waiting to surface. Yes, there was a way. But she could not see the path clearly, could not fathom how this would be possible. Bee considered the underlying message delivered. Was it possible this act could not only help his journey to the end but at some point in time have reversed his cancer? She knew she could not make him better, he had travelled too far. But she couldn't help believing it could have been possible at some point in his journey. Was the disease rooted in a part of the body that could be cured without medical assistance? After all, there were many examples of people who had managed to cure their cancer without the need for mainstream medicine.

Another question presented in her thought stream. Does Dad have to believe in all that is possible? Almost immediately an answer returned. Yes. Then Bee realised it was not enough for only her to believe in the possibility. Unfortunately, she alone could not resolve the issues. To be successful he had to believe he could cure himself. Why did she have to learn this now, when it was too late? Why could she have not held this nugget of wisdom years before, when there was a chance he could be saved? How cruel to know there had been a golden opportunity missed. One which she had not been aware of at the time. Bee felt responsibility weighing heavy on her shoulders. She should have known. She should have saved him. Frustration flowed through her body like a river in flood, bursting every bank and submerging her entirely. She often received information which could save a person's life, save their soul. But most times did not know what to do with the information. Had this happened with her dad? Had she known and hidden from the truth? She couldn't remember. Her life had been filled to the brim with looking after her young children. She had given all of herself, showered them in love and attention. She had given them everything. Too consumed to hear the important message which related to her dad? Possibly. This was not a reality she wanted to address. Had motherhood silenced the communication? She would never know. Bee stopped the thought flow and reigned it back to her current role, to deliver him to a peaceful end.

She allowed this thought to flow and a 'knowing' settled. She could only help him if he was willing to attach to his anger. But there was only one way to achieve this colossal task. The same way she had overcome her own sadness, bitterness and anger. By using an approach few seemed able to follow, to meet the shadows stored inside. Having addressed her own stored emotion she had moved to a deeper understanding of herself, to a balanced view of life, love and relationships. Why could he not do the same? Was there any more she could do for him? The enormity of these questions consumed every space inside her head as she desperately searched for a way to help him. Then she understood. He did not believe such a feat was possible. Even after all they had experienced. This reality caused a prickly sensation on the hairs at the back of her neck and every nerve tingled. She digested his choice to give up and fought back frustration. She could not give up on him. With this thought came another message, the name 'Wilton'. The communication related to a small village in Wiltshire close to where she had been raised. Once the message had been received then the recipient was identified. The message was for him. Bee wasted no time in contacting her dad. Time was precious and this information was of the utmost importance.

His voice was weak. Fatigue rasped on his vocal chords. His failing kidneys obviously affecting his ability to speak. Bee hoped he had the strength to hold on long enough to receive the operation to rectify his kidney function. With concern for his energy levels and voice, she decided not to waste his time with needless discussion.

'I can hear from your voice you're not feeling great so I won't speak for long. But I really need to tell you something. I've just received a really important message for you.' She carried on without the need for encouragement, spurred on by the thought this communication may release him from his current torment. As if driven forward by an invisible force, she asked a question, 'What does the name Wilton mean to you?'

He responded immediately, his voice frail but interested,

'It is a beautiful little village near to where you grew up. There have been people living in and around the area of Wilton for many thousands of years. I've always been fascinated by the place and its history.'

But his response did not cause a surge of electricity in her body so she asked another question,

'How does the area make you feel? Imagine you are there and tell me what you see.'

His voice took on a new level of interest, sounded less hoarse, his enthusiasm clearly communicated.

'Well, if you stand on top of the hill overlooking the village, on a clear day you can see for miles around.'

This was the response she had been waiting for; electrical energy pulsated in all her limbs. Then there followed another message. '360 degrees view.' Bee processed the words almost instantaneously and shared the details.

'This latest communication, "Wilton", relates to your situation. You need to cast your eyes around all that comprises your life. In so doing you will be delivered to the next stage of your journey. How does that make you feel?'

Bee felt buoyed by the direction of the communications, but his response was not the one she hoped for.

'I'm not really sure what I'm supposed to see. But I know you think it is important, so I promise to ponder over what 'Wilton' means to me. I will try looking around my life. Although I have to confess, I'm not sure what I am looking for.'

She could ask no more of him, for she understood this was all he could manage. She had delivered the message. All further progress was in his hands.

Chapter 33 — ARTHUR

When Bee called he had been sitting up, propped against the headboard. But this was not the most comfortable of positions, so Arthur shuffled himself down the bed and relaxed back onto his pillow, his weak body searching for extra support. Each day delivered a heightened level of kidney discomfort, depleted energy levels and diminished hope for normal kidney function. But even though pain tormented every second, of every minute, he managed a small smile. Only Bee could get away with telling him he needed to do something about his situation. The problem was, she did not understand. He was not like her. He didn't possess her strength or vision. During their conversation he had felt a sensation like an electrical buzzer inside his head. A silent experience instigated the moment Bee mentioned 'Wilton' and then again with the reference to '360 degrees view.' In addition to the unnerving vibration in his head, he had also experienced the sensation of an icy cold blanket wrapped around his body. Why the strange experiences and what did the message mean? If he were being completely honest with himself, Arthur knew exactly what they meant, but he was not yet willing to head in the direction in which he was being encouraged. He was required to consider all that comprised his life to date. This would deliver him to a situation where he accepted all he had achieved and at the same time, faced up to all the choices which had not delivered a positive outcome. Arthur had an abundance of dark shadows stored away. He had not always been the most pleasant person to live with. But on the flip side he had carried out numerous good deeds and had a positive effect on many lives. However, he could not hide from the dominant thought. One which could not be ignored. Why had he allowed a multitude of dark shadows to be stored? There was no answer. His response to the silence was fear, which slowly consumed his mind. He could ignore it no longer. He knew the weight of his dark thoughts would hamper his journey and he had no intention of meeting his God consumed with guilt or darkness. Who knew where that would deliver him? He had to take charge of his passage to the next life. He must release the darkness. A task which seemed almost impossible to achieve due to his ignorance. He was still unaware which shadows required release. Maybe he should ask Bee for help. But then he would have to share his shadows and he did not want that, he would rather she did not know the depths of his darkness and the reality of his choices. What Arthur did not realise was she already knew. She had been aware of his darkness for some time. This was her gift of 'knowing'.

The only way forward was to release himself to the process of unloading. This would not be easy. He was controlled. To allow inner thoughts to be released would weaken him. He did not allow weakness in his life. Arthur had never enjoyed this feeling. This is how he had felt as a small child. He had felt weak. The experience had taught him to rely on no one. To let no one in. What damage had this done to his relationships? He could never be totally sure. But Arthur knew he had never really given all of himself for fear of rejection. He had kept many secret thoughts to himself for fear of letting them out in the open. He had kept his feelings to himself in fear of letting someone know the intensity of his need for them. How many times had he spoken of love in his life? Few. Even though he had been in a happy long term relationship for years and should trust love, he seemed unable. Something stopped him. Silently he wept. He had never really given of himself. Arthur wondered what it was like to be free with love and emotion. He had been shackled by his past, never able to achieve such a feat. He wondered if Bee was able. Of course she was. She gave all of herself. Although, he was well aware she would give all until a point. If the gift of love was quashed then she would move on, apparently unaffected by the trauma. Almost as if she were protected in some way. He wished he had the ability to give all of himself before he died. Was it a possibility? It was certainly something to aim for. His life was not over yet. Although he did not have much physical strength left he had plenty of mental agility. Life still had possibilities. He smiled. He would not attempt it today. But he would think about it when he was next in a situation where he could share himself. Maybe he would leave this life having given freely of his love.

Chapter 34 — BEE

He needed support and in response, Bee travelled to his bedside. She stood on the ground floor bedroom of his home. A small room, only just large enough to house the brass king size bed, antique dark wood chest of drawers and two bedside tables. Upstairs in the guest bedroom she heard the sound of James and Edward playing with the yellow plastic railway set, which she too had played with during childhood. There was little comfort to be found on the rickety wooden chair with spindly struts for back support and a threadbare fabric seat, but then comfort was not her mission. Very gently she gathered his left hand and enfolded it within her own hands. Then she cast her eyes over his body. His appearance communicated one thing and one thing only; a person ready to move on to pastures new. She felt a sense of hopelessness building inside, then caught the train of negative thoughts and banished them. She hoped he had not been able to read her face, seen the despondency which clamoured for release. At all costs she wanted to protect him from his reality and any thought she might have given up on him.

In all the years since the illness had taken hold Bee had not witnessed his current level of frailty. His pale, milky white skin tinged with yellow and his eyes lost, without their twinkle. Was he ready to go, to leave life behind? Bee thought not. She sensed there was still a battle waiting for him; one he was intent on pursuing. But in order to succeed he needed elevating from his current position of pain and sorrow. He needed more energy and she could provide it. Bee was still unsure how the energy transfer worked. But it did. Who was she to question the obvious benefit to another?

'Dad, I think you could do with a session to increase your energy. Shall I go ahead and then we talk afterwards?'

He nodded and responded in a weary voice,

Yes please. I really want to talk, find out what has been happening but I am so tired.'

Bee smiled,

'That is why I am here, to help. Why don't you close your eyes and relax.'

But before she could commence the channelling, a message appeared inside her head, the word 'Faith.' With this word in the fore of her mind Bee asked,

'Do you still have faith in where you are going?'

She observed him take a large gulp, as if to clear a blockage in his throat, then he answered awkwardly.

'Yes. I still believe in God. That I will be collected,' his voice cracked, 'but I don't understand why I have to make this journey, enduring this excruciating level of pain. Everything I have been dealt during this long and drawn out illness challenges my belief in the idea I am looked after. I find myself constantly asking the question. What have I done to deserve suffering in this way?' As if floodgates had been lifted he released his frustration. 'I'm at the end of my tether. My patience is diminished for this life. To be honest with you I would happily be taken today.' He took a moment and then resumed his offloading. 'The pain I endure every single day is like torture. To be put out of my misery would be a blessing. Right now I would be delighted to meet with my maker.'

At first Bee had not noticed the tears that slid silently from the outer corners of his eyes and rolled down the side of his face. Seeing him in a highly emotional state was not something for which she was prepared. A tidal wave of emotion engulfed her senses and her own tears threatened to escape. She must not cry. She must remain strong for him. With his hand still encapsulated in her own, Bee focused on providing him with strength and support. Inside her head there was only one word. Love. Using this thought Bee released the need to dwell on sadness and instead channelled the power of love to her dad. As thoughts of love were transferred, she became acutely aware the day had manifested into the most emotionally draining encounter to date. The act of witnessing his endurance of tortuous levels of physical pain coupled with mental anguish, made approaching the subject of his choice to leave earth even harder. But the crucial message had to be delivered. Seemingly without any choice, she approached the difficult question and cautiously asked,

'You know you have the key to leave whenever you want?'

In response there was silence. Their eyes connected and he silently communicated the message,

'I don't understand.'

Bee found the courage to continue,

'Dad, you have the choice to leave. This is your life; it does not have to be extended. I firmly believe you are able to make the choice to stay or go.'

A strong 'knowing', the need to continue with the line of communication, drove Bee forward. This was an important moment for him, to understand he had a choice to make. Bee knew she was the only living person who could help him. He looked confused,

'I don't know how that can be. I do wish I were dead. But I still wake up each morning. What can I do?'

She had to keep reiterating the information.

'You can choose but it is not as simple as wishing you were dead; you need to close the chapter and the book. Be ready to go.'

His next words deposited Bee in a void of hopelessness, as if all of which she had spoken meant nothing. In a voice overcome with anger and frustration he spoke,

'I don't know how to make myself ready to leave.'

She had tried, had conveyed the message, but did not seem to be getting through, or maybe he didn't want to hear. Bee could see quite clearly the power of choice, of how he could succeed. Thoughts of failure dominated as she realised there was little chance of communicating everything visible inside her own mind. She must release the message. Further attempts were futile. He could not hear the communication. Silence descended like a heavy rain cloud, which forced Bee to focus inwards to a peaceful space inside. She could not be angry with him. She looked upon his weak body and imagined what a vicar must feel when sat beside a dying parishioner. Bee felt as if she were providing this service. But there was a difference, the person with a death sentence wasn't just any person. This was her dad, a friend who she desperately wanted to save, or at the very least help through the process of accepting the end of his life. The day and all of its parts was turning out to be one of the hardest days of her life. But she had to stay strong. He was unable to share his inner most fears and thoughts with anyone else. Even though she was treading water in a very difficult set of circumstances, Bee was determined to continue supporting, for this was the only way he could be delivered to a place of greater peace and understanding.

The period of silence communicated there was nothing more to be said on the matter of his death, which meant the channelling could begin. In preparation for the sharing of energy, Bee released the raw emotion which had built up during their conversation. Firstly, she closed her eyes and connected to the calm space in the centre of her body. Next, she connected to the unseen energy she could sense in the space all around. As with all others, the session began with the placing of hands over the top of his head. Bee sensed calm, an unusual and new sensation not felt during any of the previous channelling sessions. He must have made progress, maybe released some of his shadows. Bee felt happy at the thought and allowed her contentment to gently wash away all sadness. She continued with the session by moving her hands to various positions above his body. When her hands hovered over his heart she heard the words 'Earth Angel.' A message transmitted for the recipient of the session. Bee turned all mental focus to the meaning of the communication and a thought flow delivered her to an understanding. She was his Earth Angel. As Bee accepted the fact, electrical energy tingled and spread to every extremity, then tears escaped. With the flow of tears she felt fear grasp hold of her heart, as if attempting to twist, squeeze and wrench all life from the organ. Quickly she opened her eyes and stole a glance towards his face; there was no sign of recognition, he had not seen her reaction to his state, his eyes were still closed. After a further five minutes of sharing energy, Bee completed the session and sat down on the chair. An action which caused a loud creak and prompted his eyes to open. Their eyes connected and they shared a smile. Then she spoke,

'A few moments ago a message, 'Earth Angel', came through.'

He responded almost immediately,

‘I too have heard these words. I think only of you, that you are my angel on earth helping me through these difficult times. You have been there for me whenever I’ve needed you. I also know you will be with me whenever I need you in the future. I have no doubt you are an angel who walks alongside me.’

Bee looked once more into the eyes of the frail man and in a fraction of a second shared a ‘knowing’, the look communicated everything. Theirs was a bond of blood which had transformed into a deep spiritual connection. One which neither of them had anticipated. One which had delivered them both to a place they would never have visited without the other. Bee interrupted the magical moment with a newly delivered message,

‘I am walking alongside you always. You know I will continue to do so until your very last breath.’

In all the time she had been in the room Bee had not thought of anything else but their connection. All of a sudden she became aware of time, noticed the late afternoon light diminishing and evening drawing near. She had no choice but to slip back into her life as mother to James and Edward, they needed her attention. Although she did not want to leave him, she must.

‘I have to go. As much as I’d love to remain with you for the rest of the evening I really must feed the boys.’

He nodded in understanding and smiled weakly. She raised herself off the chair, replaced it in the corner of the room then walked over to him, took his hand and smiled. A smile that said, 'I love you', 'I will be here for you no matter what' and 'Goodbye for now.' Then she disappeared through the door.

Chapter 35 — ARTHUR

Arthur hoped sleep would deliver him to a peaceful place. But before he allowed slumber to steal his conscious thought he reflected on the afternoon. His thought stream turned to Bee and her ability to assist him even when he thought all hope was lost. Without fail she could draw him out of himself and see with absolute clarity that which held him back. Arthur knew Bee was right when she said he was in control of his life. But he could not admit this to her. After all he was struggling to admit this to himself. The realisation of his level of control had dawned a day or so earlier as he lay in the pit of despair contemplating his future. On this day he had witnessed a small sphere of white light, beyond the bed, in the corner of the room. Accompanying the unusual light was a strong sense of warmth and a knowing, that if he wanted to he could join the visitor in his room, the glow of light. Why had he not shared the details of the encounter with Bee? Did he not trust her? Or, did he not want her to point out the reality of the visit? Arthur felt confused. Each day delivered new feelings he did not understand. His logical mind struggled to make sense of them. Could it be true? Was it as simple as wanting to go to the light? Bee said not. She told him he needed to make peace with himself and all those around him. He had to prepare himself for departure. What did this mean? Why couldn't she tell him exactly?

The trauma of his life was so great he seemed unable to see the path which she laid out for him. In the moment of contemplation he could not think of any reason to stay. But equally he did not want to leave. Perhaps he was holding on too tight to his life and that is why he suffered so. Maybe he should follow her guidance, release the emotion and experiences which bound him to his life. But how? Then he remembered the message he had received before, the one which encouraged him to give freely of his love. That was it. Why had he forgotten? He guessed it mattered not. All that was important, he had remembered. He had to understand how to love, to walk into the field of life and scatter the seeds of love without any fear, without the need to control the outcome. Could he do it? He had to. He did not want to continue his life of suffering. He wanted to be free of pain, to be free of life. Although, not before the date he had set in his mind. This thought cast light on another problem. On the day of the prostate cancer diagnosis he had set himself a target. Having been advised 1 in 6 people could survive for a further five years after diagnosis, he had vowed to be the one. Arthur had never been concerned whether this choice was in his best interest, he had only been determined to fight that which threatened his life. He had been driven by the desire to control his outcome. In the moment of clarity he realised this may not have been the best choice. However, there were still a few months until the 5th anniversary of the day he had been delivered his death sentence, which meant he had time to ready himself, time to be free with love and achieve his final goal.

Arthur applied logic to his situation. He would attend hospital for his kidney operation and then return home to make peace with his life. He had been gifted time. Many people were not given this opportunity. They were struck down by surprise with no chance to make peace or say goodbye. Although the latter part of his life had been dominated by pain and heartbreak, he was suddenly aware of how lucky he was. He smiled, that word again, luck. He was a lucky man. He had been given time to put his affairs in order.

Chapter 36 — BEE

With the operation to rectify his kidney function complete, her dad had been reinstated in his own bed. She sat to his left on the rickety chair and looked upon his weak form. Her thought flow focused on the reality of his situation. The operation had been partly successful; although the surgeons had found one of the kidneys beyond repair they had successfully managed to open up the tube to the one functioning kidney. The stark reality of his condition which hit hard, his one remaining kidney would not last forever, would probably only manage a few more months. Bee sat quietly and with his left hand bound by her own she listened to his outpouring of grief.

'I am alive but I feel as if I should be dead. I know I don't have long. The prostate cancer won't kill me, my failing kidney will. I'm not sure what's worse. By which sword I would rather be slain. If it is the kidney which fails then you know this will not be pretty. I have googled the condition and it tells me there is a painful end ahead for me. The bugger of it all is, I know the end will come soon, but I'm not ready.'

He paused, his eyes glazed over, tears threatened. She did not know what to do and so sat in silence; communicating her strength of support telepathically. Then his voice took on a lighter note, as if he had never spoken of his impending death.

'After the operation, when I had regained consciousness, I could not escape the thought of Bach. I still can't. The word is constantly dominant in my mind, as if there is a purpose to the name. We both know he is my favourite composer, but the number of times I have thought of him since returning home is ridiculous.' Bee smiled and communicated silently with her eyes, willed him to share more. 'I'm being driven to purchase the entire collection of Bach music, as if this is the next step for me, the only way I can be delivered to peace.' He continued, 'I can't explain why, all I know is, I need to hear the music.'

His words warmed her heart. He had shone a light upon his path. He was listening to his own guidance. The passion for Bach had injected a renewed enthusiasm for his existence. In the hope of helping him further, inside her head she silently asked for a greater understanding of the Bach connection. But disappointingly no response was forthcoming. In the absence of a communication Bee presumed there was nothing for her to add and she turned focus on an energy channelling session to aid the restoration of his strength.

'Dad, I'm not getting any messages to support your Bach focus, so I am guessing I just need to do some energy channelling. Does that sound okay to you?'

He responded as if his thoughts were somewhere else, 'Err…yes please. Thank you.'

He communicated his readiness by closing his eyes. In response Bee connected to the quiet space inside her head and heart, then moved quietly around the bed with hands held just above his body. She allowed energy to flow unseen through her body. A process which required ultimate faith in the connection. There was no room for doubt. Only belief that absolutely anything was possible by the transference of energy. With unerring belief Bee shared thoughts of love with her dad. Then after half an hour, when the transference was complete, Bee silently challenged her faith. Had she made a difference? Was she really capable of helping him? A strong response was delivered in the form of electricity, which surged through her nervous system causing her arms and legs to tingle as if they were alight with electrical impulses. Then she heard the word 'Yes.' But she had no proof. Only a 'knowing' that she had and would continue to make a difference to his life. As was now common place, emotion rose from somewhere inside and became stuck in her throat. Bee fought back the threat of tears and focused hard on containing any outward response to the journey she knew was coming to them both. She took a couple of deep breaths, making sure they were not obvious to him. With each breath she released the fear and emotion which dominated her thought flow. Once her emotions were stabilised another 'knowing' presented. In some inexplicable way his trauma assisted her own path, delivered her to places she would otherwise not have visited. How could this be true? How could his suffering deliver her forward? This was not right. Surely his pain should not benefit her life? There seemed no rhyme or reason to the thought, and yet Bee knew she could not hide from this fact, for it had been clearly presented. Had to be accepted. Only then could she see clearly enough to help him further. Her thought flow halted. The energy channelling session was clearly at an end. Bee did not argue within the confines of her head. Instead she accepted the end and returned to the chair where she sat quietly until he opened his eyes.

She did not have to wait long. No sooner had his eyes opened then he spoke,

'Thank you. I feel so much calmer now—more at peace with myself. But at the same time, absolutely determined to follow up my connection with Bach. This seems to be my sole focus. I must reconnect with Bach music. Although I still have no clear idea why. Yet I feel incredibly enthusiastic about the prospect.'

He was clearly driven toward absorbing himself in Bach, and yet she had received no further communication on the subject,

'Dad, I don't have any specific messages regarding Bach. However, I do feel the need to encourage you to not only listen to his music but also research the great man. As if the search for information will deliver you an answer, the reason for your quest.'

There was no more to give. She had other responsibilities and must switch back to her role as wife and mother. She must leave his bedside.

'It's time for me to go. I guess you feel pretty tired anyway? Shall I tell mum you're resting or do you want her to bring you something?'

He replied with a weak smile on his lips,

'I think I'll rest for a bit. See you soon Sweetie.'

As she left the room one thought dominated. Within his seemingly hopeless existence there did exist a small shard of hope. Bach.

CHAPTER 37 — ARTHUR

Although the visit had caused further levels of fatigue, in conflict to this feeling, Arthur also felt more alive. Bee had inspired him to a new depth of understanding and had ignited a passion not seen in a while. There was still hope in his life. Though short, he could still achieve the impossible. He enjoyed her company and observing the light which represented the intelligence in her eyes. There was something unusual about the way she looked at issues. He was constantly amazed by her clarity of thought. Problems for which he could not find answers, she would offer an obvious solution, one that seemed to have been plucked from thin air. Observing Bee at work was truly fascinating. Seemingly she connected to an unseen intelligence, quite unlike any other person he had ever known during his life. Arthur recalled the many conversations they had shared on life, the universe and the unseen. He had often glimpsed something inexplicable in her eyes, beyond the light, an element he may never be able to comprehend. Although, there had been many times when he had also observed frustration buried deep in the brown of her eyes. A reaction to why everyone else could not see what seemed so obvious. During their latter years together he had developed a finer understanding of his daughter, of her differences. As if a light had illuminated his thoughts. Arthur suddenly knew. He understood her better than ever.

She would deliver a catalyst for change. But he did not know the details, the what, why or where. Arthur caught his thought flow and laughed. Now he sounded like her. 'I just know' is what she would say. He frowned at this thought. How did he know?

In a magical moment Arthur appreciated the feeling of 'knowing' and understood his daughter more than he had in years. His eyes filled up with tears at thought of the lonely and isolated path she had trodden from a very young age. More recently she had shared the truth of her existence with him. The reality of the knowledge which had been present throughout all of her years. A solitary life. No one with whom she could confide. All of a sudden Arthur was overwhelmed by guilt. Could he, should he have helped her earlier? He didn't know. He was certainly helping her now. A strong bond had developed between them. She had an outlet for her thoughts, for the experiences in her life. Him. He also had an outlet. Her. How had this come to fruition? On a telephone call. Arthur recalled the day she contacted him. They had been chatting and then she delivered a message. By sheer chance she had received contact from his mum. Or was it chance? Since that day she had guided him through a minefield and lifted him when all seemed lost. Maybe she had planned this. Maybe she knew exactly what she was doing. Arthur felt sure he could not have made the journey without her. He shuddered at the thought. Then smiled in wonder. Had she stepped in because she knew something? Had greater knowledge of his life? Yes. He believed so. His thoughts drifted to love. He loved her. He could not help it. She gave so freely of herself. Arthur caught his thought. Had he too given freely of his love? No, he had not. He had maintained his guard. In moments like these he did feel as if he was giving freely. He could feel the love bursting from his chest. But he had never presented this reality in her presence. He had always needed to be in control. However, he had promised himself he would try and give freely of his love. Before the end of his days he hoped to learn this art with Bee. Although he knew it would be hard. Maybe he should start with a simpler opportunity. Maybe he could give freely of his love to Sheila. This thought shocked him to the core. They had been married for more than forty years. Had he really never truly given of himself? The harsh reality was obvious in his thoughts. He had not. Arthur considered his choice. He had never shown his true self to anyone. But it was not too late. He would start the process with Sheila. He could not leave this life without her knowing how much he cared for her, for all they had achieved together.

Chapter 38 — BEE

Bee made a conscious choice to retain all conversations which occurred in the confines of her head. There could be no imparting of information to another. She could never share her vision of his departure. No one else would be able to deal with the truth. Everyone with whom she interacted saw the wife, mother and daughter. There were very few people who had the capacity to see her in a different light, to open their minds to the reality of the unseen communication. Even after all of her experiences, Bee herself was not fully understanding of the presence in her life. How could she expect another person to accept all of the unknowns?

The hour was early but this had never stopped the flow of communication. As she entered the kitchen, words were thrust into her conscious thought. Bee looked heavenwards. Why? The words filled the entire space inside her head. There was no room for thought, only the words. Do you really have to communicate this early in the morning? James had woken her only five minutes earlier; had crept alongside her bed and gently prodded at her arm. He was an early riser. Although she was not always in the best of moods in the early hours, she had always welcomed him, never told him to go back to bed. They had shared many mornings lying on the sofa, watching a kids TV programme or reading a book. Her thoughts returned to the task in hand, James required a drink.

On the way to the fridge she spotted the time on the cooker clock, 5:34am. Standing at the open fridge looking for the apple juice carton, the words played over and over inside her head, clearly an important message.

'You're breaking my heart, you're shaking my confidence.'

Experience told her the words would not depart until she understood the content. There was no point in attempting to re-join the land of slumber, it was hopeless to even try. With a plastic cup of apple juice in hand, she crept along the landing past Edward's room to the playroom at the end of the corridor. James was snuggled into his beanbag in front of an episode of Power Rangers. She had never seen the attraction in the programme but understood it was a way for him to connect with the boys at school. From his post school-day chatter she had learnt that during break they played a game which involved mimicking the characters. If he was not able to watch the programme then he would be at a disadvantage. She did not want that. School was a hard environment in which to thrive, especially for a boy. There could be no sign of weakness. She left James to his entertainment, tiptoed back down the landing and two short flights of stairs to the small sitting room at the bottom of the house. She settled into an armchair. Once seated, Bee closed her heavy eye lids and placed a hand on each thigh. Her first thought was directed at the impractical cotton pyjamas which provided little protection against the cool air of the room. To eliminate the thoughts of the chill air which encapsulated her body, Bee focused on a new thought inside her head. 'Bach, relaxing, it is a message.' Puzzled by the communication Bee pondered for a moment. First the words and then a link to Bach. Her thoughts bounded towards the obvious. The recipient for the message was her dad. Next she asked, 'Whose heart is broken?' This seemed a very reasonable question to ask, as the words transmitted earlier had hinted of a broken heart. There was no response. Silence filled the space inside her head. Clearly this was not an avenue to follow so she transferred focus to the word 'heartbreak.' Almost immediately an understanding developed. Bach would help mend his heart. His heart had been broken. Her dad struggled with his life. There was a strong possibility the music of Bach would ease his pain. As soon as the message became a 'knowing' the connection terminated and her conscious thought transported back to the room. Bee opened her eyes and once more was aware of the blanket of cold air numbing her extremities. She smiled at the reality of her physical state. She had been completely oblivious to the cold during the entire connection, as if the part of her brain which processed these messages had been halted for a short time. Bee stretched out her chilly limbs and joints then reconnected with her physical senses. Next, with the lightest of footsteps she returned to the playroom to check on James. Peering round the half open door she could see he was still absorbed in the programme. With her brain still fogged by lack of sleep she chose to leave him to it and headed back to bed to snatch extra sleep. On the way she stopped at Edward's room, where she sneaked a look through his half open door and saw he was snuggled on his tummy, heavy breathing signified he was still fast asleep. With both children catered for she returned to bed. The warmth which she had left was no longer in evidence but she ignored the chill of the sheets. With her head clear of messages and a thick duvet to warm her cold body, she closed her eyes and submitted to sleep before the routine of the day took over.

On waking Bee wanted to ring him immediately and deliver the message. But this wasn't practical. After all she had a household to run. Having assisted Adam in leaving the house to get to work early, she then focused on feeding the boys their breakfast and readying them for school and nursery. Only when they had been delivered to their respective establishments and she had returned home could she make the call. As usual they exchanged pleasantries expected of the introduction to a conversation. Once these were over, they wasted no more time on triviality and she delivered the communication.

'I received a really strong communication for you this morning. Bach, relaxing, it is a message.'

Electrical impulses flowed through her nerves as if in support. More intense than usual. The strength of electricity meant only one thing; this was important. But why? Her lack of knowledge meant she had to question him. There would be no further understanding until his thoughts had been heard.

'Dad, I'm not getting any supporting information regarding this message. How do you feel about it?'

After a few seconds of silence he responded,

'Every time I think of J.S. Bach I am overwhelmed. Basically I become really emotional and I can't control myself. I cry. I don't sob as if in grief, more like I weep as if in release.'

Bee could hear his voice breaking as he spoke. Clearly struggling to control his need to weep. She connected with his sadness and felt his sorrowful state saturate her soul. The act of sinking into the depths of his misery caused a protective reaction. She closed the channel to his sorrow. There was no option but to pullback. She must not be consumed by his sadness. As he regained composure Bee focused on identifying the full meaning of the message. A 'knowing' became resident. The whole of the message is important in ways you cannot yet fully comprehend. This meant it would become obvious in time. Bee understood the limitation and chose to focus only on the 'relaxing' element. Almost immediately another 'knowing' became present within the bounds of her consciousness. He must listen to the music of Bach. This will enable him to achieve a much greater level of relaxation. Which, in turn, will elevate him from the depths of despair that would otherwise bind him to sadness during the housebound days to come. She shared the words which had become present inside her head then explained how he must listen to the music, must lose himself in the sound and allow the vibrations to lift his spirit. He must learn to relax. With her work complete and the message delivered she left him to his thoughts.

Chapter 39 — ARTHUR

Arthur reached towards the bedside table to retrieve the half full glass of water in an effort to relieve the uncomfortable dryness in his mouth and throat. A seemingly constant need, which he guessed had something to do with the drugs he ingested. After taking a few sips of water he laid his head back against the padded headboard and reflected on the latest conversation. He still didn't fully understand her powers. Again she had connected with him in a way he had not thought possible. She had communicated on the subject of Bach. He had heard the message. He must connect with the music of Bach to elevate himself. The telephone call had come at a most welcome time, as if by divine intervention, in a day filled with the darkest of shadows. The daylight hours had been filled with gloom. Life had once again become unbearable and he had plunged into the pit of despair. A destination which had forced his hand. He had been at the point of letting go, of cutting the lifeline holding him in place. His current thought stream was interrupted by a piercing, agonising pain which shot through his lower body, making each breathing moment unbearable. The nausea which developed after each episode of pain overload, and there were many throughout the day, overpowered any craving for food. His life was not a life at all, just an existence. But the day had changed. As if by magic he had been hauled from his misery during one short telephone call. One which delivered a seemingly simple message regarding Bach. A communication which had catapulted him onto a new path. Arthur understood the benefit which would be delivered by listening to the music. He was ready to embrace the idea whereby the act of listening would provide relaxation no matter the level of pain. After all, there were few other options on offer. The alternative choice, painkillers, made no real difference. This was much better medicine. He would have control over the pain. The concept of this new reality drove a fresh motivation for life. No longer in the dark abyss in which he had lain. Not only was he inspired to listen to the music and use it to medicate his situation but also to embrace the life of Bach. Bee had advised him on this subject before. He had readily agreed to research the great man but had not been able to achieve this feat. Instead he had become overwhelmed by the painful existence which was his life. But on the call she had reminded him of his purpose. There was work to be done. He had an important task to undertake, to understand what Bach meant. The reconnection with the composer had given him a sense of purpose, something he had not felt in a long time. With a new lust for life feeding his mind he asked,

'Could this be my way out?'

There was no answer. He knew the music would assist his health but was unconvinced it could actually save him from death, or even buy him more time. This mattered not. Arthur drew comfort from the thought he was not alone. Not only did he have purpose, but Bee would walk alongside as he undertook the perilous journey ahead. She would support his spiritual journey. He would never be able to bestow his gratitude for her support; for fear he would become paralysed by the awkwardness of baring his emotions. Instead he would remain in a much safer place and silently send thoughts of love and gratitude across the unseen network.

Chapter 40 — BEE

Awake. Her stream of conscious thought flooded with communications. Every one related to him. Unusually the thoughts had no associated messages, only an intense undeniable need. He was calling for assistance. The intended recipient was obvious. Bee received an instant and absolute understanding of all that was required, she must channel energy to him immediately. A solemn promise had been made to support him through all of the pain and suffering, no matter how unusual the request. Determined to fulfil this promise, from her position in bed, she closed her eyes and connected to the light in the centre of her body, relaxed and allowed the light to flow in which every direction it chose. The light rose out of her body. She couldn't see it but definitely felt the lift upwards. Then she was weightless and part of the light. Unafraid she embraced the prospect of travel. How was it possible? How could she separate from her body? Inside her head a white pathway became visible. Then an entrance. Having made the choice to enter she found herself speeding along a network of passages until she reached her destination in Dorset. Although the experience was of an unusual nature Bee enjoyed the sensation of travelling to a remote destination. The art of placing herself in a split second next to another person. There were very few who had the capacity to understand such a phenomenon.

Unfortunately, there was no science to prove or disprove. Or maybe this was a science. After all, every science project began with the need to investigate. However, the issue with her encounters, they involved the brain and as yet unidentified pathways. Few were able to comprehend because there was no proof and she was unable to show them. There was still so much to learn about the brain and also the power contained within cells of the body. She was often amused when others were judgemental on this subject—one they did not understand. Like her experiences. A theory dismissed because it had not passed through rigorous scientific testing. The funniest thing, scientists were constantly learning, disproving or identifying new theories. Therefore science was a changing landscape with new findings to be uncovered all of the time. Whether it was a mechanism of the brain, an element of the body or something else entirely, she had the ability to connect with other people, alive or dead. It was very real. Bee understood people might find the concept scary. She did scare people. Their eyes said it all. She had often wondered why people were so fearful of that which they did not understand. She had always believed, to be open minded to that which is outside of your current learning is to live, evolve and progress beyond limitations set by others. Bee loved nothing more than to fathom a complex problem, even if she had no basis of understanding to begin with. She accepted her brain was a powerful organ and one that did not need to be limited by other people's definition of its power. However, she had learned a long time before to keep her thoughts to herself. Her ability to connect with others, the power of her brain, were parts of her whole which could not be shared. But this was not her current focus. She had a job to do.

The pathway delivered her to his bedside and at once she channelled energy. First she focused on the top of his head. As the need for focus in this area diminished she moved down his torso, directing energy wherever required. Unsurprisingly, she was drawn to his left kidney, where she spent what seemed an eternity focused upon the organ. When the energy transference to the area was complete she turned her attention to another part of his body. But was halted with no further need identified. In response she disconnected from him and returned conscious thought to her own body. How had she connected? There was no doubt she had travelled to his side, to share energy, to relieve pain. How was this possible? Bee wanted details, confirmation of what had been achieved. But there was nothing. Instead she was left with knowledge she must trust the connection, believe in her comprehension of life, of all that was possible. She must not be restricted by the reality of life for the rest of the population. Bee knew she would never turn her back on the truth of her reality. After all, her ability to tune into all possibilities would ultimately assist her dad and deliver him where he needed to be. With the connection complete she settled herself for a return to sleep but was interrupted as another request was delivered. She acted immediately on the new communication which dominated her thought. There was no option but to listen. Instinct told her all was not well. Bee closed her eyes once more and imagined connecting with him. Within moments she was present in his bedroom, at his side. But this time there was a difference. A vision was present in the fore of her mind. A patchwork of green fields on a hillside, the colour green dominant and a message '*green and pleasant land.*' Quickly, before the communication diminished, Bee attempted a greater understanding. What does the image represent? Then a 'knowing' became present. She needed his help. He knows what the image means. Bee disconnected from him and her conscious thought returned to the room. She would have to call him later. With the message parked for later discussion Bee closed her eyes and fell into a deep sleep.

Even though his voice was laden with the burden of the painfully ill, she still heard the essence of delight.

'Hello Bee. To what do I owe this pleasure?'

Details of the connectivity and communication gushed forth.

'I know you haven't been feeling well because you contacted me last night. In fact I visited you twice. I sense your need is great. When I visited for the second time I received an image, which I am compelled to share with you, I feel hearing the message will assist your state of health.'

She described the vision, the patchwork of green and the message of the 'green and pleasant land.' His voice changed, excitement replaced the earlier weary tone.

'I know the place of which you speak. A couple of weeks ago I found a small hamlet a few of miles from here, where a burial place nestles within a patchwork of green fields. The tranquil resting place is set within what can only be described as the archetypal English green and pleasant lands.'

His words created an electrical response. Energy flowed along her nerves causing a tingling sensation and then came knowledge; her vision had meaning. No matter how many times Bee conveyed a message to another, the thrill of delivering content that meant something to the recipient never diminished. His voice cut into her thoughts,

'How can you know the details of this burial place? I haven't told you of my latest plan.'

Bee smiled, 'Dad, this is like all the other communications. Although I must say, this had stronger imagery than usual. I saw the picture and then received a few words to ensure I understood the important elements. This is becoming the norm for me. But I understand if a bit freaky for you.'

He didn't seem overly unsettled by her knowledge.

'I've no idea how you do it. I guess it doesn't matter. It's just amazing. Anyway, I've spent the past few weeks considering my options and have decided I want to be buried in isolation, more connected to nature. You have just described the place in which I propose to rest.'

A flurry of thoughts deposited in her head. But they could not be shared for they represented the reality of his situation. He had chosen to leave and loose ends were being tidied. To prevent the sadness of this truth taking hold of her emotions, she cleared all thought from her mind and directed the conversation elsewhere,

'How are you feeling in general?"

'To be perfectly honest I'm not good, not good at all. The pain in my prostate and kidney is abominable. As if this is not enough punishment I also retch continually. Every day is ruined by my illness. I really can't comprehend how my life can get any worse. But I know it will. Bee, I'm really scared of what will come. I already feel as if I've been tested to the limits of physical pain. But I know there will be more and there is nothing I can do. With the exception of taking my own life. Which I can't do. I have thought about it. I have even planned it in my head but I cannot take my own life. My will to live is too strong.'

Bee heard his hopelessness then as if a plug had been pulled her own hope drained. The fear of loss developed and slithered into every nook and cranny of her mind, body and soul. Was her assistance actually making any difference to his wellbeing? Why did this have to be such a messy end? He was in so much pain. Why could he not choose to leave and be done with his life? A 'knowing' presented. He could choose to leave at anytime. Silently, she asked the obvious questions. Then why hasn't he chosen to go? Why has he put himself through torturous levels of pain? There were no answers, only guidance. She must employ a greater level of patience and accept her observer role. She was not there to save his life. But Bee still found this hard to accept. What had he said? She had missed a great swathe of his offloading whilst tuned into the thoughts inside her head. The art of listening to another person whilst listening to her internal communication was not easy. She had lost focus on his voice whilst facing realities she did not really want to see. But she had to live her life seeing the whole truth. No matter how painful. This situation could be no different. Had she missed a critical support moment? Retuning into the conversation, she made a suggestion,

'Maybe you should rest. Your voice sounds weak and I don't want to wear you out.'

With resignation in his voice he agreed,

'You're right as always. I am tired. But I'm really glad we've had the chance to speak. Hopefully we will get the chance to speak again later this week? Take care Sweetie.'

Then he was gone. With the conversation at an end Bee released all sadness dominant during the call and allowed tears to fall. The product of her knowledge. The inevitability of his end. The outcome of the call delivered vulnerability and sorrow, both very apparent on her face. With a thought for her family, she wiped away all evidence of the grief which had possessed her only moments earlier. At all costs she wanted to protect her family from the truth which was present in her head. She did not want to share her anguish. She must not let anyone see how much it hurt. This was not only her sorrow, but his too, she was connected to his pain, his life, his end.

Chapter 41 — ARTHUR

Arthur didn't have the energy to place the telephone back on the table. Instead, he laid the device beside him on the bed and hoped Sheila would deal with it. His thoughts carried him to a reflection of their conversation. She never failed to amaze him. The messages were always relevant to his situation at the time. This communication was no different. For the past week he had been consumed by a yearning to be buried under a tree, in a place of isolation, surrounded by countryside, embraced by the land he loved so dear, amongst the green fields of England. An idea contrary to that of Sheila and close friends. They all believed he should be placed amongst friends, near the grave of his best friend, within the graveyard of the village in which he used to live. He had ignored their input and pushed ahead with his own burial plans. He wanted to be free in death and be buried in a haven of solitude. Bee had seen this imagery. How she knew baffled him. No matter how many times she communicated a message he still had no idea how she did it. What else had she seen? What else did she know about him? Arthur sincerely hoped she couldn't see everything. He did not relish the idea of his daughter knowing the depths of his truth. There had been many times when she had attempted to allay his fears, told him the gift only allowed her to see or hear that which another was willing to share. He wasn't convinced. However, Arthur knew he would never know the truth because Bee would never confide in him. She had lived with the gift for too long to trust anyone with the knowledge of its power. There had been many moments when she expressed fear at sharing too much; how other people did not have the capacity to deal with all that defined her person. Arthur knew there was no point following the thought—he would never know her fully. With this in mind he turned to comfort. As he moved the pillows behind his head to provide greater support, he smiled. She was very strange but in equal measure completely loveable. A warm glow embraced him, as if she were present. He was left in no doubt she would be okay when he departed, would forge ahead with life and challenge all that had to be confronted. This action would deliver her to a place he had never been able to reach, to a place of peace.

His current hope. His only hope of peace, was to be buried in a place which blanketed him in green and connected him to the earth he loved so dearly. A place he did not want to leave. She had delivered the message for a reason. He needed to understand. Was it for his highest good to be buried in a place of isolation surrounded by trees? He thought so. This was his dream. One where he would be laid to rest, immersed in nature. His waking dream would become his dying dream. Seemingly he was being asked to consider this choice. Why else had she communicated the message? Was this not the right choice? Oh, how difficult the process of dying! Not only did he have to contend with the prospect of being wiped off the planet but also to understand the right choice. The right choice for who? This burial decision would benefit him. But would it? He would be gone. Did his burial place have any bearing on his wellbeing? Once he had thought so. But now he was not so sure. Reality stared him in the face. At the end of his days he would meet his maker, he would no longer be present on earth and therefore his burial place had to benefit those left behind. The remote position he had chosen would not afford his wife, children or grandchildren the opportunity to visit often. Although beautiful, the setting was miles away from any of his family, the people he was leaving behind, those who needed a connection with him. Bee had not actually told him he should not be buried in the remote location but the message had lead him to a thought. He could not be buried there. The choice was not for him. This was for them, for those left behind. He had to think of them no matter how hard the thought process. They needed each other and they needed access to his resting place. Arthur made the right decision. He would tell Sheila of the new plan when he awoke. She would be mystified by his change of mind but would welcome it. His decision would see him laid to rest in the graveyard of the village in which he had once lived, a place filled with happy memories of raising a family. He would also lay in the same ground as Bob, his best friend. He would be delivered home.

Chapter 42 — BEE

Bee had not been prepared for the early morning call. She listened intently as her mum conveyed the details of the previous evening. Unwelcome news. He had taken a turn for the worse and been admitted to hospital for twenty-four hour care. Bee heard the words spoken but could not digest the reality. Her throat tightened as her voice threatened to break under the weight of emotion. Apparently he had not eaten for days. The debilitating pain had put an end to his appetite. The doctor had been left with no choice but to make the decision to let the professionals deliver care with the aid of drips to provide food and pain relief. She sensed relief in her mum's voice. The heavy burden of responsibility for his care handed over to another, someone who would know exactly what to do for him in his hour of need. Bee could only imagine the strain of constantly caring for someone who did not want to be cared for. Her dad was a very independent man. He would not be easy to look after, would never accept the idea of needing anyone to help him with daily activities. She felt sure her mum needed the break as much as her dad needed to be looked after. In a way this was good for them both. But the rationalisation of the situation did not make her feel any better. Tears still gathered behind swollen eyes, leaving her no choice but to end the call. There could be no sharing of grief. Only when she had said goodbye and replaced the phone in its holder did Bee let the barricade down. The tears erupted, impossible to stop, no matter how hard she tried. In accompaniment to the flow of tears were sobs, which originated from a place somewhere inside her stomach. After what seemed an eternity of release eventually the tears stopped, leaving her empty, as if she had been hollowed out and stripped of all feeling. Fully aware of a need to change this state she focused on the ache in her heart. The news had caused a pain to develop in the centre of her chest, one which gripped and squeezed at the primary organ. There was only one solution. To connect. Bee imagined white light filling her entire body, then very slowly balance returned, powering her equilibrium. This new lighter state allowed her a moment of contemplation. He had entered the next phase. Bee dreaded the depth of feeling and knowledge she kept hidden. The absolute knowing he was sliding on a freefall to the end. She begged whoever was listening. Please don't make this knowledge a constant in my mind. Do I really need to know this level of detail? But the plea was fruitless. There was no choice and no time to dwell on all she did not care to know. Instead she must act upon the knowledge and not be consumed by the misery associated with the outcome. She must visit him.

The moment Bee drove into Axminster she was embraced by a sense of homecoming. The hospital was situated only a few hundred yards along the road from the Awareness Centre.

A place, where together, they had progressed their knowledge of the spiritual. But no more. A mourning veil of sadness hung before her eyes. There would never be another trip to their safe haven. Worse than this thought, soon she would be left alone. How soon his departure? Bee couldn't be sure. But she knew there was not much life left in the old man.

Collecting her thoughts she focused on parking the car, then took a solitary, gloomy walk towards the hospital entrance. Her boots tapped and echoed in the corridor as she walked towards the ward. Bee wished she had worn a pair of rubber-soled shoes, yearned for footwear that didn't sound like death marching through the building in search of a poor unsuspecting individual. As the noisy march continued, she entered the quiet space inside her head and asked for the strength required to support him during the difficult times ahead. A sign on the wall to the left caused her to stop. She recognised the name of the ward and turned toward the half glazed double doors.

Ceasing all conversation in her head, Bee walked through the open doors and cast her eyes around the ward in search of a familiar face. She could not have prepared herself for the vision which met her eyes. He looked more poorly than she had ever seen him. His cheeks bereft of a healthy pink shade, instead a sickly pale colour somewhere between white and yellow. Exhaustion dragged his features. He looked ready to give up the fight for life. As she stepped closer towards the bedside his fragility became even more apparent. With each footstep Bee focused on one thing only, remaining composed. She had to present a friendly face, one that did not reflect the multitude of emotions which craved for release. But no matter how much effort she employed tears still threatened. Inside her head she pleaded, 'Please take the emotion away. Don't let me cry in front of him. Please remove the burden of knowledge regarding his passing so that I can help him.' Bee attached to the power of strength inside and found a smile. She was rewarded with a strained smile in return. His face, though starved of light, showed signs of pleasure for her visit. Holding tight to this positive thought Bee sat down on the visitor chair by his side.

'Hello' his voice croaked, *'You made it then?'*

Bee took his right hand into her own hands. A most precious object which might break if too much pressure were applied. They connected and she smiled,

'Of course I made it. You don't think you can hide from me in here. I'm always here for you dad, you know that.'

Bee felt tears threaten once more but would not allow them to fall. Instead she focused on his outpouring.

'I hate it in here. The noise is bloody awful. I can't think. There are people everywhere. Noisy, sick people. I can't stay in this hellhole.'

Bee connected to his despair and a searing pain pierced her heart. Then he continued,

'I have nothing to live for. My life is one miserable mess, laden with pain. There is nothing to look forward to. No hope.' He faltered for a moment then continued, 'It seems like a long time ago, but before the illness I had a life, I could eat, walk, cycle and drink pints of beer. Now I have nothing. Not one pleasure in my wretched existence.'

His words cut right to her core. Bee could not only hear the words but could feel his pain as if it were her own. This experience was nothing new but she was unsure if she could endure his pain on top of the agony she already felt for the imminent loss. With great resolve she released the power of his turmoil by connecting to the white light resident in her core, seemingly the only way to reduce the impact of their connection. Then she took a closer look at him and observed a man, who however ill he appeared, still had the power of fight. The knowledge gleaned from his eyes buoyed her spirits. In his power she witnessed the existence of hope. Even though he was not verbalising this belief she knew he could lift himself out of his current predicament. She was there for one reason only, to raise his energy levels to assist this process. With his hand cupped in her own she channelled energy into his weak body. She focused on the love she felt for him and transferred the warmth of this feeling through her hands to his. He lay silent and still, with eyes closed he accepted her gift. When the invisible connection between them was established, electrical pulses journeyed through her body and flowed into his. At the point where enough energy had been transferred Bee ended the connection and waited.

No sooner had she disconnected than he opened his eyes. Bee felt time was short and so she moved swiftly toward an exchange which needed to occur.

'Yesterday I felt compelled to draw a picture for you.'

She picked up her brown leather satchel handbag, pulled out a hand drawn image on a piece of A4 paper and handed it to him. He sat with his head propped up by three pillows and cast his eyes over her work. As he consumed the communication in pictorial form, she conveyed as best she could, the message which accompanied the picture. A stream of words were delivered in a steady flow inside her head and escaped through her mouth. 'There is a shadow over your heart. You must unlock your heart in order to be free of this shadow.' Bee allowed her thought to flow freely and the name Bach appeared, followed by the word 'relevant'. Then she knew, why had she not thought of it before? He needed music.

'Would you like to listen to your Bach music in hospital? Would that help to relieve the noise and agitation at being here?'

Once the questions were out then electrical sensations fired through her nerve endings confirming he would undoubtedly benefit from the uplifting sound of Bach. He responded positively with a faint smile,

'That would be wonderful therapy; I don't know why I didn't think of it before. It will also relieve the boredom of every waking minute.'

Bee felt compelled to deliver more,

'I'll look for a portable CD player, I'm sure I have one at home.'

With the promise of music therapy he relaxed back onto his pillows and cast his eyes over the artwork once more. She watched as he connected with the picture. More words bubbled to the surface to be aired, 'The shadow over your heart is preventing you from seeing all that is available to you and the way forward.' This latest message had a new level of intensity and a 'knowing' attached. The time had come to face up to the reality of his situation, his choice. Electrical energy flowed through her body like a river in flood, rushing, engulfing everything in its path. He must be told.

'Dad, you have a choice. You have always had a choice. But today you need to know that it is your choice to stay or to go.'

To her surprise he agreed.

'I think you're right. I had a strange experience last night which has led me to believe I can go if I want. Yesterday, when dinner had been served and cleared away, the lights turned down and all of the occupants of the ward settled down for the night, a strange feeling came over me. Then I became aware of a presence by my bedside. It was my best friend Bob. I couldn't really see him, I just knew he was there.

I felt he had come to collect me and this was okay. Although I also knew I didn't have to go with him straight away. I can wait until I see him again and then I can choose to go if I wish.'

Bee felt electrical energy again, this time down her right side, coupled with a connection to Bob and confirmation he was very close. He was present to assist her dad at a time of great need. She had to share what she knew.

'Bob was here last night. I can feel him now. He is here to assist. Welcome him and accept his presence. He will help you.'

Then without invitation Bob descended into her own space. In the moment of occupation Bee felt uncertain if she would ever get used to the experience of connecting with a member of the departed. Their presence felt as if they were part of her, inhabiting her physical body. A feeling very hard to explain to another. She had tried. But had learned the connection to the departed was for her only, to understand where the communication had come from. The message was the important part for the recipient. Those who needed to understand, did, they understood without question. Within the great order of things this would always be so.

Although the process of dying was new to them both, this did not stop them from having a view on the visitation. In the past they had discussed this subject at great length. Both intrigued by recounts of people close to death who had seen loved ones appear before their very eyes. Bee felt excitement. This latest revelation proved he would not be alone. There was already activity from the other side and very soon she would be able to hand him over to them. They sat quietly for a moment, each digesting the meaning of Bob's visit. Then a memory appeared in her conscious thought. She had to ask a question, one that had already been asked but must be asked again,

'Will you accept your dad and forgive him when he comes for you?'

Electrical impulses exploded inside her body like a set of fireworks ignited together. The subject had to be raised again; he must come to terms with how he feels about his father. Bee knew not only Bob, but Grandad was coming too; he would take hold the hand of her dad to make the giant step from this world to the next. Would her dad accept the assistance? He looked shocked to have been asked again. He smiled uncomfortably. Only he could make the choice. What if he didn't accept his own father? Bee banished the chilling thought as a patrolling nurse encouraged visitors to leave. There were to be no more conversations that day. Instead she would have to leave him to ponder the question. Before she left there was just time to whisper,

'I'll be back as soon as I can. I love you.'

When Bee reached the swing doors at the entrance to the ward she turned and was surprised to see he had pulled himself up to standing position with drip still attached. He waved. She waved in return and disappeared from his view. She was stunned by his action; only moments earlier he had been lying in bed with barely enough energy to speak. Retracing her steps along the corridor which led to the main entrance, she considered his actions and terror gripped her in the stomach. He did not think he would see her again. He had just given her a memory of a man still strong. Her throat choked and bottom lip quivered as she tried to contain the sorrow of his situation. Could this be their last physical contact?

Chapter 43 — ARTHUR

Pain was all he had left; unrelenting suffering had embraced his life, every single part including his heart, mind and soul. There was no reprieve. Even the visit from Bee had done little to lessen the pain, although Arthur had been glad of the distraction. Her presence had gifted him a fleeting moment of peace. But her exit had seen him tumble back down into the dark and gloomy pit of despair. Was there any hope for him? Any point in remaining? No, there was not. Yet he could not leave. Bee had told him he had a choice. Arthur shouted out silently within the confines of his head, 'Let me bloody well leave this miserable existence then.' The act of asking to leave delivered nothing but an increase in anger levels focused on his current predicament. The fury fuelled his mood, turned him against the medical staff and all the sick people who surrounded his bedside, all of whom had a part to play in his miserable existence.

Arthur caught his train of thought and shifted focus away from the anger which threatened to dominate. Instead he reflected on the shadow Bee described. He really didn't understand the meaning of the darkness of which she had spoken. He was supposed to do what? He had no idea how to progress. A situation which occurred with regularity. Whereby Bee would plant a thought in his mind, a way forward, then leave him lost without a hope of understanding what to do next. Time after time she had explained to him, she was only the messenger. Once he was in receipt of the communication then he was supposed to deliver the appropriate action. How? There had been many moments when he witnessed frustration in her eyes because he did not understand what she was asking. What seemed like second nature to her was nigh on impossible for him. Effortlessly she could follow a thought, a thread of understanding. Whereas he could not. As hard as he tried he was unable to lift the shadow which had been draped over his existence. With no progress on the subject of the shadow, he turned his thoughts to the acceptance of his dad. Arthur remembered the day Bee had first raised this question, they had been returning home from a visit to the Medium. She had asked the question more than once. Each time he had not answered in truth, still he could not, for he did not know the answer. Then in a brief moment Arthur decided he could not accept his dad, for too much water had passed under the bridge. He knew how frustrated Bee would be with this decision. She believed this choice was an important part of his journey. He must accept. But he did not agree. Arthur believed he would be greeted by a much higher order than his dad. With this thought he drifted into sleep.

Chapter 44 — BEE

Another visit was required but this time she had company—Adam and the boys accompanied her to Dorset. They had arrived early afternoon and occupied a family room in a hotel close to Axminster. Bee enjoyed having them alongside and had delighted in seeing the joy in the boys' faces at the thought of the whole family sharing a room. Since their arrival, beds had been bagsied, a picnic tea consumed and baths completed. She left them watching television, dressed in their pyjamas, snuggled up on the king size bed, one either side of Adam. She was glad they had come along but did not require their company at the hospital. The visit was one she had to make alone. This choice driven by a 'knowing', one that had dominated her thought for the entire day. She must spend the evening with him. There was an uncertain feeling which accompanied the thought. Would he depart that night, make the choice to go? As Bee negotiated the dark country lanes which led to the hospital she felt excitement at the thought of seeing him again so soon. In the silence of the car she asked, 'Is this his last night?' The question triggered greater knowledge which flooded into her mind. Something not of the earth was working with him. She tried to fathom what. But no matter how much effort she employed she could not determine the identity of the presence at work. However, she could feel the full force of its power, which seemed to be growing in strength. All thought was put on hold as she entered the hospital car park. Bee reclaimed her mind from the communication channel feeding her thoughts and remembered she must not lose sight of the time. She must leave the hospital at 7:45pm to have any chance of returning to the hotel by 8pm. Because at precisely 8pm she had a date; the chance to spend time alone with Adam. They were going to embrace the opportunity to consume fine food and wine in beautiful surroundings. A rare chance since they had become parents and one not to be missed. Bee set her internal alarm and then banished all thought of dinner.

On entering the ward, Bee took the familiar walk to his bedside where she found him resting peacefully. She settled herself on the high-backed visitor chair and gently placed her hands over his right hand. They exchanged a knowing smile and a few words, then without further delay she focused on channelling energy to him. Usually she would have moved around his body focusing energy where appropriate but she could not draw that level of attention in the hospital ward. There was only one option open, to stay seated with eyes closed and channel energy through her hands into his. In the quiet space inside her head thoughts floated gently through her consciousness, one of them a 'knowing.' This could be their last time together. The knowledge ripped through her like a tornado and panic grabbed hold. Could it be true? Will I lose him this night? The time was right for him to leave. But she recognised the fact he would have to choose to leave, he would not be taken. As thoughts tumbled over one another a new one became dominant. He was driving the exit from his life. He had been contemplating the messages delivered during her hospital visit the previous day and was seriously considering his exit strategy. This was her chance to increase the level of support. With this in mind she focused her love and shared all that could be shared through her hands to his. There were no assurances. Bee could not be certain her assistance would help him, and yet, she had to continue the focus of energy flow between them. When she felt enough had been shared then she resurrected the conversation about the shadow over his heart.

Lovingly she connected with his eyes and then spoke gently,

'I still believe you need to clear your past and remove the shadow from your heart. If you don't then you will struggle to move forward from this point to any destination.' Taking a deep breath she continued, 'I believe there are two steps you need to take. Firstly, you need to listen to the music of Bach. This will lift your spirits and energise your body, and hopefully eliminate the shadow from your heart. Secondly, you must address the issue of your father. You must forgive all that was done to you. If you don't then you'll carry the burden of emotional discord and your transition to the other side will not be straightforward.'

In speaking the words out loud Bee transferred the responsibility of action firmly onto his shoulders. Feeling more like a life guide than a daughter. He raised a weak smile and spoke in a monotone voice which lacked enthusiasm,

'OK. I'll listen to my music because I love the way it makes me feel but I'm not sure where it will deliver me. I will also try to forgive. But I can't understand how a conversation in my head with my dad, who is dead, will help the situation. I just don't get it.'

There was no more she could do. The message had been delivered and she was free of responsibility, it was now down to him.

As Bee comforted him, a thought entered her mind regarding a conversation they would not share this night; to the place of goodbye, to the moment they would lose sight of one another. Instead their conversation traversed a much safer path, to the process of passing. The pathway to death intrigued them both and they never shied away from sharing their thoughts on the matter. Bee could not stem her desire for answers,

'Have you seen anyone from the departed? Or heard any signs of a party to welcome you across the divide?'

Such questions would have fazed many but not her dad. Many times they had discussed the possibility of a party to assist his passing to the other side. When he responded his voice did not contain an ounce of fear, nor despair, but was filled with hope,

'So far I've only felt the presence of my good friend Bob. I haven't seen my dad or a welcome party to guide me on my journey.'

Suddenly her thought flow was interrupted as she received a 'knowing.' She heard the words but not in the conventional way. She learned that very soon he would see someone from the welcome party. The outcome of this encounter would be his ability to see through the mist which clouded his eyes, a fog which obscured the reality of everything waiting for him. Once the 'knowing' had been received and interpreted then Bee understood the visit had come to an end. Everything she had been required to deliver, had been. All that was left, was for him to reflect on his situation and move himself forward. Even though Bee knew her job was done she didn't want to leave him alone. What if this was his last night? She wanted to help him. She wanted to stay. But she knew the best thing was to leave him to make sense of his own journey. Could this be the last time she ever saw him? Bee knew he had the choice to leave if he wanted. She had no power to keep him. She could not save him. She could only guide the lost and lonely man. With these thoughts in mind, before leaving his bedside, she found the courage to carry out an unusual act. She leant over and gently kissed the top of his head. But the loving act was not enough; there was more to give, just in case, just in case she never saw him again. With a slight tremble to her voice she delivered her parting words,

'Dad, I love you. Take care of you and I will see you tomorrow.'

As she stepped away from the bed Bee felt sure her weakened legs would collapse and the sobs waiting to be released would escape. But neither happened. She turned to wave goodbye. His pale face lost in a pile of pillows caused a chain reaction, whereby an unseen hand grasped her heart and squeezed hard until an unbearable pain seared through her chest. The first rip in their connection had occurred. Would she see him the next morning? No, she did not believe so. A dark and shadowy notion informed Bee he would probably make the decision to leave that night. With this level of knowledge there was no stopping them, the tears could be contained no more. Having found the car through a blur of tears she climbed in and drove carefully through dark country lanes back to the hotel. As each mile passed under the wheels, another layer of sadness wrapped around her heart, until there came a point when the centre of her body felt full to bursting. There was a distinct possibility she might lose him that night. In response to the thought a wave of misery flooded her senses. But as she made the turn into the hotel driveway she reclaimed her senses. There had to be balance. There would always be happy and sad times in life. She must learn to employ a greater level of self-control. After all, she had been afforded the chance to spend time with Adam, to share conversations missing from their lives thanks to his intense working hours and the focus on her dad. No matter the thoughts which pressed for release regarding the possibility her dad might leave that night, she had to leave the emotion behind, accept everything which could have been achieved, had been. Even though her dad was an important male in her life he was not the most important. She had chosen to spend her life with Adam. An incredibly special man, who loved her enough to allow her freedom of thought, who would love her to the end of days even though she was just a little bit different. Bee knew how lucky she was. This night they would have a chance to connect, truly connect in a way they had not been able to for months. She released from her mind the predicament her dad faced that night. As she snuggled next to Adam on a sofa in the hotel bar, with a large glass of white wine in hand, she welcomed the promise of a special evening into her heart.

Chapter 45 — ARTHUR

Arthur felt as if an invisible blanket had been wrapped around his body, delivering a chill which seeped through every layer of skin into his core. The reaction to her departure did not end there. Thoughts of desolation descended as feelings of loss and isolation snowballed inside his head. The moment she exited he had wanted to scream out, 'Stop! Come back!' Instead he allowed his bereavement to overpower all other feelings. He had lost a dear friend; she had been taken from him. Arthur loved her presence. She brought warmth, glowed in a way which could not be seen but could most definitely be felt. The inexplicable and invisible energy which she shared helped him in ways he did not fully understand. Once again she had lifted him from a state of darkness in which he had wallowed. When she was not there he felt utterly empty, cold and alone. Arthur knew he had no right to complain. After all, she had a husband and family to tend. In his heart he felt the power of everything which had been conveyed that night. She had delivered energy and a message. A very clear directive. He must find space and time for quiet reflection. He must deal with his shadows before the journey to the other side. Inside his head Arthur was bombarded by thoughts about the voyage he was to make. He could never have predicted the force and intensity of emotion involved. The predominant and most terrifying thought was his lack of belief in the destination. Throughout his life he had held strong to the belief in the destination following death. Yet as his departure date crept closer he found himself challenging his philosophy, questioning the certainty of life after death. As if this was not enough, Arthur also felt a deep sense of grief in response to the disconnection from his daughter. With each passing day he felt a stronger level of detachment. He was powerless to stop the process. He also had no control over the strange voices which had taken up residence inside his head. Voices which could not be ignored for they eliminated all other thought. The message delivered was very clear. There was a reason to remain alive. Yet in conflict, his body told him to leave. As if under a spell, all of a sudden clarity cleansed his thoughts. Arthur realised he did have a choice. Ever since admittance to hospital he had consciously chosen to let go of his grip on life. But he could not leave yet.

On the previous evening he had been visited by something not of the earth. He had not told Bee of the encounter because he feared the presence might signify his imminent departure and he did not want to her to worry. Every single detail of the encounter had been retained in his thoughts. No matter how hard he tried they could not be erased. The night before, as he lay in bed listening to the irritating sound of the other inmate's night time sleep noises, a visitor arrived. Out of the shadows of the ward a pale coloured shaft of light appeared, an object which glowed as it hovered alongside his bed. Upon seeing the vertical shaft of light he had made an automatic connection to the Holy Ghost, the only appropriate label at the time. After a short period, when he had become accustomed to the unusual presence, a communication occurred. Not out loud so all the other ward dwellers could hear but inside his head, almost a whisper, 'It is not time yet. First you must clear everything blocking your path. This will greatly assist your journey.' Once the message had been delivered the vision disappeared into thin air, leaving behind a residual warmth on the right hand side of his bed.

Arthur contemplated the experience of the previous evening and realised the message was exactly the same as Bee had delivered. The time was nigh to clear the unseen debris in his path. There could be no escape. Finally he understood; to ignore the message would mean a traumatic crossing to the other side. He could not determine how distressing. But sensed a dark cloud, one he knew would weigh heavy as he tried to push through to that which awaited beyond the bounds of his earthly existence. Even though his body felt ready to shut down and much of his spirit too, he could not depart. Bee had warned him many times, and more recently, so had an entity not of the earth. He would be foolish to ignore the communications. Often, Bee had warned him not to ignore a message. She had explained they could only be presented a certain number of times. Arthur was no longer willing to take the risk of delay. He would face his shadows.

He wasn't quite sure how. But knew he must. He must find the elusive state of peace. The decision to stay was made and he began planning. First he would accept the efforts of the hospital staff and regenerate his physical strength. Then he would return home to finish off all that should have been completed months before.

Chapter 46 — BEE

Bee had been surprised when he had not departed on the night of her visit. She was left somewhat confused by messages received in relation to an imminent departure. Yet she was overjoyed by the reality of his choice. He had stayed. Having stayed she hoped he had made the choice to clear his path, to understand what was required of him before he left. She vowed to keep working with him but knew she must be careful. In the days which followed her visit she had been bombarded by surges of emotion. The like of which had never been experienced before, each stronger than the last. Her balance was threatened. Bee was left with no other choice but to protect herself from him. She had to prevent his negativity from adhering to her form. He had no idea of his effect on her life. Without realising it he was sapping her energy. She knew a healthy connection should not feel this way. There were major differences between a connection with the unseen in all its forms and another person. When she attached to the unseen energy stream and channelled it, the sensation was tolerable, energising. But when she connected to the energy of another person, like her dad, the sensation was depleting. Bee knew if she were to successfully manage the walk alongside, to support him to the end of his life, then she had to receive and deliver messages without collecting his residual negative energy. She must not bear the weight of his sadness on top of her own. The dark shadows he faced were not her burden; they were his and his alone.

In an attempt to release the impact of his emotion on her life Bee found a quiet spot in which to connect. A thought floated into her awareness. He will be departing in the near future. Then, more thoughts. There is a small window of opportunity. Just enough time for him to put his life in order. Hope embraced her thought stream and then knowledge. The months to follow will be challenging. In order to survive you have to put your own needs first. Bee recognised this would be one of the hardest challenges, for she still harboured a desperate need to save him, to keep him near. But she could not save him. Guilt became entangled in her thought flow. She was giving up on him. The process of letting him go was more difficult than she could ever have imagined. She did not want to give up on him. But the certainty of his demise remained. Seemingly, there was only one way to make it through the coming months. She must learn to allow the flow of knowledge regarding his state to be presented within her conscious mind but not let his emotion attach to her thoughts. This would not be easy. However, there was no room for failure. She must remain in a centred and safe place in order to deliver him to a place of wholeness and wellbeing. In the quiet space inside her head a new communication came to the fore, the need to record a transmission.

You have knowledge; use it, for it will serve you well.
Forgive all those whose path is not yours and you can remain balanced.
Your dad is okay. He is making his journey and must learn to accept.
He will get there in his own way and peace will come soon.

River of sadness brings great strife,
You must remember that this is life,
Embrace it, believe it, and you can be free.

The words in black ink upon the white pages of her journal could not have been clearer. They communicated one thing and one thing only. His departure was imminent. The whole process was more than a little confusing. Even though he had chosen to stay, she understood his departure would be soon. How soon she could not be sure. Maybe she had to hear the message over and over in order to prepare for the reality. Tears fell in response to this latest knowledge. When the flow stopped she received a 'knowing' and clarity was delivered, as if a light illuminated the space inside her head. Their relationship would soon come to an end. Despondency momentarily engulfed her mind and then withdrew. Subsequently, a small thread of their connection fell away. This severing of the connection, the first stage of their separation, was imperative in order to allow her to let him go.

Chapter 47 — ARTHUR

Arthur was very pleased by the distinct change in his circumstances. He felt better than he had in a long time. The hospital staff had successfully fed him through a drip, relieved his pain with medicines and repaired him in a way he could never have imagined possible. Having returned home, he had a job to do. In the comfort of his study he pondered the way forward. With renewed physical ability he felt able to achieve anything. Hope had been reinstated. The one element of life which kept him going, which enabled him to believe in another day. Life without hope was not a life at all. However, he was realistic, he knew the current level of hope was not powerful enough to save him. But it was strong enough to guide him through the challenges he faced and would propel him toward a brighter end. Even with this knowledge Arthur still felt inclined to attempt the impossible, to find a way to stay alive. But he did not follow this thought. Instead he listened to the nagging thought which told him the gifted time of good health was not to be wasted on new adventures, rather was to be used to make sense of his life. Could he do it? Could he address the shadows blocking his path? He was still not convinced and so turned his attention to the view of the garden, where a rambling rose trailed along the garden wall to the front gate until it met with lavender bushes swaying in the breeze. The sight empowered him. He was overawed by the beauty of nature. Then, as if by magic, he was suddenly inspired. He believed in himself. He could do it. He could achieve all that seemed so impossible and yet he had no idea where to begin. As always his first thought was Bee. But the nagging voice spoke up inside his head. 'You have to move forward by yourself. You must not rely on Bee.' Arthur recoiled from the voice and the idea he should make the journey to the shadows alone. After all, he had witnessed the effects of turning to the shadows when Bee had attempted the same feat at the Awareness Centre. Arthur did not believe he could attempt such a difficult task alone.

As belief in his ability slipped away Arthur placed his head in his hands. How could he do this alone? He knew he should be able to. Bee had explained the process so many times. All he had to do was find a quiet space inside his head and then listen for a thought. Arthur closed his eyes and waited, and waited. There were no inspiring thoughts, only frustration. Then all of a sudden his head filled with the thoughts which he had carried every day for the past five years. Why me? Why do I have to die before my time? I'm too young, I still have so much left to do. I will be forgotten, erased. Who is going to remember me? My grandchildren will not remember. I will not be present at my youngest child's wedding, will never meet his wife or children. The negative thoughts spiralled until he put an end to their flow. He couldn't do it. Every time he tried to connect to the silence his head filled with negative thoughts, there was no quiet space. He was left with no option but to ask Bee. She would be able to help him. Then, as if gripped by a large hand, Arthur felt pressure applied to his right shoulder followed by a voice in his head which boomed, 'YOU must to do this. YOU have to try. She cannot do everything for you. She has done all that can be done. YOU have had more than she should have given.' With the words still echoing inside his head Arthur wept as he accepted the reality of his situation. In the past he had relied heavily on Bee. He still wanted to use her magical touch to elevate him from his current position and yet he knew this could not be. Instead he had to find the resolve to keep pushing towards the knowledge which remained hidden. Arthur wished he had her strength and resolve. But he did not. However, he could not give up. He had been given a chance. He had to keep trying. He must attempt the impossible, in the hope one day he would catch a glimpse of everything which had to be seen. With this in mind, Arthur selected a track from his Bach Collection and pressed the Play button. The heavenly music rose and fell in waves, each permeating his skull, transmitting vibrations to his brain. He closed his eyes, absorbed the purest of sound and connected with hope. Then he connected with his God and prayed to be shown an image or hear a message before it was too late.

Chapter 48 — Bee

He had returned home, but she had not spoken to him for a week or so. There had been too many other responsibilities to deal with. The boys deserved her attention too. Much of her time had been spent supporting their needs. She had been consumed by their activities, family playtime and bedtime reading. She loved their company, still cherished the gifts she had been given. They had a way of helping her to see what was important in life, to keep her grounded. She loved them with all her heart. Her favourite time of the day was the evening. More precisely, bath time. A time when the boys laughed and splashed together, playing with boats and divers in the water. In quiet moments, when they were drying off, they would discuss the book they would read together that night. With the bathroom next to her bedroom there was an easy flow from one activity to the next. Once dried and dressed it was a short hop onto the king size bed which was usually shared with Adam. There was an order to the evening event, she always lay in the middle with Edward snuggled to her right and James to her left. Sometimes one would go off to play whilst the other read their school book. When all school reading was done they dipped into the fun books. Recently they had been introduced to a childrens' poetry book. She had been unconvinced by the idea, but had been pleased to see the boys lap up the silly rhymes and expand their reading. However, most of the time they read humorous books from the Hundred Mile an Hour Dog or Cows in Action series. This was a precious time of connection. She loved to play up to them by reading with silly voices for the different characters. These were cherished times and she never swapped them for chores; to answer the phone or even to call her dad. This was time to lose herself in their childish innocence, in silly jokes and the joy of being a mum. During this time her mind was empty of communications. She did not have any responsibility to her dad. This was her private time.

But she could not hide in the childish space forever. She had a responsibility to hear the communications. The message of his departure grew stronger. Bee knew she could no longer rely on him to provide the friendly ear for discussion which they had once enjoyed. Their relationship had changed. Had moved beyond the father and daughter space they once shared. Now more than ever he needed her listening ear and guidance. He needed her to shine a light on his path. Was he really ready to go? She thought not. Otherwise he would have left during his hospital stay. What had kept him? Bee still believed he harboured shadows relating to the unhealthy relationships in his family. She was in no doubt these complex relationships required the focus of his attention. He must speak the truth to each person in his troubled relationships, and in so doing, would shed the ties which bound them together in their dance with darkness. This burden of 'knowing', more than she wanted to know, meant she was fully aware of his situation. She understood the implications if he were unable to achieve this task. His journey to the other side would be a very rough crossing. However, she was also completely cognisant of the fact he would not be the only person affected. Those left behind would carry a burden of grief which would likely weigh them down for many years. She had to help him. She still had a responsibility—which is why she had travelled to see him. A telephone call would not solve the problem. Only a face to face communication would do.

Bee halted all thought of his situation as she entered her parent's house. The time was a gift for him, a chance for conversation and an opportunity to assist with his progress. On entering his bedroom Bee almost stopped dead in her tracks. The man in the bed was not well; his appearance snatched her breath, there wasn't a glimmer of life in his eyes. His face had aged to patchy, grey parchment. What had happened? The last time she had spoken with him he had been a rejuvenated man released from hospital? What could have occurred in the space of two weeks? Immediately all hope and excitement for his future slipped away. But she must not allow him to see her disappointment. She caught her breath, found a smile and spoke in the cheeriest voice she could summon,

'Hi, how are you doing?'

Quickly followed by the ceremonial handing over of a 'welcome home' card. A tired smile broke out across his face in reaction to the offering. Then as his eyes consumed the picture the smile developed into a quiet chuckle. Bee had known the image would brighten his day; the picture of a smiling face fashioned from a couple of fried eggs for eyes, a tomato for a nose and a sausage for the smile. She watched as he read the 'welcome home' message, and with each word his smile broadened. This had been the best way of communicating how glad she was that he was still alive, and of how much she loved him. She could not speak the words for fear of breaking down in tears but she could write and share them. When he had finished reading he gave her the card to place on the window sill. She found a position which would afford him a view of the smiling face at all times. Once the card had been settled in place then Bee took her usual seat upon the old and rickety bedroom chair to his left side.

No sooner had her bottom landed then Bee felt she had to mention his shadow, something she could clearly see blocking the view of his heart. With this detail in the fore of her mind she delivered a message.

'Dad, I feel we urgently need to speak about the shadow. That is where we must start. I have to share all I know.'

He responded with a resigned nod. He had learned long ago not to argue when she had something to deliver. His acceptance opened the invisible gate to her knowledge and out flowed thoughts.

'You have emotions locked inside that relate to events in your life. These are the residual outcome of your actions. Each needs to be reviewed and processed.' Bee closed her eyes, took a deep breath and picked up the next level of communication. 'These stored emotions from the past, are within your heart, not your physical organ but in your core, the very centre of your body. They will not aid your journey. They will cripple you if you don't address them.'

Unusually there was no emotion accompanying the message. She conveyed the information without any sentiment whatsoever. In this situation she was only a messenger with no space for feeling or judgement. When the flow of words stopped she looked to him for a response. There was none. In his deep hazel-brown eyes she saw recognition. He understood the presence of the shadows. This visual confirmation encouraged her to repeat the message.

'You know. You know you have stored hurt throughout the course of your lifetime and yet you choose not address this problem. Why? This really should be possible for you.'

He found the strength to speak but his voice was weak,

'I don't know what to do. We've tried so many times before and never got anywhere. I'm not sure I can achieve what is needed. I know I need to. I know coming out of hospital was the chance for me to put right all that needs addressing and yet I'm still lost. I have tried and I'm still trying. Do you think it is because I'm male and you female? Females attach to emotion easily and yet males do not. Is this my problem? If so, then we may need to find another way to attach to the issues because I have tried the way you've described and I can't do it.' He paused momentarily and then continued. 'Do you really believe addressing the shadows can save me? What on earth does saving mean? I know I'm going to die anyway. I will never have my life saved.'

The hopelessness in his voice only served to compel Bee to try harder. She knew there was a way. She must guide him to the place where he could see all that was required. She had never understood why he was unable to discuss his emotions. Maybe it was because he was male and this was not in his nature. Or maybe he didn't have the energy to drag up the past. Perhaps he didn't trust her with the knowledge. She would never know. But she understood one thing. She could not force him to dredge up the past. Therefore she was left with no choice but to leave the message behind and allow him to choose his own path, no matter how detrimental she perceived the choice. During the course of her life she had learned to guide people and to curb the desire to control the destiny of another, knowing each person had to accept the truth of his or her choice before moving forward.

Instead of pressuring him further she offered to channel energy; in the hope the act might illuminate his shadows. In response to her suggestion he visibly relaxed. Seemingly relieved she had stopped pushing him towards the torturous process of uncovering emotions from the past. There were no more words required. He closed his eyes. She raised herself off the chair and moved forward to perform the energy transfer. A 'knowing' was delivered. Almost like a whisper floating through her consciousness. The need to ask a question.

'Would you like to listen to Bach?'

He opened his eyes and responded in a weary but positive tone,

'Yes, I think that would help.'

Bee picked up the earphones from the bedside table, placed them carefully in his ears and then switched on the music. He closed his eyes again. Then she placed her hands over the top of his head and closed her eyes. Next she focused energy through her hands into his body. After a few moments she opened her eyes to check he was comfortable. This act caused her to witness tears falling silently onto the pillow which supported his head. Emotions were being released. A smile developed on her face and inside she felt elation for his discharge, accompanied by hope. The tears would assist his chances of accessing the issues he had stored away. With renewed confidence in the energy being channelled she moved her hands towards his heart and once in position, allowed the warm electrical energy to flow. Then the quiet of her mind was disturbed as a message was delivered to her ear. Without hesitation she released the words to a place outside of her head.

'You must look through the windows at those things which have marred your life, for these are the issues which are shadowing your heart.'

Bee felt the warmth and clarity of the message but he did not. His response formed another layer of sadness around her heart.

'I really don't know what the issues are and I can't see any windows. What does the message mean, look through the windows?'

Frustration bubbled to the surface but she had to help. She must not be angry with him.

'Dad, the windows are like a view on your life. Think of a point in time and then focus by looking through an imaginary window at the view. This should be the point you need to address.'

Why could he not see what was troubling him? All that was so obvious. Why would he not go to the place of shadows? Bee knew her levels of frustration wouldn't assist him, so she released the build-up and turned her focus to his relationships with women.

'We both know your heart was damaged by your mum in your early years. You have to release this emotion. If you don't want to share the details with me then you will have to release the past on your own. This is the only way you can lighten the load for the journey to the end.'

But no matter what she said there was no shift in his behaviour.

'Mmm…I kind of get what you are saying. But I still don't understand how or why it will have any impact on my situation. I really will try but I don't seem to see things the way you do.'

Many times they had spoken about her ability to return to past memories and release them from her consciousness. She had explained the simplicity of the process and yet this seemed to have no bearing on his situation; he was still unable to talk about the past. Bee knew the gravity of his circumstances, how important the discussion would be in easing his journey to the other side. She dearly wanted to push him to the place he needed to be and yet she could not. As much as she loved him, as much as she knew this was the right way forward, she could not make him walk the path he needed to travel. However, there was to be no escape from the channel of communication as a message repeated over and over in the confines of her head. A stronger message than before, one that would give a very clear directive. The words 'guilt' and 'rejection'. These two words were emblazoned across her mind. The intensity meaning only one thing. The need to share them. Dutifully she passed the words on. There was no response and so she left him to his thoughts and continued channelling energy. Obviously there was to be no respite from the open communication channel. Another 'knowing' developed. If he is to have any chance of achieving a smooth passage to the end then it is crucial his mind, body and spirit are kept in balance. Bee did not divulge this thought, instead she allowed the information to pass through her mind and released it to the place from whence it had come. With her attention refocused on channelling, she delivered the only possible help remaining. She balanced his mind, body and spirit. After ten minutes had passed, when all of the required energy had been delivered and she felt sure he was more balanced, she sat back down on the chair and waited for his eyes to open. She watched his restful face. He seemed to be entranced by the music. Eventually he opened his eyes and greeted her with a smile.

'Thank you. I feel much lighter now. Thankfully my head has cleared of the negative thoughts which have dominated in recent days. I know I can be difficult but I have heard the messages you've delivered. I will try and address the emotions you think I've stored. I am not sure how but know I must.' He took a sip of water from the glass on the bedside table to refresh his dry throat, then continued, 'I've really enjoyed seeing you today but now I'm exhausted. There is a lot for me to process. I'm not sure I have the energy to get up and socialise. Would it be okay if you leave me to sleep now?'

Bee could not argue, after all, her job was done. She left him in peace.

She spent the next hour with her mum. Over a cup of tea they discussed his situation. During this time Bee did not speak of the conversations shared with her dad. She did not mention his shadows. She had never told anyone of their conversations, of the messages received. This was not her information to share. This was private. However, the time spent with her mum provided space for another offloading. It allowed her mum to share thoughts on the trials and tribulations of the battle against cancer. Bee listened. She did her best to support her mum, but there were no communications. She was not a guardian for her mum. She was a daughter only. The role of guardian was reserved for her dad in his time of need. After all, she only had so much energy to share around. This meant she had to concentrate on him, had to deliver him to a place of peace before he left. When the conversation and tea had dried up, Bee left her parents and their traumatic life. Another day spent within the walls of their home had been emotionally draining. She had been required to deliver the same message, to encourage him to uncover emotional issues harming his journey. The need to expose his stored memories and emotions was not her own. She was driven by an unknown factor. In his room she had sensed an unseen assistant working alongside, moving her towards a place where she would enable him to see. On the drive home Bee reflected on the day and came to the conclusion she had achieved as much as possible. Although she knew there was no more she could have done, she couldn't help but feel dissatisfied with progress. Why could he not see? If he ignored communications then his journey would be more difficult. Bee reminded herself of the need to forgive those who chose another path which was not her own. In the moment of forgiveness, even though she did not want to, she accepted the path her dad had chosen.

CHAPTER 49 — ARTHUR

She had gone. He tumbled into a void of loneliness. Unable to climb from the depths he allowed the darkness to consume him. She had been different. This time their interaction had been different. Arthur couldn't quite pinpoint the change but she had been more distant than usual. Why? He most certainly did not like this new sensation of Bee slipping from his grasp. He wanted a connection, needed a connection. She fed his life with an energy which could not be found from any other source. Almost as if she were life itself. How could this be so? She was not just his daughter, he knew that. The more their lives intertwined, the more he did not really understand who she was. His life had become confused, boundaries blurred and focus shifted. Thoughts dominated by death, a constant noise which demanded attention. How to save himself. How to end his life. What would happen to those left behind? What if he had caught the cancer in time? He pushed the thoughts away. With resignation weighing heavy on his heart Arthur knew no matter how much he wanted it, he could not control the connection with his daughter. Instead of wasting time on this fruitless activity he chose to focus on the analysis of the messages she had delivered. Bee had directed him to the shadow over his heart, which in turn led back to his childhood. She always directed him to this place. When in hospital he had agreed to try. He really wanted to.

But he still couldn't see how it would help. Was he just being stubborn? Maybe, or maybe he was terrified of attaching to the emotion lurking in his depths. Could he address the sentiment stored? Could he let go of the wealth of feeling? No he could not. He could not travel to the destination on offer. Besides, he had no idea how to get there. There were no maps to follow. She had explained how he, himself, needed to find the way there. This was the only way to confront the past. He had to look through windows in his life. Find the windows which stir up emotion. She had explained many times before, he must flow with the thoughts, the windows. Some of these would be filled with joy and others, with emotion which would weigh heavily on his heart. Those shadowed by hate, by guilt, and by sadness must be seen. She had been very clear. Yet still he could not focus his mind. How did she achieve this so effortlessly? Arthur came to the same conclusion as all the other times. An identical decision made. This was his choice and he chose not to return to the past. No matter how this action may affect his future.

He slipped into sleep. The promised land of peace. That was it. He was awake. Peace. He was looking for peace. Why had he forgotten? Why did his thoughts always slip back into the misery of death? His mission was to find peace. He must remember this elusive state was his purpose. But how? With sleep forgotten his mind raced towards his goal. A light illuminated his path and shone upon his children. He would not start with his mother, with the distant past, she would wait for a future moment. Instead he must focus on his children. They would be affected by his passing. They would themselves need to find peace. Arthur was overwhelmed by the power of knowledge. His mind buzzed with activity. He knew. At last he knew which windows to look through. He would find memories of his children and in turn find peace.

CHAPTER 50 — BEE

The days which followed her visit delivered further severing of the threads which formed their connection. Each fell by the wayside and in turn their bond lessened in strength. With clear knowledge of this erosion, a dense fog of gloom descended upon her days. Sadness which threatened to snuff out her light. His final day would come soon. There was no denying the fallout of this event. Bee knew what would happen. She would transition to a state of isolation. But this thought did not dominate. Instead, her first thought each morning was for him, the dying man. Always, she sent him love across the unseen channel of communication. There was no time to dwell on how she would feel when he was gone. The time remaining had to be spent supporting him. He had to make it across in one piece. Having figured out she could not save him from the clutches of death she had only one mission. To assist his search for peace. To help him leave. To deliver him where he needed to be. In every spare moment she considered how. If only she could wave a magic wand to transform his state. But the harsh reality was, she could not. With each desperate wish for his salvation she burdened herself further. The responsibility for his care weighed heavy upon her shoulders. Dark oppressive storm clouds closed in on her thought flow. But she could not allow these shadows to overwhelm. Yet she seemed powerless to their advancement. Bee had no intention of taking a step back into the gloom, a place from which she had once escaped. There was only one way forward; to find balance. She had to protect herself. This was the only way. She would not live each day with the shadowy cloud of death blocking out the light. After all, she required light in order to survive. A solution presented in a moment of clarity. She would lose herself in the loving shelter of her family. She would embrace the joyful moments of her life instead of the doom laden future to come. The choice would not prevent her from supporting his journey but would provide balance.

As she waited for another call to be answered Bee wondered in what state she would find him. Would he be more energised or slipping closer towards the end? On hearing the tone of his voice Bee believed the latter to be true. He had plummeted into a depressingly dark and cheerless place. To receive this information she required only a connection, an attachment to the vibration of his voice, there was no need for detailed dialogue. She heard the despair in his greeting and caught her thoughts. Immediately she protected herself from the hopelessness. However, no matter how much light she channelled into her form, the desperation in his voice catapulted her into a downward spiral of misery. Bee fought against the heavy burden of his sadness. She wanted to help him and in so doing was connected to every part of him. But the need to save him would deliver her to a dangerous state. He could easily consume all of the light she had on offer. He couldn't help himself. He wanted to be saved. She had to be strong. She must prevent him from dragging her into the depths. Once their connection had served them equally well but not anymore. His recent change in state meant he was not the only one to feel the hopelessness of his slide toward death. Within the bounds of their connection she too felt the impending death, as if it were her own. The conflict which dominated her thoughts was new. Bee had never experienced the reality and close proximity of death before. She was driven by a desperate need to support his every waking moment and at the same time to protect her own life. All thought came to a grinding halt. Instinct took over and Bee focused on light to eliminate the darkness. She imagined a bright white light pouring through her thought stream. Then allowed the light to expand and fill her entire body. She hoped this was enough, would provide the protection she so desperately sought. Guilt seized her mind. How can I stop him from connecting to me? Surely he needs me every moment of every day? Is it not my responsibility to support him? How can he possibly make the journey ahead without me? All of a sudden her mind emptied of questions and was filled with knowledge. She must halt her obsession to support him. She must never again allow their connection to drag her into the depths of darkness. He must be allowed to walk the path alone. Her job was to walk alongside. Her responsibility; to offer a listening ear, to guide and channel energy. Her job was not to walk the path connected to his every thought as if she too were close to death. She did not have to be that connected to provide the support required. Having accepted this fact she turned her attention to his conversation.

'I feel completely wretched. Almost as if I'm already dead. My insides feel cold, murky and hollow, like a dark and empty cave. I could almost believe my insides have been ripped out.'

Bee felt her chest tighten as an invisible hand gripped hold of her heart. Within the confines of her head a silent scream shattered the silence. She must not connect to his feelings. A connection would be easy. She would be able to take his pain, dispose of it and relieve him. But she must not. She held strong. She prevented him from attaching to her light and subsequently offloading his pain. He continued to spill his sorrow,

'I've never felt quite like this before. I really do think I would be better off dead. If I died today it would be a good day.'

He had appealed for help. He needed her more than ever. But she could not help. Bee maintained her resolve and prevented his emotion from violating her protective barrier. She had one thought only. He needed her to be strong. She responded in a calm and collected voice,

'I believe this is your choice. If you really want to go then you can. The power is within, you just need to access it.'

Conflicting thoughts ricocheted off the walls of her mind. What gave her the right to speak these words? How could she encourage him to go? But the reality was plain. She was a messenger. As messages were communicated she delivered them. This was the way. This was the nature of her existence. It mattered not what she wanted. This was not her choice to make.

During the initial stages of conversation she managed to maintain a level of protection, was able to shelter from his grief. But as the level of trauma increased Bee felt her defences crumbling.

'Every day I develop more debilitating responses to the illness ravaging my body. Each one removes my ability to function as a normal healthy person. I can no longer consume large volumes of food or liquid. There seems to be no space inside for sustenance and yet I feel hollow. My ability to walk has diminished to a shuffle and that is if I manage to get out of bed. I have no energy left. Then there is the pain…'

Her thoughts turned to his kidney pain. Bee knew no matter how hard she tried, no matter how good the connection, she would never have a full comprehension of the suffering he endured. How could she help him when his physical symptoms threw him off balance, scything through all of the good work achieved to date? Any chance of balancing him both mentally and spiritually seemed hopeless as his illness grasped a stronger hold. Did she truly believe balance was possible in the state of departure? Could a person really maintain all three, mind, body and spirit during the final stages of a terminal illness? Bee believed it was possible for some but was not sure her dad could achieve such a feat. What made people so different? Why did she believe she was one of those people who could achieve this mind, body and spirit balance, and her dad not? What made her so different? Why did she have an absolute knowing in this regard? Questions rained down and flooded her mind. Then fear crept forwards, followed by doubt, both tugged at her consciousness. Why did she have the right to say another could choose to save themselves or not? She had never received an answer to this question but held out hope one day an answer would come.

In the present she had only one aim. She must support her dad. He was suffering at the hands of his body's response to the enemy within. He was looking to her for answers. But how could she advise him on what to do? All she felt capable of was listening. When he had finished sharing the despair and with his voice at its lowest ebb, she made a suggestion,

'Don't try and address any issues. Don't try and fix your problems. Instead, why don't you listen to your music? Lose yourself in Bach and elevate yourself out of the pit of despair in which you find yourself.'

The inspirational idea to direct him towards Bach came from a space inside her head, the place where all messages were delivered. This was not her conscious thought but the process of 'knowing.' Then she offered further support, the only other option on offer.

'When we have finished talking I'm going to perform a remote session of energy channelling. Hopefully this will work in tandem with the music and help you climb out of your current predicament.'

This was all she could offer to the desperate man at the end of the line. After they had spoken their goodbyes Bee collapsed, no longer able to contain her emotions. She climbed onto her bed, curled up into the foetal position and sobbed. Thoughts exploded in her head, each demanding airtime. First came frustration. Why was he unable to make himself better? Next came hopelessness. There was no more could be done. Finally, pity, she felt great swathes for the man who would be meeting with his death very soon indeed.

Chapter 51 — ARTHUR

As he leant over to place the telephone on the bedside table, internal pain fired up again. Wincing, he cried out silently inside his head in anguish, 'For God's sake will this pain ever stop?' Tears threatened. He was at his wits end. He desperately wanted his life to end, or did he? This was a quandary he faced daily. After all, he had been to hospital and almost died but for good reason had chosen to stay. There was no escaping the reality of his choice. He had stayed to sort things out, to square off a number of relationships within his immediate family. Could he achieve this goal? He was not entirely sure. Once more he had lost his way, the path ahead no longer illuminated. Perhaps he could make a new deal with whoever was in charge of his departure? He would swap the pain for doing exactly what was required of him, a fair trade. But Arthur knew the reality. The passage to the end didn't work that way. How he wished it did. He heard her words again. 'You have the power to manage the pain and your exit. But in order to do this you have to be willing to see into the very depths of who you are.' Just the contemplation of this suggestion caused fear to restrict the function of his heart. He couldn't do it. He didn't believe in the path she offered. Therefore he could not even attempt the process. If only he possessed her power and courage. However, he did not. Instead he would have to figure his own way to the end.

His journey was not the life of which he had dreamt. His current existence akin to a roller coaster; trapped in a vessel from which he could not escape, dropped to depths never before experienced and delivered to an abrupt end. Although Arthur did have a get out clause. If the weight of his journey became too great to bear then he could take his own life. This particular option was easier to talk about than actually accomplish. He and Bee had already discussed this option months before, at a point in time when he had felt able to share his thoughts on ending his life before the cancer became unbearable. Arthur was now in the very situation of which they had spoken. There was no hope for his existence. The pain he endured was intolerable. But he could never execute the plan. The choice to kill oneself did not sit comfortably with his faith and belief in an afterlife. When they had discussed the subject, Bee had been very vocal and supportive of his choice, saying a person who took their own life would not be damned forever as some religious folk believed. But Arthur could not take the chance, would not test a scenario which had been argued over for centuries. Therefore he was left without a choice. He had to endure the pain and torture of a slow death. Arthur felt confused as he contemplated the journey which had delivered him to this point. He had not been a bad man. Although not perfect, did he deserve the current level of pain and suffering? He had hurt a few people along the way but not committed any serious offence towards another. He had not always been entirely honest with people. At times he had abused trust. However, on the flip side he had supported many people during times of hardship. He had never turned his back on his children, even in difficult times. He had been a good husband. He had not turned away from difficult situations, had always offered solutions to people in need. He had given freely of his time.

Arthur reconnected with memories from his late thirties through his forties. A time when he had been presented with a new opportunity, a new career. An acquaintance in a neighbouring village had heard he was looking for a new challenge and had offered to train him in the field of agronomy. This gift, which came from out of nowhere had changed his life, had inspired him. Although the choice of securing a large overdraft to cover the costs of a year without salary seemed daunting, he and Sheila had concluded future gains would be worth the short term pain. He had thrown all his energy into the new career and his mentor David had provided unwavering support. The years which followed saw Arthur grow in strength until he was a most highly regarded member of his profession. He had never forgotten the gift which had been presented to him by David, had felt eternally grateful to the man who had opened his door to another. Some years later, when David died prematurely of a heart attack, Arthur had been devastated by the blow. He had not been able to comprehend how a man of such kindness, who shone the brightest light onto other's lives could have been taken in his forties. At the funeral he had made a vow to his dear friend, that he would take the mantle, he would support those who came to his door. Arthur had been true to his word. In his voluntary role as church treasurer he had provided support to many of the church community. After meetings or services he would lend an ear to a troubled soul. He had opened up his heart to others. A seemingly endless supply of people at work and in the village community needed a friendly ear or required guidance. As he reflected, Arthur remembered three of those people. They had lost their way in life either through redundancy or the breakdown of a relationship. He had been there for them. The outcome of his support for these three, was their choice to join the church in a ministerial role. He smiled on the reflection. He had been a good man. Although he had lost this focus on supporting others when he moved to another village, the one in which he and Sheila had devoted their time to renovating an old cottage. Soon after they moved he had become lost, had drowned in a sea of politics at work. The stress levels he endured had been too much. He had become broken. Once again he had to make a difficult career decision. This time to take early retirement. The only way to save his soul. With Sheila alongside he had made it through the difficult times. They had made the choice to sell the cottage and use the proceeds to support their pension pot. When the decision had been made, he received the next blow, one which paralysed his ability to support others. He had been delivered prostate cancer. Although later, after he had come to terms with the fact his life would be taken, he had once again found the space and time to share kindness and generosity. He had been a good man.

Was the end of your days a reflection of your path through life? Did you have to walk a path of goodness and light the whole way in order to die peacefully and without pain? Did the quantity of light you shone on other people's lives outweigh the darkness you shone on your own? Would his good deeds balance the bad? Arthur wasn't entirely sure. He wasn't sure of anything anymore. All he really wanted was to fall asleep one night and never wake up. But apparently life was not that simple. Instead, he would have to find a way to get through the next five minutes, hour, day, week or month until the day when he was allowed to leave his godforsaken existence. The only thing which made life worth living was music. Arthur understood the power of the Bach music; whereby every note conspired to elevate his spirit. Whenever he listened to the compositions of this great composer Arthur felt as if he were receiving a special gift meant only for him. An undeniable level of elevation and ecstasy, which in turn motivated him to delve deeper into the connection with the famous composer. Driven by a thirst for knowledge, Arthur turned to the bedside table where Sheila had placed a new book, a biography on the great man himself. Arthur cast his eyes over the front cover and was overwhelmed by an unusual tingling sensation which rushed into the space inside his head and then electrified his scalp. He recognised the picture. After grappling at the edge of the front cover, he turned over the first few pages and happened upon another picture which he recognised. His excitement grew, as did a need to check out the theory developing in his head. He slipped out of bed and shuffled slowly to the study where he searched the filing cabinet for a hanging file labelled 'Spiritual.' With the file open, Arthur hunted for the picture drawn by the Medium Marjorie many months before. His hands shook, causing the paper to wobble to and fro before his eyes, but this did not prevent him from recognising the face. The picture which Marjorie had drawn was an exact match of the image in the book. A sketch of Bach. Fuelled by his excitement, Arthur searched for the notes made in parallel to the drawing. He poured over the scribbled text and found the description of the man and his physical ailments matched exactly with those written in the Bach biography. Gripped by the euphoria of enlightenment all pain was forgotten. Was there no end to the magic of life? In one moment he had been lost to despair, trudging a lonely path towards death. Then in the blink of an eye he had been delivered to a magical interaction with two pieces of paper and a book. He remembered Bee had advised him Bach was an important element in his life. But she had not known why. Arthur was left with one overriding thought. He must submerge himself in the music of one of the greatest composers on earth. He collected the notes and picture together and went back to bed. Once there, he laid them on the bedcovers to his left. Arthur lay back and nestled his head deep into a plumped feather pillow, then placed earphones into his ears and pressed the play button on the CD player. Whereupon his head filled with the glorious notes of the chosen Bach composition. There was nothing else on earth to compare with the music soaring through the space inside his head. Within moments peace enveloped his mind, body and soul. He smiled, closed his eyes and slept.

Chapter 52 — BEE

There was to be no escape from the intensity of support required. Bee found it nigh on impossible to balance his needs with her own. All she could do was connect within to find her strength and allow it to dominate all thought. With the added demands of family life this proved hard. Although the luxury of alone time was in short supply, it was possible to connect to her inner silence wherever she was. Her most favoured position being the kitchen, where she spent many hours preparing food and clearing up after her family. Bee stood at the kitchen sink washing the dishes and tuned into a silent connection. As her mind shifted, a flow of information poured through her consciousness and she saw the issue. A light shone upon her path and she realised once more, she had allowed his pain to penetrate her space and deplete energy levels. She had to stop the behaviour. Although this was easier said than done. Bee had always been able to feel another person's pain, had never managed to eradicate the feeling of a mild, but aggravating, tingling sensation in her own body. An experience she did not particularly enjoy.

Her thoughts galloped back in time to possibly the worst example of feeling another person's pain. An accident involving Edward. Whilst on holiday, he had run into a wall at the corner point where the two walls connected. The result of the collision had been a large gash which ran nearly the whole length of his forehead from top to bottom. Bee recalled the gut wrenching fear, as momentarily, she thought one of her beautiful boys was about to be taken. Within half an hour, having been ferried by a kindly taxi driver, she and Edward had been deposited in a hospital room. A sterile place, in the company of strangers, is where she had experienced the greatest sensation of pain from another. As Edward lay on the table, she had stood by his side and held his hands to prevent him from moving. She had spoken comforting words and channelled energy to ease his pain. As the doctor stitched the wound without the benefit of anaesthetic, Edward had howled like a wounded animal. Bee could still recall the harrowing sound of her little boy as he accepted the inner and outer stitches required to bind his broken head. Bee never, ever, wanted to hear this sound again. But almost as unpleasant as the sound was the pain itself. Bee could still recall the level of pain Edward endured. The sensation of his pain had not been received as nerve endings on fire, but as nerve endings being manhandled, squeezed and manipulated to mimic the pain endured by another. She had experienced this reaction many times but had never turned the gift away; as if she knew one day this form of messaging would serve. Until the day arrived and its worth realised, she would continue to manage the strange feelings she felt when another was in pain.

Her mind had been momentarily distracted. She refocused on the job in hand. She must release the pain absorbed through the connection with her dad. She knew how to, for trial and error had delivered a method. First she imagined a state of peace, a blanket of white wrapped around her form. Then she spoke silently in her head, 'Please release all that is not required from my mind, body and soul.' Next, she imagined a bright white light shining upon her body, converting all shadows to bright white. Then calm descended. All thought of pain disappeared. The result—a sense of self. Within moments of finding peace a thought tumbled into her mind and encouraged her to pick up a pen. Bee responded to the request. She wiped her hands dry, found pen and paper and recorded a message.

Be peaceful,
Be truthful,
The shining light will come forth one sunny day,
You shall see it and in it see yourself,
You will be calm,
You will embrace it for you will know that it is safe,
You know that is true,
We are here for you,
We are waiting for you,
Love all those who are you.

When the last word had been transferred to paper Bee placed the pen to one side and read the words. There was little or no comprehension as the words were recorded. This was a peculiar experience, as if she were not in control, not physically writing. Yet she was. A detached state, where all other physical input was muted, barely accessible. Bee found the experience hard to describe to anyone, even to her dad. In the early days she had been convinced she was controlling the pen. Over time she had conducted many experiments, whereby she tried to control the process and write what she wanted, but this was never allowed. As soon as her mind shifted to control the channel then the communication dropped. Once Bee had come to terms with the unique delivery of information, she had learned to trust everything transmitted. Using this form of communication she had delivered messages to many people. Always words they needed to hear at a given time. Bee had vowed never to hide from this gift, to always find a way to deliver the transmission, no matter how awkward the situation. Looking upon her writing, Bee realised the message was for him. This would give him direction. Help him to see the pathway. These were beautiful words. Words to be treasured. Although she ought, Bee could feel no sadness for the content. All emotion had been paused. In its place a clear directive which fired electricity through her body. She must not waste time. She must call him and pass on the message.

Chapter 53 — ARTHUR

Another day passed idly by as Arthur lay in bed contemplating life. The shrill sound of the telephone at his bedside interrupted his thought flow. He rolled ever so gently onto his left side so as not to ignite the fire in his prostate region, then picked up the handset. He smiled at the sound of her voice. Then his heart lifted. Arthur wondered what news she had to deliver. The excitement in her voice was obvious. Whatever she wanted to convey had to be valuable.

'Dad, I've just received the most incredible message for you. A very important one.'

The words filtered through into his consciousness. He loved the thought of another message but in equal measure was wary of the reality coming his way. Although he was not yet aware of the content, and even though she was incredibly excited, Arthur knew this was something he did not want to hear. Although he felt no excitement, he was fully aware of how foolish it would be to ignore a communication. There had always been, and he guessed would always be, a reason for the information received. Reluctantly, he accepted she might be able to assist his journey to the end point, a place he both desperately sought and anxiously fought. What if Bee handed him a message that projected him towards the end more quickly? Could she do that? His stream of thought was rudely interrupted by a question.

'Do you want to hear the message? You may not want to as I think it relates to the end.'

Arthur thought for a few moments, facing the same dilemma as every other time she had asked this question. Of course he wanted to hear her words of wisdom. But he did not want to actually face the reality of moving ever closer towards his death. Arthur felt his heartstrings pulled, stretched taut, a sign he had to listen to the message. If he truly believed as she did, that everything in life happened for a reason then he had no choice but to embrace all that was divulged. Unenthusiastically he answered,

'Yes.'

Arthur felt dizzy, as if he had been knocked to the ground by a powerful right hook. Inside his head words exploded like fireworks, ricocheting off the walls of his mind with nowhere to escape. The output of this reaction, tears. In plentiful supply they streamed down his face. The time had come for goodbye. Arthur used his hands to wipe his face dry and composed himself before responding,

'How would you interpret the words?'

He asked the question but did not really want to hear the answer. Bee responded with enthusiasm,

'I think it will be a sunny day when you leave and when you see the light that comes for you, you will see for yourself that in essence you too are light. You will see a light. You must embrace this light and you will know without doubt it is safe to do so.' With every word her voice sounded more assured, 'In this safe place there will be a party, not the kind you are used to, but a meeting of energy and a celebration as you move across to the other side.'

At this point Arthur felt compelled to speak,

'But what does the last line mean, "Love all those who are you"?'

Bee knew exactly what it meant,

'You must love all the parts that are you, the dark and the light, those you like and those you don't. You must learn to feel love for all the parts of your life.'

In an instant Arthur understood what he must do. He had heard the message before. He must allow love to flow for the children he had created. He had been challenged by this thought for weeks but unable to progress. A nagging thought told him this was the reason he was still alive. Once more she had cast light upon his path. She had put him back on track. He could see with clarity. The parts of his life which needed to be loved were his creations. The most important thing for him to do was address his feelings for his children.

Chapter 54 — BEE

As Bee shared the message she had focused only on her purpose. There had been no emotion. Even though the communication clearly related to the end of days, no tears fell. Afterwards, when they had fully discussed the meaning she asked a question of him,

'Will you tell me when you sense a presence coming to collect you?'

She mulled over the response he had given.

'Of course I will, that is if it's not too late.'

Another solemn promise had been made. She mused over what other people might think of their frank discussions regarding his journey to the end. They may well think the pair would be better off living in the now and ignoring what might be. But Bee knew the unusual, verging on morbid conversations, helped. He wanted to be prepared. He wanted to know someone was going to be there. He did not want to be alone. All of a sudden a thought came into view. She recalled the point in their conversation when she had delivered the last line of the message. At that precise moment an unseen force had almost pushed her backwards. An unusual occurrence. Very rarely was physical force used. Fear flooded her senses. Had she over-stepped her role? Who was she to tell him what he should or shouldn't do on the path to his departure? But the message had been undeniably strong. Traces of its power still lingered, which indicated one thing only, she was following the path for his highest good. She was correct to guide him. This was her role. He needed her to be strong. He was still lost. There was no way she could allow him to wander aimlessly to his end. She was privy to all he needed to see. She had to help him to see. Bee hoped this latest transmission had done the job. That he was now able to take the next step toward accepting all he had become and then find a state of peace within himself. Bee knew, how she knew was irrelevant, she just knew that in the process of passing a person had to find peace. Had to understand who they were and what they had become. For her dad, this would be one of his hardest challenges. Yet she still had faith he could achieve success. She would make sure of this. The grave undeniable situation, she was preparing him for death. Alone, without a soul to tell, Bee fell to her knees and sobbed like a small child. With arms wrapped around her bent legs she curled up on the floor and let go of the pain of losing her dad. She could not tell anyone of his plight. This was between them. She had to help him. These were to be difficult days ahead. But she was his only hope. She would move heaven and earth to make sure he reached his end in one piece.

Chapter 55 — ARTHUR

Blissfully unaware of her depth of sadness, Arthur dealt with his own grief. Another communication delivering the same realisation had landed firmly in his lap. But this time the message was stronger. He was actually on his way to the end. There had been previous indications. He knew he would not be physically saved. But there were stages to the journey. Information provided along the way to assist the traveller. This latest stage indicated he was no longer actually able to sustain life on earth. The reality produced a response. Tears of sadness, anger and frustration rolled down his face as he contemplated the mammoth task overshadowing his existence. If Bee was correct, he must face up to his lifetime of creations. His mind filled with reflections of past mistakes, pain he had caused others and the pain he bore for his children. Arthur did not once reflect on the joy his life had brought to the many he had met along the way, the people he had inspired. He seemed unable to attach to any positive element in his life. A few weeks earlier, during his stay in hospital, Bee had tried to focus his thoughts on the joyful interactions he had experienced over the years. But he had struggled then, as he did now. For the darker thoughts were much, much stronger. He would not dwell on his life; instead he directed all thought to his four children.

As a young boy, the eldest son Richard, had been the apple of his eye. But all that changed. As the boy grew older, with little in common, they had grown apart. Eventually hurting each other with their words and actions. Arthur knew it was imperative they spoke of the past. Otherwise when he departed, his son would struggle with the grieving process. Arthur vowed to make a telephone call to his eldest son. They would speak of the past and hopefully come to an understanding. Maybe they would once again be able to share love freely.

His second child, Bee, was the daughter with whom he was able to share love. Although he could never tell her, he thought she knew how much he loved her. Arthur had recorded a message for her, so that when he was no longer visible she would be in no doubt of his love. Their regular conversations and her support throughout his illness meant everything. He was in no doubt all was well with them. He felt a very deep sense of love for her, and knew, even when he was gone, she would be able to feel his presence and love. There were no more words to be spoken, for they were at peace with one another.

His third child, Lizzie, was another daughter with whom he was able to share love. They had always maintained a good relationship, shared the same sarcastic sense of humour and never had reason to fall out. Arthur did not converse with her to the same degree as Bee, for they did not have the same relationship, but that did not diminish all they shared. In later years Lizzie had helped him greatly by supporting his visits to the specialist in London. Their time together had afforded them the luxury of closing off any outstanding conversations. They had a healthy relationship and there was no more to say.

His fourth child, Andrew, had been a most welcome surprise, born some years after the other children. In the early years they had enjoyed a very close relationship. Then Andrew attended boarding school and the connection became frayed. What had seemed like a perfect choice for his son, to provide him with the company of other children of his own age, now seemed to be the wrong choice. As the years passed Arthur had become alienated from his son and their connection broken. They needed to reconnect, to find common ground, to make peace.

His mission was clear. He had to make peace with both of his sons. Not only was it important to his journey, but was equally important to their future. They needed him to reach out and connect with them before the end.

Chapter 56 — BEE

A new day and another set of saucepans required attention. Bee scrubbed the evidence of the previous evening meal from the enamelled pans and allowed her mind to wander. She recalled the moment her dad shared his revelation regarding Bach. He had excitedly told her of his findings, an exact match of the image in his book with the sketch drawn by Marjorie. The result of which had increased his belief in a relationship with Bach and highlighted the importance of this thread in his life. Bee felt happy for him, pleased he had established a connection with the power of music. Bach music was his medicine, could deliver him to a state of peace, if only for the duration of the piece. She had known Bach was important but not why. Now she had a better understanding. The powerful uplifting pieces were to comfort his soul through the days to come. But only Bach could elevate him to the required level. Bee had always believed music was important to the soul and therefore was not shocked by the understanding he would benefit from its power. However, she was surprised at the focus on one form of music only. Bach. She deduced the compositions of this famous musician delivered a connection not available through any other. There was no need for her to know why this was so, just that it was so. Throughout her life, on happy, sad or even regular days, she lost herself in music. She loved to connect with the notes. No matter the instrument, the notes always danced in her mind. White against a black background. They rose and fell in time with the music. They were part of her, as if she were the instrument. They danced with her soul. Her latest game was to use the shuffle function to release control of what she played, to allow her mind and soul to be cleansed by whatever appeared on the playlist. This method delivered smiles, messages and relief from the events in her life. The funniest moments were delivered with the Christmas tunes, which played even though it was nowhere near the festive season. This music annoyed fellow listeners, but not her. She loved Christmas. This was a time of light. She loved the light. The light cleansed her soul and so did the music. Bee dearly hoped her dad would benefit in the same way and find his peace. In contemplating the sketches drawn by Marjorie, Bee realised she had never identified the person in her picture. Did she believe the lady drawn was relevant? She wasn't sure it really mattered. There were more important things to consider. Like how she was going to take the difficult step backwards from her dad. To allow him to take control of his path and to give her the space to focus on herself and family. She felt sure this was the only way to ensure survival through the rocky times ahead. However, she was fully aware this was not her only issue. There were many other people who demanded attention. She would not only have to find a way to balance requirements from her dad and household but also the others.

As she walked along the path leading to school, with one boy at each side, she was struck by a communication relating to a parent walking in the opposite direction. The message came like all the others, without any warning. She could not outwardly react, as she had to retain composure for the sake of the children. Bee continued walking as if nothing happened. But something had happened. The woman who was closer, nearly alongside, had a departed father who wanted to converse. Bee was the only open channel of communication and felt the uncontrollable change of state. She smiled at the boys and accepted the electrical energy which set all nerve endings on fire. This was not an unusual occurrence. She had received many communications in public places and long since learned how to accept and deliver a message, or alternatively, allow it to pass through. There were times, like this, when it was impossible to deliver the message. No matter the heartbreak. She could not walk up to a complete stranger and explain that a departed family member wanted to communicate. She had to go about her business as if nothing had occurred. Only she was aware of what had transpired. Bee allowed the communication to pass through, dropped James at school and returned to the car with Edward. Then as if nothing unusual had happened she emptied her mind of the connection and returned to her own thoughts. On the drive back home a memory appeared in her thought flow.

A few months earlier she attended a lunch with the mums of James' classmates. Not something she had done before and not something she would do again. She had said too much. There had been a tirade of questions about the unusual occurrences in her life, brought about by a well-meaning but loose-tongued friend with whom she had shared a few details of the events with her dad. She had become the centre of conversation. The sole focus. There had been no escape from the ten sets of eyes which bored into her soul in an effort to comprehend her world. Bee remembered feeling excited about the act of sharing, opening up, allowing other people to see all she had to give. But as always, too much had been expressed. Many of the mothers had open hearts and faces, they clearly wanted to believe. But there were a few who were not able to see beyond the barrier which had formed in front of their eyes. At the time Bee had not, and still did not judge them for their disbelief. Rather, she questioned her reasons for sharing stories with people who were not ready for her truth. No matter the reception, after every imparting of truth came bereavement. But not at the start. To begin with, the process of speaking about her life, her reality, set off butterflies in her tummy. Excitement grew as truths were uncovered. Then, as those listening processed the details and their faces showed disbelief, fear suffocated the enjoyment, like a snuff eradicating a candle flame. Afterwards, she always felt the same. Desolate. Why did she not learn? Why expose herself? Why share what could not be understood? It was as if she harboured a childish dream. Of one day finding someone who might understand, might be the same. The follow-on from every disclosure was an overwhelming sense of remorse. She would attack from within, chastise herself for believing someone would understand. She would speak to herself in cross tones, tell herself, there is no point in trying to share who you are. But she couldn't help herself. She knew, as proved in her dad's situation, she had a multitude of gifts for a reason. She could help people. She wanted to help people. Where they saw complex choices, she saw solutions as clear as day. She could see the path which would be for their highest good. She possessed a window to their soul. But clearly this was not her intended path and having accepted this, the lonely space to which she returned was colder and more desolate than before.

Her mind emptied of the recollection and she returned to the present. The contemplation of the memory had served to tell her one thing. She needed to develop a survival technique for the near constant flow of messages. But she faced a dilemma. The choice to protect herself from the bombardment of communications made her feel as if she were not fulfilling her duty. She felt a grave responsibility to those speaking through the channel. Often times feeling as if she were the only one listening, were the only person able to pick up the transmission. How could she decide what to hear? Was it right to select only some of the messages? There was no directive available. No one ever explained how she should deal with the transmissions. There were only knowings. In the absence of direct guidance she came to her own conclusion. All messages that came and could not to be passed on, would have to be discarded. Having decided on a positive way forward. Bee felt compelled to call her dad to discuss the topic.

This was not his voice. Bee sensed danger immediately. There was nowhere to flee. She had to listen to the unwelcome news.

'Your dad has gone downhill fast. In his mind he is not strong enough to do anything. He no longer wants to eat. He doesn't have any energy. He is in a really bad place. There doesn't seem to be anything I can do, other than keep out of his way. Bee, he doesn't want to speak with anyone, even you.'

The severity of this reality caused despair to lodge in her throat and threaten to strangle her voice. Helplessness engulfed her senses. If she couldn't speak with him then how could she help? Why had he shut her out? After all they had been through. She had promised to help him to the end. He couldn't shut her out. She wanted to escape and process the news. But instead she felt it only fair to listen to the plight of her mum and help as much as she could. They spoke briefly and then ended the call. After she disengaged, the state of helplessness was replaced by a veil of misery. One that threatened to drown her in a shroud of grey. Instead of feeling rejected she felt sorrow for his soul, as if she were connected to a greater knowledge of his journey. A 'knowing' developed. He would leave within six weeks. In the moment of understanding Bee made a silent vow. She would do anything, absolutely anything to assist what was left of his life. A humanitarian need demanded she be at his side at all times. Yet in her heart she knew this action would not serve either of them. A harsh reality remained. He had to figure the journey for himself. He had to come to terms with the passage to the end. She would have to be content with the delivery of remote channelling with no sight of achievement. She must develop a greater belief in her remote support and remember it was he who had requested privacy. His demand had to be accepted. Bee was left little option but to wait for the moment he was ready to talk.

A few days later, she thought the moment of reinstatement of conversation with her dad had arrived. But the caller was her mum. A messenger of further bad news. A voice hampered by emotion delivered the latest update.

'Your dad has got much worse. He has physically deteriorated to a level I've not yet seen. I've been finding it really hard to cope with him. He doesn't want me to help and when he does I can't do it right. He is so bad tempered.

I don't blame him. He is really distraught by the pain and his lack of energy due to not being able to eat. I didn't know what to do yesterday when it all came to a head, so I called the nurses for advice. They suggested he be admitted to the hospital in Dorchester. They came to collect him this morning. I have to say, I felt a huge sense of relief when he was gone. I know that sounds really bad but the responsibility for his life, for having to make decisions on his pain relief is sometimes overwhelming.' Her mum paused for a moment as if to swallow the emotion and then continued in a brighter tone, 'I'm heading off to the hospital now. There was no need for me to follow the ambulance. By the time I get there they will have settled him in a bed.'

Bee could not attach to the situation. She could not connect to his pain, neither could she connect to her mum's anguish. There were very few words to say. Without any sign of emotion she responded to the news,

'Please let me know what the doctors say. You head off to the hospital. We can catch up later.'

Bee ended the call. Afterwards, she sat on the edge of the bed, dropped her head into her hands and wept. Tears were becoming common place after a telephone call. As she wept her body shook, sobs which indicated the pain she felt for all that was to come. Bee had known the day would arrive but could not believe it to be true. Fear tortured her soul. What if she were never able to speak with him again? This thought caused a fresh batch of tears. When these eventually dried up she wiped her eyes, cleared her nose and slumped back onto the bed. Almost immediately a 'knowing' presented. To have any chance of coping in the weeks to come, she had to learn how to release all emotion associated with his passing. Otherwise she would be suffocated. Bee closed her eyes and an image of a heart displayed inside her mind, followed by an understanding. She must focus on this part of her body. Immediately she tuned into the organ. Once connected she felt the horror of imminent loss then the agony of detachment. With knowledge she would soon lose the ability to speak with him. Bee was deposited in a void of sadness. But once visited, miraculously, the emotion smothering her existence dissipated. She felt able to move forward without the burden of sentiment. This new state allowed Bee to return to the reality of her day and a very real need, to collect Edward from nursery.

The journey to the nearby village took less time than expected. With five minutes to spare, Bee chose to avoid the nursery mother chat and park her car next to the village church, away from prying eyes and busy mouths. There, she was engulfed by another wave of emotion in response to his situation—emotion which needed to be released. Even though she was dealing with every reaction there seemed no end to her sadness. She had parked face on to the churchyard. There she felt the close proximity of death but she could not allow it to dominate. The knowledge accessible in her mind regarding his journey to the end; a sad and lonely trip. These thoughts threatened to drown out all other thought. She felt compelled to help him. He needed her assistance. But she could not help, must not help, for both their sakes. In the solitary space of the car, very quietly she spoke, 'He has to make the journey on his own. No matter how hard this is to accept. His time has come. He has to face up to his life and accept the transition across the great divide.' Bee fought the desire to make the journey for him and instead reflected on the burden of knowledge, one carried for years. She had tried to shut out the details. But could not. The gift, to know that which others did not, had to be dealt with and not ignored. Information which presented as if she were connected to a central data repository. For all the pain the knowledge delivered, Bee knew there would be a time when it would assist. This comforting thought allowed her to continue. However, there was no time to dwell on sadness or the information inside her head, Edward needed to be collected. Then he required her undivided attention.

Chapter 57 — ARTHUR

Arthur suffered another humiliating journey to hospital. When would the circus end? He had allowed himself to slide further down the slippery slope towards the gaping hole which awaited. Instead of fighting against the slow free fall, in the moment he wanted only to be taken. Although he didn't feel this way during every waking hour. Many moments were spent trying to figure out how to deal with his children. But mostly, his hours were spent considering the beauty of being wiped off the face of the planet. This was one of those moments. He had no energy. He had not been able to consume food or drink for days and the pain in his prostate cried out with a level of agony that negated the need for sustenance. What awaited him in Dorchester? The end? He bloody well hoped so. His life felt like a fairground ride. One which made him feel desperately sick. Yet he could not get off. He was to endure the torture until the ride ended. His life was a miserable, vomit-inducing fairground ride. What could they do for him in hospital? He could not be saved. He had faced this reality the day the doctor had diagnosed his condition. He had known there was no cure. He could only hope for a few years of respite. Those years had passed quickly and his time was most definitely up. Did he want to see his family again? Arthur knew he must. There were still conversations to be aired. He had realities to face. No matter how ill he perceived himself to be, he would not be taken yet. He had not changed a single thing since his last hospital visit. He had tried. But there had been no progress, and until there was, Arthur knew he would not be released from the hell endured.

By the time he slipped between the crisp sheets of the hospital bed his mood had changed. Arthur sincerely hoped the doctors would be able to perform another miracle. He needed to be saved. To be given enough painkillers and drip fed enough food to get him back on track. He didn't want to die. But didn't want to live either. This was a painful process. Did this always have to be so? Arthur did not wish this painful passage to death on anyone else. He turned to prayer in the hope of salvation. Arthur had always connected with prayer when in church. But more recently he had taken to creating his own prayers; prayers for his soul, a soul that needed help. The pain in his body was enough to drown out any connection to this special part of himself. But the prayers helped. He still had a job to do. He had not yet resolved the issue with his children. He needed to be saved. With this thought he pleaded to his God. His prayer was answered.

Chapter 58 — BEE

All communications came without warning, this one no different. Suddenly she felt the need to draw a picture. Bee collected her journal and box of colouring pencils from the bedside cupboard. Then she selected a blue pencil and began to draw. On the page appeared another keyhole. But this was different to the last, the one she had presented during his last hospital visit. This picture depicted a three-pronged fork, like a toasting fork, dominant in the foreground and in the background a keyhole. As she examined the drawing she felt sure the fork was the main element of the message. From a place unknown, words streamed into her mind. She scribbled each one down on the paper. *'I have kept locked, you are the one, open me.'* Once the words had been recorded, she wept. Then an awareness developed. She could unlock everything hidden away. She placed the pencil and journal on the bed then focused on this one thought. Almost instantly a 'knowing' developed. Only she could unlock the pain in her dad's heart because only she knew what was ailing him. He could not unlock the details. He was unable to face all he had become. This inability, to face up to the facts, was the basis of his frustration. Why were people unable to face and address their greatest fears? After all, she seemed able to do this with ease. What were they scared of? She realised that for most, the choice to hide from their deepest knowing was simpler.

Therefore they accepted their fate; an empty journey. This was one of her life lessons. To learn how to deal with those who were unable to face up to their past. A flow of electrical impulses forced a passage through her body, igniting every nerve ending as they travelled. A thought entered her mind. She had to help him unlock his heart. But how? In the past she had encouraged him to face the shadows and channelled energy to deliver him from darkness, but without success. The situation seemed hopeless. But she could not give up on him. She would not. She had no alternative but to keep on trying. After all, she had promised to support him all the way to the departure point. She had to find a way. There was absolutely no option to leave him to make the journey with the shadows he bore. This reality would deliver only one outcome. His transition would be a torturous mix of darkness and terror. Bee could not knowingly allow this to happen to a man who had encouraged others to find their path and connect to their dreams. A good man, who had looked after his family; provided them with a comfortable home, supported them in times of difficulty and given generously when needed. He must leave with an open heart and an understanding of all he had given and achieved.

Following a week of hospital care, Bee was pleased to learn he had been released and was ready to talk. The sound of his voice was like birdsong, a gift to be cherished, not one to be taken for granted. After the pleasantries of opening conversation had been dealt with he launched into the details of his hospital visit. Bee listened avidly. There was a story to tell. For the first time, in a long time, she heard excitement in his voice.

'One night I was woken by a sound beside my bed. I opened my eyes and there was my father. This vision of my father did not utter a single word but just stood silently beside my bed.'

Bee felt a tingle of excitement and craved to know more,

'How did you feel when you saw your dad?'

He responded with enthusiasm,

'I felt happy to see him. No words were exchanged. He smiled at me, I smiled back at him and then he was gone.'

Bee could not have been happier. In seeing his dad and accepting the presence, he had taken another step towards smoothing his transition. He had climbed out of the shadowy hole in which he had once wallowed and had cleared the issue relating to his dad. However, the late night encounters had not ended there.

'But that was not all. You will love the next bit of my story. Well, maybe not this first bit as I need to describe the horror of the ward. What a depressing place, filled with the unmistakeable sound of the sick and dying. A mixed ward of old men and women. No matter the gender, they all snored. Horrendous! Thankfully I had my music to drown out the surroundings.' The reality of his situation did not dampen the excitement for the story told. 'Well, there was an elderly lady in a bed near to me. Poor thing had been surrounded by her family all day. I couldn't help but watch with morbid fascination as they clung to her life. It was obvious to me the old lady wanted them all to disappear. She wanted to depart. But couldn't, not while the family were in residence. I don't know how, but I knew she wanted them to go. Anyway, at last they left, at about one in the morning. Almost as soon as they had gone a blanket of peace and quiet deposited over every bed in the ward. Then not long after, this sense of calm and peace was replaced by the sound of voices, laughing and glasses chinking. The sounds of a party. I couldn't believe my ears because there was no obvious cause for the noise. I could not see the source of the sound and so curiosity got the better of me. I went to investigate. I climbed out of bed and went directly to the nurses' station. On the way I passed the elderly lady resting peacefully in her bed. I thought it odd how quietly she lay when I could clearly hear voices. At that point I questioned myself, had I really heard the sound? But I didn't give up, I carried on to the nurses' station to find answers. I asked them if they had a television or had heard any unusual sounds. The oldest nurse responded, "Nope, we're not allowed a television. We haven't heard a thing." With that I returned to my bed. I walked past the elderly lady, whereupon I saw she was still at rest. Then I climbed back into my bed and settled down to contemplate the peculiar encounter. My first thought was to the sound. I quite clearly heard the sound of a party. You know like the drinks parties we used to have when you were growing up. As I lay in bed and questioned my sanity my thoughts were interrupted by another sound, this time a curtain. I watched two of the nurses draw the curtains around the bed of the elderly lady. Then in muffled voices I heard them discuss the latest passing.'

Bee had contained her excitement throughout the long description of the encounter. She wanted more details. Many times they had talked of a party, a gathering which occurred when a person was ready to make the journey across to the other side. His experience supported their theory.

'Dad, what did the party actually sound like?'

She had to know. Once again he described the sound of a very jolly event.

'What I heard were the unmistakeable sounds you would expect at a large party. Lots of people chattering, laughing and the clinking of glasses.'

Bee could not hold back her enthusiasm and communicated her hope for his exit.

'How exciting to know the party actually happens. You will undoubtedly be met by friends.'

He had been shown the passing to the other side would be okay, a celebration. Not wanting to dampen his spirits, but knowing she must speak of her latest message, Bee changed the subject,

'I received another picture message for you. In this one there is a keyhole with a three-pronged fork. I am sure the picture is linked to the one I drew when you were last in hospital. I think I am the key to unlocking your heart. I must help you achieve this before you leave.'

His voice communicated tiredness and uncertainty,

'But I don't know what I'm supposed to be unlocking.'

This was not the answer she hoped for. Yet her response must be tactful and diplomatic, without a hint of impatience, even though she overflowed with frustration at his lack of sight. Why did he not understand how close he was to taking his final breath? Why did he not see how to simplify his journey? She could see so clearly, as if it were displayed on a fifty-foot by fifty-foot billboard. Taking a deep breath she prepared herself for that which had been explained many times before,

'You must allow love to flow through your heart, release your bitterness and come to terms with all you have achieved in your life. You have to open your heart to all we have discussed in the past, all you know to be true. Accept there is life after the earth. Admittedly, a different life, but life all the same.'

Words had been delivered. The responsibility for action was back in his hands. There was little more to say, especially as his voice had taken on a strained tone. She left him with a promise of a call the next day and an exclamation of love, as if he did not know already,

'I love you Dad.'

Once disconnected, Bee struggled to manage the emotional battering which attacked from the inside out. The day had surpassed all others. This was now the most difficult to date. During the call and still resident inside her head were the details of his journey. A vision as if she were actually making the journey herself. Why was she unable to communicate the message to him in a way he could understand? This was the most important stage of his journey. If he did not apply the advice given then his passage would not be straightforward. Every day this knowing grew stronger. Yet she could share the reality with no one. They would not understand. She picked up information the rest of humanity seemed willing to ignore. Which was something she could not do. She had always been this way, different. Why? She had no idea. Who was she to tell people how they should and shouldn't die? There was no answer. Just one troubling thought. The one person in the whole world who she most wanted to help seemed out of reach.

Chapter 59 — ARTHUR

After such a long break in communications Arthur had enjoyed the opportunity to converse with his daughter. They had not spoken at all during his most recent hospital visit. He had missed the strength of love she delivered. After their call he felt strangely alone, as if she had disconnected from him, almost as if he did not matter anymore. He could not judge her for this feeling he had inside. After all, she had been there for him through many complex and emotional situations. She was still there for him. Always willing to share messages and advice. She had never once given up on him, not even when his response did not meet with her approval. He took a moment to reflect on how this latest episode must be affecting her. Arthur marvelled at how she did not show the strain or any sign of withdrawing support. Yet he sensed something had changed. Once more she had raised the subject of his locked heart. What was he to do? He still had no idea how to unlock his heart. Bee had told him explicitly. He needed to allow love to flow, to resolve relationships and understand all he achieved in his life. She had even lengthened the list further during their last call. He had been instructed to lose all bitterness stored, forgive all others for their actions and forgive himself. How did she know? She spoke with such clarity, as if she were connected to the font of all knowledge. Even after all this time, after all the messages, Arthur still found this hard to comprehend. He chuckled quietly to himself on contemplation of her likely response. Bee would tell him she was indeed connected to a knowledgeable source. Then she would say he was too. But he was not so sure. However, of one thing he was sure, before he could leave he had to speak with members of his family and make peace with all relationships. Then and only then, could he begin the process of letting go. Although he was well aware that even if he could achieve this mighty feat, there was still one more to overcome. In order to leave his life he had to let go of the will to live, his natural instinct for survival. Having already tried he knew this would prove to be the most difficult task of all. Was he damaging himself by hanging on so tightly to the threads of his life? Right now he seemed to have no choice. The path was carved. With each day he held on to life his mind cleared of debris, he was able to see his final destination more clearly and the eventual peace he would embrace. Bee was right to direct him to reflection in order to move forwards. He knew he had to leave behind the pain and sadness of this life before embracing the next. There was still so much work to do. But if he could achieve peace, maybe the hold on this life would lessen. With this in mind Arthur began the process. He closed his eyes and relaxed, then turned all thought to reflection. In this space he contemplated his achievements and also those moments where he inspired others to believe in themselves, to make difficult decisions and choose a path which was right for them. He had always helped another if they asked for assistance, never more so than after David died. This was probably his most prolific stage. A time when he had shone a light on the path of a wide number of people in his community. In the moment of reflection he admitted to the reality of his life. He had a positive effect on many lives. Arthur had found the next level of peace. This newfound state, delivered through contemplation, caused Arthur to fall into a deep sleep. Where only one thought remained. Hope.

Chapter 60 — BEE

Bee found comfort in her journal. She filled the pages with thoughts and emotions relating to the situation in which she found herself. Although not all thought was focused on her dad. She also noted her thanks for the love shared with Adam and their two boys. How had she allowed this depth of love to develop? How had these three males managed to creep into her heart? Although she had always been a loving person, from a young age Bee had protected the sacred space of her heart and not allowed anyone to connect at a deep level. This management of her heart was an absolute necessity, driven by the intensity of the knowledge stream and the need to protect herself from others. She had always been fearful of anyone knowing the real her. The unusual person who could sense others thoughts, see a presence which no other could and receive messages from an unseen channel. She had kept these attributes well-hidden for fear she would be unlovable. Even when she did trust someone with her heart, allow them to love her, they only saw what she wanted them to see. The number of connections with her heart was kept to a minimum to keep life simple. Strangely, in recent times, she had shown more to her family of three than to any other person throughout her entire existence. She trusted them. They would not harm her. Could she ever share herself totally? No. There was much that could never be shared. But she could share the majority of herself, which was enough.

As the pages of the journal flicked through her fingers in a moment of review, a message presented in her thought stream. She allowed the words to pass through her mind and flow through her hand onto an open page. Sorrow grabbed her by the throat and held her in a vice like grip. *I feel grief at the passing of time, at the loss of love, at the moment.* Then a 'knowing' descended. The communication was about him. She double checked her understanding of the message. Do I have these feelings? No. Although she had to admit being distressed by his illness and imminent departure, she did not harbour the feelings recorded. The message belonged to someone else. In order to gain a clearer understanding she released the sorrow which had been delivered. Once the emotion had receded then she reread the text. She emptied her head of all clutter, leaving only the words delivered, then waited for clarity. Initially there was nothing and then a name was presented. Three letters appeared inside her head. DAD. This message was from him. Not from the unseen channel or the departed, this was her dad. Bee could hardly believe it. He had never managed to communicate in this way before. But there was no doubt it was him. The message and associated feelings were very strong, unmistakably him. She smiled in wonderment. At last he was opening up. He was working with the unseen channel. He had made a giant step. She wondered if he knew he had communicated or whether he was in a state of unawareness. He could be transmitting without even realising. She decided to park this discussion until she saw him face to face.

As the days passed there were no more messages from him. But her knowledge increased. Predictions of future events became heightened, almost as if she were playing a game or practising for a greater challenge yet to come. On a daily basis she was inundated with insight into events that would occur during the course of the day, as if she were connected to a vision of the future. A similar state to that which she had enjoyed in childhood, a time when she had hidden this gift because it had made her unusual. She felt differently now. As a woman her confidence had grown and with it belief, it was safe to develop foresight. A gift she knew would be required in the very near future. In parallel to the future visions, she learned to trust every feeling and thought as soon as it was delivered. The most recent dominant thought, one that would not leave no matter in what activity she was engaged, was actually more like an instruction. She must visit him. Time was of the essence. She must visit very soon. Bee didn't need to be asked twice.

Bee left home and embarked on a journey to the house in Dorset. Unfortunately, Adam was unable to make the trip, so she travelled with James and Edward for company. They raced along the A31 cutting a path through rolling green Hampshire hills bathed in morning sunshine. Bee attempted to reduce the boredom of the journey for the boys and started a game of I-Spy. This was one of her favourite and least favourite games to play whilst driving, depending on her mood and need for silence. When in the right frame of mind, listening to three year old Edward attempt to play the game induced side splitting laughter. There had been countless moments when she and Adam had almost lost control of their bodily functions whilst playing this game with their youngest son. As Bee hurtled along her mood lightened, the sound of Edward's young but confident tone instigated a change, enabled her to connect with the beauty of her life. She could not help but smile as he delivered another corker,

'Spy with my eye something beginning with T.'

Based on past experience, both Bee and James knew full well Edward would not have an object in mind, and even if he did, it would not begin with 'T'. But they played anyway, for the fun of it, for the hilarious reference to objects which never existed. This time of amusement delivered them to a place of togetherness where nothing else mattered.

After many games of I-Spy, they arrived at their destination in the best of spirits. As Bee pulled the car into the driveway a persistent 'knowing' entered her thoughts. This was the last chance the boys would have to play with their Grandad. Time was short. Unable to show the impact of this knowledge, the tears which pushed for release, she acted as if nothing had been communicated. Then climbed out of the car, stretched her legs in the warm sunshine and walked confidently towards the already open front door where he waited. To her boys, the man in the doorway looked like Grandad, but not to her. The strain of his illness presented a very different person. A stranger with a bloated stomach. However, other than the obvious bloating and pink cheeks, he actually looked remarkably well for someone whose body was almost at the point of giving up on life. Bee employed the greatest resolve to push aside thoughts of his appearance and imminent departure. Instead of collapsing under the weight of the reality she threw her arms around his frame and hugged him as never before, as if she would never get the chance again. Following the embrace, they filed into the house and arranged themselves around the dining table where lunch was waiting. Over a bowl of deliciously spiced chilli, which had been prepared by her mum, they talked of the boys' accomplishments at school and nursery. Once upon a time, to prepare and then indulge in lunch would have been one of her dad's greatest pleasures. He loved to cook. But not anymore, he did not have the energy or inclination to stand for the length of time required. When all food had been consumed he made excuses to leave,

'Do you mind if I go for a nap? All this food and chatter has worn me out.'

Throughout the meal she had noticed the development of fatigue on his face. Also how he struggled to chew and then swallow the food. She concluded there wasn't enough room inside for food, with most digestive space dominated by either excess water or cancer tumours. The fun of eating had been revoked. Once he had loved food. He had savoured the very best of what the butcher, greengrocer, baker and wine merchant could deliver. But no more, one of his favourite pastimes had been stolen.

After an hour or so, once his batteries were recharged, she was summoned to his bedroom. As at all other times, she took her seat on the rickety chair at the side of his bed. There was not much to say as they had chatted at length over lunch. There were few new topics to discuss, except for one. She had to ask about the communication.

'A couple of days ago, did you try and communicate with me?'

He looked confused then smiled,

'No, I don't think so.'

Surprised by his response she asked,

'Are you sure?'

He was certain in response,

'Yup. I've just been lying here in bed, reading my prayers, some poetry and finding texts to assist the passage to the end. I have written a few prayers too. But most I've taken from the book on my bedside there. They seem to be the only things which provide comfort right now. In fact I spend a lot of time considering Jesus and how to connect with him. This feels important. The words give me strength. They help me to believe I can get through this.' He paused for a moment in reflection and then spoke again, 'I have also recorded a few for you. So that you have them to remember me by. They are stored on my laptop. Don't forget to access them when I am gone.'

He gave her a weak smile. They both knew crying about the reality of what was to come would do no one any good. She smiled in return,

'Thank you, I will seek them out. Strange question I know, but do you want me to read any of the poetry at your funeral? Is there anything you want to share?'

He pondered for a couple of seconds,

'There is one. Funnily enough I have been thinking about this too. It's not by my bed. I would have to find it in the study. Leave it with me and I'll find it later. The poem is to remind those left behind to move on. As much as I don't want to be forgotten, I also don't want people to mourn my passing either.'

He stopped talking, not out of choice but because his voice cracked under the strain. Bee filled in the silence,

'Don't worry dad I'll find it for you. About my earlier question—I had a strange communication and I was positive it was from you. Maybe you sent it without even realising.'

His eyes lit up with the unusual nature of the conversation, 'What did I say?'

She wasn't sure what to tell him, she couldn't give him the exact wording, what was the point?

'You were obviously having a bad day. It wasn't so much a call for help but a message to say you were struggling. I didn't want to call because I wasn't sure about it. I have never had a message which felt like this one and I thought it better to discuss when I saw you.'

There was no more to be said. He smiled, obviously not wanting to know anymore. He looked tired, too worn out for heavy conversation. They both knew why she was really there. He wanted an energy channelling session. He wanted to feel lighter, relaxed and to get relief from the pain. Her focus was to keep him balanced. She knew her role and commenced the process. As was the norm, first she closed her eyes and then imagined a peaceful space inside. Next, she focused on the light that emanated from within the centre of her body. Finally, she leaned over the bed, placed her hands over the top of his head then allowed the energy and love to flow between them. There were no accompanying thoughts placed in her head. Instead she felt a state of peace developing in his body as he relaxed beneath her palms. After half an hour of holding her hands above various points of his body, the session was complete. He had relaxed into sleep and she left him to rest.

He reappeared later and joined them in the living room, where he took a seat on the leather two-seater sofa near the fireplace. No sooner had he relaxed into the space than Edward hopped up onto the sofa and snuggled up to his body. Seated on the floor, Bee watched as the pair spent nearly an hour happily playing with a wind-up toy record player. She loved to observe their bond. They shared an undeniable link, an inexplicable connection. One soon to be broken. Bee felt twinges of sadness but could not allow them to show. There was no escaping the reality. Edward and James would lose their Grandad very soon. She hoped they would remember this special man. Then her thoughts were interrupted by Edward. Not content with just listening to the music, Edward nagged his Grandad to sing,

'Sin dandad, sin.'

Although her dad loved to sing Bee knew he lacked the energy. But this did not stop him from delivering entertainment to his grandson. He dug into his reserves and sang along to the music playing on the toy record player, as if he did not have a care in all the world. The 'knowing' returned. This would be the last chance for games. Not a thought to be shared. With the knowledge still present in her thought flow Bee gathered all three together and took a photo. Capturing a memory of good times, to remind them of the games they played on this special day, the last day spent with Grandad. As the afternoon drew on, much as she did not wish to go, Bee knew she must leave him to rest. This was the final farewell for the children. She did not share her knowledge with anyone in the room. To take her children away from a man they would never see again was the last thing she wanted. But she had to. Life had to go on. They would continue to exist whether he was alive or not. As Bee stepped across the threshold of the front door and out of the house, the stark reality embraced her like a damp mist. He was slipping further away and there was nothing she could do about it. Could this be the last time she would see him? No. She knew there would be another time. She hugged him as tightly as she dare, not wanting him to know how she felt inside.

After the boys had fallen asleep, the gift of quiet time in the car afforded Bee the chance to replay the conversations with her dad. She considered how she would feel if this were the last time they saw each other, spoke or hugged. Tears rolled down her cheeks in response. The knowledge of his departure had been with her for so long and yet she was still not ready to come to terms with the reality of her forthcoming loss. The journey home seemed to last an eternity even though it was only two hours. When at last she parked the car at the top of the drive and her feet met with the ground, all the strength in her body slipped away into the stones below. As her strength evacuated, all that remained was fear, coupled with misery. But she would not give in to the negative spiral. Instead she sought her inner strength and there found a reserve, which she used to carry the sleeping boys to their beds. With James and Edward tucked up in bed, she crept downstairs to the kitchen, where she found Adam preparing dinner. As she entered the room he looked up from his preparations. He stopped what he was doing and offered her a glass of wine. Gratefully Bee took the glass and placed it carefully on the work surface to her right. Although she craved the relaxant which the drink would deliver there was a more pressing need. Bee wrapped her arms around his middle and buried herself in the comfort of his chest. Within the safety of his arms she wept, releasing the emotion of the day. As she sobbed into his chest, knowledge of the departure grew ever clearer in her mind.

Chapter 61 — ARTHUR

Arthur had enjoyed their visit. Bee and her children delivered light into his life which could not be gleaned from any other source. They were easy to be with, gentle and mild, but fun too. Each of them possessed a light which burnt as bright as a candle in the dark. He loved to share in their existence, particularly Edward. He had never quite understood the connection between Edward and himself, but there was most definitely a link. From the very earliest days when Edward had been a baby he had sought Arthur out, demanded to be in his space. During their visit Edward had connected with him through music. He had not wanted to sing the nursery rhymes and yet somehow he had managed to fulfil his grandfatherly duty. Where he had found the energy for the activity he could not be sure, it was as if he had been miraculously gifted with just enough for the visit. Each time he had believed the fuel store to be empty it had been refilled just enough to take him through the next activity. There had been good reason for the assistance. This was the last time he would see the boys. The reality ripped through his mind, sweeping aside all other thoughts and eliminating any sense of balance which previously existed. The contemplation of his imminent disappearance transformed his state into one of panic. He didn't want to leave everyone behind. But most of all, he didn't want to be forgotten. Tears escaped. Soon he would be gone. Soon after, forgotten.

Chapter 62 — BEE

On picking up the phone Bee heard a strained voice without hope, one close to breaking point. She listened to her mum describe the latest turn of events.

'Yesterday, the day after your visit, your dad took a turn for the worse. He refused to eat. His pain was unbearable. But I couldn't, and can't deliver the level of pain relief he needs. He is now at the point when he needs more than I am allowed to administer. The only thing I could do was speak to his doctor and Macmillan nurse. They told me I had to let your dad go to the hospice, so the staff there could provide him with the level of care he needs. This is it. He is coming to his final days.'

Although she shouldn't have been, for she knew it was coming, Bee was still shocked and saddened by the news. After a few uncomfortable moments she found her voice,

'I'm glad he is being looked after by professionals. You've done the right thing. I only hope he actually gets the level of relief he needs. It seems crazy the amount of pain he has to endure. I really wish he was able to leave this life without any more discomfort. Do you know what the incredibly sad reality is? If he were an animal he would have been put to sleep by now. How can he be allowed to experience this level of torture? They know full well he will die within a matter of weeks.'

Then words failed her. What more could she say? Nothing would change the reality of his situation. Her worst fears had come true. He was leaving. Bee became lost inside her head, thoughts of his departure drowning out all others until she heard the words for which she did not care.

'Bee, your dad doesn't want to talk to anyone. He does have a phone by his bed but he wants to come to terms with this latest change in his circumstances.'

As much as Bee understood the need for the request, she did not care for the demand. The request for silence pierced through her heart like a dagger, making her want to scream out. But she did not. Instead she screamed inside her head, 'He can't cut me off. We have too much left to say.' But Bee did not impart all she felt. Instead, she released her mum to the duty of delivering the same news to her brothers and sister. Left alone with her thoughts, at her bedroom window she placed elbows on the sill, rested her chin in cupped hands and absorbed the dramatic view of pine trees which dominated the valley ridge. She hoped the magnificence of the tree line against the sky would lift her spirits. They did not. Misery clung to her and threatened to smother all hope of happiness. There was nothing more to be done. No words could be spoken. He did not want to communicate. All that remained was hopelessness. She had no control over his journey. She had no option but to wait until he was ready to converse. Bee connected with the beam of light in her heart and found a 'knowing.' There would be another chance. She would have at least one more conversation before he departed. She embraced and trusted this knowledge then turned her thoughts to the practicalities of the household.

Bee did not have to wait long in the space of radio silence. Communication was reinstated as soon as he had been stabilised through pain relief and a food drip. A request had been made for her to call the telephone at his bedside on Friday evening. As requested she placed the call. His voice sounded much stronger, not at all like a person ready to slip away. Without waiting to be asked he told his tale of woe.

'Bee, my life has come to the point where I can't keep any food down. They are having to feed me through a drip. The one kidney I have left is failing. I spend most of my day and night retching. I'm at my wits end. Because I can't eat, I don't have anything to vomit. I think the pain of constant retching is worse than anything I've suffered up until now. This is not a life. I really wish the end would come soon.' He paused as if in thought and then continued, 'Although, I guess there are a couple of positives. The nurses are wonderful and they can give me stronger doses of pain relief than I received at home. But really my case is hopeless. There is nothing they can do but watch me sink further and further into a pit where they cannot help me.'

For once she was left speechless. There were no words on the tip of her tongue, no message of support. Bee felt more useless than she had in all the years they had journeyed together. All she could do was listen. Then she heard a change in his voice, it lifted slightly.

'Strangely, in amongst all of the pain and anguish, I have found a level of peace afforded by my stay in the hospice. I feel safe on the ward. I take comfort in the knowledge there is medical expertise and pain relief to hand.'

There was no escaping the realisation. Although the medical staff had stabilised his pain, he was realistic, there was no cure. All they could do was make his final steps less arduous. Their conversation stirred up sadness of all that was to come. But she did not allow this to dominate. Instead she cast it aside and focused on the enjoyment of their time together, although she would have preferred they were face to face. If she had been allowed, she would have spent the whole evening on the phone. But this was not practical. After all, her family needed support and her dad needed to rest. Reluctantly they spoke their goodbyes, gladly spoke of their love for one another and promised to speak again soon.

Within two days of the promise being made, it was broken. Bee could no longer speak with him. Having initially reacted positively to treatment, everything had changed, his pain levels had increased and in turn he lost the will to live. Apparently he did not feel like speaking with anyone. He was at his lowest ebb. Bee reacted badly to the news. She careered down a slippery slope into a dark cavernous area of her mind.

To counteract this sense of hopelessness she connected to the light within, to her heart. The connection instigated a series of messages. The time for departure was nigh. There were difficult choices to be made, which he needed to make alone. She had to record this in her journal.

The Lord hath given you a lease of life,
You can choose to end your lease.
Be sure in your heart that you have chosen wisely and you shall be delivered to your beginning.
Be free from all that chains you to earth,
Be free from your desire to hold onto something that no longer serves.
When you release your heart to the highest you will feel your soul lift and you will be happy.
The strength of all who surround you will ease your burden and you will love them forever more.
Be silent, be strong, be of free will, and you my child will be with me once again.

Forever and ever, Amen.

Bee analysed the words. The reality of the communication slowly dawned. The message was undoubtedly for her dad, had been delivered to provide support through the days to come. She must deliver the words immediately. Without delay,

Bee searched for a card on which to write the message. She found one with a photograph of a red poppy field. With knowledge this was one of his favourite flowers, she chose the card and then copied the message. When the words had been transposed then Bee conveyed her love by adding a message of her own. Next she sealed the envelope, wrote the hospice address on the front and placed a stamp in the top right hand corner. At the front door she slipped her feet into a pair of Crocs. Then walked the precious mail to the post box at the end of the lane. On her return, the very moment she stepped through the front door, the telephone rang. Her mum was the messenger of more bad news.

'I'm really sorry to have to tell you this, but the hospice have asked for all family members to be advised, your dad has only a matter of days left. You will need to visit him soon. Let me know when you plan to come and I'll make sure I'm there too.'

There were no words to express her grief. Bee maintained a sense of calm. There was no point in upsetting her mum any more than she already was.

'Okay. Thanks for letting me know. I'll come tomorrow morning. I'll text you when I leave here.'

Although her dad had expressly asked for no visitors, a wish she had respected, Bee knew one last visit to express her love would be accepted by the dying man.

CHAPTER 63 — ARTHUR

He had been told. They had all been told. He did not have much time to put right all that had gone before. He knew they would all come. Each one would arrive with a need to make a connection before he left. Would these visits help them or him? Arthur was unsure who would benefit most. Affected by the heady mix of pain relief and despair Arthur could not think straight. A part of him wanted the family to visit, to have the chance to say goodbye. Yet another part wished he could leave immediately. Was this any way to die? Holding on until the bitter end. Drowning in a sea of pain and turmoil. Maybe not. But it was the way in which he would depart, slowly and painfully, experiencing the agony of every last breath. For him, life had been more like a box of liquorice allsorts than a box of chocolates. Plenty of sweet moments, but mixed with a healthy dose of distasteful tongue tingling moments too. Had he lived his life to the full? Yes and no. Was that always the answer in the days before escape? Probably. How many people could actually answer with honesty that they had lived to the full? Enjoying every moment and having only a positive effect on all others. There could not be many. Maybe this was not the point of life at all. Maybe he was not here to have fulfilled his life but to have achieved something else. If the point was to have created life then he had achieved that in the four children fathered.

But could there have been more? Could he have learnt more about life? Bee would answer, 'Yes.' She would categorically support the theory there was more to life than the obvious. Arthur felt the need to ponder, and as he did, fell into a deep sleep. Not a sleep to take him to places unknown but a sleep to replenish his mind and body.

When Arthur awoke he felt more refreshed. He had some serious thinking to do. The past had to be addressed. He must speak of issues which had marred the relationship with his sons. For one, the problem related to Arthur's sense of guilt. For the other, perhaps he had overreacted. Peace had to be made with them both, for his sake and their own. Arthur felt as if all that had not been said over the years, needed to be. He wasn't sure if either of them were as concerned as he. They probably wouldn't want to bring up the past with a dying man. But Arthur felt this was the right thing to do. He was their father. He had been their main role model. When he left they must consider him in the highest regard. This was the male code. A father had to show the rightful path, no matter that he was dying. Once a father always a father. Arthur felt duty bound to his children. Not until he had taken his last breath would his role be complete. But where should he start?

His eldest son Richard. The issue had developed around the time Richard left the family home. His son had caused a rift between himself and Sheila, had played them off against one another to get what he wanted. He had lied. Arthur hated lies. Arthur could see no excuses for Richard's behaviour. In his late teens and early twenties Richard had lacked direction and had not exhibited any signs of responsibility or respect. Arthur had been left with little choice but to stand strong. He made the difficult decision to push his son out into the big wide world. He determined this was the only way. Richard had been angry to have the support line fractured. Sheila had been torn between the two. She wanted to stand by her child at the same time as her husband. Arthur had made a stand. He had told Richard to take responsibility for his life. He had not been a popular father or husband. In the years since, he and Richard had buried elements of the past but had not made peace with each other. Instead they had plastered over the cracks. Arthur knew this had to change. He needed to forgive Richard for making the same mistakes he too had made as a young man. Maybe he also needed to forgive himself. He also wanted to give Richard the opportunity to air his grievances. Although painful, Arthur knew this was the only way to be delivered to a peaceful state.

Then there was his youngest child Andrew. The one he had lost. Arthur had been overjoyed when Andrew was born, an extra child to boost the family. He had desired the largest of families but finances would not allow more than three children in the early years of his career. The late addition of another had been a most welcome gift. His other children were grown up and had either left home or were nearly at that stage. With only one child to focus on he had been able to enjoy the early years with Andrew. But as his son grew older and entered the school system, a problem arose, one which he had not foreseen. Arthur became obsessed by responsibility, by the need to provide other children for his son to live with, to play with. This need had consumed him. He had felt duty bound to provide his son with a proper family life. As he and Sheila were too old to produce another family there seemed only one sensible option, to send Andrew to boarding school. At the tender age of nine he had been shipped to Gloucestershire.

With the benefit of hindsight Arthur realised this was one of the biggest mistakes of his life. At the time he had truly believed he was doing the right thing. But the decision had meant he lost the chance of nurturing his son to adulthood. The opportunity to experience mundane daily activities, to connect over dinner, in the car to school or watching a comedy show in the evening. He had missed really getting to know his son. This lack of bonding had an adverse effect on their relationship as Andrew grew older. His son had connected only with Sheila. A rift grew between father and son. There had been little Arthur could do. When his son left school, he went to a local college where he grew further away from his parents, then he went to University. The connection was broken. Theirs was not a deep relationship. Arthur needed to be forgiven for the decision he made. He also needed to forgive himself for the chances lost.

Although Arthur knew what needed to be said he did not know how to say it. He had never been an emotional man. Had never spoken of affection to his children. Instead he had demonstrated to them in material ways by providing a roof over their heads, food on the table and clothes on their backs. This was his way of saying I love you. When they were children he had made sure every day ended with a shared evening meal. Seated around the dining table had been their connection time, his moment to communicate, to hear about their day and views on the world. Had this been enough? At the time this was all he could manage. He had worked all hours to provide well for them. He could not have done more. He had done his best. But this was not his focus. He needed to decide how to begin? He did not have the energy for high drama but had to provide a forum for disclosure. He had to listen to their emotion as well as sharing his own. In a moment of clarity he knew how to start the conversation. He would do something he had never done before. He would tell them of his feelings at the thought of losing sight of them, of missing the rest of their lives. Within this conversation he would also be able to reference the past and seek the forgiveness he desperately craved. With luck, peace would follow for all parties.

Chapter 64 — BEE

They discussed the benefit of James and Edward seeing their Grandad one more time. The fact he was struggling with a constant need to vomit and spent much of his time retching into a receptacle, caused them to decide against it. A week and a half earlier the boys had spent a truly wonderful day playing with their Grandad. This should be their final memory; a playful and cheeky Grandad, not the shell of a man who lay in a hospice bed. Having parked the car outside the hospice Bee embraced the serenity of the location. Although beautiful, the colour of late spring flowers did little to lift her mood. Why did he have to die? Why did he have to leave her? In the past few years they had developed a special connection both mentally and spiritually. Why did he have to leave her alone? Why did her children have to lose their Grandad? Why did he have to die so young? With question after question dominating the space inside her head Bee struggled to concentrate on the task in hand. Thankfully, Adam helped her find the visitor room, where she left him with James and Edward. Bee had chosen to see her dad first. As she followed her mum along the corridor to the ward conflicting emotions developed, excitement at the thought of seeing him again and fear at the thought of witnessing his physical state. Bee knew as soon as she set eyes on him she would connect to his pain. Something she did not want. Inside her head she prayed for it not to happen. Even though this was one of her gifts, on this particular day she did not want to feel its force. There was only one way to prevent the connection. She must attach to the light inside. Bee searched for the energy to protect herself from the pain she knew was coming. Once connected to every ounce of internal strength at her disposal, she strode confidently to the bedside of the weakening man. Standing at the end of his bed she surveyed his frail state. Surely this man was not her dad. He did not look at all like the man she had left a week or so earlier. This man had a puffed face with rounded bright pink cheeks. He was barely able to breathe, speak or even keep his eyes open. This man displayed all the signs of the end of his days. The vision in her line of sight caused more surges of emotion to overwhelm her senses. But she would not let him see the depths of her sadness. She was there to support, not to fall at his feet burdened by her own grief for the loss of his life. His grief at the loss of his own life had to be dealt with first. Bee summoned a smile and he responded with a weak smile in return. The effort level required to produce the smile showed on his face. He was trying to be her dad but quite clearly could not manage this anymore. Written all over his face and deep within his eyes were the telling signs, there was very little left to give.

In a small croak like whisper he managed a few words,

‘Thank you for the poppy card and the words inside. It came at a very timely moment when all hope for my life was lost.’

His voice weakened and her mum took over,

‘The doctor has told us that there is nothing more that can be done for your dad. They will continue to administer painkillers until his body shuts down, which is likely to happen within a week seeing as he has chosen not to take on food.’

Bee took a few moments to register the news, connected with his eyes and then deep into his soul. There was nothing left but resignation. He had come to the end of the road. His body could not hang on any longer. All he had left was to accept his last breaths and leave whether he liked it or not. Bee had known the day would come but the prior knowledge did not make the reality any easier to accept. Emotions ran riot inside her head and heart looking for escape, but she could not let them out, would not let them out. The brave man lying in the bed deserved more. He needed her to be strong, now more than ever. Still smiling, Bee sat down on the visitor chair to his left and ever so gently took his swollen hand into her own. Then she tenderly channelled love and energy to his body. She did not speak, for words were not required. Even if she had wanted to she would not have been able. Tears fought for release. She could not speak for fear they would escape. This was to be their last conversation and she could not spoil what little was left. Bee was very thankful when he found the strength to speak.

'I want to leave you something to remember me by.'

Inside her head she cried out, 'I don't want any gifts. I just want you to live.' But she did not have to say this. They both knew there was no possession which could ever replace him. She was very happy just to be left with the memories of their times together. But there was no stopping him. He was dying. He wanted to leave something behind. There could be no argument.

'I want to leave you the pocket watch my father left to me, and his father left to him. Remember, this watch must be passed down through to the next generation. I want you to have it because I know how much this old timepiece will mean to you. I think you will enjoy the energy it holds.' He paused, clearly in discomfort, then continued, 'My second gift is a Bible that has been in the family since the 1700's. Although you're not a religious person, I think you might like it and know you will care for and respect this heirloom for me.' His voice now a whisper, 'Finally, I want you to have the picture you have admired since you were a girl. The field of poppies photograph that hangs on the wall in my study will be yours, a final reminder of me.'

She didn't want his gifts. But she could not deny his last wishes. She had no choice but to accept everything bequeathed. His departure could not be ignored. All of the tears held at bay threatened to break through their barrier but she would not let them. Determined not to spoil their last moments together she pushed them back from where they originated and smiled. But there was no escaping the reality. She must prepare for his departure. All of a sudden their tender moment was interrupted by his retching. Bee could not bear to see his frail frame in pain. He looked uncomfortable with her presence and so she left his bedside to allow him the privacy of his torment.

With weakened legs she stumbled back along the corridor to the visitor room. All of the strength with which she had connected prior to the visit had escaped. She was drained of everything except tears. They threatened to breakthrough but she would not let them. She could not cry. The boys must not see her cry. As she stepped through the visitor room door the boy's faces lit up, they raced towards her and threw their short arms as far round her body as they could reach. Whilst embracing two of the dearest people in her life, her eyes met with another, Adam, and there, she saw a reflection of her pain. He placed an arm around her shoulders in comfort. Bee was thankful he had come. She needed him more than she realised. Heartache was hurtling in her direction. This was one journey she did want to make alone. After a short interlude with her family, she was recalled for one final conversation with her dad. Once more sitting on the visitor chair to his left, she took his hand then connected with his eyes. This was the only way she could convey the love she felt in her heart. She could not speak the words for fear of being overcome with grief. But time was precious. She had to speak it. There might not be another time. Quietly, in soft tones so that only he could hear, she shared her sentiment,

'I love you. You are a lovely dad.'

He smiled weakly in response and whispered,

'And you are a lovely daughter.'

The invisible dam erected to prevent tears from escaping, burst, there was no hope of stopping them. During their last moments together they held hands and communicated silently through connected eyes. The moment of parting had arrived. In it they shared a 'knowing.' This was their end. But he had one last message. He winked an eye and whispered,

'See you around.'

There was nothing else to say. Bee held his hand until he fell asleep, then raised herself quietly from the chair and walked away from the ward. Away from the father she loved with all her heart.

Each step away from his bedside delivered a new depth of sadness. Unable to control the tears, she hastened toward the main entrance and out into the car park where she collapsed on the nearest bench. Bee allowed the tears release. There was no point in denying them. As if the flow of misery unlocked a door, a 'knowing' presented, information she did not want to acknowledge. The conversation had been their last. There would be no more talking. Comprehension of this fact tore through her insides, ripping and tearing as it wreaked its havoc. The fallout, more tears. When all seemed lost, Bee felt Adam wrap his arms around her body to protect her from the pain. Safe within his arms she sobbed for all that would be lost. When the tears subsided, Bee wiped her face, blew her nose and pulled herself together. She had to be strong. She had duties to fulfil as a mother. There was no time to dwell within the sadness of her heart.

Back in the visitor room Bee focused all mental strength on pushing thoughts of her dad to the back of her mind. But she could not. The image of their last meeting had been burned into her consciousness. She wanted to be alone. To have the space to come to terms with all she knew was coming. She dreamed of escape, of putting distance between herself and the reality of his untimely demise. But she could not leave yet, for her dad wanted to meet with Adam. When Adam left the room, Bee gathered James and Edward for a walk in the garden, a chance to enjoy a breath of fresh air before their long journey home. Embraced by the tranquillity of the green open space dotted with flower borders, Bee escaped the reality of the day and found herself smiling as wild rabbits hopped frantically across the lawn in an attempt to escape her two boys. Life carried on. There was no mistaking this reality. When he died she would carry on with life, with raising her two children. There would be a gap which he had once filled but this would not prevent her from existing. She would be alive. How tough the cycle of life but equally how beautiful. She had said goodbye to one life, but had given life to two others and had a role to play in nurturing them into adulthood. She could mourn his passing but not be lost in grief. He had his time. This was her time. Then it would be her children's time. And so, the cycle of life.

Chapter 65 — ARTHUR

Arthur lay in a bed next to the window. Thankfully every hospital bed had afforded him a window. Maybe there was someone looking after him after all. The moment Arthur had entered the hospice he had known his time had come. This is where he would close his eyes and switch off. The past week had been a bearable existence. But not the last couple of days. During this time he had been required to face facts. There was no way of saving him, no other route. Time to head for the hills. The card Bee had sent contained words which filled his heart with a mixture of terror, grief and hope. Arthur understood the importance of the message. He did have a choice. He had made the choice to finish the act and drop the final curtain. He had asked not to be drip fed anymore, and in turn the doctors had advised him this act would end his life within a week. He accepted the outcome. However, there was one element of his departure which Arthur feared more than death itself. The stream of visitors. He could barely speak and had little strength to deal with the emotions his family had on offer. Was it unfair to put his needs first? He didn't think so. This was his time. His last week. Surely he could spend it however he chose? His desire to achieve a state of peace before departure was unlikely to be achieved with a flow of visitors to his bedside. Which is why he had asked Bee not to visit again. She had agreed to this wish. He knew of all people she would respect his request. She was not a selfish creature, would not put her emotional health before his own. There were few who understood his journey to death. But Bee knew. Quite how she knew was beyond all earthly reason, but she did, she had secret knowledge of his voyage to a granular level of detail. This would spook many, but not Arthur, for this was his daughter at her finest. He looked up to see a visitor had arrived. At the end of the bed stood Adam. Arthur was suddenly aware of the beauty his daughter perceived in this man. In his line of sight stood a man, and behind him a light, one he had never seen before. A faint glow radiated from his body. Arthur took the view of radiance as a sign his daughter would be well cared for. Adam stepped forward awkwardly and then sat on the visitor chair. Under the circumstances both men found conversation difficult. Really they only had one thing in common, Bee. Arthur had asked to see Adam for one reason only. He found his voice and communicated his last wish,

'Please look after Bee for me. I'm handing over my duty to you, as her husband.'

Adam smiled,

'Of course I will look after her. She will be safe with me.'

There was nothing else to say. Although short, their conversation had delivered all that was required and had come to an end. Adam understood and got up from the chair. He left without saying goodbye. Obviously he could not go to the place of goodbye.

Arthur lay quietly and reflected on the day's progress. He had spoken to Adam and handed over the reins. He felt much better having relinquished his responsibility for Bee and was in no doubt the young man was up to the job. He did worry about her. She looked strong but she was sensitive too. This is why she let few people in. They could never deliver the strength of love, trust and truth she required. Adam obviously did. This was clear in the way she looked at him, and he her. They shared a love which others could only dare to hope for. In fact it seemed to Arthur, they were more in love now than when they were first married. He smiled and wondered what it must be like to live with his daughter. He could only imagine what it would be like to be truly loved by her. He had experienced this to a degree. She had a strength of love second to none, which could be felt most when in close contact. When nearby there appeared to be a stream of energy which flowed from her to him. Although he had observed this many times he was still amazed by the power of the connection. He wondered if this is what it would feel like where he was going. He hoped so. He could cope with his final destination if it felt like the energy Bee shared with him. He was glad to have been given the chance to speak with her one last time even though they had both struggled to maintain composure. There had not been much need for conversation, other than to bequeath her the gifts. He knew she didn't want them or need them. But he wanted her to have things that would mean something, which would be dear to her heart. She would not hide them away. Instead she would enjoy all of his gifts and he would be remembered. He had chosen well. Then his thought stream emptied and he took a step toward sleep. With eyes closed he could see peace in the distance, like a dusk cloud covering the sky, peace was coming.

Chapter 66 — BEE

A shadow flitted outside the kitchen window. Excited by the activity Bee connected with the presence, which caused the activity to increase to include every window at the front of the house. Electrical surges ignited all of her nerve endings and a 'knowing' was delivered. He is ready to fly. He is ready to leave his body. Bee felt sure she was in receipt of a message regarding her dad. Not wanting to forget the unusual occurrence she recorded every detail of the shadowy movements in her journal. As the words tumbled onto paper Bee realised the shadows manifested at the exact moment she contemplated the loss of her dad. There was a reason for this. With this in mind she focused her thought and travelled back to the memory. An idea unravelled inside her head. Their journeys were about to take on different directions. Bee connected to this new thought and to the reality of his imminent departure then his presence entered her mind. Bee trusted him and the interaction then allowed his energy to merge with her consciousness. Next she conversed inside her head, 'I miss you already.' The words spoken ignited a need to record a message.

'I know. But we can be together. I will be here to help one day when you need me, until then you will be fine. You have so many around you and they have enough love to support all of your needs. I am needed elsewhere. Rest assured though that we will speak later, much later, take care of you and never forget that you are special.'

Bee reviewed the words. She could hardly believe her eyes. He had communicated. She was not sure whether to be happy or sad. The fact he could communicate meant he had gone past the point of no return. All of a sudden she was overwhelmed by sadness which enveloped her entirely. To protect herself she lay down on the bed, snuggled under the duvet and closed her eyes. Sleep did not come easily, after all it was not yet evening. But she needed respite—to shut down external input and regenerate her weary soul. First there were tears to shed, which fell silently. Her dad had been there for her, someone with whom she could share truths when there had been no one else. She spoke to him without making a sound.

'Thank you for your support. I'm not sure how I would have managed without you. Thank you for listening, even though you did not believe all I had to share. Most of all, thank you for sharing your journey with me.'

Then she let him go. In the moment of release she allowed his soul to be liberated and detached from his existence. As their connection severed he broke free. Tears fell for all that had been, for everything shared and for all that would be no more. Then finally, sleep took her to a place of peace which could not be found during wake time.

Chapter 67 — ARTHUR

Arthur spent most of his time lying on his back unable to move. Mercifully, the sickness and retching had subsided. Halting all food intake had the desired positive effect. Even so, he still felt vile, which was hardly surprising. As his body degenerated so did his voice. Thankfully he had just enough left of his voice to speak with his children. This day he would close the book on the past. In the moment of waking and before opening his eyes, Arthur indulged the one sense which had not yet deteriorated. His ears picked up the sound of birds making merry outside his window, taunting him with their happy chatter. His initial thought was to be grumpy at the loud noise but he could not. Arthur had always loved birds, even if they had the habit of waking him at dawn. The day had begun well. Although obviously there was no cup of tea or breakfast to follow. His was not a life filled with these pleasures. After all he had decided to end his existence. He was starving himself to death. Not a pretty end. With every day that passed he became less interested in food. The fun had gone out of it.

His first visitor was Sheila. She came every day. They didn't have many new things to say. Without fail there was always the question about how his night had been. For the past few days his answer had been different. Before, every night had been a living hell. But since he stopped eating his nights had become a whole lot better. There had been no retching whatsoever and the pain relief had actually worked. If he hadn't felt so weak he could almost have believed he was okay. Had he dozed off? Sheila had disappeared from his bedside. Moments later she returned with Richard. A man stood at the end of the bed, his son. Love washed over Arthur like a warming wave. Not a feeling he had often. An unusual and powerful sense of love. He likened it to the feeling he experienced the day his son was born. A new love, one without past crimes to muddy the water. Arthur took this as a good omen. All would be healed between them. Richard sat down on the visitor chair to his left. There were two chairs but they always chose the one to his left. His son looked uncomfortable, so Arthur encouraged him to share a few details of the journey down from London. When Richard visibly relaxed then Arthur moved to the conversation which needed to be aired.

'We both know I am not long for this world. I want you to know how much I am going to miss our banter. We have had a few laughs haven't we? Although I'm sure you'll agree there have also been a few moments of anger, it has not all been rosy. Before I go I need to talk to you about the past.' Richard looked uncomfortable again. Arthur smiled and continued, 'As I get closer to death I realise I need to clear out the cupboard, metaphorically speaking of course. You and I have not always seen eye to eye across the years but we need to find peace. I cannot leave without speaking to you of the past.'

Arthur looked deep into Richard's eyes and saw the painful truth of the imminent death. Richard resigned himself to the conversation.

'Okay Dad, but are you sure? Do you really want to dredge up the past? I am okay with it. We are talking years ago.'

Arthur remained firm in his stance. Richard clearly did not realise how much this would mean to them both. Arthur had to make peace.

'I think I need to talk of the time when you left home. When I encouraged you to go. When I told you the lifeline would be no more. I was so frustrated with you. You were so capable and you had ability. You just couldn't be bothered to put the effort in. At that time I felt so angry. I had supported you, nurtured you, but it wasn't enough. You always wanted more. So I had to stop it. Do you realise you were not only damaging our relationship but you were damaging your mum's and mine? I couldn't let you do it. So I made a stand. Looking back I realise how hurt you were. I am not sure we ever resolved the bad feeling that was generated. But I need to now. I need to forgive you for being a little like me in my early years. I need you to forgive me for doing what I thought was right. I fear if we do not settle this today then we will both be damaged in the days and years to come.'

Arthur stopped, he had said enough. Richard looked ready to surrender to emotion but he did not. Instead he flashed one of his cheeky grins and spoke in hushed tones.

'Look Dad, the past is the past. Yup, I was really mad at you. Really bloody angry. But I hate to say it. You did the right thing. I always whinge about all you have given my siblings but in reality you gave me so much when I was young. I just didn't appreciate it. You kicking me up the backside got me where I am today. I have never looked back. Since then I've never been an idle layabout, as I recall you used to label me. Of course I forgive you. Can you also forgive me for giving you such a hard time?'

Arthur smiled and took his son's hand. They sat silently for a few moments. Neither wanting to speak. Each protecting their emotions. Arthur didn't want to die. His children were good people. They were interesting people to be with. All he wanted was to chew the cud with Richard over a nice bottle of claret. But this could never be. Those days were gone. How he wished they were not. They conversed for a short time on nothing of any great consequence and then Richard left. Arthur had closed the chapter called Richard. All he had left was to face the one called Andrew.

He had been asleep. When Arthur opened his eyes he saw Andrew seated on the chair to his left. Was it really him? Arthur was still dozy. He couldn't trust his eyesight. But he could trust his heart as he felt the warmth of love pour through his chest. How he loved this boy. He often thought of his son as a boy, probably because he was the youngest. In reality he was a young man. Arthur sensed the love he felt in his heart being returned. Andrew was able to give love with ease and he enjoyed the feeling of warmth emanating from his son. The quiet moment inside his head was broken as Andrew spoke,

'Hi Dad, how are you doing?'

Arthur wasn't going to pretty up his response, it was too late for that,

'Not good son.'

Andrew looked relaxed considering the situation. He had always been that way. Sometimes Arthur had taken this relaxed attitude to mean his son did not care or could not be bothered, but he understood better now. In the moment he realised Andrew was more like Bee. He allowed life to flow. He was comfortable with love, relaxed in its presence. Although relaxed, Arthur could see the pain buried in his son's eyes. There was no option to avoid the truth. Arthur had to speak of all that burdened his soul whilst he had the opportunity.

'We both know I don't have long now. I want you to know how much I am going to miss being part of your life. But I also need to talk of the past. I feel we have unfinished business and I can't go to my grave feeling this way. I'm sure this will not be good for either you or me.' Arthur paused, choked by tears. This was going to be difficult. 'I need to tell you of a mistake I made and I sincerely hope you will be able to forgive me.' Arthur saw confusion in Andrew's eyes as if he had no idea what was coming. This was the most difficult conversation he had experienced with any of his children so far. 'You know I wanted the best for you, for all my children?' Andrew nodded in response. 'Your situation was different to the others. You came later. Which was great for us as parents, we had more time for you because the others had left home. We also had the advantage of knowing the ins and outs of raising children, as we had learnt with the other three. However, for all the plus points we had, I could not get over the negatives for you. Once Bee had left home you had no siblings. Even she wasn't what you really needed. I felt you needed boys of your own age to muck about with. To be perfectly honest I have never liked the idea of an only child. All children should have other children to play with. You were like an only child and I couldn't do that to you. So I talked your mum into sending you away to boarding school. Whilst you were away I quashed the nagging doubts that this was the right thing for you. I had made the decision and I stuck by it. I lost you.'

Arthur's voice broke, he couldn't hold back the tears. Andrew sat quietly with tears running down his cheeks. Neither wanted to speak. Then Andrew wiped his cheeks dry and spoke,

'I missed you and mum so much when I went away. It really hurt. All I wanted was to be in my home. But I learnt to enjoy it at school. I had the best of both worlds. I got to live with my mates and was able to come home to you guys. Yes, it was really hard to begin with but then it was fine, it was better than fine, it was good fun.'

Arthur smiled and wiped away the tears. They had spoken on the subject he had not been able to face for fear his son hated him. He had carried this burden for years. At last he was free. His heart felt lighter. He did not need to beg forgiveness. There was nothing to forgive. Andrew stayed for a while. They shared school boy stories and other memories of Andrew's childhood. Their last moments together were spent without the past overshadowing the present. They were free with each other. Another chapter closed.

He had one more visitor to welcome. Lizzie arrived later in the day. They did not have any past to rake over, for they were at ease with one another. Arthur felt the same warm glow in his chest as he had with his other children. As with Andrew, Arthur often thought of Lizzie as a child. Once, in the years before Andrew was born, she had been the youngest and with her position in the family had received the level of attention the youngest demands. He loved her in a different way to the boys but was not sure why. There was a different bond with his daughters, a much softer connection. He smiled in her direction to welcome her to his bedside. She sat to his left as all others. A face altered by grief communicated everything she felt inside. He had not yet passed and yet she looked as if he had. Clearly she was applying a great deal of effort to hold it together. They had a lot in common; shared the same sarcastic sense of humour and neither liked to speak of emotion. Instead they preferred to demonstrate their love by giving, whether it be time, support or gifts. Both were much more comfortable with this method of delivery. In the last moments together they did not speak of love, they spoke of family. All of a sudden Arthur was compelled to ask his daughter to look after the family. He had not planned the conversation and yet knew this must be spoken.

'Look after your mum won't you. She will be okay but is sure to need support. You're the one who keeps the family together. Can you do that for me? My family is the most important thing to me. I have still not fully accepted that I have to leave you all, miss out on all that is to come. Can you make sure the family doesn't fall apart? Will you take this role for me?'

Her face transformed and delivered a smile, one which warmed his heart. Grief had been replaced by love. Love for her father and family.

'Of course I will Dad. You know me. Life and soul of the party. I'll keep the family going. At the very least I'll make sure everyone has somewhere to go at Christmas.'

He couldn't ask for any more. His family would stay together, she would make sure of that. Another chapter had been closed, one he had not been aware of before. He had not planned to ask Lizzie to look after the family. But whilst they were talking he had become aware this was the right thing to do. As if the earlier conversations with his sons had delivered peace and with this new state he was able to see more clearly. This new line of sight had delivered him to an important conversation. Lizzie would keep the family together, their bond would be strong enough to deal with the trials of life. He would be remembered through them. He would not be forgotten.

His children had come and gone. Now he could spend the days as he wished. He was alone. Well, with the exception of the daily visits from Sheila and her friend Pat. Arthur could see Sheila would have plenty of support following his departure, so he did not worry about how her life would be when he was gone. He also had no worries about how his children would cope either. They would be fine. Each had made their peace. The path ahead was clear, refreshed. However, there was one small problem. Even though he made peace with his family and accepted his journey to the other side he was still alive. There had been greater evening activity. As if he were close. Since his acceptance of the end he had been visited every night by something not of the earth. His visitors were quite unlike anything he had ever seen. Bright shining spheres of light in a variety of colours. Although always pale, except for the white ones, which were brighter than all the others. Arthur looked forward to their appearance at his bedside. They lifted his spirits and lightened his existence. Then as if the very thought of these light sources instigated a chain reaction, his thoughts wandered off. How had he forgotten? Which day was it? He could not remember. Was it the day his children came? Or maybe the day before? Maybe it had been a dream? He did not know. Arthur was confused. But he replayed the thought anyway.

He had been lying in bed contemplating his existence when a strange electrical tingling spread to all nerve endings and he felt motion, a sense of being lifted out of his body. In this new state he had looked down from ceiling height to his body below. Upon seeing his frail form, a river of sadness had engulfed his consciousness. Surely the man on the bed was not him? He had not dwelled on this thought for long. The new vantage point afforded him a detached view, one which had delivered him to a place without concern or fear. Instead he had been intrigued at the concept of travelling without his body. Maybe he had been at ease because he sensed support in the form of a guardian alongside. As if in a parallel existence he had embraced the experience. Once connected, he had entered a tunnel which appeared in his mind's eye. He had accepted the journey without hesitation and within moments was outside of her home.

On remembering the encounter, Arthur realised he must have utilised the same method of travel Bee had used when delivering a remote channelling session. Arthur wished he could tell her. But knew this would not be possible. There would never be another conversation between them. The end of their time for speaking had come. However, there had been an opportunity to communicate, but it had been difficult. No matter how hard he tried, he had been unable to penetrate her home, almost as if a protective shield prevented him from entering. Although this had not stopped him from trying. He had travelled round and round the outside of the house, passed every window in the hope she would see him. For a long time she didn't seem to notice him. Then he saw a reaction when she gazed into the space which he occupied and smiled, as if she could actually see his new form. Once connected he had not wanted to leave. All he wanted was to communicate. An opportunity presented when he saw her recording the experience in her journal. At this point he made his move. He communicated and then watched as she recorded his words. After, he stayed and observed the tears. He had been desperate to speak with her, to tell her he was ready to go, that death was okay. He wanted her to know death was not the worst thing that could happen but merely the passing from one existence to another. All death was timely, there was no such thing as an early death, only your time. But he had not been allowed to speak. He had only managed to communicate the few words which she had recorded. The moment she closed the pages of the book and his words disappeared, Arthur had felt the severing of their physical connection. Unwillingly he returned to his frail and silent body. Once there he had no option but to accept his destiny. Having remembered, he felt ready for sleep, then drifted into a state of peace and allowed sleep to encase him in a blanket of quiet.

The morning which followed delivered a shocking truth. Arthur found that not only had his voice deteriorated but he could no longer speak a word. As if a thief had crept up to his bed during the night and stolen his speech. Words would not come, no matter how hard he tried. His tongue and vocal chords seemed beyond his control. This new disability made the art of communication virtually impossible. However, all was not lost as he had one communication mechanism left, his sight. He contemplated the option of looking directly into the eyes of anyone who came to visit. However, the only person he knew with this skill was Bee. Therefore there was little chance of getting a message across this way. Once again the prospect of communication seemed hopeless. There seemed little point in visitors sitting with him. The passing of time to his end would be much easier without them. Then he wouldn't feel so bloody hopeless. But this was not to be, the visitors still came. Instead of slipping into despondency Arthur devised a plan to make use of their presence. Although he would struggle to make any sense, he knew there was one person who would understand. The first message formed inside his head and then all he had to do was encourage his vocal chords and mouth work. This was not easy. But it was the only way a message could be passed on. When his voice erupted with a guttural sound, Sheila nearly jumped out of her skin. There was something faintly amusing about the whole episode. But the message was serious. He needed their help. With the first message delivered he took the opportunity to formulate the next. But by the time he was ready to communicate his visitor had disappeared to find refreshment. The longer he waited for them to return the larger the message loomed. Arthur was consumed by a need to communicate that he was ready to go and prepared for the journey ahead. But no one was bloody well around to receive the message. It was like waiting for a bus, never there when you needed one. With each passing minute Arthur grew more impatient. Then he spotted Pat walking towards his bed. She smiled at him then sat down and made herself comfortable in the chair to his right. With a level of effort that really shouldn't have been necessary, Arthur slowly turned his head toward her and focused on presenting a smile on his face. The muscles in his face were not responding as they once had. He hoped the poor woman was not looking at a grimace. With determination he forced the words inside his head past his vocal chords and out of his mouth. The blurted words caused Pat to look both surprised and bemused. Once Pat had processed his gobbledegook words and recovered from the surprise outburst, she relaxed, smiled and continued reading her newspaper. He had absolutely no idea if she had actually heard him correctly or if she would deliver the message to Sheila. There was nothing more to be done. The message could not be repeated. He could only hope Bee would receive the words just delivered. Time was short and there was still one more message to deliver. Arthur forged ahead with the delivery of the final communication. He employed every ounce of strength left in his feeble body and forced his dry mouth and vocal chords to move. When the delivery was complete he hoped the herculean effort had been worth it. Just to be safe, in case Pat had not understood, Arthur looked directly at her, connected to her eyes and implored her to pass the messages on to his wife. He felt sure she would. In his experience, a woman's prerogative was to dredge up all conversations from the day and share them with someone, anyone.

His daughter, the target recipient of his messages would understand. He felt sure she would be able to decipher his messages and trust the source. Arthur slipped into a moment of reflection. As a child Bee had been a most determined creature and yet had not shouted or screamed. Instead she had a way of silently being. Through the course of her life she had experienced a roller coaster ride of highs and lows.

The crushing lows had been hard on her existence, yet somehow she had managed to pick herself up from each one. With every challenge she seemed to have grown stronger. Within his newfound connection he saw the magnificence of her future and dearly hoped he would be able to watch her life unravel. Then all thoughts slipped from his mind, his day was done. There was nothing left to do but sleep. Arthur shut his eyes and immediately saw the dusk cloud, the same one from the previous night but it was no longer in the far distance, now it was almost within reach. Peace was closer than he could have ever imagined.

Chapter 68 — BEE

Having released her dad to his future Bee felt the pressure of responsibility slip away. All that remained, to wait for knowledge to be delivered. Bee knew with certainty the departure day would be delivered to her stream of conscious thought when the time came. With trust in this thought she released control of the communication link. Without the weighty burden of responsibility she embraced family life and the opportunity to live without a care. But however much she tried, her freedom was still hampered by what remained of their link. Although not as strong as it had once been, a connection still existed, one which delivered a heightened sense of his wellbeing. This constant data feed informed her of his status. He was still alive. The 'knowing' felt like a fine thread of silk which bonded them to each other and allowed a trickle of information to flow along its length. Bee was aware that when he left the thread would be broken, there would be a slight pull on her end and then there would be nothing. Although this was not the only information resident. In addition, Bee knew details of his departure day, including her role. She would be transported to his bedside to deliver her parting gift.

Another call delivered more sad news. Bee listened in silence as her mum spoke.

'Your dad is slipping in and out of consciousness, which is a clear sign he is on his way. He must be losing control of his brain because he has taken to blurting out random sets of words.'

The words were important. Bee felt electrical energy ignite all nerve endings and broke her silence,

'Mum, whatever they sound like, the words spoken will not be random.'

A 'knowing' developed quickly. They were definitely not random words, but a message.

'You must tell me exactly what happened.'

Her mum needed little encouragement,

'Well, yesterday when Pat and I were sitting beside his bed he blurted out strange words. Last night when we were eating dinner and chatting about the day, we found he had done the same thing to both of us. I realised the words sounded like a communication but I wasn't sure, so I thought it best to ask you.'

Bee listened as her mum shared details of the previous day. She stopped the flow of chatter when she heard the first message and recorded it on a piece of paper. The next stream of words delivered another pearl of wisdom, which she also recorded. When the conversation was almost at an end the final message was delivered and this too was noted. Bee scanned the words and smiled, a 'knowing' developed, then she explained the meaning.

It's time for prayers.
I've nearly squared the circle. Of course it was the dark powers of the devil.
The essential end of the night music thing.

Bee understood their meaning almost immediately, as if there was already a definition planted somewhere in her mind. Electrical impulses charged throughout her body, intensifying as her 'knowing' increased in stature. Bee spoke slowly and confidently,

'It's time for prayers. Means his time is coming. Because of this, he would benefit from listening to the prayers.'

Bee understood the reason why but did not share this part of her 'knowing.' The prayers he had written were an important part of his journey, for they raised the level of his vibrations and enabled greater balance to deliver him to the end. The next message would sound odd to others but not Bee. The meaning was obvious.

'I've nearly squared the circle. This sounds like a term Da Vinci used. I think Dad has finally worked out how to move from our physical world to the non-physical. He has figured out how to let go.'

Bee sensed this message was for her. Her dad was communicating his major achievement. He was able to converse on the matter of leaving the earth. He was trying to tell her an important step had been taken.

'It was the dark powers of the devil. I think this is linked to the previous message and is part of squaring the circle. Dad understands how he was delivered to the place in which he finds himself. He has come to terms with the darkness to which he desperately clung.'

Many times she had attempted to clear the darkness from his body but he would not let her assist. At last it seemed he understood. Then Bee turned her attention to the third and final message. This one, if he could accomplish, would lift him up to the level required for a smooth transition to departure.

'The essential end of the night music thing. This relates to Bach. The music he has been listening to. He needs to hear this music in order to open his heart.'

He was clearly asking for the music to be played. With very little physical function left he could not achieve this action alone. Another message became manifest in her head. There was an urgent need for the music. In support of this, electrical energy powered through her mind and body and in accompaniment a 'knowing.' He required the music immediately.

'Mum, you must call the hospice without delay. Ask the nurses to play the Bach CD for him. He needs his music.'

There was no time for further conversation as her mum had a job to do.

The next day, when morning arrived so did a message, one which played over and over in her head. There was only one valid response. Bee had to call her mum. Thankfully her mum had not already left for the hospice.

'Mum, I woke today with words inside my head, a message that needs to be delivered to you but relates to Dad. The message is this; if you take a look inside a book who knows what you might find.'

As the words were released from her mind a realisation dawned. The book was his Bible.

'Go to the study and find the Bible that Dad has been using.'

In the background Bee heard the rustle of paper as her mum searched for the book. On finding the bible, Bee heard the turning of pages and then an exclamation. The prayers written in his own hand had been found.

'You must take the prayers with you to the hospice, they are part of the message, are urgently required today. Then you must promise me you will read the prayers to Dad. It is imperative they are delivered as soon as possible.'

With her job complete, and her mum released to the task, Bee contemplated their conversation. The message had been delivered to her that morning because he needed his prayers. If she had not listened and acted upon the words, not called her mum, then the prayers would have been forgotten. The words written in his hand were an important part of his journey, together with the music of Bach. He needed both to raise himself to an elevation which would allow smooth passage to the next world. Bee had always believed a level of elevation was required prior to and during departure. Her theory seemed to be proven. Her dad had quite clearly requested items which raised his spirits. But this was not the end. There was still one major step left. One that involved ultimate belief.

Chapter 69 — ARTHUR

With almost all of his life force eliminated, Arthur contemplated that which remained in his head, the communication of words to Sheila and Pat. Bee had interpreted the messages correctly and consequently his request had been delivered. The product of one message was seated by his bedside. Sheila sat with his Bible in her hands and contained within, his prayers written on notepaper. Arthur listened to the words he had written to assist his passing to the other side. Although he possessed a strong belief he would be travelling to a peaceful space, way beyond his imagination, Arthur still feared departure into the unknown. The visitors, who no one else could see, had become ever present around his bed, waiting. Although Arthur could not fully see the detail of their form he could feel their undeniable presence. An unnerving experience. But he held strong to a small comfort. They meant him no harm. He felt their support, which in turn strengthened his belief in an absolute certainty of a life ever after. Although unable to fully perceive the enormity of the transition from his body, Arthur knew without any doubt whatsoever he would be transported to a safe space. With eyes closed and time nearly at an end, the voice of Sheila drifting in and out of his consciousness, Arthur floated outside of his body. High above the bed he looked down upon his wife. She was looking at him and probably thought he was asleep. The sadness she felt in the moment was written all over her face. He felt deep sadness for their parting and the end of their journey together. But he did not feel sorrow for her loss. Instead he felt elevated. Knowing he would soon be free of pain and liberated from the constant battle for life, and in turn, his wife would be free to live again.

Chapter 70 — BEE

Bee needed respite from the reality hurtling in her direction. There was only one place to achieve such a feat. Sleep. Knowledge pursued her throughout the day, always within reach of thought, relentlessly present. There was no true escape from her 'knowing.' But sleep delivered reprieve. Sometimes people asked if she was afraid of the knowledge. They did not understand. There was no option to be fearful of the information. More frightening was the thought a message had not been delivered correctly or missed altogether. That was a terrifying thought. Having been placed in a position of responsibility, there were so many chances to get it wrong. But she would not let this happen. She possessed a fierce determination to do her duty no matter what. There would be a message delivered very soon. She needed to be ready. He needed her to be strong. The only way to maintain strength was to enter a self-preservation state in sleep. However, the luxury of peaceful sleep did not last for long. She was awoken by a vivid dream. With her heart pumping at five times normal speed Bee opened her eyes and tried to recall what had woken her. This was not an unusual occurrence, messages were often received during night time dreams. But there were no sounds and nothing to see but darkness. Bee enjoyed the dark, the mystery of that which was hidden in the shadows. But there was nothing lurking in the room and so she turned her thoughts to the dream which caused her to be bolt awake. As with all dreams, if there was a message with relevance then she would recall the details, and if not, then she would return to sleep. Bee ignited the remembering process. A thought became present inside her conscious mind. The dream replayed and she saw her dad. He was standing in Edward's bedroom doorway. Then she heard the name Uriah Heap. Why would her dad refer to Uriah Heap? Then she remembered. Over the years he had often copied the hand wringing actions of Uriah Heap. But why at Edward's door? She was wide awake, her brain on high alert processing the input. A desperate need clung to her, smothered her like a damp cobweb. He required her support immediately. In the middle of the night there was no option to travel by car to be at his bedside. But she had to respond to the request. She had promised to be there for him. There was only one avenue of support, to provide an energy channelling session from afar. Instantly she cleared her head of all that had existed moments before. Then inside the void of her mind she pictured him in the hospice and travelled to his bedside. Once there, she connected to him and imagined love flowing from herself into his frail form. Next she focused energy into the top of his head and waited until it had been transported throughout his body. During the long and painful journey to this day there had been many visits of a similar nature but none had the same intensity of exchange.

This time was different. There was a deadline and no room for mistake. Bee placed all her trust in the night time call and never once questioned the reality of the request. Faithfully she delivered support. When all that was required had been transferred she attempted to leave his side and return to her own bed. But she could not. For some reason she could not get home. Bee sensed she had been locked out of her own body. Panic paralysed her thought. Previously, returning to her home had been simple. But something was different this time. Bee fought against the panic response and imagined herself reunited with her body. Much to her dismay this didn't work. But she could not give up. She refused to allow the shadows control. However, a shadowy existence still surrounded her form and darkness shrouded her view. Then a solution presented inside her mind. She must travel to the light. She had to connect with the light which dominated her home. Over and over she focused on the same thought, of lying alongside Adam. Eventually, after many attempts she made it back home. Although her heart still raced, thankfully it had lessened in speed to only beating at twice its normal pace. Her mind whirled with all that occurred but she would not let the strange occurrence knock her off balance. The encounter was no different to any other, which meant the terror could easily be released from her mind. Determined to be rid of the fear which had been present moments before, Bee imagined a bright white light cleansing her mind. Then she disconnected from him and closed her eyes in search of safety. With trust in the state of sleep, she released herself to the night.

Chapter 71 — ARTHUR

The other inmates were sleeping. He could hear their snoring. He, however, was wide-awake and attempting communication with his daughter. Bee had explained many times the simplicity of such an action. 'All a person has to do is close their eyes and connect.' With these words in the fore of his mind Arthur considered contact. On this night more than any other, he needed help, for he had begun to disconnect. He craved to remain inside his own body, in a place he felt safe. But the unseen collective had other ideas, they had increased in power and reached closer. Arthur felt powerless to stop them. Suddenly he did not welcome the idea of release to the unknown. Fear suffocated his every thought. But there was no escaping the reality, departure was imminent. But he couldn't go yet. He needed Bee. The journey could not be made without her help. Arthur knew she would help if he asked. But how could he ask from his hospice bed in the middle of the night? The only way was to attempt communication. She had made the process sound easy. But Arthur did not find the method easy at all. He tried, with eyes closed he imagined talking to her. No response. He tried again and again. Nothing. But he would not give up, he needed her. Then inspiration delivered Arthur toward a new method. He imagined a request for help written on paper and dropped this into an imaginary post box. Then he waited for a response. Arthur had absolutely no idea if the message would be delivered. In fact he had very little faith in his ability to connect to the unseen channel. He waited and waited. Nothing. The same response as all other times. He had failed miserably. Had he been clear enough? Would Bee know without doubt he was calling? Arthur tried again. This time choosing to send a message which included a character from a Dickens story. He hoped the larger than life figure would stand out in the communication, that Bee would remember all the times he had impersonated the character. As if to reinforce his identity as the sender, Arthur chose to link the message to Edward. Surely Bee would have no doubt the message was from him. After all he and Edward had an undeniable bond.

His second attempt at communication reaped reward. Soon after delivery Bee appeared at his bedside. She wasn't actually there and yet she was. He had never seen her this way before. Once at his side, she channelled much needed energy to his body. Arthur had asked for help too many times to recollect. Once again she delivered. In a moment of clarity, Arthur understood the importance of his mind, body and soul balance on the success of his journey ahead. He must endeavour to achieve balance and at the same time reduce the fear which dominated his every thought. After a while Bee finished the transfer of energy and tried to leave. But she could not. Arthur sensed her desperation. Was he holding onto her? Suddenly he was struck, as if by a lightning bolt to the chest. He was. He was clinging to her life form. He felt safe when they were connected. He didn't want her to leave. But there was no denying the truth in his heart. He had to let her go. As much as he loved her, he had to travel the next part of the journey alone. She must not witness all he was about to see. It was not her time. Arthur delved deep into his soul for the courage to release and allow her to return home. Without delay he released her and a moment later she was gone. In her place an icy cold blast. The warmth she effortlessly delivered had been stolen away. Arthur tumbled into oblivion and allowed sleep to take him into the peace of the night.

The sound of birdsong woke him. His eyes did not want to open, he was too tired. When he eventually coaxed them into an open state he observed a visitor standing alongside the bed. An uninvited guest not of the earthly kind, more precisely a sphere of white light had taken up residence.
As his eyes became accustomed to the illumination Arthur recognised the face of his departed friend Bob emanating from within the sphere. An arm was extended and a hand offered. All of a sudden Arthur was struck by a searing pain in his heart, as if someone was squeezing it hard enough to end his life. Fear flooded his consciousness, consuming every space. His time was up. Inside his head he heard Bob speak,

'Do not fear. I am here to assist. You are right, it is time and I have come to lead the way. Do you trust me?'

Silently Arthur responded inside his head,
'Yes of course, you were my best friend.'

The admittance created panic. He was not ready to leave. As much as he trusted the man he could not take the hand offered.

Chapter 72 — BEE

The departure point was nigh. The call had to be made. His daughter had to deliver her last gift to elevate him to a point from where he could make the transition. If she were not by his side during passing then he would still make the journey but the passage would not be easy. Fear dominated his departure. In parallel to his requirements, the daughter needed to experience death. This was the only way to develop the level of belief she required in order to succeed in life and make it to her end. And so, the orchestra of life came into being.

Sunshine streamed through the bedroom window, lit up the room, warmed her face and woke Bee from a dreamless sleep. As soon as her mind connected to conscious thought, the change of state from sleep to awake, the sound of a choir in full song resonated inside her head. 'Ding dong merrily on high in heaven the bells are ringing.' The words and music filled her head as if she were seated in a cathedral with a full choir singing out the Christmas song. Electrical energy fired up all nerve endings and ignited a sense of excitement. The song had been received and a moment of understanding followed, an absolute certainty. Bee knew this to be the magical day her dad would depart the earth. The excitement she felt previously transformed into a need. She must get to the hospice as quickly as possible. Motivated by an unknown factor Bee jumped out of bed, showered and dressed. Energy flowed through her body and drove her forward. She possessed a seemingly endless supply of electrical excitement, a force that could not be managed or contained. Why was she so enthusiastic? He was about to leave her behind. But there was no denying the force. She could not attach to any sad thought for the day ahead. This was the beginning of a great day, a momentous occasion and she had to be at his bedside as soon as possible. Before Adam left for work, Bee informed him of the need to visit her dad, explained that it was probably his last day. But she did not share the detail of the messages received. Adam begged her to drive safely. She knew he worried about her state and ability to drive that day, about the safety of the three most important people in his life. But he didn't have to, for she always looked after them. When Adam had left for work, Bee turned her thoughts toward how to make the day more fun for the boys. She decided on a picnic. She would take them to Maiden Castle after the visit to the hospice. Having prepared the picnic lunch and with a sense of urgency driving her forward, Bee herded the boys into the car.

Bee could tell time was tight as the intensity of the call to his bedside dominated every thought. However, once the journey was underway she was able to relax, and in turn the intensity of 'knowing' reduced. As she drove through countryside bathed in sunshine, Bee smiled inwardly and recalled the message delivered to her dad a few weeks earlier. There had been a line indicating 'one sunny day he would be gone.' The day was sunny and Bee knew without doubt this was the day he would disappear from view. Despite her 'knowing' Bee felt no sadness. She felt only elation for the imminent freedom he would be afforded. But her faith in being delivered to his side in time to say goodbye was tested each time the journey ceased to flow. There were a succession of traffic incidents to hold her up but they did not dampen her good humour. Bee understood the flow of life. For reasons beyond her control she was being held back. Would her mum understand the late hour of arrival? Bee had informed her mum she would be at the hospice by midday. Bee laughed at the thought. With current levels of traffic she would be lucky to arrive by teatime. But she was not defeated. In her heart there existed faith, coupled with a 'knowing,' if she were meant to be at the departure point then that is where she would be.

Having arrived at the hospice later than originally predicted, Bee took the boys by the hand and hustled them towards the entrance doors. There, she was greeted by her mum and Pat, who kindly took the boys into the visitor room to play. With time running short Bee hurried with her mum along the corridor to the ward. As they reached the entrance to the ward her mum stopped and delivered a warning,

'Your dad does not look as he once did. Prepare yourself for a shock.'

At his bedside Bee consumed the view that was now her dad. His face had changed. He had been transformed to a deathly pale colour and grey hair hung limply against his head. His face devoid of expression. The body resembled her dad but no longer represented the man he had once been. This was a life form ready for the light to be snuffed out. There was but a fragment of the man left. All elation and excitement felt earlier slipped away, replaced by the harsh reality of his passing. Tears threatened but Bee stemmed the flow. The backup of emotion almost engulfed every one of her senses. She was determined not to let him down and pushed the emotion away. In the background she heard her mum retreat, leaving them alone. There was only one plausible way to deal with the trauma of the current situation. She struck up a conversation inside her head. How can I help you dad? What am I supposed to do? She had never seen a person ready for immediate departure. Had absolutely no idea where to start. Then in an instant she knew. There was only one thing to do. Smile. After searching hard she found the light to smile and shared the gift with him. Was that a smile in return? No, the shaking of his head did not reflect the sentiment she had delivered. There was an intensity to his eyes as his head shook from side to side. He was attempting communication. Excitement for his attempt was dampened by frustration for she could not identify his message. Was that fear in his eyes? Was he still fighting against the inevitable departure? Her heart ached for him, a searing pain, as if the vital organ were being ripped apart. Then from a place unseen Bee felt support as the weight of responsibility lifted from her shoulders, strength replaced sadness in her heart and her head cleared of all thought.

She had promised to help him on the day he made the journey to the other side. The time had arrived. She must draw upon reserves of courage and focus on helping him from this world to the next. With a new sense of strength and an air of calm, Bee stepped closer to the bed. She sat upon the visitor chair and inside her head asked for the power to deliver all that was required. With newfound confidence Bee made a positive move and placed her left hand over his heart then right hand on his shoulder. Thoughts of love for the dying man tumbled over one another in her mind. In accompaniment to the love, a surge of energy from an unknown source. Bee channelled both to her dear departing father. The intensity of energy exchange like no other she had experienced. A stream of electricity flowed through her body and into his. Then Bee felt him loosen his grip on life. In the softest of voices she spoke,

'Dad, I'm here to help. You will be okay.' Her throat became choked with tears but she managed to speak one more time, 'You look beautiful.'

The choice of words seemed strange and yet had to be spoken. Although there existed discord between his mind, body and soul, Bee could still see the beautiful part of his existence in the flame of life which bound him to his body. As her strength of focus became threatened by emotion Bee pleaded for help. Immediately extra support was delivered in the form of electrical energy which provided the connection and strength required. Then she felt calmer and more able to focus. In her supportive role she continued to aid his passage. Closed eyelids flickered as energy surged through her hands into his body. Although distracted by the need to deliver him to a safe place Bee could still feel the very real pain in her heart. A sense of despair which developed with each second that passed and yet she could not allow this to divert her from the task in hand. She would not lessen the impact of her assistance by allowing emotion to take control. With determined focus on his journey Bee balanced his mind, body and soul. An act of selfless giving, one of paramount importance to his safe departure.

Chapter 73 — ARTHUR

The moment Arthur saw his daughter walking towards the bed he knew his time had come. There would be no more chances to grasp at the remnants of life. His last thoughts were dominated by the comprehension of what her presence represented; these were his last breaths. Although he knew this to be true he could not help but be distracted by the vision. As Bee stood above him a bright white light emanated from her body, a radiance he had never before observed. Arthur was overwhelmed with love. He attempted, by utilising every connection left in his brain, to raise a smile. But he knew the effort was futile. He could not control his face. There would be no more smiles shared. In response to this reality a chain reaction caused fear to suffocate his consciousness. There was to be no escape. The time to leave had arrived whether he liked it or not. His daughter was in place to ensure he left intact. He knew he was going but did not want to leave. Arthur employed every last ounce of energy to shake his head. Inside he cried out and implored Bee to stop. His last attempts to cling onto life. But this was not an option. Initially he had been oblivious to the vision but as it moved into the space behind Bee, he saw the presence which had come to collect him. He must release all that had been his life and with grace pass over to the other side.

When Bee touched him he felt love and warmth emanating from her body. In an instant he realised she felt exactly like the energies who had visited him in the hospice every night since his arrival. She was one of them. In the moment of passing he realised the importance of her role in helping him to leave. She gifted him unconditional love without a thought for what had gone before. Her desire to keep him alive forgotten in order to provide the level of love required to assist his journey. In the final moment of his life Arthur felt himself, the part that no longer belonged to his body, leave. The connection was cut and he was free to rise up. Way above his body Arthur viewed Bee sitting below. Her hand still rested over his heart channelling energy. But he did not require her support anymore. He had left his body and was in the hands of friends. A gathering of light surrounded him entirely, beckoned him to follow, and follow he did. He accepted his journey on earth was at an end.

Chapter 74 — BEE

With her left hand still placed upon his heart Bee felt the life giving organ stop beating, his body relax and his breath no more. With the last breath came peace, which washed over her mind and soul. Then she felt freedom and in response smiled. He had been released from the torment of his body. She had not noticed the arrival of her mum and the vicar. Their questioning eyes searched for a reaction to her loss. But there was nothing for them to see. His passing would eventually manifest in tears but not in front of them. She would release grief in the privacy of her own space. What she could not explain and feared they could not comprehend, was the current of warmth and love which still flowed through her body. The tears would fall but not until her body had experienced the deep chill of loss. In the moment of passing she was filled with jubilation. She had achieved everything required. She had helped him across to the other side and delivered the most precious gift she could ever bestow. With his life force no longer in view Bee could not remain next to an empty body. She escaped the death bed, exited through the main entrance doors and out into the warm sunshine. As fresh air hit her lungs all of the strength she once possessed dissipated. With a desperate need to sit, to support her trembling limbs, she found a bench on which to collapse. Once seated, she calmed her mind and released the trauma of the passing. She had to be in a stable mind set to call her brothers. At the death bed her mum had offered to make the call to Lizzie, which left two calls for her to make. When she felt able, Bee took the mobile phone from her handbag and dialled the number for Richard, her eldest brother. On hearing his voice she delved deep for the strength to speak calmly, to delicately deliver the news of the departure. She managed to explain the reality of their father's demise but did not possess the strength to engage in extended conversation. There was nothing else of importance to discuss. Next, she made a call to her younger brother Andrew. There followed a similar conversation, where again she dug deep for the strength to deliver the news without tears. Where she had not felt concern for how Richard would deal with the news, she was worried for Andrew. After all, he was fourteen years younger than herself and still in his twenties. This news, no matter how expected, would deliver a severe blow to his life. But she had nothing left in the reserves. She did not have the strength to assist him in his hour of need. After the delivery of wretched news to her brothers, Bee still remained unnaturally chipper and brimmed with happiness for her dad. She seemed unable to connect with the sadness of the event. With one more call to be make she lifted the phone to her ear. On hearing Adam's compassionate voice, all emotion associated with her dad's passing crept slowly from its hiding place. With Adam she felt safe and could express her sorrow. But this was not the time. She must not crumble in public. Later, when she returned home she could express her grief. Bee stemmed the tears and connected to the last of her strength. When all calls had been made and the news delivered, she placed her palms on the warm bench and pushed herself upwards. The sunshine felt good on her skin and she gratefully accepted the heat on offer. Having been gifted a few moments of solitude Bee felt ready to return to the others.

Back in the visitor room she was reunited with her two hungry boys. The well intentioned plans for a picnic at Maiden Castle were pushed aside. Instead, the group in mourning chose to eat their lunch in the hospice garden. They left the visitor room by the patio door, stepped out onto the lawn and found a sunny spot in which to sit. There, Bee carefully laid a rug down on the grass upon which she sat with the boys. Alongside on their own blanket, the vicar Gerald and his wife Ann, her mum and Pat sat. Under a clear blue sky they shared food and basked in the warm sunshine. The act of slipping back into the normality of life might have seemed strange to some, to be enjoying a picnic within an hour of a loved one passing. But for everyone in the group this seemed exactly the right thing to do. As lunch was consumed they shared stories of the man who had left. Within the light-hearted chatter they spoke of their love for him and each other. This was their way of sharing the loss, the only way they knew how. When enough had been said, when she had exhausted all avenues of discussion and there was no more left to give, Bee left the hospice seeking the solace of home.

From the moment they climbed into the car, James and Edward asked a steady flow of questions, each needed an answer. Their enquiring minds searched for an understanding of death. Drawing upon the very last of her energy reserves and utilising a little humour, Bee managed to field their questions. Thankfully, when all questions were answered they fell asleep. The car became a haven of peace, giving Bee the time to reflect upon events of the day. But still she could not shed a tear. She recalled the moment of his passing. She had not expected it to be such a joyous event and yet it had been. Although she had felt sad on arrival at his bedside, she had not when she left. Almost as if the passing were a celebration. There was no rhyme or reason to the feeling. The sadness for her loss had been balanced by the knowledge of his release. He had been released from pain, no longer hanging onto a life which did not serve. But Bee knew the balance would not last. With each mile put between herself and the hospice, sadness crept forward in search of release. The balance experienced earlier in the day now weighted in favour of loss. There was to be no escape, she would have to address the underlying sadness currently masked by the joy of his release. But not yet, first she had to return to the safety of home. When Bee turned the car into the drive she engaged autopilot and parked the car. Then gathered the boys, fed them a light tea, bathed them, shared a story and then put them to bed. With all motherly duties complete, only then did she allow herself the time and space to grieve her loss. She found Adam in the kitchen, collapsed into his arms and lost herself in the safety of his embrace. There, she sobbed into his chest and released the pain of the day.

Bee awoke feeling drained and hollow. A dark cloud had settled over her life, one that smothered all hope and showed no signs of shifting. From within the haze of bereavement a 'knowing' appeared. She must address any and all of the emotion stored before and during his passing. Everything must be released. But she had given everything, every ounce of strength to support her dad. This effort had left her depleted. Surely she didn't have ability to visit the stored emotion. And yet she must. She had to move forward. She must connect to the feelings of loss. She must stop being strong and admit the emptiness inside. This focus on herself proved difficult. Never before had she felt emotion at such an extreme level and at the same time possessed an unstoppable flow of tears. She spoke to the empty room,

'How am I ever going to get over losing him?'

The physical disconnection felt as if parts of her insides had been ripped out, leaving behind a dark empty space. As she sobbed into another tissue Bee attempted to rationalise her loss. She considered her life and in a moment of realisation understood she had not lost everything. She was surrounded by the love of friends and family. More importantly, she had a husband and two children whom she loved, and who loved her. On connecting with this thought she felt immediate comfort. However, even though Bee recognised the love and support in her life, she could not ignore the fact she had just lost a very dear friend. The sense of loss continued to hurt, as if a knife was repeatedly twisted in her stomach. Unable to leave the sanctity of her bedroom, Bee stayed seated on the bedroom floor with her back rested against the bed frame. There she remained. She wept until there were no more tears to shed.

When all emotion had been released Bee turned her thoughts to the accomplishments of the previous day. She wanted to make sense of the visit to his bedside. The channelling of energy had been quite unlike any other. The energy more intense, the pressure of the external force more powerful, as if holding her afloat. A need to write developed. If she recorded the events of the previous day she would see how her efforts had made a difference. This would also ensure if there were any remnants of emotion hidden away they would be released. As the details of the day were transferred to paper, Bee understood how she had assisted his passing to the other side. She had shared unconditional love. She had not grasped at his life for her own selfish need. Rather, she had allowed him to go with the gift of love. She could hardly believe how lucky she was to have been given the right to see him die, to be there at the magical moment of departure. Her heart raced and electrical energy fired to all nerve endings. Bee understood the beauty of the moment, whereby he had given her the most precious of gifts. There were few people lucky enough to share the departure of a loved one. But she was one. In sharing his exit she had been shown the magnificence of release, the beauty of every element of human life, including death. She smiled at the thought. The first smile of the day. But her heart did not join in. However, she couldn't ignore the sense of a warm glimmer of light deep within, a sparkle of knowledge that all would be well. Bee looked down at the journal, to the sentence just written, and realised a message had been delivered.

Fear not for he has been returned to his beginning, to his creator. Just as he knew he would be.

She hadn't asked for a message to confirm his wellbeing. Why had she been told he was okay? Did she not believe in his deliverance to the other side? Her conscious thought demanded she face up to the reality of his departure. However, this thought stirred up a storm. Bee had thought she was comfortable with the knowledge he had moved onto another existence. Yet a shred of doubt lingered. She questioned the reality of the presence, the energy she experienced which no others could see or feel. An energy which had been present throughout her life and also at his death bed. Bee had known this would be a difficult time. She had known this would test her belief to the limits. As she questioned his death, dark matter filled her soul and crept into the crevices of her mind. The bright light which usually shone upon situations, smothered, barely visible. The power of the shadows dominated, they pressed down and forced all light from her mind. Then a 'knowing' presented. All emotion should be allowed to surface, no matter how difficult to address. She must accept all that had been and all that would be no more. In essence, his exit must not affect all she had become. There was still so much for her to achieve in life. This was only the beginning. Yes, she had lost sight of him. But she had not lost sight of the love they shared, of all they enjoyed, learned and experienced together. She was one of the lucky ones and would be able to communicate with him through the unseen channel. His passing was the end of their journey on earth and the moment of departure had been the culmination of their learning. He would always be part of her future, with memories of their shared past forever resident within her heart.

Chapter 75 — ARTHUR

No longer as he had once been, Arthur existed in a space quite unlike earth. A place where he reviewed his life and faced up to all actions. An opportunity to understand those life experiences helpful to his cause and those which were not. In this space he evaluated his treatment of others.

The remarkable process felt like a dream, with no physical elements or bounds. When the review was complete, Arthur felt monumental sadness for the way in which he had allowed his life to flow. The ability to feel surprised him as he was no longer in a body capable of emotional reaction. Instead he was a fragment of energy in a parallel reality, neither in one place or another. But there was no space for deliberation of this existence. He had a job to do. Once more focused on his life Arthur realised all had been well until he allowed others to eat into his spirit. From an initial small and seemingly insignificant bite, a wound had grown, leaving behind a gaping hole. Arthur had allowed himself to become resentful and this had developed inside his body until there was no chance for change. Once bitterness and sadness had become embedded in his body there was little hope for him. He felt profound sorrow for his lack of belief during Bee's endeavours to uncover his true pain. He had been too blind to see. But this stage of his passing had given him another chance. Arthur replayed the events which comprised his life. Images displayed like a cinema film show for him to digest and accept. A painfully slow process where the edges of his existence blurred, neither in this world or the next. The presence who had gathered him at the point of departure remained close. Arthur was left in no doubt as to his responsibility. He must accept and come to terms with all choices made. Only he could deliver himself to the next level. He alone must believe in the difference he had made to the great order of things during his life. There was only one way to achieve this, and that was to watch those he had left behind, his family.

He watched as Sheila busied herself in the kitchen making a cup of tea. They had enjoyed a long and happy marriage and had successfully raised four children. This had been a successful union and he had no regrets. Arthur knew she would be okay. She would be sad for her loss, after all they had been together for nearly fifty years. But she was a strong woman and would find a way forward. Next he checked on Richard. Having cleared the past with his son there was nothing to review and accept. The end had delivered them to a healthy father son relationship. Arthur observed Richard eating lunch with his wife in a brasserie near to their home. Although torn apart by the sadness of losing his father, Richard had the support needed to make it through the difficult time. His eldest son would manage without him. Then he looked down upon Andrew, who sat at home staring at the television, having taken the day off work. Arthur worried about his youngest son the most. Not because there was any ill feeling between them but because he did not have the support structure his other children enjoyed. He hoped Lizzie would hold to her promise and keep an eye on her brother, for it was Andrew who would require the greatest support of all. Then he turned attention to Lizzie. She had surrounded herself with children. This had often been used as a coping mechanism in times of strife. Arthur could see she would suffer during the grieving process, however he was sure she would be able to utilise the positive nature of her children to transport her into a bright future. Finally he visited Bee. Although the connection he had once enjoyed with Bee no longer existed, remarkably she was still able to connect to his journey and comprehend his transition period. Arthur watched as she recorded all perceptions on the pages of her journal. He observed her interactions with the rest of the family and how she avoided all direct questions regarding his journey. She knew much more than she was letting on. He felt sure when she came to review her life, her experience would be different, for she had lived her life in absolute truth and made conscious choices to serve her wholly.

But he was not allowed to dwell on the lives of his family members. Instead he had to accept all he had become. The good and bad, the light and dark. But this was not all. Once all had been accepted he faced another difficult task. Possibly the hardest task of all. To remember from whence he had come. Once the review process was complete and he had accepted the past Arthur was ready to make the connection with all he had once been. Arthur released the bonds to his earthly life and then followed the guide, the one which had remained alongside for days. They moved toward a pulsating sphere of bright white light, larger than anything he had seen previously. As they merged with the outer edge of the sphere, the pair were consumed by radiant light and Arthur transitioned from the place of shadows to a place not of this world.

A LIGHT

A light shines yonder,
A glimpse of what will be,
No more to fear the burden of truth.
A shadow caught,
A life fulfilled,
The heavens have opened, a life redeemed.
All seems lost,
There is no need to fear,
A light walks with you, shines upon your path.
Welcome the past, the present, the future,
See the beauty in all,
A life to live.

Author

D.H. Knight lives in the U.K. with her husband and two children. She has worked in various guises; from first job as a papergirl whilst still at school, to a waitress when at college, then a career job as a software consultant, and at one time as a learning assistant supporting primary aged children in their Maths and English lessons. However demanding these roles, they are not the ones which have shaped her life. Instead, it is the parallel roles into which she has thrown her heart and soul which have delivered the greatest experience; that of wife, mother and daughter. Within these roles she has found a voice. Her aim is to share this voice in order to support those in similar circumstances, whilst at the same time, to raise money for worthy causes which relate to the subject matter of her writing.

For more information on the author please visit www.dhknight.co.uk

ACKNOWLEDGEMENTS

There are many people to thank for their support in the creation of this novel. Firstly, my dear dad, without whom there would be no story. Then my family, my very special husband and two children. Who have put up with my ramblings and supported me through the years as I have written and revised, written and revised. Next, my sister who spent hours reading through the text and advising on structure, content and dialogue. My friend Tamsin, who gave many hours of precious time using her skills in design and editing, in order to get this book over the finishing line. Not forgetting two more friends, both called Debbie, who read the book for me and provided much needed feedback. There are also a multitude of family and friends who have positively supported my desire to create this novel, one which has been a long time in the making. Thank you to all for your patience, support and belief in me.

What next I hear you ask? The next novel, currently in production, sees the return of Bee but in a different phase of her life. The theme of the book focuses on another topical subject, which touches many lives, often with devastating effect. A subject close to my heart, for which I have very real experience. For more information on a release date check www.pinkpigpublishing.com.

READING NOTES

Many books include book club reader notes. However, you may not be a member of a book club. But you may have read this book and thought, 'I don't want to stop here, I have been affected by the content and need to contemplate how I feel about it.'

For all those who would like to ponder on the text, I have created a page on my website which is appropriate for both indviduals and book clubs. A place to understand how you feel about the topics raised in 'The Knowing'. Please visit www.dhknight.co.uk

If you have been moved by the book and would like to send me an email then I would love to hear from you. You can find my contact details on www.dhknight.co.uk.